SUPER
TRIPTYCHS

SUPER
TRIPTYCHS

Storyboards Screenplays / Novels

Written solely for motion pictures audiences

Warning; these writings are all (factual) based & are the extremely controversial of these times.

Everett C Borders Jr. PhD.

To order additional copies of this book, contact:
Xlibris
1-888-795-4274
www.Xlibris.com
Orders@Xlibris.com
797825

The brief bio of Everett C Borders Jr. Ph.D.

He was born in 1951 at Cook-county Hospital in Chicago ILL. He was the fourth of six children & son of the late Everett & Mary Borders.

He grew-up on the west side of the mean streets of the cities Rockwell garden projects with hard living & extremely violent gangs.

His passion for writing started in the early sixties attending & graduating with a scholarship from Westinghouse vocational high School.

He began writing poems & lyrics as expressions as he started playing bass guitar & drums, keys & 4track recording learning from his brother. He graduated from Loop College in Chicago ILL.

He started working for Ford Motor Co. As an apprentice in Dearborn Mich. & joined the Chicago Police Dept in 1973.

He excelled in worked in tactical, special operations, gang enforcement HBT (Hostage barricade terrorist) & vice.
In 1976, he joined the United States Coast Guard reserve port security; he worked with agencies of the US

After receiving over one hundred & fifty awards for valor & meritorious city/state/ federal service work, he left Chicago in 1989 arriving in Denver Colorado where he started ECB (Clandestine).

He continued academic learning & began to work in industry of, addictions, Counseling, social services, and sitting on the Colorado state board for mental health.

He started working in fast-paced engineering & advanced concepts in innovations.

He worked in the assisting & mentoring in small theater productions with local & at risk adolescents & adults.

He received numerous letters of praise for service & civic efforts. He received his Ph.D. in Counseling Psychology in 2006 from Cambridge S. University.

He has publications in, Publications.

He consults, mentor, writes scripts, articles, commentaries & considers himself as an innovational scientist as he has more than several, groundbreaking inventions & is a constant collaborator in theoretical scientific projections, as an Independent Think Tanks Professional of real world innovations a LinkedIn professional.

Storyboards legends;

Storyboards Triptychs Index;

1; Planet Black

2; Little Miss Pantomime

3; the Ghosts of Vegas

4; short scripts/short skits

1- **Planet Black screenplay movie**; exert;

This storyboard is about a high action & very high science fiction high drama, about a race of black warriors who come to earth after witnessing the genocidal & treatment atrocities on planet earth, as they attempt to correct what's been a historical global effort to denigrate the black experience on planet earth. The story is science fiction & futuristic; it has extreme drama, with scientific, biblical & historical facts as its back drop is in years 2020 and thirty five thousand years in earths past.

This screenplay is harvested upon presentence of real factual historical & scientific evidence, perceived science fiction & futuristic interpretations, along with this writer's personal highlighted original theoretical scientific innovational concepts, and part (original story movie) screenplay novel; *included within this screenplay, all complete movie scripts, dialogs & soundtrack forthwith.*

In the real history of earth, as to when, mankind first crawled out of the jungle & began the first civilizations & how they first started ancient civilizations, is extremely relevant based upon the (now history) of all subsequent civilizations that we all take for granted & follow, even now.

In the realm of planet earths real history, it is recorded that symbols found from archaeological digs, from all over the world has resulted in civilizations, all separated by time, distance & bio-geographically, all worshiped

& studied the same pictograms of Orion star constellations.

In the year of our planet earth year 2020, here is what we do know now, as scientist would all agree, that several ancient civilizations that are reminiscent of the Aztecs, Egyptians, Mayan, Seminarian, Babylonian, Cambodian, Mesopotamia, Hawaiian, ancient civilizations separated by centuries that shared no contact with each other except, they all studied & deified the Orion star constellations, is the same pictograms of, Orion star constellations.

The second storyboard/screenplay is named;

2- **Little Miss Pantomime short screenplay movie**; exert;

Included within this movie screenplay, all complete movie scripts, dialogs forthwith.

This story is about very dark true life story about a little homeless girl living on the streets of a big city. The tale has many twists & turns of high drama, about street children & pedophilia, child prostitution & children being trafficked.

This story is a grave tale & very difficult to write; however, the laws of candor must always be obeyed in order to seek out all truths, however painful & grotesque.

This storyboard depicts real actual accounts of the facts of life and the ultimate fate, for so many children in the United States & around the world.

Many homeless & at risk children, all whom scrounge around to attempt to just survive, until the next day, all face the horrors of the streets worldwide, being at extreme risk of being exploited, trafficked, sold & preyed upon by adults & maniacal organizations.

For so many children live on the streets of our cities, all around the world, eating out of garbage cans, begging & stealing food, sleeping in dumpsters or whatever they can find shelter to attempt to appear safe. Many grow up unfortunately to adulthood only knowing the (ravishes of the wind) & the people & conditions that make it, & allowing it so.

Children & babies should be protected against all mannerisms of any harm, as they are representative of our own future historical building blocks of our own natural evolutionary progressions.

When a person lies, they murders, some other parts of the world;

3- The third novel is named;

*The third novel (**the Ghosts of Vegas**) is another material that could very easily be converted into another movie.*

The Ghosts of Vegas; exert;

The storyboard is a snapshot about the fate of so many street people, in Vegas & all over the world living in shantytowns, as it depicts the whys of a growing & concern, as so many homeless people who live on the streets.

A foreword;

We are but the wind, & kindred spirits in this place, as we have no footing in this place & no place of our own, as we all are ultimately only shadows & dust.

Alias, we are in the mists of dammed fools and presence, of false, evil, & terrible prophets, the Invasion of the booty & mind snatchers. What is being done, to you, is not as disturbing & as important, as why, it's being done to you, at this current time & place; There are many ancient legends out there, that has passed down through the ages, however; there is one tale that is repeated, from one end of this planet till the other, that all say the same things, they all say, "If you want to deal with a parasite/human being, who preys upon people, you need to use silver, but when you want to deal with a demon, you need to use gold"

A slight poignant & poetic reference;

Somber tumbris, Solutions missed,

Mumblings stumbling,

Miseries bliss,

Many are crying, as the few lavishly laugh,

Very reminiscing of the medieval past

Twisted rituals

True meanings missed

Many are blinded by, sleight of hand tricks—; Poem by, E-Borders; @

Languages, we count on them so much, & they mean so little; however; in the domain & realm of communication, there is another language unspoken that is commonly spoken amongst all global brethrens that are currently caught up in this manically, sadistic, ritualistic, ridiculous demonic struggle on this planet, as it transcends any & all other languages on this planet & is only spoken through the eyes & the souls and aura of the many.

This language could only be described as the non-spoken language, of the struggle of all global brethrens.

When the words & knowledge of the Wise men & Women, all fall on deaf ears, then mankind is surely lost.

In this world, there is too much needless, suffrage & pain, death & despair, as the needs of the many cry out to the cruel laughter of the twisted few.

Millions & millions of people, from all around the world visit, (Vegas) every year.

They arrive & are taken/herded to their hotels & motels, connived & cheated by, the crooked taxi cab thieves, also the (sodomistic) (Bluber) & (if) drivers.

They get over charged, by the hotels & motels, with exorbitant resort fees, on top of other assorted fees, and Are pocket rifled, & become blinded by the lights by the factious ambiance of the strip.

These three storyboards now Convenes;

Planet

Black

Screenplay Written by:Everett C Borders Jr. Ph.D.

The brief bio of Everett C Borders Jr. Ph.D.

He was born in 1951 at Cook-county Hospital in Chicago ILL. He was the fourth of six children & son of the late Everett & Mary Borders. He grew-up on the west side of the mean streets of the cities Rockwell garden projects with hard living & extremely violent gangs. His passion for writing started in the early sixties attending & graduating with a scholarship from Westinghouse vocational high School. He began writing poems & lyrics as expressions as he started playing bass guitar & drums, keys & 4track recording learning from his brother. He graduated from Loop College in Chicago ILL. He started working for Ford Motor Co. As an apprentice in Dearborn Mich. & joined the Chicago Police Dept in 1973. He excelled in worked in tactical, special operations, gang enforcement HBT (Hostage barricade terrorist) & vice. In 1976, he joined the United States Coast Guard reserve port security; he worked with agencies of the US Government. After receiving over one hundred & fifty awards for valor & meritorious city/state/ federal service work, he left Chicago in 1989 arriving in Denver Colorado where he started ECB (Clandestine). He continued academic learning & began to work in industry of, addictions, Counseling, social services, and sitting on the Colorado state board for mental health. He started working in fast-paced engineering & advanced concepts in innovations. He worked in the assisting & mentoring in small theater productions with local & at risk adolescents & adults. He received numerous letters of praise for service & civic efforts. He received his Ph.D. in Counseling Psychology in 2006 from Cambridge S. University.

He has publications in, Publications. He consults, mentor, writes scripts, articles, commentaries & considers himself as an innovation scientist as he has more than several, groundbreaking inventions & is a constant collaborator in theoretical scientific projections, as an Independent Think Tanks Professional of real world innovations a LinkedIn professional.

Planet-Black

A foreword;

Sometimes, just sometimes, when you wish upon a shining star, it does, make a big difference on whom; your real ancestors are, as it is within all of nature; for even a (dog), distinguishes between being stumbled upon & being kicked.

Some conditions are like a poison, soaked into the ground, as no amount of cordial words, no amount of civic protests, or wishful thinking can sometimes divert from what is, what was, or what ultimately could be.

The writer of this story & being a lifelong personal eye witness to these most egregious of all retched existence of the most chronic deplorable of all conditions of being on this planet, constantly dreams of a world without (them).

As in most dreams, real purgatory exist in real time, right here & now, with billions upon multitudes of real unfortunate souls that privies of both, conscious & subconscious subliminal twilights of their own personal narratives.

As so many are Amorally & cryptically managed, and at times, sink into morbid states of temporary contentment or manically managed micro increments of predilections of bliss, a few, always have the same reminders of this place, every time they listen to the twisted, demonic, deplorable & demented talk radio stations & turn on their TV sets, or just step outside their front door.

The greatest strengths maniacal entities that are currently perched upon & feeding upon you have, are their arrogance & blatant anonymity, of (you) never really knowing they truly exist.

This storyboard is a high action science fiction & high drama, about a race of black warriors who come to earth after witnessing the genocidal & treatment atrocities on planet earth, as they attempt to correct what's been a historical global effort to denigrate the black experience on planet earth.

The story is science fiction & futuristic; it has extreme drama, with scientific, biblical & historical facts as its back drop is in years 2020 and thirty five thousand years in earths past.

This screenplay is harvested upon presentence of real factual historical & scientific evidence, perceived science fiction & futuristic interpretations, along with this writer's personal highlighted original theoretical scientific innovational concepts, and part (original story movie) screenplay novel; included within this screenplay, all complete movie scripts, dialogs & soundtrack forthwith.

In the real history of earth, as to when, mankind first crawled out of the jungle & began the first civilizations & how they first started ancient civilizations, is extremely relevant based upon the (now history) of all subsequent civilizations that we all take for granted & follow, even now.

In the realm of planet earths real history, it is recorded that symbols found from archaeological digs, from all over the world has resulted in civilizations, all separated by time, distance & bio-geographically, all worshiped & studied the same pictograms of Orion star constellations.

In the year of our planet earth year 2020, here is what we do know now, as scientist would all agree, that several ancient civilizations that are reminiscent of the Aztecs, Egyptians, Mayan, Seminarian, Babylonian, Cambodian, Mesopotamia, Hawaiian, ancient civilizations separated by centuries that shared no contact with each other except, they all studied & deified the Orion star constellations, is the same pictograms of, Orion star constellations.

The first ancient civilizations on this planet earth and every other ancient civilization that preceded it, all shared the same interest, Orion.

Whatever the true mysteries of the Orion star constellations, at this current time & place, are scientifically & currently unknown at this time, however; it may be the answer, we as humans, all seek as to who, we really are & most important, where we all came from, or the key to our ultimate humanoid survival.

The story of planet black is a possibility of what was, & what's most important, the possibility of future horizons of mankind & the ultimate way mankind may have become, as half of writing history is hiding the truth, as this story pits mankind's ancient fears, against the summit of mankind's current knowledge.

Real history has been white washed to disguise much of the real truth of the past, as in anything, the real truth, like real history is relevant, only if you truly seek the perceive knowledge & plot your own life's course of your own futures past.

This is the most controversial work ever written to date

This Screenplay Novel is dedicated to the memory of HS

Planet Black

(Story-Board)(Movie/ Screenplay)

The (**storyboard**) starts in the Orion belt constellations with a (blue star) of (Rigel).

Rigel about 40,000 times brighter than our local sun, Rigel Temperature Rigel is estimated to have surface temperatures of around 12,000C (22,000F), more than twice as hot as the sun.

Rigel Luminosity (energy emitted) Rigel is a blue supergiant star with a luminosity more than 100,000 times that of the sun of earth. A planet named (Planet Black), just the correct distance from (Rigel), not too close & not too distant to sustain humanoid life.

It was named (**planet black**), but not because the (**inhabitants were black**), but because from the planet orbit, & shining with the (blue star), the entire planet looks & appeared black because of its very rich mineral complexities, from its seas, lands & mountains, as it appeared the entire planet looks like a shimmering, glittering black ball in space, from the high orbit of the planet.

Planet Black

Their appearance, of its inhabitants, It is said their appearance, was that of an extremely dark black, almost blue/deep purple color, humanoids with black curly hair & brown eyes.

They highly resembled the indigenous humanoids of earths, as what is now known as, Australian & African continent; the forerunners of all now generations of earth.

Where, the (inhabitants) of planet black, ultimately came from, was a mystery; however their presence on planet black seemed to be most curious & intentional.

They all had a natural Genoa maturation type Melanin of 99.9%, far different from humanoids on earth as their (DNA strains were in the hundreds), far more than earth's humanoids.

The planet inhabitants used an ancient methodology of calculus & measurement, with laws promoting & directing the prime directives.

Their legal & all working methodology's were systems all done by a series of bio-super computations, in algorithms to imply, direct & instruct the outcome of any legal proceedings, without the corruptions of senators, presidents, & royalty.

All or most proceedings & legal briefs/case management were imputed in a series of bio-super computations, as the outcome is based upon all known planetary & galaxy laws, relevant throughout the constellations, conveyed in algorithms to imply, direct & instruct the outcome of any legal proceedings.

Each individual or inhabitant of planet black, all strive in their own perfections of the arts, science, management, maintenance, navigation, & etc; in order to seek a more perfect world.

Example; if an individual or inhabitant of planet black, wanted to be a planetary waste collector & disposal unit, that humanoids designations will be as such & all rights & privileges were to be afforded to that individual or inhabitant of planet black, with the same as if the person was an associate supreme prime council member.

On planet black, all of its inhabitant have & enjoy the same privileges, with no rich & no poor, a zero class systems with no corruptions or greed, ever, as they had no need for currency, as credits were assigned to every citizen inhabitant of planet black or (apportionments) enabling the inhabitant to purchase anything from food to garments, & etc.

When purchasing anything out of the planetary systems, they all sometimes used ancient pieces of the currencies of gold & silver.

Their trade & barter systems throughout the two galaxies of Orion & Andromeda were done with commerce of trading deeds for services & services of goods.

Planet black, so rich in minerals wealth with gold, diamonds, silver & titanium & etc, did not trade their mineral wealth to other systems; however the inhabitants of planet black provided services in aggressive law enforcement throughout the two systems & received bartered goods & services in exchange for those services.

Planet black, under the blue sun/star of (Rigel), emitted, gamma rays that gave the appearances of translucent & iridescent colors in all plants & animals, oceans, rivers, along with the molecular chemical content of the planet being so rich in so many minerals, that (even on the dark side) of planet black, the planet shined ever so brightly, in the dark.

Planet black shimmered like glitter in both day & night, as wealth is so abundant, system & planetary wise, the need to attempt to hoard & connive was absent.

For instants, this entire system was so streamlined & efficient, if an individual or inhabitant of planet black, ever wanted to move or relocate to another side of the planet, or off-world planet, all they had to do is file a request, listings family size & home size, & the matter would be extradited by council member with a new relocating & employment placement unit designated, so forth & so on.

Individuals or inhabitants of planet black, all enjoyed, great dances, joys, native wines, ales, & other refreshments, and off-world delicates for trading with Andromeda constellations systems wide, they all celebrated in vast sports & musical cathedrals, when vacationing, they climbed the jeweled, rubies & emerald mountains, they worshiped in the crystals & diamond caves, they swam & enjoyed, in the golden & silver glistening & shimmering very warm waters.

They were enthuses of universal solemn brotherhood, as they were the gate keepers/

law enforcers of the Orion & the Andromeda constellations systems wide.

Planet black scientists were of the most advanced in the constellations, with a wealth of innovations in bio- humanoid evolutionary advancements, such as; (EveBor),

The Pneumatic internal human heart pump system,

This writer's theoretical projected concept of total heart replacement has evolved around the nexus phase of the dawn of artificial human heart replacement projects.

Inline aortic implantation-al device that has a self-backup pumping system,

1-primary system device is visualized by a bio-electric fifty-year perpetual self-charging capacitance cell system using **sonic** calibrated pumping action.

2-second stage of this device is using the human body's own everyday **Pneumatic compression** movement action, using sonic **Pneumatic compression** pumping of necessary body blood transfer.

3-when the recipient of the device is asleep or lies

Dormant for a period of three hours or more, the device automatically switches to the primary system.

While the recipient of the device is awake or moving about, the system reverts back to the secondary system, using the human body's own **Pneumatic compression** pumping movement action.

In concepts of a one way valve, allowing fluid transfer to only go in the direction of the sonic pulse valve reciprocal directed direction.

The device is about the size of a human's hand, including the self-contained power packed, bio-electric fifty-year perpetual self-charging capacitance cell.

The self-contained power packed, bio-electric fifty-year perpetual self-charging capacitance cell is replaced every fifty years.

Any failure to either, primary or secondary systems, the device is designed to run on a single system until such times that corrections can be made to either system.

Concept or concepts, of this system designs would allow the recipient of the device to virtually extend lifespan of many years beyond a normal humanoids heart.

The inhabitants of the planet all had limited mental & kinetic telepathy abilities, allowing them to share thoughts, even control other life forms, without verbally speaking, as pets they had lions, tigers, leopards, jaguar, cheetahs.

The inhabitants of the planet were all individually implanted with rice sized chips, constantly transmitting signals to a fifty trillion channel liquid bio-micro super computation computer, alerting presence, area, vital signs & locations in real time.

As there were **no zoos on the planet**, all creatures enjoyed all freedoms of movement within the entire planet, with the exceptions of the more dangerous ones that were all chipped, for dangerous zones & crossings implantation radius chipped signals.

Their scientific methodologies, allowed them to fully synthesize the natural bio-camouflage elements of the chameleons camouflage, in order to mask their always war like stance appearance.

Part of their bio Ergonomic self cleaning, disinfecting clothing apparel, also used a series of bio-electric capacitor panels, or slats that could jolt any object for a distance of fifty feet, from one to seven hundred thousand volts of electric current for five minutes in any direction, by sheer will, much like an electric ell.

Their bio-electric Nanette-micro (led) apparel allowed them to fully design their outer garments, specialize in military readiness & enjoy everyday freshness with a different look, while being optimum in total safety & security at all times, with the comforts of using over seven million color & design pattern styles.

They were a very compassionate people, strong determined but without malice.

They were definitive outcome driven, but were never imposing.

They were very bold, strong in stature, but never offensive, or over bearing towards any other life forms.

They all strived towards total perfections, harmony of the, mind, body & spirit of all humanoids, & other creatures as well.

They only engaged (warfare) to protect their own planetary systems & that of the Andromeda constellations.

They only implored the most fiercest, (galaxy O rangers), to patrol the Orion & the Andromeda constellations, in order to maintain mutual respect, reverences, of the prime directives throughout Orion & the Andromeda constellations to ensure peaceful cohabitation living for all, & in all systems.

(Galaxy O rangers), were comprised of male & female humanoids from the toughest parts of the both Orion & the Andromeda constellations.

They all carried out & enforced all laws relative to the prime directives & the orders of the supreme council on planet black.

Where ever there was, lawlessness, the (Galaxy O rangers), always prevailed, & where there were specific threats towards any inhabitant in either the Orion & the Andromeda constellations galaxy, they very vigorously, addressed & eliminated, the threat in their small numbers, using smart nano containment weapons & micro pulse blast cannons.

The police/rangers, as part of their clothing apparel was a series of bio-electric capacitor panels, or slats that could jolt, any object for a distance of one thousand feet, with a half million volts of electric current for five minutes in any direction, by sheer will, like an electric ell.

Their bio-electric Nanette-micro (led) apparel allowed them to fully design their outer garments, specializing in military/police mode readiness at all times.

Whenever the tasks were too large for the (Galaxy O rangers), their massive military armadas, from both the Orion & the Andromeda constellations galaxy addressed any threat, with their thousands of monstrous super warships, that could destroy any planet along with steering comets & asteroids to destroy any & all finality obligatory orders, set forth by the supreme high council.

As it was in always rotational, inhabitants on planet black all enjoyed natural surroundings, wealth, comfort, meaningful employment, spiritual reverences of contentment of self being, they lived in total harmony with other known galaxies worlds & all its inhabitants.

They developed & used smart bots, infused with programmed (**Ai**) intelligence; all manufactured using micro-gyro stability systems, this allowed the smart bots to walk & run, bend & balance upright with micro nuclear fusion (cell) unit with strong titanium indo-skeletons covered by a bio-synthetic living humanoid outer shell, lasting two hundred of earth years capable of driving, doing house work, tutoring/teaching, to pleasure, to Manuel labor, as none were ever programmed for tactical combat or war.

Each inhabitant of planet black was assigned two bots per person or two per household, as they all looked & had the real appearance of a regular humanoid, with exception of distinct markings in the eyes & hairline of each bots, making them very noticeably identifiable to all other humanoids on & off the planet.

Smart bots, did everything from tutoring, to operating crafts in & off world of planet black.

The planet black inhabitants all lived, laughed, smiled, dined, wined in total peace at each other's company & other life-forms as well, however, **(all was not well)**.

Eons ago, a peaceful accord was established within the Orion constellations as a universal law established guarantying the safe & peaceful existence/coexistence within the galaxy to promote, respect, & abides in accordance with the general planetary sovereignty of the general harmony of the entire galaxy.

An elite law enforcement element was established to promote, enforce & bring forth (order), to the entire galaxy, this accord so ratified, by all peaceful systems in the entire galaxy that even the Andromeda galaxy also joined the same accord; thus the (galaxy 0 Rangers) were established, a methodology to ensuring peaceful coexistence of all sentient life forms, that is in the two systems, with basic law & order, and most of all, general planetary sovereignty,& territory respect, to all systems within the two galaxies.

All identified & registered sanction sentient life forms agreed, to this accord to promote law and order throughout the two galaxies signed & agree to the lawful accordance of the rules & regulations set forth by the high councils of both the Andromeda galaxy and Orion constellations, as a universal law enforcement established entity guarantying the safe & peaceful existence/coexistence within the galaxy to promote, respect, & abides in accordance with the general planetary sovereignty of the general harmony of the entire galaxy.

Now comes the realm of the (galaxy 0 Rangers), one million personnel strong, beyond bold, beyond fearless, beyond corruption, they all flew in threes (plus three smart bots), their ships (special jumper attack ships), were well equipped with smart weapons, built for attack & destroy and enforcement.

They used extremely intense ultraviolet & infrared scanning weapons, discreet ultrasonic emitters to disrupt all the neurological impulses of all whom that were under the attack.

They always approached every incident with disruptive sound & music blaring & forward micro observational array drones, as they shot (molecular acid) the size of tennis balls, self adhesive at supersonic speeds towards their enemy's ships to disable & breach their hulls integrity, for extreme breach of any barrier or hull in a fire fight to confuse & disrupt, disable.

When they arrived on surface of any planet, they all rode on hydrogen powered jet rocket bikes, ascending & descending in and out of orbit, armed with smart targeted smart micro-missiles & pulse cannons.

Their heads up display indicated on their helmets face shield aids the weapons targeting & navigational display.

These bikes allowed the rangers to speed towards any aggression & confront any adversary with ease of speed, weaponry & tactical edge; however, they were limited in range to only twenty thousand miles, but rangers always carried spare fuel cells to spike the bikes range to forty thousand miles.

They micro transmitted in real time, back to both of the high councils Andromeda galaxy and Orion constellations in real time actions after seeking assistance.

They wore chameleon apparel, even their (special jumper attack ships), were equipped with the chameleon cloaking capabilities.

Each ranger was equipped with a personal bio blaster, capable of firing five thousand rounds with ten thousand degrees with plasma rounds, at any target, with settings from stun to total thermal destruction at will. (Galaxy 0 Rangers), were true gunslingers in every sense of the word, a no nonsense philosophy & ensuring the order of two galaxy's.

Whatever they decided on was final, in accordance with all rules & laws by the high councils of Andromeda galaxy and Orion constellations in real time actions after seeking assistance.

The next step up from lawlessness in the two galaxies', were the extreme military super starships, with untold fire power & ten thousand men strong, per ship, capable of destroying entire planetary systems with directing comets, asteroids to any target.

Their military weaponry was ten times the fire power of the (Galaxy 0 Rangers), with settings on destroy only.

Military operations were only used when all other methods of diplomatic efforts had failed or abandoned, in relative orders & accordance with the high councils of the two galaxies.

Relative order needed to be maintained throughout the entire systems & the (Galaxy 0 Rangers), were the advanced guards of police law enforcement.

Galaxy 0 Rangers

Introduction & sound tracks ;(four beat measure) sounds starting from very slow

& faint & gradual semi to strong & violent thunderous African war drums, African war drums sounds of thunderous;

https://www.youtube.com/watch?v=tR2fgsEjyp4

https://audiojungle.net/item/african-war-drums/10894670

https://www.youtube.com/watch?v=kZxEI9E9aP0

https://www.youtube.com/watch?v=BLZTOiKBHVA

https://www.youtube.com/watch?v=DYvNAHByKPM

https://www.youtube.com/watch?v=H2hfzX5XaXg

https://www.youtube.com/watch?v=N9IWpYgEaug

https://www.pond5.com/stock-music/8535478/battle-war-drums-main-154.html

https://www.pond5.com/stock-music/8535478/battle-war-drums-main-154.html

https://www.youtube.com/watch?v=B2qfCy_UTZo'

https://www.youtube.com/watch?v=qGnodTjD6QM

https://www.audiomicro.com/african-drums-music-musical-african-drums-1-sound-effects-44886

https://www.audioblocks.com/royalty-free-audio/heavy+african+drums ;background sounds of growling lions, tigers, leopards, jaguars;

Live recorded sound of a leopard roar;

https://www.youtube.com/watch?v=xW4R8Gp4J8s

https://www.youtube.com/watch?v=Zi3350uEvE8

https://www.youtube.com/watch?v=AA2uS9VG7B

Live recorded sound of a tiger roars;

https://www.youtube.com/watch?v=SkFx45lxlvA

https://www.youtube.com/watch?v=tbylGZuMU7c

https://www.youtube.com/watch?v=fWd_b0IOsGM

Live recorded sound of a lion roar;

https://www.youtube.com/watch?v=_22gJ5kB31k

https://www.youtube.com/watch?v=qSu4gx-yIgs

https://www.youtube.com/watch?v=qDoMWd3OS5Q

Live recorded sound of a jaguar roar;

https://www.youtube.com/watch?v=tlMHz-eQdDA

https://www.youtube.com/watch?v=_ORmL-PlU_

https://www.youtube.com/watch?v=1v_kzNpnnF4

https://www.youtube.com/watch?v=_ORmL-PlU_I

https://www.youtube.com/watch?v=tlMHz-eQdDA

Other wild cat sounds;

https://www.youtube.com/watch?v=pHZm52nvBB4

& very slow & hard fusion music with an extreme hard riff lead guitar, as the sounds of war drums get faster & faster with backup low vocals, "g0-rangers, "g0-rangers, death no strangers, g0-rangers, death no strangers, g0-rangers, death no strangers, g0-randers, g0-rangers, death no strangers, g0-rangers, g0-rangers, g0-rangers, death no strangers."

Side & frontal view of three Galaxy 0 Rangers, sitting in the main cockpit of a (special jumper attack ships), cruising at sub light speeds in sector qlb426.

They get an alert (crises) of problem activity in that sector & hone in on a group of (semanoids monsters), large ("Veloster-Raptor" Lizard like garrotes), highly intelligent carnivorous monsters with very big teeth that enslave & feed (alive) on any humanoids for food they can find.

Three galaxies 0 Rangers, (Capitan AAma), (Commander Gham), & (Pilot Methim), are getting the (crises) alert to responds to a planetary crisis, in sector qlb426.

They are cocked & loaded & all have their extreme game (Mandrill) mean war faces, as their faces, all with downwards frowns & grins, & all smoking a cigar like, (vapor adrenaline, high O2, vitamin sticks).

Their cigars, tilting from the side of their mouths, their brows, poised & firm, their chins straps very stern & their nerves are at full & extreme aggression, and their determination is in its full readiness.

As they get closer & closer to the crises, they get more & more excited & prepare for anything, with weapons all at max & power at all full.

They go in, very quickly, and red hot, prepared to blaze with full cannons first.

(Semanoids monsters), are spotted by rangers, from high orbit, are attempting to devour & enslave humanoids, on a small obscured planet on called (Quiroz), within the Orion constellation galaxy.

(Semanoids monsters), have already captured twenty of the (Quiroz), humanoids, on the surface of the planet & have murdered and devoured alive nine others, on the spot, as the level of carnage & blood splatter is extremely devastating.

(Semanoids monsters), are from the planetary systems of the mouhara nebula, from the Andromeda galaxy, that conducts frequent raiding parties, outside their galaxy, for the purpose of enslaving & devouring humanoids, as they are (fully sanctioned) by both the Orion constellation galaxy and the Andromeda galaxy, by all reigning councils, for misconduct & crimes against two galaxy's, under punishment of pain of death.

On their own planetary systems of the mouhara nebula, (Semanoids monsters), have all the food sources from their own indigenous animals they would ever need, however, they prefer the taste of humanoids, in their semantics, and it was a difference of lobster, verse crab, as they had absolutely zero regard for other life forms, especially humanoid, life forms, as they all considered humanoids as a delicacy, to assist in their diet.

The (Semanoids monsters), have large slave cargo star ships, armed with electrostatic plasma bursts, to stun, however the Galaxy 0 Rangers, all have (special jumper attack ships), armed with pulse cannons, electro plasma, tungsten discharge rods, along with their tactical armament, they deployed one hundred tactical space grenade/molecular acid smart drones, used for extreme hull breaching & deploying bio micro weaponry & meteor pulse phase cannons, even gravity cannon bursts to direct meteors to any direct target.

Their hundreds of space drones would encapsulate their opponent's ships, breaching the hull & disrupting their communications, transmissions, weapons.

The (Semanoids monsters), are well over three meters in height, personally armed with stun cannons to be used in quickly stunning & devouring its alive prey, compared to the three Galaxy 0 Rangers, standing just over two meters in height, they are personally armed with, phazers bio cannon blasters pistols with six extreme capacitor power settings, from stun to destroy mode.

The three, Galaxy 0 Rangers, all, quickly set down their star ship just about two hundred meters aft of the (Semanoids monsters), star ships, as they are immediately fired upon by the (Semanoids monsters), star ship.

The result became a ground shooting war & from ship to ship until the Galaxy 0 Rangers, fired an electro plasma, tungsten discharge rods, rendering the (Semanoids monsters), star ship, incapacitated.

All twenty of the (Semanoids monsters), were held in containment on the planet surface as a real time holographic council court, was in-fact held, with three council members from both the Orion constellation galaxy and the Andromeda galaxy.

The holographic council courts, all deemed that the invading ships to be destroyed, or given to the humanoids of the planet (Quiroz), & the (Semanoids monsters), all to be imprisoned on a barren ice cold planet in the kaliem nebula, or terminated forthwith, under pain of death by the discretion of the Galaxy 0 Rangers.

The humanoids of the planet (Quiroz), were very pleased & delighted, to have a little solace from the terrible ordeal & were given planetary systems, kinetic weapons systems & repulsar cannons for any other futures contingencies & eventualities. While leaving the orbit of the planet, (Quiroz), the Galaxy 0 Rangers, (special jumper attack ship) was once again attacked by two other invading ships piloted by, more (Semanoids monsters).

Galaxy 0 Rangers, (special jumper attack ship) fired, their pulse cannons, electro plasma, tungsten discharge rods, & meteor pulse phase cannons, even gravity cannon bursts to direct meteors to their direct targets.

As the results of these star ship battles, the two attack invading ships were destroyed in the battle, and three other attacking invading ships were destroyed.

A real time viewing of the entire spectacle was recorded & transmitted to, both the council members of the, Orion constellation galaxy and the Andromeda galaxy.

As to the (Semanoids monsters) on their own planetary systems of the mouhara nebula, were all deemed quarantined system, and their entire planetary systems, were on future (warning notice) ordered for total planetary destruction, by three super ships from both the Orion constellation galaxy and the Andromeda galaxy, combined, end of transmission.

Banter of the encounter

On; the planet, (Quiroz), in the Orion constellation galaxy, a planetary crisis, in sector qlb426.

Three galaxies 0 Rangers, (Capitan AAma), (Commander Gham), & (Pilot Methim).

(Capitan AAma),

"Stand by to get out of sub-light speeds at my mark, five, six, and seven, mark, now!"

(Commander Gham),

"Slowing to internal navigation on my mark, (Pilot), at three, two one, mark, now!"

(Pilot Methim),

"Coming in red hot Capitan & Commander, orbital geo scan, reveals we can set down hot, just about two hundred meters aft of the (Semanoids monsters), star ships."

(Commander Gham),

"we have a tactical advantage with weaponry, and the element of surprise, I recommend attack pattern bull three."

(Capitan AAma),

"The old full flanking maneuver, sounds like a plan commander, you guys flank left & right, & ill take the fight to the middle and hit them straight in their big ugly faces, check!"

(Capitan AAma),

Sits inside the main cockpit of a (special jumper attack ship), his weapons on the trigger, with, all the ships armaments to bare, facing the enemy ship, armed with pulse cannons, electro plasma, tungsten discharge rods, & meteor pulse phase cannons, even gravity cannon bursts to direct meteors to any direct target.

They come in red hot, blazing using extreme high intensity ultraviolet & infrared scanning weapons, discreet ultrasonic emitters to disrupt all the neurological impulses of all of all whom that were under the attack.

They always approached every incident with disruptive sound & music blaring & forward micro observational array to confuse, (**Commander Gham**), He took the right flank, with pulse cannons on full settings & blazing towards the enemy ship.

(**Pilot Methim**),

He took the left flank, with pulse cannons on full settings & blazing towards the enemy ship.

The tree advanced meter by meter, with the (special jumper attack ship), giving the other two physical cover, left & right, up the middle, with steady cover fire, encroached meter by meter, until the entire threat analyses was fully neutralized.

Battle above, the planet, orbiting (Quiroz),

While attempting to leave the planets orbit after the attack.

(Pilot Methim),

"Capitan we are being fired up by two invader ships."

(Capitan AAma),

"Start the maneuver, attack pattern (roni)", *a (zigzag pattern & x movements to confuse the enemy's targeting systems)*

(Commander Gham),

"Targeting their aft engines on three, two, one, firing now Capitan, using ultraviolet & infrared scanning weapons, and discreet ultrasonic emitters and pulse cannon, now."

(Pilot Methim),

"A direct hit Capitan, ship on starboard disabled on their main engine & the port ship destroyed broadside full hull breach".

(Capitan AAma),

He's looking out at the scanners & says,

"Well, gents, looks like we have more coming to the party, give me an attack pattern (bulha), a (pattern the goes in semi circles & quickly centers)."

(Commander Gham),

"We have three other attacking invading ships aft of us closing at mock point seven."

(Capitan AAma),

"Give them full spread gents, and give them plenty of spare sauce."

(Commander Gham),

Approaching with disruptive sound & music blaring & forward micro observational array to confuse,

"Firing, on full focus ultraviolet & infrared scanning

weapons, discreet ultrasonic emitters, pulse cannons, electro plasma, tungsten discharge rods, & meteor pulse phase cannons."

(Pilot Methim),

"Direct hits on all three, Commander, great shot as always commander."

(Capitan AAma),

Transmitting all images in real time, of battles out to high council to Orion constellation galaxy and the Andromeda galaxy.

"Good job gents, it's time for some R & R."

The inhabitants of (planet black) were a race of warriors, however, in their vast history, they did not always rule, other or lesser civilizations.

They all had the ancient & inherited ability of their enhanced primal adrenal gear, a seventh sense, fight or flight mammalian methodology, the same as the humanoids on earth, but much stronger, the same bursts of adrenal strength as gorillas & lions on the planet earth.

This allowed them to be much stronger & much more agile relative to their earth's counterparts.

They observed & learned other systems, & only intervened when they were directly threatened, as they were extremely formidable

& feared throughout the Orion constellation systems & beyond.

They all walked with a definitive confidence & purpose and self-assurance.

Their mannerisms were like & resembled that of the warriors, warlords of the Moors & Egyptians on earth.

The rhythm of their walk & talk resembled that of several mixed ancient African (kata movements) Passed down from old ancient African warlords of the Zulu, & Mau Mau, the Maasai, the Timbuktu, the Oyo Empire, the Opobo, Ghana Empire and the Ashanti Kingdom, as well as the Bambara Empire Moors & Egyptians on earth.

Whenever they spoke, it was always of an instructional dialect of definitive information of what was to be done & how it was to be carried out.

Their armies all moved with such great (stealth & rhythm) of the keen stalking aspects of African great predators as the lion, the leopard, the cobra, the black mamba & Nile crocodile.

On planet black & on earth, they mastered the arts of flanking & (taught), bred & used the rhinos & elephants, the Cape buffalo & hyenas, Lions, Leopards, Cheetahs only to influence advanced guards of warfare, always, in front of advancing hoards as an armored stampede.

They mastered & doctrine the arts of tactical flanking & encompassing, & like the horns of the bull, with the stealth of the cobra.

Their vast armadas, all mastered the arts of night stealth, as it was the night ambush & in the night, as well as the day, that made their war campaign almost invincible to any other defending force.

In their vast history, they admired & influenced, the Moorish warriors that took on all comers, all opposing forces, with no quarter, no mercy, no possible means or possibility of escape.

They mastered & left behind in their wake of conquest, the techniques of the old ancient African arts of building, aqueducts, barter, farming, animal herding, music, dance, pottery, weaponry, poetry, spices, masonry & carpentry, ancient irrigation, conservation, in all systems so deemed.

Moorish warriors, whenever or whomever they conquered, they would leave behind their great generals, like (Othello), a Moorish prince, & general Tariq ibn Ziyad, with small garrisons in an occupying force & always for a tactical Intel apparatus.

They tried not to influence, peak periods in the evolutionary humanoid history on earth, however they were always there, like the rule of the (moors) conquered, & (ruled all of Europe for seven hundred years).

They were there when the Egyptians, ruled, https://www.history.com/topics/ancient-history/ancient- egypt

Also the warlords of the **Zulu**, https://www.sahistory.org.za/article/zulu

https://www.britannica.com/topic/Zulu

http://en.lisapoyakama.org/the-religion-of-the-zulu/ & **Mau Mau,**

https://www.britannica.com/topic/Mau-Mau

https://www.sahistory.org.za/article/mau-mau-uprising

https://www.merriam-webster.com/dictionary/mau-mau & etc.

They were there observing the genocide of hundreds & hundreds of millions of blacks & (Black slavery) on a global scale of the planet earth. https://www.history.com/topics/black-history/slavery

https://www.history.com/topics/black-history/black-history-milestones

https://www.theroot.com/slavery-by-the-numbers-1790874492

https://www.smithsonianmag.com/history/slavery-trail-of-tears-180956968/

They were there when Neapolitan was defeated on the island of Haiti, by the black islanders. https://www.history.com/this-day-in-history/haitian-independence-proclaimed

https://library.brown.edu/haitihistory/9.html

http://caribya.com/caribbean/history/napoleon.haiti/

http://www.milwaukeeindependent.com/syndicated/haiti-became-an-independent-nation-when-enslaved-blacks-defeated-napoleon/

https://www.quora.com/Is-it-true-that-Haiti-defeated-Napoleon-s-invasion-attempt-in-Hispaniola

They were there when (Caucasians) would dress up with white sheets on their heads, murdering millions of innocent (black) men, women & children & church goers, https://www.history.com/topics/reconstruction/ku-klux-klan-video

https://www.splcenter.org/fighting-hate/extremist-files/ideology/ku-klux-klan

https://www.britannica.com/topic/Ku-Klux-Klan

https://www.pbs.org/wgbh/americanexperience/features/flood-klan/

https://www.pbs.org/wgbh/americanexperience/features/grant-kkk/

They were even there observing the Nazi, murdering their own people, on a worldwide genocide scale.

https://www.holocaust.cz/en/history/final-solution/general-2/the-start-of-the-mass-murder/

https://encyclopedia.ushmm.org/content/en/article/the-murder-of-the-handicapped

https://www.livescience.com/64420-holocaust-jewish-deaths.html

http://www.projetaladin.org/holocaust/en/history-of-the-holocaust-shoah/the-killing-machine.html

https://www.history.com/topics/world-war-ii/adolf-hitler-1

http://www.historyplace.com/worldwar2/defeat/mass-murder.htm

https://aeon.co/ideas/drunk-on-genocide-how-the-nazis-celebrated-murdering-jews

They observed the following historical events of; murders by the Caucasians;

Murders by the Spanish & Aztecs/Incas,https://
sites.google.com/site/thecolonistsjournal/
spanish-conquer-the-aztecs-and-incas

https://www.classzone.com/net_explorations/
U4/U4_article5.cfm

http://www.ushistory.org/civ/11e.asp

http://www.aztec-history.com/fall-of-the-
aztec-empire.html

https://www.spanishwars.net/16th-century-
conquest-inca-empire.html

Murders in Australia with the (black
aborigines),

https://www.google.com/search?q=
Murders+in+Australia+with+the+
(black+aborigines),&tbm=isch&source=
univ&sa=X&ved=2ahUKEwiTpJX
g1trhAhUBrZ4KHblWCDsQsAR6
BAgJEAE

https://www.google.com/search?q=Murders+in+Australia+with+the+(black+aborigines),&tbm=isch&source=univ&sa=X&ved=2ahUKEwiTpJXg1trhAhUBrZ4KHblWCDsQ7Al6BAgJEA0

https://www.theguardian.com/australia-news/2019/mar/04/the-killing-times-the-massacres-of-aboriginal-people-australia-must-confront

https://www.theguardian.com/australia-news/2019/mar/23/murdering-gully-settlers-killed-35-in-aboriginal-camp-and-threw-bodies-into-the-water

https://atlantablackstar.com/2015/06/09/8-facts-may-not-know-extermination-australias-aborigines/

http://theconversation.com/we-just-black-matter-australias-indifference-to-aboriginal-lives-and-land-85168

Murdering of millions of American Indians,

https://www.history.com/news/native-americans-genocide-united-states

http://endgenocide.org/learn/past-genocides/native-americans/

https://www.youtube.com/watch?v=jUeAYiKHcvo

https://www.aljazeera.com/indepth/opinion/thanksgiving-annual-genocide-whitewash-171120073022544.html

http://oxfordre.com/americanhistory/view/10.1093/acrefore/9780199329175.001.0001/acrefore-9780199329175-e-3

https://worldwithoutgenocide.org/genocides-and-conflicts/american-indian

Murdering millions of east Indians,

https://www.history.com/news/native-americans-genocide-united-states

https://www.theguardian.com/world/2007/aug/24/india.randeepramesh

http://endgenocide.org/learn/past-genocides/native-americans/

https://www.independent.co.uk/news/world/world-history/winston-churchill-genocide-dictator-shashi-tharoor-melbourne-writers-festival-a7936141.html

https://www.npr.org/2017/04/17/524348264/largely-forgotten-osage-murders-reveal-a-conspiracy-against-wealthy-native-ameri

https://guestlist.net/article/92742/how-the-british-heartlessly-murdered-one-million-indians

Murdering millions of Asians in Southeast Asia,

https://thediplomat.com/2015/12/1975-the-start-and-end-of-conflict-in-southeast-asia/

https://www.nbcnews.com/news/asian-america/forty-years-after-resettlement-thousands-southeast-asian-refugees-face-deportation-n466376

https://densho.org/asian-american-opposition-vietnam-war/

https://www.counterpunch.org/2015/10/02/southeast-asia-forgets-about-western-terror/

https://www.google.com/search?q=southeast+asia+during+vietnam+war&sa=X&ved=2ahUKEwjRjqDA2NrhAh UEv54KHYHsAAwQlQIoAnoECAoQAw

Murdering Canadian Eskimo Indians,

https://www.thecanadianencyclopedia.ca/en/article/aliko miak-and-tatimagana

https://www.macleans.ca/culture/books/lawrence-millman-revisits-a-grisly-mass-murder-in-canadas-north/

https://www.google.com/search?q=Murdering+Canadian+Eskimo+Indians,&tbm=isch&source=univ&sa=X&ved=2ahUKEwj7-4SA2drhAhXIo54KHd-zD_0QsAR6BAgJEAE

https://www.google.com/search?q=Murdering+Canadian+Eskimo+Indians,&tbm=isch&source=univ&sa=X&ved=2ahUKEwj7-4SA2drhAhXIo54KHd-zD_0Q7Al6BAgJEA0

https://www.canadiangeographic.ca/article/inuit-injustice-and-trial-changed-everything

Murdering over a million, in South American Indians,

http://endgenocide.org/learn/past-genocides/native-americans/

https://www.history.com/news/native-americans-genocide-united-states

https://www.survivalinternational.org/tribes/brazilian

https://www.nytimes.com/2017/05/29/opinion/the-genocide-of-brazils-indians.html

The civil war, First World War, & Second World War,

https://www.history.com/topics/american-civil-war/american-civil-war-history

https://www.battlefields.org/learn/articles/brief-overview-american-civil-war

http://www.historyplace.com/civilwar/

http://www.civilwar.com/

https://www.britannica.com/event/American-Civil-War

https://www.britannica.com/event/World-War-I

https://www.history.com/this-day-in-history/world-war-ii

https://www.history.com/topics/world-war-ii/world-war-ii-history

https://nationalinterest.org/feature/the-spanish-civil-war-trial-run-world-war-ii-17086

They witnessed & monitored the Asian wars, and Arabic wars.

https://www.google.com/search?q=causes+of+middle+east+crisis&sa=X&ved=2ahUKEwiv5pLc2trhAhXF854KHZvVAasQ1QIoBnoECBIQBw

https://www.britannica.com/event/Arab-Israeli-wars

https://www.aljazeera.com/indepth/opinion/2015/11/arab-world-war-151125115525462.html

https://en.qantara.de/content/civil-wars-in-the-middle-east-the-arab-issue-of-kith-and-kin

https://www.google.com/search?q=yom+kippur+war&sa=X&ved=2ahUKEwiv5pLc2trhAhXF854KHZvVAasQ1QIoAno ECBIQAw

Some (emissaries) inhabitants of (planet black), observed from a distant, but at times, were caught in the middle of the (indigenous earth black population) ramblings & fray of the nonsensical raving's of the lunatic minds they encountered on earth, always perpetrated by Caucasians.

The inhabitants of (planet black) were there, when the now continent of North America, (elected) the first black president, **Obama**, as some (emissaries) inhabitants of (planet black), observed and recorded, him from a distant & all thought that he had great promise.

The inhabitants of (planet black) were there to witness it all, as some inhabitants from (planet black), sent to earth as (emissaries) were murder, enslaved, imprisoned, raped, beaten along with the rest of the (indigenous earth black population) on planet earth.

The inhabitants of (planet black) came to earth, not to rule, but to observe, in accordance of their (prime directive rules).

The inhabitants of planet black lived on a planet where, all things were possible for all its inhabitants.

All of the inhabitants on planet black were true vegetarians, & refused to ever consume animal matter, as it was in-fact deemed all poisonous & (illegal), not fit for nutritional humanoid consumption, on their home world of planet black.

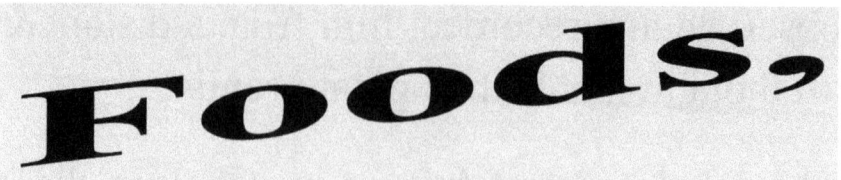

Foods,

They consumed many exotic fruits & vegetables, native to (planet Black).

They used & consumed Algae protein, Sugar kelp and seaweed as super-food human food source.

(They perfected to art of food sensitizes) as many exotic fruits & vegetables, native to (planet Black), from algae protein, sugar kelp and seaweed as super-food human food source. Foods containing;

- **Iodine and calcium-rich, kelp also has natural antioxidant properties**
- **Seaweed contains 46 minerals, 16 amino acids and 11 micro-nutrients**

The natural diuretic also helps with weight control and cleanses system

- **Nori:** 37 mcg per gram (25% of the RDI)

- **Wakame:** 139 mcg per gram (93% of the RDI)
- **Kombu:** 2523 mcg per gram (1,682% of the RDI)

Dried Spirulina can provide

- **Calories:** 20
- **Crabs:** 1.7 grams
- **Protein:** 4 grams
- **Fat:** 0.5 gram
- **Fiber:** 0.3 grams
- **Riboflavin:** 15% of the RDI
- **Thiamin:** 11% of the RDI
- **Iron:** 11% of the RDI
- **Manganese:** 7% of the RDI
- **Copper:** 21% of the RDI

Contains a Variety of Protective Antioxidants

Provides Fiber and Polysaccharides That Can Support Your Gut Health May Help You Lose Weight by Delaying Hunger and Reducing Weight May Reduce Heart Disease Risk

May Help Reduce Your Risk of Type 2 Diabetes by Improving Blood Sugar Control, Raw kelp is a good source of calcium (healthy bones), magnesium (important for overall bodily health) and sodium (helps muscles and nerves work properly).

Raw kelp is also a good source of vitamin A, important for eyesight and overall eye health, and vitamin K.

Vitamin K plays a key role in helping blood coagulation, which is especially important to control bleeding. Aside from basic nutrition benefits, eating seaweed may have a number of other benefits.

Consuming seaweed can help with diabetes management. It's low in calories, rich in fiber, and full of micronutrients.

How many fibers does seaweed actually pack? Well, 8 grams of seaweed per serving can provide up to 12.5 percent of your daily fiber requirement, which helps blood sugar, stabilize throughout the day.

Seaweed also delivers functional foods like, such as polyphenols and carotenoids, which can act as antioxidants.

Nori, seaweed often used in sushi, is the most suitable plant-based source of vitamin B12. Vitamin B12 is critical for cellular metabolism, brain and nervous systems, and blood formation.

Nori also contains high levels of other nutrients that vegetarian diets might be missing, such as iron and some types of polyunsaturated fatty acids.

Most sources of Vitamin B12 are animal-derived foods, so for vegetarians, seaweed could be a big boost for getting important nutrients.

Spirulina Benefits

It's blue-green, absurdly healthy but often overlooked or misunderstood; Spirulina may not be from Pandora, but it grows in our version of that magical moon, Hawaii, along with other exotic locations around the globe.

These blue-green algae are a freshwater plant that is now one of the most researched, and alongside its cousin chlorella, most talked about super foods today.

Grown around the world from Mexico to Africa to even Hawaii, Spirulina is renowned for its intense flavor and even more powerful nutrition profile.

While you may have only seen it as an ingredient in your green super-food beverages, energy bars and natural supplements, Spirulina benefits are so profound those taken on a daily basis they could help restore and revitalize your health! To date, there are nearly 1,700 peer-reviewed scientific articles evaluating its health benefits.

A biomass of cyano-bacteria (blue-green algae) that can be consumed by humans and other animals, there are two species: Arthrospira platensis and Arthrospira maxima. Arthrospira platensis and Arthrospira maxima are cultivated worldwide and used both as a dietary supplement (in tablet, flake and powder form) and even whole food — and even for livestock and fish feed.

1. Detoxes Heavy Metals (Especially Arsenic)

2. **Eliminates Candida**

3. **Improves HIV/AIDS**

4. **Helps Prevent Cancer**

5. **Lowers Blood Pressure**

6. **Reduces Cholesterol**

7. **Lowers Chance of Stroke**

8. **Boosts Energy**

9. Alleviates Sinus Issues

10. Offers Neuro-protection for Brain Disorders & Memory Boosting

Spirulina Nutrition Facts

The major reason why I prefer Spirulina to chlorella? Dietary Spirulina is arguably the most nutrient-dense food on the planet.

It's why I believe that taking dietary Spirulina supplements is essential to good health.

Taken as an average of different Spirulina species, just one ounce contains the following nutritional content:

- Calories: 81
- Protein: 39 grams
- Dietary fiber: 1 gram
- Sugars: 0.9 gram

Fats:

- Total fat: 3 percent DV
- Saturated fat: 4 percent DV

- Omega-3 fatty acids: 230 milligrams
- Omega-6 fatty acids: 351 milligrams

Minerals:

- Copper: 85 percent DV
- Iron: 44 percent DV
- Manganese: 27 percent DV
- Magnesium: 14 percent DV
- Sodium: 12 percent DV
- Potassium: 11 percent DV
- Zinc: 4 percent DV
- Phosphorus: 3 percent DV
- Calcium: 3 percent DV
- Selenium: 3 percent DV

Vitamins:

- Riboflavin: 60 percent DV
- Thiamin: 44 percent DV
- Niacin: 18 percent DV
- Pantothenic acid: 10 percent DV
- Vitamin K: 9 percent DV
- Vitamin E: 7 percent DV
- Folate: 7 percent DV

- Vitamin B6: 5 percent DV
- Vitamin C: 5 percent DV Vitamin A: 3 percent DV

Sugar kelp as human food source

Like many other seaweed's, sugar kelp has all sorts of uses. The leaves of Saccharina latissima provide a sweetener, mannitol, as well as thickening and gelling agents that are added to food, textiles and cosmetics.

Seaweed is high in iodine, iron, vitamin C (which aids iron absorption), antioxidants, soluble and insoluble fibers, vitamin K, vitamin B-12 and a range of other nutrients important for human health.

Red seaweed such as dulse is high in protein. Algae as human food source

What are algae a good source of food supplements?

A typical serving of dried Kombu seaweed contains significantly more calcium than a cup of milk; Seaweed is also rich in iron, magnesium, potassium, zinc and vitamin K and contains useful amounts of vitamin E, riboflavin, thiamine, niacin and Folate.

Dabberlocks or badderlocks (Alaria esculenta) is eaten either fresh or cooked in Greenland, Iceland, Scotland and Ireland.

Aphanizomenon flos-aquae are cyano-bacteria similar to Spirulina, which is used as a nutritional supplement.

Extracts and oils from algae are also used as additives in various food products.

Edible seaweed, or sea vegetables, is algae that can be eaten and used in the preparation of food. They typically contain high amounts of fiber.

They may belong to one of several groups of multicellular algae: the red algae, green algae, and brown algae.

Algae contain 10% to 50% of protein depending upon their sizes. ... Algae contain protein with essential amino acids, which is involved in the metabolic processes like enzyme production.

Hence, high demand is observed for alga products from the food.

Planet black was a (water planet), vast oceans, lakes, streams, extremely comfortable shelters; wealth was in so much abundance, as there was never a want or a need for anything.

As all of the inhabitants owned everything equally, they were (void) of any adverse corruption, greed, malice & their advanced humanoid society was well beyond the frailties of other humanoid life forms.

On the planetary scale, they used; **Blue energy, "osmotic power";** along with direct solar & hydrogen power, Blue energy, sometimes called ocean energy, is a term for the method of generating electricity through the convergence of both fresh and salt water.

This energy can be extracted through a variety of means, including tidal power, current power, wave power, Image: Potential of the technology of using the salinity gradient for energy is estimated to be around 2000 terawatthour on an annual basis.

This energy source relies on the energy that dissipates when two solutions with different salinity's mix.

Salinity gradient energy is based on using the resources of "osmotic pressure difference between fresh water and sea water."

[9] All energy that is proposed to use salinity gradient technology relies on the evaporation to separate water from salt.

Basics of salinity ... · Efficiency·

Methods·

Possible negative...Osmotic power, salinity gradient power or blue energy is the energy available from the difference in the salt concentration between seawater and river water.

Two practical methods for this are reverse electrodialysis (RED) and pressure retarded osmosis (PRO).

Salinity gradient energy, also known as blue energy and osmotic energy, is the energy obtainable from the difference in salt concentration between two feed solutions, typically seawater and river water.

It is a large-scale renewable resource that can be harvested and converted to electricity is based on using the osmotic pressure difference between fresh water and seawater and relies on evaporation to separate water from salt.

Osmotic pressure is the chemical potential of concentrated and dilute solutions of salt.

Osmotic power, salinity gradient power or blue energy is the energy available from the

difference in the salt concentration between seawater and river water.

Two practical methods for this are reverse electrodialysis and pressure retarded osmosis.

Both processes rely on osmosis with membranes. The key waste product is brackish water.

This byproduct is the result of natural forces that are being harnessed: the flow of fresh water into seas that are made up of salt water.

The (**planet black**) was one hundred times the size of earth, with its oceans, vast & rich with so much abundant life forms, mineral & wealth.

The mineral wealth was beyond rich, with the total abundance of pure gold ore, silver, titanium, Platinum, is a chemical element with symbol Pt and atomic number 78. It is a dense, malleable, ductile, highly un-reactive, precious, silverish-white transition metal.

Its name is derived from the Spanish term platino, meaning "little silver."

The white silver metal known as platinum is the heaviest of the precious metals, weighing almost twice as much as karat gold. It is dense, ductile and impervious to corrosion. ... It's color, which mixes well with gold, and its resistance to tarnish.

Diamond (Geo) boulders, the size of houses, so much that they made their homes & buildings out of pure gold, silver & titanium, Platinum, & other materials not on the periodic table.

Some (inhabitants of planet black) lived in coastal floatable domicile cities, as others lived in the mountainous regions of cities of the planet, some even lived, sub surface oceans system, even manufactured asteroid moons that surrounded the planet.

Radiation shielding, used in (ship & craft) making, transports, homes & buildings were made of pure gold & silver.

Of all the metals, silver is the best conductor of heat and electricity known; in fact it has the highest electrical and thermal conductivity known for any material.

It is strong, malleable and ductile, and can endure extreme temperature ranges.

Silver is also able to reflect light very well.

They used pure gold, as electrical conductors,

High capacity batteries can be made with silver and zinc and silver and cadmium.

Gold as Radiation Shield, GOLD, one of the heaviest chemical elements, is the basis of new lightweight plastic foam under development as a radiation shield, Gold as Radiation Shield. ... The polymer is 11 percent gold by weight and the gold atoms in the substance efficiently scatter or absorbs most forms of radiation, including X- rays.

Chemically incorporated into a polymer, gold is less poisonous than other heavy metals that also block radiation, gold-coated Mylar sheets to protect them from solar heat/ radiation.

From vapor-deposited gold taping to gold coating, gold is used because of its multiple benefits in outer space.

Conductors conduct electrical current very easily because of their free electrons.

Insulators oppose electrical current and make poor conductors. Some common conductors are copper, aluminum, gold, and silver.

They used pure cut & uncut diamond boulders, as diamonds has fluorescence, it will glow to some degree under a "black light", a fluorescent light.

Here, again, the reason is because the boron in the diamond is stimulated by ultra-violet light.

The presence of fluorescence in diamonds is considered good when it enhances the appearance of a diamond.

When a diamond is exposed to ultraviolet light (also known as black light) it glows blue.

Sometimes you might see another color too like yellow, green, red & white, but blue is the most common fluorescent color in a diamond.

The way that diamonds reflect light is unique: Inside the stone, the diamond will sparkle gray and white (known as "brilliance") while outside of the gem, it will reflect rainbow colors onto other surfaces (this dispersed light is known as "fire").

Fluorescence refers to a diamond's tendency to emit a soft colored glow when subjected to ultraviolet light (such as a "black light").

Roughly 30% of diamonds fluoresce to some degree. Colorless (D-F) fluorescent diamonds sell at up to a 15% discount since the fluorescence is perceived as a defect.

They also used **Rubies**, the Meanings of Ruby — Stone of Divine Creativity. Ruby is a stone of Divine creativity.

It boosts your energy levels and promotes high self- esteem, intuition, and spiritual wisdom.

Ruby is a symbol of good fortune, pure love, and loyalty. As an aphrodisiac stone, it brings vigor into your life.

Rubies, as illumination

Ruby is a powerful stone to shield against negative energy, psychic attack, and energy vampirism, especially of the heart energy.

Working with Ruby one may feel that all sense of limitation has been removed, strengthening courage, joy, leadership qualities and selfless work in all spiritual endeavors.

Emeralds, emeralds, illumination, It brings loyalty and provides for domestic bliss.

It enhances unconditional love, unity and promotes friendship.

Keeps partnerships in balance and can signal unfaithfulness if it changes color.

Emerald stimulates the heart chakra, having a healing effect on the emotions as well as the physical heart.

The most desirable emerald colors are bluish green to pure green, with vivid color saturation and tone that's not too dark.

The most-prized emeralds are highly transparent. Their color is evenly distributed, with no eye-visible color zoning.

It is believed that emeralds contain the energy that is necessary to bring creative form to your work.

And it was once believed that a high quality emerald would change hues to alert the wearer to impending danger.

They also help one express love, devotion, and adoration. Emerald (Synthetic Overgrowth Hydrothermal) Gemstone & Information. ... One of the most popular methods for creating synthetic emerald is the hydrothermal process, which uses heat and pressure to imitate natural conditions deep in the earth that formed natural gems.

Inhabitants of planet black used them for the purposes of lighting & computer systems apparatus.

As Gemstone & Gold, Silver & platinum was so plentiful & abundant on planet black, it was used in many aspects of navigation, ship building & natural laws of quantum propulsion systems.

From the outer most upper atmosphere of the planet, The planet looked (Black) from the planet being so rich with its rich mineral & diamonds contents.

It was named (**planet black**), but not because the (inhabitants were black), but because from the planet orbit, & shining with the (blue star), the entire planet looks & appeared black because of its very rich mineral complexities, from its seas, lands & mountains.

Its (black) inhabitants, extremely advanced in celestial navigation & mastery of galaxy systems, they dwelled on a planet where the mineral wealth were so plentiful, in diamonds, gem stones, pure gold, silver platinum & copper, that they made hovercrafts & starships from the same material.

They were a very proud race of humanoids, genius, noble & compassionate & highly intellectual people.

As a compassionate race of humanoids, they never attempted to interfere in any other inter civilizations historical relevance or evolutionary in-furtherance.

Their entire civilizations used hovercrafts, ships, & entire transportation systems used hydrogen, solar, & fusion drive systems & other complex gravity drive systems.

They were disallowed the taking of other (humanoid life) forms; however they did create **(human & non-human bio-disrupters)**.

They used **(human & non-human bio-disrupters)**, weapon only to disable, and as they're military weapons were even more powerful.

The body composition of the study subjects was measured using **(bioelectrical impedance)**, which involves running an electrical current through the body, from a distance.

Muscle allows the current to pass more easily than fat does, due to muscle's water content.

They also had the ability to (using **the Sun's rays, as a Weapon)**, using the sun to concentrate the suns ray to bring sun to almost any part of the world, at any time, & just imagine using the sun to destroy virtually anything.

> 1- A fifty foot (concave) reflective, adjustable double (lens), able to spread focus beam points in any descended direction, from any orbit.

2- pin point concentrate heat rays, from the sun would descended in any direction, even to destroy another orbital satellites / destroy space junk / make agricultural fields more fertile / spread focus in a fifty foot wide radius upon any army / any aircraft / missile / empire.

They used electrical fields in the buildings & homes, as well as on their (Mother super galaxy class Ships);

Rudimentary force fields

In physics a force field is a vector field that describes non-contact force acting on a particle at various positions in space.

Specifically, a force field is a vector field, where is the force that a particle would feel if it were at the point.

A force field in physics is a map of a force over a particular area of space. ... Since force is a vector - it has both size and direction, like an arrow - all force fields are vector fields.

Examples of force fields include magnetic fields, gravitational fields, and electrical fields.

Field forces are also called non-contact forces or at-a- distance forces.

There are four types of field forces: gravity, electromagnetic forces, and the strong force and the weak force found in atoms.

These four forces constitute the most fundamental forces in the universe.

Force field may refer to: Force field (fiction), a barrier made up of energy, plasma or particles to protect a person, area or object from attacks or intrusions or as a means of containment or confinement.

Force field (physics), a vector field indicating the forces exerted by one object on another.

There are the 5 types of forces

.

1- Applied Force.

2- Gravitational Force.

3- Normal Force.

4- Frictional Force.

5- Air Resistance Force.

6- Tension Force.

7- Spring Force.

For the purposes of this demonstrational exercise, we will demonstrate **(one)** methodology that is highly effective & cost effective in creating a definitive security barrier of protection.

Exercise **(one)**,

Dry ice (mist) used as an electrical conductor.

If you create a dry-ice mist or use, typically, fog is created by vaporizing proprietary water and glycol-based or glycerin-based fluids or through the atomization of mineral oil.

This fluid (often referred to colloquially as fog juice) vaporizes or atomizes inside the fog machine.

A rubber six inch strip in the circumference of In a doorway, head to toe and, blow a light breeze within the mist, via nozzles, two on top of the doorway, two on each sides of that doorway & two at the bottom of that very same doorway.

A fog curtain, via six-inch depth within the doorway emits a head to toe six-inch shield of depth cushion from one side of the door to the other side of the door.

If you place a rubber six inch strip within the frame of that same doorway, if you electrify the mist in that same doorway, staggered electrical currents to match the width, height & depth of the doorway, if you charge that electrical field in that doorway to two hundred thousand volts of electricity, thus, a force field is now created.

Results; nothing, not even a mosquito, could breach this electrical or chemical field.

Exercise **(two)**,

Now, within that same doorway, introduce an ultraviolet flashing beacon & infrared beacon while using a sniff sensor & you not only have a force field, but you now have a positive identification system that will positively map each person who attempts to go through that doorway.

Since each person has its own thermal signature & smell signature under ultraviolet, infrared & sniff signature sensors, the positive identification of any person or persons can always be recorded & mapped.

Exercise **(three)**,

Removing the model of electricity from Exercise **(one)**, Within the same doorway, using an eyther and glycol mixture, forming a (Caustic), eyther and glycol curtain, would disallow or surely, Anesthetize.

Administer an anesthetic to (a person or animal); especially so as to induce a loss of consciousness.

Deprive of feeling or awareness, of any human from breaching such fog barrier.

Exercise **(four)**,

A bank or convenience store robber attempts to get away with cash from the bank or store, while using the front doorway.

The clerk has a wristband with a parabolic indentation button to signal law enforcement, at the same time, activate the force field at that doorway.

Thus the assailant is in-fact instilled/cataloged & coded, at the same time alerts law-enforcement, even tags the assailant with a definitive time, date, and thermal, ultraviolet & sniff signature, while stopping them at that doorway with a two hundred-volt jolt.

Ultraviolet sensors activate & discharge the electronic capacitors to jolt/charge the systems field.

Infrared sensors activate the thermal heat signatures; time & date stamp, also activating the sniff sensors.

All recorded information is recorded on a micro SD card for cost effective affordability. Even, if the assailant leaves the establishment, the DNA signature is time & date & stamped for law-enforcement & court purposes.

Transportation systems

Their normal (high-speed) transports were fully autonomous magnetic lift self-driving crafts, & hydrogen powered hovercraft personal crafts.

Complex (high speeds) road systems were a series of embedded (solar) metallic chip systems, throughout the entire planet, allowing fast total access to any part of the planet using the magnetic lift transportation, at any time.

Since the entire road system was solar, the totality of the solar power on the weak & the strong side of the planet were always charged, even on the dark side of the planet, for greater transport efficiency.

Hydrogen powered personal hovercraft, were implemented to hover at the height of one to five hundred feet, using the vector approved highway transportation systems, in furtherance over, water, & mountainous terrain, & high rise domiciles & building offices.

Each inhabitant of (planet black) was assigned a personal hovercraft; however their smart bots, most of the time piloted the crafts, as fully autonomous magnetic lift self- driving crafts, were of daily twenty four-hour public transportation systems.

Every, car, craft or ship in and around planet black all had hull chip designs for instant identifications of crafts & ships, this allowed traffic designators then could best direct the craft or ships towards its intended destinations through a self driving mode with more traffic fluidity.

Any foreign craft or ship attempting to enter the terminal control area of planet black or within its orbit that does not have the intended sanctioned isolinear hull chip design would be directed in furtherance to an inspection or quarantined area.

Highway direct solar power strips

There is, thousands & thousands of miles of roadway systems on (planet black), powered by direct solar, & blue energy systems.

The general planets power systems were made from (Blue Energy) & hydrogen power.

The planets upgraded its energy grid to meet the needs of the needs of the populous, by implementing a solar electrical highway & street grid system.

This methodology addressed effective needs of this entire planet populous.

Highway solar strips that run the length of all highways & street systems, effectively boosting, even overriding; all of the planets power grids.

1-solar strips are designed to work in series of succession & as if one panel fails, the system automatically by passes & goes to the next panel in succession, boosting the grid. Luminance solar panels have two functions:

A; collect the stars energy & provides power 24/7

B; illuminates in the dark to mark all road systems without the need to exert more power from the grid, as Luminance is highly visible from dawn till dusk.

The system power grid is managed from sector to sector to best protect the overall grid integrity & security.

Simplistic, in its design with (positive fields) on one side of the highway & (negative fields) located on the other side.

This grid would allow power for magnetic Light rail systems, electric cars & bus commuting, & boosting all local existing communities in & around the interstate, & large city systems.

Luminance solar panels strips run the length of the highways & all sectors that they will serve.

All highway markings are Luminance solar panels strips to ensure in total continuity of the overall system.

For maximum cost effectives & to ensure the system peaks at an always eighty seven percent all the time, all Lighting, by high yield /low cost led systems using the light apparatus.

All rural, urban & suburban communities can very easily match the overall grid using the existing technology & existing infrastructure to improve the needs of all five billion of residents in & around the planet.

Electric cars all need to rely on an energy converter to allow the cars to work after being purchased from the states.

Buses, trains & light rail will have their own type of converter to ensure in power continuity.

Conclusion;

This proposal by (Dr. Borders) (EveBor) address three scientific plausible & highly creditable scenarios:

1-adds a cost effective new power grid with the length of the entire planet.

2- Allows fully none & autonomous, electrical vehicles, trucks, cars to travel along the grid with drivers using a converter from the planets transportation sector.

Allows fully autonomous, electrical vehicles, trucks, cars to travel along the grid, using the grid power by way of an onboard converter, & exit the grid using their own battery/ super capacitor, more over; regular vehicles using hydrogen will use the same highways with no new obstructions or hazards, in any way.

Note; fully autonomous, electrical vehicles will all travel in the same middle lane, with contact strips embedded into the pavement of the center of the highway, & when exiting the highway electrical grid, the vehicles will automatically change to their own battery/ capacitor systems, or hydrogen.

If the fully autonomous, electrical vehicles approach an obstruction, they will slow down & stop, allowing the onboard passenger to take command manually of the vehicles, any obstacle, within ten feet, the fully autonomous, electrical vehicles will stop & will not proceed until the passenger is fully apprised & can again manually take command of the vehicles.

More refined technology in fully autonomous, electrical vehicles in reference to guidance systems became forthcoming with the advancement of high altitude Hovercrafts & more sophisticated magnetic lift crafts systems.

3-residual power from the grid, in conjunction using (blue energy) will be used to power all highway lighting systems, simply by changing to cost effective led's, using the same apparatus, powering local towns, cities, & etc.

The massive amount of electrical power generated from to grid will be managed sector by sector to allow for the Maximum security & more fluid continuity across each sector.

All solar panels run the entire length of the highways with positive polarity on one side & negative polarity on the other on the other side, of the highway, with electrical contact strips & ground in the middle of the asphalt or highway to allow connections for electric cars & trucks using a converter.

Water or moisture, even snow, will not be a factor by reasons of the fluidics of the grid matrix, as sectors, offering year round peak power surges in the solar matrix being more than enough to add to the grid with less weather overcast, at intervals in other sectors, as all sectors contribute to the overall hive grid matrix, via (blue energy) & direct solar.

By location, areas of the grid can be thermally controlled, allowing better ice melt, & more clearing of safer travels.

Ultimately, it envisioned that this solar & (blue energy) electrical grid, totally replaces all other known systems.

The entire vehicles in and around the planet, in a total solar electrical grid network, using extremely cost effective methodologies & infrastructure that is already in place.

Ultimately, the goal is to drastically reduce any carbon foot print, virtually eliminating all smog on the planet.

This methodology makes electrical power, a non relative financial factor, for all the government, counties, cities, towns, in & around planet black, as the new nexus, in the new area of vehicle passenger, light rail, & cargo transportation & automation was at hand.

Final consideration; billions & billions of people all around planet black are personally driving & moving cargo & flying all over the world all using, **a none mode** polluting **transportation** methodology of the planet black.

They all used a more common sense, cost effective, approach to their planets energy needs, and their next generations.

conveyance, & plausible methodologies, to address the nexus of new energy (grid) needs, for the planet black & the cost effective methodologies of the nexus needs in clean electrical (grid) transportation in and around the planet black.

This proposed, methodology, transportation program, one mile at a time, sector by sector, of total operations, to achieve the overall targeted goal.

UVEB-7-(super ship)

Mother ship was (**one of eight**) in the fleet/ armada.

Three circular disks, each disk measuring (two miles in circumference diameter) X, five hundred feet tall.

Each disk is detachable, with its own power systems.

Attached within the center, is a solid (titanium) shaft connecting at three points to reinforcement super structure, though all three super structure disks.

Weapon systems, emits a plasma discharge, under hypersonic discharge, plus an electrical discharge harnessed by onboard (nucleonic), super storage capacitors, with a three hundred & sixty degree discharge.

Each disk rotates & counter rotates for assistance in propulsion, flight mode & inertial gravity drives systems. All disks are coated & layered with three feet of solid gold, less than three feet of solid silver, less than five feet of pure hull titanium, and a natural radiation barrier.

Diamonds & gems stones are used for aids of instrumentation & navigational systems.

Maximum personnel of mother ship are crewing quarters of well over five thousand personnel, as apparatus could hold in stasis tubes, ten thousands in war stance.

The ship records, (one thousand personnel active) at any time, while four thousand in (stasis tubes) at any given time, even additional five thousand personnel in war settings in rotational patterns.

UVEB-7 had (eight different types of propulsion systems);

Inertial mass navigational systems Focused concentrated lens-light object to lens-light object

The inhabitants of (Planet Black) used this system for a method of navigation, & types of propulsions in navigation, as planet wise, they daily used (hydrogen), & (magnetic drive systems) for daily transports; however their space drive systems were much **more** sophisticated by designs.

It was known that eight different systems were used in space propulsion systems, in stellar & interstellar space travel.

One of systems or methodology; whereby focusing & pinpointing & dialing, an exact celestial address of a stars/sun, propulsion could be achieved by an object that has mass, reaction-less drive is a device producing motion without the exhaust of a propellant.

Using inertial light source of that target star/sun; in other words, the intensity of that target star/sun, & homing in on that star/sun would gravitate towards that star/sun after using slingshot inertial navigation methodology.

Example; using a pinpointed, focused concentrated lens- light to light (type solar sail concept, (however extremely precise), the focused light could gravitated towards that target object (star/sun).

Between a distant light source and an observer, that is capable of bending the light from the source as the light travels towards the observer.

A star acting as a gravitational lens, high-intensity starlight, focused by such a lens, in some cases, background objects are made brighter because otherwise diverging light of the more distant object is focused into our line of sight by the gravity of the foreground object.

So gravitational lensing sometimes enables us to see faint objects we might not otherwise see.

The gravitational field of galaxies and clusters of galaxies can lens light, but so can smaller objects such as stars and planets.

Even the mass of our own bodies will lens light passing near us a tiny bit, although the effect is too small to ever measure.

A system of lenses which helps to focus light directly on the (target) that is mounted on a host (target/ship), Example; once the pinpointed object is fixed/locked in meaning, light target the lens will gravitate towards that target, as the target light intensity continues stronger the closer it gets to that target light sources.

Light source, diaphragm, stage, (target), objective lens, body, relates to the ability of the objective lenses to retain the same central FOV when the user switches from one objective to another of an objective.

Power System 1,

Blue energy, chemical (kinetic),

The concept of blue energy – otherwise known as osmotic power – was developed upon the realization that through electrochemistry, researchers can create a concentration cell with salt water on one side and fresh water on the other, which results in a novel way to power devices.

But how exactly can this method generate energy? Just look at fresh water and seawater.

Imagine on one side of a tank there are fresh water, and the other side houses seawater.

The only thing standing between the two tanks is a semi- permeable membrane, which allows only water molecules to pass through.

The sea water is going to naturally have a much higher salt concentrate than the fresh water, and that large difference will cause the molecules from the fresh water side to rapidly pass to the sea water side.

This causes pressure that can be turned into electricity.

Blue energy, "osmotic power",

Blue energy, sometimes called ocean energy, is a term for the method of generating electricity through the convergence of both fresh and salt water.

This energy can be extracted through a variety of means, including tidal power, current power, wave power, Image:

Potential of the technology of using the salinity gradient for energy is estimated to be around 2000 tera-watthour on an annual basis, This energy source relies on the energy that dissipates when two solutions with different salinity's mix.

Salinity gradient energy is based on using the resources of "osmotic pressure difference between fresh water and sea water." [9] All energy that is proposed to use salinity gradient technology relies on the evaporation to separate water from salt.

Basics of salinity ... · Efficiency · Methods

Possible negative...

Osmotic power, salinity gradient power or blue energy is the energy available from the

difference in the salt concentration between seawater and river water.

Two practical methods for this
are reverse electrodialysis
(RED) and pressure retarded osmosis (PRO).

Salinity gradient energy, also known as blue energy and osmotic energy, is the energy obtainable from the difference in salt concentration between two feed solutions, typically seawater and river water.

It is a large-scale renewable resource that can be harvested and converted to electricity is based on using the osmotic pressure difference between fresh water and seawater and relies on evaporation to separate water from salt.

Osmotic pressure is the chemical potential of concentrated and dilute solutions of salt.

Osmotic power, salinity gradient power or blue energy is the energy available from the

difference in the salt concentration between seawater and river water.

Two practical methods for this are reverse electrodialysis and pressure retarded osmosis.

Both processes rely on osmosis with membranes. The key waste product is brackish water.

This byproduct is the result of natural forces that are being harnessed: the flow of fresh water into seas that are made up of salt water.

Power System 2,

Inertial propulsion engine
Gravity manipulation and amplification is the key that unlocks the Milky Way galaxy and the rest of the universe.

Gyroscopic Inertial Thruster (GIT) - The Gyroscopic Inertial Thruster is a proposed reaction-less Electromagnetic propulsion (EMP) is the principle of accelerating an object by the utilization of a flowing electrical current and magnetic fields.

The electrical current is used to either create an opposing magnetic field, or to charge a field, which can then be repelled.

The Em-Drive engine, which is designed to generate, thrust by bouncing microwaves around inside a cone- shaped chamber. ... The engine works by bouncing microwaves around inside a chamber; it requires no propellant and could therefore usher in a new era of super-fast and efficient space flight, advocates say.

They used a propulsion system that uses an alternating series of magnetic forces, inertia, and gravitational drops to propel a magnetic object along a pathway.

The pathway can be an undulating track that can retain an object thereon.

A plurality of magnet pairs is placed along the track, one of each pair on either side of the track, the pairs in spaced relation from each other along the track.

Magnetic and inertial propulsion systems

Graviton-static and the graviton-magnetic field intensities, the graviton is a hypothetical particle which is thought to be responsible for transferring the force of gravity.

Like a photon it is mass-fewer particles, however it is a spin 2 particle rather than a spin 1 particle; a propulsion system that uses an alternating series of magnetic forces, inertia, and gravitational drops to propel a magnetic object along a pathway.

The pathway can be an undulating track that can retain an object thereon. A plurality of magnet pairs is placed along the track, one of each pair on either side of the track, the pairs in spaced relation from each other along the track.

Power System 3, Gamma propulsion energy concepts,

Which is then used to power some types, of (kinetic) electric space propulsion system?

Power System 4,

Antimatter power generation. ... Antimatter annihilations are used to directly or, indirectly heat a working fluid, as in a nuclear thermal rocket, but the fluid is used to generate electricity, which is then used to power some form of electric space propulsion system.

The antimatter rocket could hit speeds of 72 million mph.

Power System 5,

Once again, a nuclear thermal electric drive, Ion thrusters that have top speeds of 200,000mph.

Power System 6,

Solar Sails,

The top speed of a solar sail craft is estimated to be about 18,600 miles per second, or about 1/10 the speed of light. This speed would be achievable if a laser or magnetic beam transmitter was attached to the spacecraft to give it a constant flow of photons.

Power System 7,

Nuclear energy converted to (kinetic) electrical power

Power System 8,

Deuterium & helium plasma mixture

Plasma & Fusion rockets for maneuverability

(Point & Click) celestial navigation computation

Traveling times X-ten around their (star), Celestial address of **Rigel in Orion** constellation; **Riel's position is** RA: 05h 14m 32.3s, dec: -08° 12′ 05.9″.

Slingshot to & towards target address of;

Celestial address of our (earth's) sun, azimuth = 15.68_deg, altitude = -17.96_deg. The Sun (or Sol) is the star at the center of our solar system and is responsible for the Earth's climate and weather.

The Sun is an almost perfect sphere with a... Surface Temperature 5,500 °C Diameter 1,392,684 km

Mass 1.99×10^{30} kg (333,060 Earth's) Age 4.6 Billion Years

Sun live position and data.

Right Ascension: 16h 17m 21.6s
Declination: -21° 20' 34.1" (J2000)
Magnitude: -26.77 (Estimated: JPL)
Constellation: Scorpius
Sun Distance: 0 km [0.0 km/s] Earth Distance: 147,577,724 km [30.2 km/s]

Using the navigational lens, (Inertial mass navigational systems), **(**Focused concentrated lens-light to light methodology), pinpointed solar sail (type), concentrations towards the target objective.

Once launched & targeted in, the inertial mass stays on course towards the (target address), as the focused beam speeds up the mass, faster & faster towards the target objective.

Objects sun/star in focus of (blue) means the object is moving towards the focus beam thus the object sun/star in (red) means the object is moving away from the focus beam.

Using the eight onboard different propulsion systems makes any necessary course corrections.

A system of lenses which helps to focus light directly on the (target) that is mounted on a host (target/ship),

Example; once the pinpointed object is fixed/ locked in on the destination, meaning, light target the lens will gravitate towards that target, as the target light intensity continues stronger the closer it gets to that target light sources.

Inertial calculations of slingshot gravitational launch,

(EveBor) Space launch theory;

It was estimated that, after leaving earth's atmosphere, by using normal kinetic propulsion systems, via; (ion/nuclear/chemical/fusion), equations, sub-light speeds could be reached with the least minimal efforts.

A course plotted towards the suns outer gravitational rims & using the Inertial slingshot gravitational launch, of X-10, or ten loops around the sun vector towards another sun/ star, using the (six dimensional space model), of using six points to map out the destinations & one point to plot the point of origin.

Using a gravitational (push/pull lens), towards the (target sun/star), can be plotted by locking on to the next suns, vector/address, via; concentrated light focus methodology by homing in, on the nexus light source focused in that address.

Using this methodology, & after the completion around the X-10th rotation, the course plotted towards the next sun/star, & the distance directed towards that next sun, via; distance & concentration of the (push/pull lens), would draw/increase the intensity, of that (target sun/star) beacon, based upon magnifying focus lens methodology towards that (target sun).

As the target course is locked, upon that (target sun/star), the space ship would be traveling an incredible speeds through space & (increase speeds) though the gravitational (**intensity**) (**push/pull spectral concentration lens**), towards the next target star/sun.

Using any, (ion/nuclear/chemical/fusion), equations can mitigate course corrections from any object proximity, within the flight path.

In theory, a space launch/jump can be achieved from one system to the next, using this methodology.

To define a Position in four-dimensional space you need 5 points: 3 points to define a plane, and 2 points to define a line that will intersect that plane at a specific location. Now use a point of origin to target that 5-point location in space.

Celestial address of our sun
Azimuth = 15.68_deg, altitude = -17.96_deg.

Sun Facts - Interesting Facts about the Sun - Space Facts
https://space-facts.com/the-sun/

The Sun (or Sol) is the star at the centre of our solar system and is responsible for the Earth's climate and weather.

The Sun is an almost perfect sphere with a...
Surface Temperature 5,500 °C Diameter 1,392,684 km
Mass 1.99 × 10^30 kg (333,060 Earth's) Age 4.6 Billion Years

Celestial address of **Rigel in Orion**

Riel's position is RA: 05h 14m 32.3s, Dec: -08° 12' 05.9".

Science of stars Rigel. We could not live as close to Rigel as we do to our sun, because its surface temperature is much hotter, about 19,000 degrees F (11,000K) in contrast to about 10,000 degrees F for the sun.

Overall, Rigel about 40,000 times brighter than our local star. Earth would need to be about 200 times farther away, or about 5 times as far as Pluto, to bear life in orbit around Rigel.

Even then the light would not be the same, as much would be at higher, bluer, wavelengths.

Counting all its radiation (not just visible light, but infrared, ultraviolet and so on), Rigel is 66,000 times more powerful than the sun.

With such enormous energy, you might be surprised to find that it has only 17 times more mass, and 70 times the width, of our sun. Yet Rigel is not one of the galaxy's largest stars, as the great video above, by Jon S. on YouTube, shows.

At magnitude 0.18, Rigel is the seventh brightest star in the heavens, the fifth as viewed from North America.

It is a blue supergiant star, designated as type B8Ia, some 773 light-years from Earth (by Hipparcos data).

Rigel Statistics;
Also known As: Rigel A, Beta Orionis

Distance from Earth: Approx. 800 light years

Constellation: Orion

Star Type: Class B Supergiant

Mass: 18 x Sun

Luminosity: Approx. 117,000 x Sun

Diameter: Approx. 65 million miles (105 million km) - 75 x Sun

Temperature: Approx. 12,000C (22,000F)

Age: Approx. 8 million years old

Rotation Period: Unknown

Rigel Radius Rigel has around 75 times the radius of the sun; if it were placed in the center of our solar system it would almost reach the orbit of the planet Mercury.

Rigel Mass Rigel is estimated to have a maximum mass of around 18 times that of the sun.

Rigel Temperature Rigel is estimated to have surface temperatures of around 12,000C (22,000F), more than twice as hot as the sun.

Rigel Luminosity (energy emitted) Rigel is a blue supergiant star with a luminosity more than 100,000 times that of the sun.

Rigel is around 800 light years from Earth and is the brightest star in the constellation of Orion.

Rigel is actually a three star system consisting of the blue supergiant Rigel A and two distant and much dimmer companions.

Even though much of Riel's energy is emitted as invisible ultraviolet light it is still around 40,000 times brighter than the sun.

High Mass stars such as Rigel exhaust their fuel at a far quicker rate than smaller stars; as a result they exist for only a few million years.

Rigel is only around 8 million years old and has already exhausted the supply of hydrogen in its core.

Our sun, which is already 4.5 billion years old, will continue to fuse hydrogen in its core for another 5 or 6 billion years.

Over the next few million years Rigel will expand to an even greater size as it becomes a red supergiant and may eventually explode as a supernova.

If Rigel explodes as a supernova it will become the brightest object in the night sky apart from the moon. https://astrobob.areavoices.com/2013/01/05/meet-rigel-in-orion-a-star-with-supernova-potential/

(Scouts), Spaceship approaching earth's atmosphere

The final approach was always on the dark side of the (moon) of the (planet earth) using winged scout ships.

The indigenous humanoids of planet earth all thought the scouts ships were giant beasts/ dragons & gods, like caciquato the plumed serpent, Quetzalcoatl and to the Maya it was known as Kukulcan.

Names of ancient flying deities of earth

https://www.bing.com/images/ search?q=ancient+flying+deities+of+ earth&qpvt=ancient+flying+ deities+of+earth&FORM=IGRE

https://www.bing.com/search?q=%20 ancient%20flying%20deities%20of%20 earth&cbir=sbi&imageBin=&qs=n&f orm=QBRE&sp=-1&pq=ancient%20 flying%20deities%20of%20earth& sc=1-31&sk=&cvid=262AC5B6442146448AB 530CC20FB9299

https://www.bing.com/search?q=names+ of+ancient+flying+deities+of+earth& FORM=AWRE https://www.bing.com/search?q=Names+of+achient+flying+deties+of+earth+&qs=n&form=QBLH&pc=EUPP_cosp&sp=-1&pq=names+of+achient+flying+deties+of+earth+&sc=0-40&sk=&cvid=DF08A9B5FA254FE19F27600A43459979

Ancient Hopi: The Hollow Earth, Flying shields and Ant- like Gods.

Every ancient civilization on earth has had contact with flying beings, which they called as "deities".

Osiris and Isis (among others). Thoth is known as the Ibis God, as he is usually depicted with the head of a bird known as the Ibis.

Assembly of the god's index of the gods 148 minor gods' quotes / texts 44 minor gods time-line of the god's ancient astronauts winged gods & discs planet nibiru mul, Osiris, Anubis, and Horus.

(**EveBor**), the planet black ruler, quarantined (the earth planet), only after his (ELd), planet engineering council member (six), found an obscure system in the Milky-way constellations with a younger (yellow star).

There, they found a planet, rich in life forms, ever evolving from primitive humanoids, the planet was called (earth), and the (earth year) was, five hundred thousand years of earth's past, in human history.

It was because of this obscure (planet earth), (EveBor), the (planet black ruler), quarantined (the earth planet), they instituted the

(Prime Directives);

Mission statement;

Regarding (Planet Black), other extra terrestrial worlds, any & all-exploratory settlements on any & all other worlds, planets & planetary systems.

Rule-1

Whenever there is any (approach in furtherance), of any & all-planetary systems, planets, the following must take place first.

1- a detailed & comprehensive telemetry (grid) geo/map, of the planet in questioned (must/shall), be made of its compositions via; diseases, life-forms, possible dangers, possible evolutions, purpose of study.

2- after the study is (concluded), at all times, a safe distance must be maintained to mask the (visitors/studies) existence.

3- contact the (Supreme Counsel), for further instructions, as in such time, either, an approval to (quarantine the planet), (bypass the planet), (proceed to the planet) on the dark side in unpopulated areas for further analyses.

Rule-2

Their (shall never) be (any!), interference in any, on & off planetary, functions, involving any conflicts, commerce, politics, and methodology of living, in any way, as failure to abide by this directive or to violate this directive shall be swift termination of any & all privileges in the future/past/present, (forthwith).

Rule-3

Observe and study only, & don't be a part of, nor attempt to influence in any way, with exceptions of the (Supreme Counsel), authority.

Rule-4

If this prime directive is violated in any way, other than following directives issued by the (Supreme Counsel), (the violator & heirs) shall be disavowed forthwith & returned to (Planet Black) for internment with no exceptions.

Rule-5

Do no harm!

Rules & regulations set forth of this celestial (Prime Directive), is to ensure all life forms, & life-forms mannerisms & methodologies are to only (evolve) at their own pace, except relative to strict instructions by the (Supreme Counsel), ultimate interpretations.

Hardly within the click of the periodic clock, of the periodic human history progressions, of, (three hundred thousand years of earth's past), the order was made by (ELd), planet engineering council member (six), to attempt to further progress/nudge, the primitive nature of (planet earth's humanoids inhabitants).

(ELd), seeking to expand his own legacy & possible empire, in another world started the process of violating directives set forth by the high counsel of (planet black).

Using two (earth's humanoid inhabitants), (Genoa), slicing with the (Genoa), of the (planet black inhabitants), not fully knowing that process would create extremely hazardous results.

In (earth's-history) of the years (nine hundred thousand years of humanoid history, when the planet earth had one (super continent), (one large landmass), a decision was made, by (ELd), to expand its landmasses by way of directing a comet four miles wide toward the ocean strike of (planet earth).

They learned the ability to direct & (controlling comets and asteroids) by placing/landing a (*gyroscopic nuclear seismic compression converter*), on the surface of a comet or asteroids, & digging in, the process to steer the directing the trajectory of a comet or asteroids by altering its flight or orbital path.

Once attached to the comet or asteroids, the system would change to a secondary engine system, & using the (*comets own hydrogen activation system*) producing more power & much stronger (core vibrations thump).

This (gyroscopic nuclear seismic compression converter)

Could also slow down & even halt the forward momentum of any comet to any state of geo-stationary dispositions, through a series of calculated rotational axes.

Using a calculated series of (seismic compression converter, (pulse thumpers), altering the comets trajectory flight path, in segmented increments until its final course of the trajectory is achieved.

In order to reach its ultimate objectives, of a precise targeted pinpointed strike, the (heavy pulse thumper), gets much stronger & adulates much deeper to core vibrations of the (comets or asteroids), as the targeted objective becomes more proximity in reaching its final objectives.

This process allowed them to infuse water on the surface, & the bedrock, of any dead planet for future cohabitation, as long as the planetary body was near & far enough, from a desired star/sun, for a synergy atmosphere effect.

They also had the ability to reposition small planets, using the same process to match the precise gravitational orbital elliptical trajectory, in order to create any possible cohabitation zone, for sub bases.

The process for altering comets & small planets took years of precise measurement calculus, to achieve, but with great success. They also had the ability to dissolved asteroids on the inside & use them for scout ships.

This process flash boiled the seas/ oceans, and increased the levels of all seas/oceans spreading, breaking up the (one super continent) to what is now known as north & South America, Africa, Australia, Europe, Asia, north & South Pole continents.

The planets tectonic plates, shifted & changing the entire planets appearance, & regional demographics, on planet earth.

The inhabitants of (planet black) perfected (Precognition), the status of, knowing with knowing, foreknowledge of an event, especially foreknowledge of a paranormal kind.

With their development of the (Intracortical visual prosthesis, contact lens), (super quantum eye computation), along with using their perfected, bioengineer-ed., Magnetic smart bacteria, they ascended, to a state of speaking to each other, learning & understanding without Audible speaking.

They could even, communicate to other humanoid life forms, even lower life-forms without speaking, while under the influence of,

(Embryonic transference elixir)

Along with a,

(Corneal) neuron sensor @
Intracortical visual prosthesis (lens) super computation (eye lens)

Beyond Quantum Computation

The inhabitants of planet black used a series of enhanced smart bacteria for computational analysis, these (smart bacteria) added in the assist & computational spectrums of advanced computation, as these allowed all the inhabitants of planet black to compute & in real time be current in a current events, below, on the surface & beyond the planet in real time.

The (Corneal) neuron sensor, Intracortical visual prosthesis (lens) (super computation) (Eye Lens) methodology also allowed every inhabitant to vote on all issues, relevant on matters of the planetary systems, by using & computing wearing a wrist screen.

One of their leading scientists & (ruler of planet black) named (EveBor), invented & pioneered (***Embryonic transference elixir***) and one methodology of the below system.

(Corneal) neuron sensor @
Intracortical visual prosthesis (lens) (super computation) (Eye Lens) @

Just imagine a super computer that fits in a single glass of liquid, Water/emulsion solutions, with direct corneal interface by way of bio thermal activate contact lenses.

A neurological (contact lens) interfaces with the soluble liquid to quantum compute any adverse computational equations. This methodology allowed them to interface with all crafts & ships on planet black, space flight & earth.

Variables of activation of liquid computer computations;

- ten millionth of a centimeter

- Sand grains particles (**silt particles**) smaller than 0.0625 mm down to 0.004 mm).

- **ALON** is optically transparent ($\geq$80%) in the near- ultraviolet, visible and mid-wave-infrared regions of the electromagnetic spectrum.

- Chemical formula (AlN) x•(Al2O3)1-x, $0.30 \leq x \leq 0.37$

- Density: 2.14 oz/in³ (3.70 g/cm³)

- Simple glass of water, nutrient/ enzymes (fuel).

  Silica & aluminum / Silica Spherical(**Fused**) Particles

  Activity of bacteria through their multi-enzyme systems in splitting up the peptone in the medium into amino acids.

For starters, a single Fused Silica & aluminum / Silica Spherical Particles with the dimensions of less than (0.001 mm) for layer (Z) & continued layers (Y) & (X) until continued succession layers to (A) one Fused Silica & aluminum / Silica Spherical Particles can hold, Bio electrical/bacteria can form on a single layer of times (ten million) per particle.

Each (0.001 mm) particle can hold an estimate, ten million Bio-electrical/bacteria that float's on the top of said surface of a (**solution**) in question.

Bio-electrical (electromagnetic) conductivity precludes each particle to approximate no further than one half inch from the other.

At (0.002 mm) particles are (recessed) no more than one half inch depth, of solution in question.

In every recessions of strategic positioning per particle (0.001 mm) to (0.100 mm), electrical (electromagnetic) conductivity is achieved.

Activity or super computation is activated & manipulated by a layered system (independent) per layers to conduct instruction per layer & able to inter-connect with each layer simultaneously.

In laymen's terms; super computation is occurred by layers of trillions of signals per second (via) speed of (Bio-electromagnetic) electrical conductivity, of millions of manipulated electrical signals from the types of (solution & strength) or the (validity) of the (bio-electrical (electromagnetic) -**bacteria**).

(Please note) Intracortical visual prosthesis is achieved by the following two methodologies;

1- **(Rice size (interfaced) chip)** Implanted in a depth of four centimeters, over the orbital sac into the neuron receptors of any subject, as the (chip) is only a neuron- orbital (interfaced) receptor.

The **(chip)** is proxceminity & manually activated with four failsafe patterns.

Upon activation of the (**chip**), the interface from, Intracortical visual prosthesis (super computation) would carry out any instruction (**programmed**) by the (bio- electrical (**electromagnetic**) (Super-Computational Instructions) while immersed in –**bacteria solution**).

2- Less invasive direct corneal interface by way of (bio thermal) activated contact lenses, would operate in the same mannerisms.

3- (**bio thermally**) activated contact lenses, with direct corneal interface programmed to receive specified signals (microwave/ radio & sitcom) would directly receive information through (**corneal interface/ contact lenses**) could directly interface with the humans neurological stimuli (**directly to the normal brain functions**) of collecting (instructions, learning, etc).

Note# contact lenses would visually enhance the subject normal eyesight & coupled with interface would allow super instructions in super computational methodology.

Upon activation of the (**chip**), the interface from, Intracortical visual prosthesis (super computation) would carry out any instruction (**programmed instructions**) by the (bio-electrical (**electromagnetic**) (Super-Computational Instructions) while immersed in –**bacteria solution**).

(This) mannerism of (Super Computational) (methodology), does not need computer screens or hard drives, cables, Wi-Fi, & is extremely Mobil as it is replaced by the human body, as by way of using the individual (**bio-electrical rhythmic signals**) to operate its own bio-thermal electrical connections or (field).

Most of (Humans), learn through (our eyes), we receive (valued important) of our (**corneal interface lucent instructions**) of our five senses, through our eyes.

When making the relative comparisons on current computing methodology Vs (this model of computation);

A-no computer screen is needed as information is sent directly to the **(corneal interface)** (bio thermal) activated contact lenses, would operate in the same mannerisms.

B-normal vision would be enhanced through **(Bio- thermal spectral contact lenses)**, greatly magnifying range/thermal imaging/ digital distance while the wearer enjoys enhanced sight.

This **methodology** addresses several issues associated with the trappings of current computational methods:

1- enhanceing (bio-thermal activated) contact lenses for purposes of enhancer sight/ thermal imaging/range & directional seeking).

2- direct (**Bio-thermal corneal interface**), that replaces the (computer screen), as a more direct interface to the human neuron-network is the nexus phase of computation.

3- by using the above (**Variables of activation of liquid computer computations**) methodology, a super computational direct (bio-thermal interface) can be achieved, as (planetary super computation) (fifty trillion liquid channel chip matrix systems), to control all aspects of the planet from tracking all inhabitants to controlling All transports & all other areas of planetary & off planetary operations.

4- This methodology can issue specific computational instructions while the subject is both (Lucent & illucent) in variable systematic rhythm cycles.

The methodology of this **(corneal interface)** is just an enhanced method of the human body's own natural reception & disseminations of vast collection & super computational information.

5- cost cutting effectiveness of (Lenses), as they are disposable & able to be (regenerated/ recycled)

6- A single Fused Silica & aluminum / Silica Spherical Particles with the dimensions of less than (0.001 mm) for layer (Z) & continued layers (Y) & (X) until continued succession layers to (A)

One Fused Silica & aluminum / Silica Spherical Particles can hold, Bio electrical/bacteria can form on a single layer of times (ten million) per particle.

Each (0.001 mm) particle can hold an estimate, ten million Bio-electrical/bacteria that float's on the top of said surface of a (**solution**) in question.

Bio-electrical (electromagnetic) conductivity precludes each particle to approximate no further than one half inch from the other.

At (0.002 mm) particles are (recessed) no more than one half inch depth, of solution in question.

In every recessions of strategic positioning per particle (0.001 mm) to (0.100 mm), electrical (electromagnetic) conductivity is achieved.

Activity or super computation is activated & manipulated by a layered system (independent) per layers to conduct instruction per layer & able to inter-connect with each layer simultaneously.

super computation is occurred by layers of trillions of signals per second (via) speed of (Bio-electromagnetic) electrical conductivity, of millions of manipulated electrical signals from the types of (solution & strength) or the (validity) of the (bio-electrical (electromagnetic) - **bacteria**).

Finally;

When making (**quantum**) comparisons relative to computing, it must be clear that this super computing is in no way compared to quantum-computing that is already underway.

However, this methodology offers an all new (**nexus phase**) in new computing methodology for the future phases in future concepts in super computation.

Theorical projections concepts by Dr. Everett C Borders Jr. Ph.D. (EveBor)

Magnetic bacteria replicate itself building future bio- computers, Magnet-making bacteria may help build biological computers, larger storage space and faster connections, Faster, Smaller 'Nano-Magnet' Hard Drives.

Bio engineered computer bacteria cells, nano Biological Engineering, The principle of the use of modified bacteria for medical diagnosis, Synthetic biology, The internal computer communicates by engineering a cell to change color, researchers used the platform to design 60 genetic circuits, Their cells are around ten times smaller than our own, which means if a single engineered bacterial cell were to attack a tumor, it would have little or no effect.

Genetically engineered bacteria, by using genetically engineered bacteria populations. The proposed bio transceiver is capable of sensing, processing, transmitting, and receiving. To program the bacteria, molecular biologists modify the rest of the biological circuit.

There is a class of coordination polymers, consisting of metal ions or clusters linked together by chemically mutable organic groups.

Nan-ophotonic chip system using lasers and bacteria to observe fluorescence emitted from a single bacterial cell.

To fix the bacteria in place and to route light toward individual bacterial cells, they used V-groove-shaped plasmonic waveguides, tiny aluminum-coated rods only tens of nanometers in diameter.

Selection of short sequences that have affinity to (noble) metals, semiconducting oxides and other technological compounds, these genetically engineered proteins for inorganics (GEPIs) can be used in the assembly of functional nanostructures.

Branched network serves as an electricity-collecting network atop the mushroom's cap by acting like a nano- probe - to access bio-electrons generated inside the cyanobacterial cells.

Characterization of nanoscale fragments of biomaterials such as DNA, proteins, chromosomes, plant cells, bacteria, starch granules and anti-allergens are extremely important.

Nano–bio projects. Lab-on-a-chip applications, such as DNA chips and pharmacy-on-a-chip, creation of nano-vehicles that mimic the way viruses interact with specific cells.

Metabolic engineering has the potential to produce from simple, readily available, inexpensive starting materials a large number of chemicals that are currently derived from nonrenewable resources or limited natural resources.

Some of them are eukaryotic (human), but many more of them are prokaryotic, thanks to the friendly bacteria of your gut, skin, and other body systems. Jump in to learn more about prokaryotic and eukaryotic cells DNA computing is a branch of computing which uses DNA, biochemistry, and molecular biology hardware, instead of the traditional silicon-based computer technologies.

DNA (deoxyribonucleic acid) molecules, the material our genes are made of, have the potential to perform calculations many times faster than the world's most powerful human-built computers.

In DNA computing, information is represented using the four-character genetic alphabet (A, G, C, and T), rather than the binary alphabet (1 and 0) used by traditional computers.

This is achievable because short DNA molecules of any arbitrary sequence may be synthesized to order.

The "biochips" made of DNA that is able to perform billions of calculations at once by multiplying themselves in number.

Computational biology involves the development and application of data-analytical and theoretical methods, mathematical modeling and computational simulation techniques to the study of biological, ecological, behavioral, and social systems. Quantitative & Computational Biology the Division of Biological Sciences is actively building our research strength in quantitative and computational biology.

Research projects share a common interest in using advanced mathematical and computational approaches to study fundamental problems in biology.

Computational and Quantitative biology The LCQB is an interdisciplinary laboratory working at the interface between biology and quantitative sciences.

It is built to promote a balanced interaction of theoretical and experimental approaches in biology and to foster the definition of new experimental questions, data analysis and modeling.

Biocomputers use biologically derived materials to perform computational functions.

A Biocomputers consists of a pathway or series of metabolic pathways involving biological materials that are engineered to behave in a certain manner based upon the conditions (input) of the system.

The Bio-chip computer, Based on the underlying principal of digital computing based on the binary code of 0's and 1's, we start to see how a single molecule capable of being in a state of 0 or 1, or On or Off, makes the possibility of molecular computing achievable.

Bioengineering research includes bacteria engineered to produce chemicals, new medical imaging technology, portable disease diagnostic devices, and tissue engineered organs.

Students in bioengineering are trained in fundamentals of both biology and engineering, which may include elements of electrical and mechanical engineering, computer science, materials science, chemistry, and biology.

They were able to use the extreme gamma bombardment of the (blue sun/star), using, Lawrencium, verillium, Deuterium, in a helium mercury sulfide (cinnabar), pure silver & pure gold as a live active coil) matrix methodology.

This highly enriched the Genoa engineered bacteria emulsions (saturation's), to prolong their life span to a state of immortality, for thousands of years, by ingesting a (*Embryonic transference elixir*).

The only (drawback), with this methodology was that the entire process needed to be repeated, every (**five hundred of earth's years**), otherwise the subject would revert back to a mortal state.

The (*Embryonic transference elixir*) coil, had to be recharged, using the same process with the using of extreme gamma bombardment of the (blue sun/star), & using the verillium, mercury sulfide (cinnabar), pure silver & pure gold as a live active coil).

This methodology, this process, could invoke almost total immortality, & could be sustain by ingesting the (**elixir**), almost indefinitely.

They bathed and drank the elixir to the point of their DNA/Genoa spans were one hundred times of that of a normal earth humanoid.

When injured, all that was required was a twenty-four hour bath in the elixir chamber, to fully regenerate all tissue & regenerate all damaged tissue, to a state of morph genetically natural state, to that of a new born embryo. They had perfected the art of almost total immortality, however; their bodies measured molecular density a lot more (dense) as earth humanoids.

By the total immersion, of ingesting & bathing in the (Embryonic transference elixir), in and around (Planet Black), while in space flight, even on what is now known as planet earth, almost total immortality could be sustained for thousands & thousands of years.

While traveling in space flight, all crew is totally encapsulated in the total cylindrical chamber, filled with, (Embryonic transference elixir) (mist).

Comprised of highly enrich, Genoa engineered bacteria emulsions (mist), & bioengineer healing bacteria, liquid (mist) ventilation (LV) is a technique of mechanical ventilation in which the lungs are insufflated with an oxygenated perfluorochemical (mist).

Breathable liquid/mist solutions to suspend humanoids for years, as the substance is a per fluorocarbon (PFC), a synthetic liquid/mist fluorinated hydrocarbon—clear, odorless, chemically and biologically inert, with a low surface tension and high O_2/CO_2 carrying capacity.

Pfc. can hold as much as three times the oxygen and four times the carbon dioxide as human blood.

Liquid/mist breathing is a form of respiration in which a normally air-breathing organism breathes an oxygen-rich liquid (such as a per fluorocarbon), rather than breathing air.

Once that oxygenated liquid/mist, is inside your lungs it would feel just like breathing, even treating High bacterial loads in humanoid asymptomatic & atypical abnormalities.

In biology, regeneration is the process of renewal, restoration, and growth that makes genomes, cells, organisms, and ecosystems resilient to natural fluctuations or events that cause disturbance or damage, every species is capable of regeneration, from bacteria to humans, regeneration by reproduce by the methodology of budding.

On (Planet Black), the inhabitants refined & perfected the art of successful humanoid sustainability for thousands of years.

Nano blood signatures, introduced within the humanoid blood system gave rise to total methodologies of internal regeneration's & repairs, not only in humanoids but thermal replications of most bio organisms.

(ELd), not factoring in that they're own (Genoa) was altered, by the presence of their own (blue sun/star).

They thought, upon the introduction of their own (Genoa) & combining it with two primitive (earth's) humanoids, they could progress/nudge, its evolutionary progressions, with (earth's humanoids).

(ELd) was stunningly wrong!

Planet black, inhabitants (DNA/Genoa), only worked while using the, (Embryonic transference elixir) and in close proximity of the (blue/Rigel/star), as the process (could never) be transferred to any other type of humanoids.

By introducing an experimental (Genoa), of two planet earth's humanoids, as they mixed their own (Genoa), with (earth's) primitive humanoids (Genoa), creating the recessive negative (Genoa) (Germs), producing what is now known as (Albinos, then/Caucasians).

Caucasians, all attempting to convey their fictitious, pretentious, A-moral high ground, as they lack the humility of being real empathetic human beings, as their entire lives & aura was nothing but chaos & distain, the true antisepses of pure evil.

"Only (Liars), speak in alternative truths"

Case & point, who or what are you, if you can't acknowledge your own putrid origins.

The first offspring mixed with (Genoa), from (planet Black), & (earth's) (Genoa), produced monstrous offspring.

As conditions first appeared as white blotches on the upper hands of the (black indigenous) (Vitiligo), then white spots & blotches in the abdomen until the condition had completely consumed the (black host).

They were vile, chaotic, filed with anger, vile lust & wanton self-destruction; they had pointed beaked noses & canine/lizard like, some had pointed & bat ears, and evens some were dwarfs in stature.

They were A-moral & trifling, filled with all new kinds of disease, their minds were twisted & they were cave dwellers in filth, under the (earth's yellow sun), made their faces & the back of their necks turns red, in the daylight, as they preyed upon their infants & young.

Many died, from genetic blood born disease, as many couldn't dwell within the sunlight of day of the (yellow sun) & scurried about, in cave dwellings unlike other natural (earth's) humanoids, which were all black.

In the beginning, they were shunned away from the villages of earth's (black) humanoids & many were murdered as many began to migrate to colder & more UN-tempered climates of the planet.

They perpetually continued to replicate on their own to create their own (Germ/Genoa), degenerative sequences, going from white/ hair, pale skin, to pale skin to blond hair, red/ hair, straight/hair, from red eyes to Grey eyes, blue eyes, green eyes.

They were on the complete opposite ends of the (normal humanoid spectrum), from black skin, curly hair, brown eyes to the complete opposite, even in their mannerism, thinking & degenerative behaviors.

They had no grace, no future, and only a highly corrupted & vile sense of disposition.

These (Genoa) (Germs), (Albino, then/ Caucasians), behaved just like the (Germs) in natural world with no honor, no inclination of natural humanoid necessity of life of, especially neither others, nor the cranial consistency composite to have any empathy of self-concise.

They historically (coveted evil), & were ravenous, (historically demonic) towards the natural world, as they practiced in perpetual continuous cannibalism & not only humanoid but in animal degradation.

With every generation of their offspring, they perpetually created even more & more, monstrous offspring, vile, chaotic filed with anger, vile lust & wanton self- destruction, they were filled with wanton lasciviousness, greed & contempt towards the fellow (earths) brethren.

They had malice & with forethought towards, even their own kind, as they were murderous

& rampant/rabid with the vile of the stench, of self-loathing.

They practiced in incest towards their offspring & corrupted their filth ways of their own surroundings.

They declared wars on their own kind, even created wars on all that were peaceful, as they all drank from the vines of wickedness & ate the bitter Erebus herbs of their own putrid compulsions.

They adorned themselves with the riches (stolen from the poor, the downtrodden, the much more poorer nations, with factious & twisted monarchy's, with king & queen- ships, lords, dukes, built on the bloody backs of the (indigenous blacks) all over the planet earth.

They have historically (murdered hundreds & hundreds of millions) of the (indigenous blacks), all over the planet with such impunity, as they really think, it is their right to do so. They are so historically proud of slavery, apartheid, genocide, rapes & murder of the countless billions of (indigenous blacks), all over the planet.

They felt self-justified their presence on planet earth, by thinking they had, their self twisted god given rights to that genocidal servitude's of millions &millions of (indigenous blacks), all over the planet earth.

They relished in the idea of sleeted inbreeding to that of accession. They hoarded the resources of the (indigenous blacks), to make themselves riches, all the while being highly obsessed with their self twisted & maniacal historical greed.

With their **historical** thievery, juvenile unnecessarily, ridiculous wars over greed & general stupidity, their weapons of mass destruction, plundering, rape & murder were their own (**self twisted created religion**), as they knew not the ways of peace, harmony & content, of their own planet.

They were void of natural empathy & natural decency, & couldn't feel in general humanoid compassion unlike their (black indigenous brethren).

They were afoul upon the lands, of nature, staining the planet everywhere they went & always with the drunkenness, selfishness of foolishness of the disdain.

They trampled upon all the lands & life forms of (planet earth), with such reckless abandon that even their children or their own kind, wasn't safe from their vile destruction.

Their (entire sub-humanoid existence) was that of rage, contempt towards all things of nature & each other, petty bickering & jealousy, blind stupidity and greed, the stains of deception soiled them & the truth was not before their eyes.

Their dorsal souls were as black as the nights that they themselves have corrupted.

(Their twisted historical religion) was taking that of others, & fouling/spoiling the lands for the own personal greed & contempt's, as well as others all whom they have taken.

When they discovered that others possessed gold, silver, & diamonds, their blind murderous rampages only added to the degenerative (historical) natures of these (Genoa/Germs), nonsensical A- mortality, and one dimensional thinking.

As some, self created themselves as (sects) & (self chosen ones), others openly worshiped in the clouds, the yellow sun, fire, the lunar moon, the water, the mountains, the wind, serpents, dragons, insets, birds, & visions & sights they did not understand.

Behold, as this is (their legacy) upon planet earth; the recessive negative (Genoa) (Germs), producing what is now known as (Albinos, then/Caucasians).

*(They) have only been, (semi civilized or just out of the forest, for **(twenty five thousand years)** & look how much damage that they have done to themselves, nature & the rest of the planet up until now 2020.*

Germs are in-fact, just germs.

No matter what other label, or façade, or attempt to alter its genetic makeup, in the end they are all just germs, an historical & habitual plague upon this planet.

Consider just another, out & out facts as presented. The planet earth, once a with pristine environments, just less than fifty years ago around the world:

Fact-1-all oceans polluted by Caucasians, Exxon Valdese, Gulf oil spill, & countless oil spills around the world in all the waterways, Ocean trash of plastics, killing sanative pristine & delicate fish environment, reef habitats.

Fact-2- all once pristine land environments in every continents around the world have all been polluted by Caucasians.

Fact-3-Ozone & air particulate's are record levels, with smog, increased Co2-levels rising every year & heating up the planet, causing dangerous climate changes, all caused by Caucasians.

Fact-4- Caucasians have polluted the upper atmosphere

With space-junk, the likes this planet has never seen. Fact-5- Caucasians have destroyed every civilization on the planet earth, since their very conceptions, North America, South America, Africa, India, Middle East, Asia, Australia, Canada, Arab states, all other outer Islands.

Fact-6- Caucasians are about to destroy; very sensitive water shed environments in the middle of this country with their endorsement of the pipelines in North Dakota (Pipeline is about to run from Canada to Texas) as the probabilities of spills are greatly apparent, as more pipelines have been approved by this administration, even imposed pipelines through Indian tribal lands.

Consider more & more Cancer deaths rates in associated from water contamination & other illness associated with the same, as in 2020, this is now a post apocalyptic environment.

Looking around this country & the rest of the planet, ask yourself the intelligent question, what do you, the readers and most true logical pragmatist, think.

According to all Caucasians, everything is just fine for them, (*a screw you, & hurrah for me, twisted & diseased mentality*), as most think this way & they really cannot help it, despite what some may say to the contrary.

There is real scientific evidence of conveyance of historical human & sub-human patterns, which existed thousands of years ago & even more prevalent in 2020.

You see they have destroyed every civilization that they have encountered, even their own, as they are so desperate to infect, infest, & destroy other planets in space, they are most eagerly beside themselves.

Stewardship is not a right; it is a privilege as if we lose what we have, then we have no one else or nothing to blame when it is gone but ourselves.

There is a saying that goes" never eat where you defecate" and as most humans & non-humans abide by that nocturne, it make one to wonder, are humans really stewards of this planet environment.

Let us begin analyzing historical recent human behavior:

Every sector, every continent, of our human and non- human society has been infected with ideals and values, not of their own.

Their intellectuals will say we have made humankind better; more advanced, but have they.

Look at what they have done on a global scale.

Colonial infestation mentality has diseased and anguished this entire planet.

They have killed tens of millions and infected many more with their twisted fantasies.

History records that everywhere they go, death, and pestilence follow.

Wide scale killing of whales, over fishing, indiscriminate killing of animals for sport, globally depleting of food & mineral supplies, fracking, the indenturing of others for personal gain.

Lynching, murder, raping of the young, institutional racism, disease, cultural disfranchises, liberty and land disfranchises, when people are deprived of land, they are robbed of their basic liberties.

Pollution and the degradation of natural resources.

Trashing of the oceans, seas, every landmass, lakes, and fresh water systems, the pollution of ground water, air quality, strip mining, cutting timber, oil spills, the pollution, and formation of space junk.

Burying nuclear waste & Co_2 gases, starving millions, ethnic cleansing, and global warming.

Genetically enhanced germinal viruses, the irradiation, and the altered behavior of pollinator, such as bees, plants and animals, cancer and aids.

The historical genocide that has plagued this planet has taken centuries, with always the same intent, greed and the need to oppress others different from themselves.

No amount of intellectual, justification of what they have done can correct what has in fact, been done.

Other scientist will agree that they are polluting the very same space they are attempting to explore.

With limited knowledge of propulsion systems such as ion, and nuclear, they have already left trials of toxic debris throughout this solar system.

Are we to live to feed & breed, thieve, heave to perpetrate more little ones just like ourselves as redundancy has sometimes-grave consequences.

In summary:

Caucasian people attempt to exploit, steal, connive, and conquer.

It is in their true nature, they are hard wired to be, poison, and they cannot help it.

"Never have so few done so much evil to so many".

The truth is what it is, no matter whom it offends, more over; fore they are, Evil aliens upon (planet earth).

If an extraterrestrial came to this planet, god helps them, if they arrive in the wrong country.

From the Dutch, to the British, to the Italians, to the French, From the Germans, to the Russians, and the Spain to the Portuguese, not to mention the self appointed so called (Jews) as they all had the same destructive A-moral mentality.

(Jews), all worship a (black Hebrew bible or Koran) that was written by the (indigenous blacks) (real black Israelites of fifteen thousand years past), as only real Israelites are all black; a definitive & historical contradiction to all that is being currently purported by all, Caucasians & (Jews).

Caucasians did not have the capacity of original thinking of their own religion, so they created it/ plagiarizing & masquerading as Caucasians Israelites (JEWS).

The Jews don't have a religion, they worship a fifteen thousand year old (black Hebrew faith/ religion), as all the Hebrews were & still are all black, which make the Jews are a cult, a sect, as they are secular.

Here is the definition of a **sect**; Definition of sect:

Sect

/sekt/ Noun
A group of people with somewhat different religious beliefs (typically regarded as heretical) from those of a larger group to which they belong.

synonyms: (religious) cult, religious group, faith community, denomination, persuasion, religious order; More

DEROGATORY

A group that has separated from an established Church; a nonconformist Church.

synonyms: (religious) cult, religious group, faith community, denomination, persuasion, religious order; More

A philosophical or political group, especially one regarded as extreme or dangerous.

Here is the definition of **secular**;

sec·u·lar

/ˈsekyələr/ Adjective
1. Denoting attitudes, activities, or other things that have no religious or spiritual basis.

"Secular buildings"

synonyms: nonreligious, lay, nonchurch, temporal, worldly, earthly, profane; More

2. CHRISTIAN CHURCH

(Of clergy) not subject to or bound by religious rule; not belonging to or living in a monastic or other order.

Noun

1.

A secular priest.

Translations, word origin, and more definitions

Three Definitions of a **cult**; Cult

/kəlt/ Noun
A system of religious veneration and devotion directed toward a particular figure or object.

"The cult of St. Olaf"

A relatively small group of people having religious beliefs or practices regarded by others as strange or sinister.

"A network of Satan-worshiping cults"

synonyms: sect, religious group, denomination, religious order, church, faith, faith community, belief, persuasion, affiliation, movement; More a misplaced or excessive admiration for a particular person or thing.

"a cult of personality surrounding the leaders" synonyms: obsession with, fixation on, mania for, passion for; More

Translations, word origin, and more definitions

Cult

Any flood of religious cuckbois who believe in a God, idol, guardian, deity or of the like. They are often ambitious/extremist zealots and can be of any culture, belief or religion, be it Christianity, Jewish, Muslim, Atheist, etc. They will often argue or fight solely for their preferred religion and deny all others just to protect theirs. They often refuse to listen to others not of their own and will fuck you over provided you oppose them or refuse to join.

The KKK cult is a cult.

By picklestein June 20, 2016

Cult

Noun UK /kʌlt/ US /kʌlt/ Cult noun (RELIGION)

[C] A religious group, often living together, whose beliefs are considered extreme or strange by many people:

Their son ran away from home and joined a religious cult. [C] a particular system of religious belief:

The Hindu cult of Shiva, Christianity, Jewish, Muslim, Atheist, etc.

Caucasians, who now masquerade as (Israelites), were still living in caves, centuries while there were (indigenous blacks) (real black Israelites (Hebrews) of fifteen thousand years past), were building civilizations, how ironic & funny is that.

The (black Hebrews), the facts are, the (black Hebrews), wrote the original book of the word, a book that almost all faiths worship, study & semi attempt to abide by even now, the (Jews) plagiarized & desecrated this, so did the Christians, Catholics, & soon & etc.

There are so many twisted versions of the (original word), by (Caucasians) that the (original message from the (Black Hebrews) & meaning is extremely (twisted), from all those who are the most twisted.

Caucasians have in-fact fully twisted the Egyptian religion, unable to interpret the Egyptian meaning, they twisted it too fully desecrated the true religions of blacks, sick is sick.

True Case in point, in the Vatican & at this very moment in earth's history, Egyptian obelisks adorn the gates of Rome, as they (Romans) cut off the tops of the Egyptian obelisks & placed their own twisted crosses on tops of another religion.

May this factual evidential information assist in guidance of your true & personal global perspectives;

The following factual informational evidence, depicts all highly plausible & definitive reasons historically, for every black Person on the face of this earth to be an 'Anti- Semite', as if you start reading for yourself, the factual information conveyed, its content (Shall), alter your true perspectives & personal opinions about all, Jews & Caucasians.

The following factual information is the real truth about all (JEWS), & all Caucasians on this planet.

Being Jewish is not a religion or faith, it's really a (CULT) & a (SECT), and disguised as a religion, as (JEWS) all attempt to worship a fifteen thousand year old (black religion of the real black Israelites, (Black Hebrews), the people whom wrote the first original book/bible of the (word).

Real history is real history, & not (**his-story**), as why do Caucasians all lie about history & slavery? https://www.everystudent.com/features/truth.html https://www.snopes.com/fact-check/facts-about-slavery/ http://www.crf-usa.org/black-history-month/the-slave-trade

https://theestablishment.co/white-people-you-have-a-lying-problem-e991c3634493/

http://www.digitalhistory.uh.edu/disp_
textbook.cfm?smtI D=11&psid=3807

https://slate.com/news-and-politics/2015/09/
slavery-myths-seven-lies-half-truths-and-
irrelevancies-people-trot-out-about-slavery-
debunked.html

https://www.smithsonianmag.com/history/
slavery-trail-of-tears-180956968/

https://medium.com/message/how-white-
people-got-made-6eeb076ade42

https://qz.com/1012692/this-is-what-reparations-
could-actually-look-like-in-america/

Texas schools teaching & self justifying, children that black slavery was somehow just.

https://www.salon.com/2013/03/13/11_
heinous_lies_conservatives_are_teaching_
americas_school_children_partne r/

https://www.latimes.com/books/jacketcopy/la-et-jc-do-new-texas-textbooks-whitewash-slavery-segregation-

20150707-story.html

https://www.houstonchronicle.com/news/houston-texas/houston/article/State-textbook-standards-on-Civil-War-concern-6373928.php

https://billmoyers.com/content/walk-through-20th-century-marshall-texas/

https://www.pbs.org/wgbh/americanexperience/features/reconstruction-schools-and-education-during-reconstruction/

https://www.houstonpress.com/news/5-reasons-the-new-texas-social-studies-textbooks-are-nuts-7573825

https://www.theatlantic.com/education/archive/2018/02/what-kids-are-really-learning-about-slavery/552098/

https://whyevolutionistrue.wordpress.com/2015/08/17/texas-textbooks-attempt-to-hide-the-history-of-slavery-but-are-exposed-in-doonesbury/

https://opinionator.blogs.nytimes.com/2014/01/30/the-young-white-faces-of-slavery/

https://www.washingtonpost.com/local/education/150-years-later-schools-are-still-a-battlefield-for-interpreting-civil-war/2015/07/05/e8fbd57e-2001-11e5-bf41-c23f5d3face1_story.html

Schools in the United States & around the world & self justifying & teaching children that black slavery was somehow just.

https://www.theatlantic.com/education/archive/2018/02/what-kids-are-really-learning-about-slavery/552098/

https://medium.com/synapse/an-education-reading-ta-nehisi-coates-s-between-the-world-and-me-279a7b122912

https://medium.com/in-medias-res/teaching-slavery-in-the-high-school-latin-classroom-ce4146827abe

https://www.nybooks.com/daily/2018/02/07/slavery-and- the-american-university/

https://www.wbur.org/hereandnow/2014/11/19/slavery-economy-baptist

http://www.ncte.org/library/NCTEFiles/Resources/Journals/CCC/0611-sep09/CCC0611Good.pdf

https://www.nydailynews.com/news/national/king-black-history-month-slavery-article-1.2513580

http://www.loc.gov/teachers/classroommaterials/connections/narratives-slavery/file.html

https://isreview.org/issue/100/w-e-b-du-bois-black-agency-and-slaves-civil-war

https://www.google.com/search?q=why+is+it+important+for+students+to+

learn+about+slavery&sa=X&ved=
2ahUKEwj3jPTsg_ThAhW5FTQIHan
XARoQ1QIoBHoECAoQBQ

Look up for yourselves;

Why isn't slavery taught in schools

Teaching slavery to elementary students

Teaching slavery to middle school Teaching slavery in schools

Why is it important for students to learn about slavery? Teaching slavery activities

How is slavery taught in the south? Slavery in America

How Dutch Jews started the black African slave trade https://www.washingtonpost. com/archive/opinions/1993/10/17/half- truths-and-history-the-debate-over-jews- and-slavery/6b2b2453-01da-4429-bd50- beff03741418/

https://www.myjewishlearning.com/article/jews-and-the- african-slave-trade/

https://www.theatlantic.com/magazine/archive/1995/09/sl avery-and-the-jews/376462/

https://www.tabletmag.com/jewish-arts-and-culture/books/137476/slave-trade-black-muslim

https://www.jta.org/2013/12/26/global/dutch-rabbi-confronts-jews-with-ancestors-complicity-in-slavery

http://www.washingtonpost.com/wp-srv/style/longterm/books/chap1/jewsslavesandtheslavetrade.htm

https://www.nybooks.com/articles/1994/12/22/the-slave-trade-and-the-jews/

https://www.youtube.com/watch?v=_Aa3Wu6ocV0

https://www.africanholocaust.net/news_ah/jewishslave.html

How Portugal Jews started the black African slave trade http://www.africaspeaks.com/articles/nacs0502.html

http://www.bbc.co.uk/worldservice/africa/features/storyofafrica/forum4.shtml

https://www.amazon.com/Jews-Slaves-Slave-Trade-Perspectives/dp/0814726380

https://www.momentmag.com/book-review-black-jews-in-africa-and-the-americas/

How English Jews started the black African slave trade

https://www.haaretz.com/opinion/.premium-labour-s-latest-blaming-jews-for-slave-trade-1.5390569

https://www.myjewishlearning.com/article/jews-and-the-african-slave-trade/

https://www.nybooks.com/articles/1994/12/22/the-slave-trade-and-the-jews/

http://www.bbc.co.uk/worldservice/africa/features/storyofafrica/forum4.shtml

https://nyupress.org/9780814726396/jews-slaves-and-the-slave-trade

How German Jews started the black African slave trade

https://www.africanholocaust.net/news_ah/jewishslave.html

http://www.bbc.co.uk/worldservice/africa/features/storyofafrica/forum4.shtml

https://www.timesofisrael.com/in-germanys-extermination-program-for-black-africans-a-template-for-the-holocaust/

https://aeon.co/essays/dare-we-compare-american- slavery-to-the-holocaust

http://www.washingtonpost.com/wp-srv/style/longterm/books/chap1/jewsslavesandtheslavetrade.htm

https://www.washingtonpost.com/archive/opinions/1993/

12/04/rewriting-the-history-of-blacks-and-jews/36f6c3db-7d16-4493-ac2a-6ebcd8199389/

https://abhmuseum.org/what-is-the-black-holocaust/

How Spanish Jews started the black African slave trade

https://arcade.stanford.edu/rofl/how-did-early-modern-slaves-spain-disappear-antecedents

https://jps.library.utoronto.ca/index.php/renref/article/download/9185/6150/

https://newint.org/features/2001/08/05/history

https://www.theatlantic.com/magazine/archive/1995/09/slavery-and-the-jews/376462/

http://www.washingtonpost.com/wp-srv/
style/longterm/books/chap1/jewsslaves
andtheslavetrade.htm

https://www.nps.gov/ethnography/aah/
aaheritage/histContextsC.htm

https://www.jta.org/2013/12/26/global/dutch-
rabbi-confronts-jews-with-ancestors-complicity-
in-slavery

http://www.writing.upenn.edu/~afilreis/
Holocaust/austen.html

https://www.jstor.org/stable/340143http://www.
siger.org/mauritsstadnewamsterdam/

http://ldhi.library.cofc.edu/exhibits/show/
african_laborers_for_a_new_emp/early_
trans_atlantic_slave_tra

How French Jews started the black African
slave trade

http://realhistoryww.com/world_history/ancient/Misc/Doc tor_clarke/Gates.htm

https://history.stackexchange.com/questions/11343/who-were-the-traders-involved-in-the-triangular-slave-trade-in-france

https://www.pbs.org/wgbh/aia/part1/1h281t.html

http://ldhi.library.cofc.edu/exhibits/show/african_laborers_for_a_new_emp/pope_nicolas_v_and_the_portugu

https://noirg.org/articles/jews-selling-blacks-into-slavery-was-extensive-irrefutable/

https://noirg.org/faq/

http://www.bbc.co.uk/worldservice/africa/features/storyofafrica/forum4.shtml

https://www.nps.gov/ethnography/aah/aaheritage/histContextsC.htm

http://www.oxfordbibliographies.com/view/document/obo-9780199730414/obo-9780199730414-0254.xml

https://www.momentmag.com/book-review-black-jews-in-africa-and-the-americas/

http://newsreel.org/guides/blacksan.htm

http://www.writing.upenn.edu/~afilreis/Holocaust/austen.html

https://www.jstor.org/stable/525389

https://abhmuseum.org/what-is-the-black-holocaust/

https://www.cs.mcgill.ca/~rwest/wikispeedia/wpcd/wp/a/Atlantic_slave_trade.htm

https://newint.org/features/2001/08/05/history
https://historynewsnetwork.org/article/41431
https://www.ncbi.nlm.nih.gov/pmc/articles/PMC2973943/

http://www.finalcall.com/artman/publish/ Perspectives_1/article_101830.shtml

http://holywar.org/jewishtr/08slave.htm

https://www.quora.com/Were-Jews-involved-in-the-Transatlantic-Slave-Trade

Consider a whole, (pie), & consider taking a piece of that pie, the piece in question is now (secular) from that original whole (pie), universal logic.

The attempted over taking of Africa was not possible through force but by their factious manufactured religion and missionaries and forced enslavement & disease.

Mentality was to make friends and deceive.

So was the same in India, South America, North America, and Australia.

Every sector, every continent, of our human and non- human society has been infected with ideals and values, not of their own.

Their intellectuals will say we have made humankind better; more advanced, but have they.

Look at what they have done on a global scale.

Colonial infestation mentality has diseased and anguished this entire planet.

They have killed tens of millions and infected many more with their twisted fantasies.

History records that everywhere they go, death, and pestilence follow.

The historical genocide that has plagued this planet has taken centuries, with always the same intent, greed and the need to oppress others different from themselves.

Other scientist will agree that they are polluting the very same space they are attempting to explore.

It is in their true nature, they are hard wired to be, poison, and they cannot help it.

The truth is but the truth, (no matter whom it offends).

After Caucasians have stolen & murdered & raped all lands from blacks, continents, countries, diamonds, gold, silver, platinum, titanium, ebony, oil, chocolates, and all natural resources, committed mass & generational genocides, past & current,; after all the chains & shacking, jailing, mass incarcerations, past & current denials of the proper education, housing, employment opportunities, health care, proper & decent human dignities, historical generational imposed servitudes, subjected to generational & current mass murderous genocidal committed by Caucasians whom are historically & generationally (**rabid**) & possessed over the possessions of all that (blacks) ever had & will ever have.

Right now & after they have historically & generationally imposed all of the above vile atrocities upon all (blacks) on this planet;

this is the Caucasians past & current worldly, sadistic & demonic logic.

Behold, the Caucasians, past & current ridiculous demonic, sadistic worldly demented logic is this, as this is what they saying about (US) at this very moment.

Why can't (black) people lift yourselves up from the generational poverty?

Why can't (black) people lift yourselves up from the generational horrors & tortures that have been inflicted by Caucasians?

Why can't (black) people lift you up from the generational self imposed dispositions of miss educational, voting opportunities?

Why can't (black) people lift yourselves up from all the generational hardships that were demonically & sadistically imposed by Caucasians, decades, centuries, & eons, of denigrating indentured imposed disenfranchisement of billions of blacks on a global scale?

After historically & generationally self conveying impedance towards the entire black global populations, this is what is strikingly & stunningly apparent, to the present day.

The (inhabitants of planet black) all used,

(batwing composite suits)

These suits worked as a parachute type of a descent mode.

A telescopic system operates by depressing twin $Co2$ canisters from the chest of the wearer of compressed air & protrudes recessed telescopic tubing from the appendages from the wearer to extend to a span of (thirty feet) of paper thin composite stretchable material.

The wearer can be dropped from a distance of ten thousand feet & glide at pinpoint accuracy towards the planet safely.

The expanded wings & telescopic system, attached to the appendages operates a solar shelter, for communications systems & heat activation.

Thigh & shin pads are equipped with one week's water & food rations.

From a distance, & looking up from the sky, the (planet black inhabitants) descending, looked like they were flying, like angels & gliding like birds.

At times on (earth's), in humanoid history; it was recognized by the (high counsel), of (planet black), that humanoids needed to believe in (deities), adverse & distinct towards, process of specialized area of the planet.

Each area by region began its own unified beliefs system of the (deities), as certain signs were introduced to attempt to somehow guide & assist, imply to all of indigenous populations of earth to promote more harmony within the general populous regions, thus;

Symbols, ceremonies, stones & other rites & ornaments, were set forth to preview of ceremonial rites of invocations.

Within the brief history of earth's humanoid mankind, several prophets, omens, prophecies had some influence from time to time, these people were all ostracized, or murdered at the time for attempting to inform, imply & enlighten, such as; Methuselah, Hadith of the Moorish Prophet, Mohammed, BLACKS ISRAELITES, Moses, Noah, black Hebrews, black Muslims, Gandhi, Mandella, Lincoln, Kennedy, Malcolm X, Dr, king, Ali, Obama.

Their influences, effective in time & however limited in their scopes of reach, somehow only fueled brief, segmented moments of prolong suffrages of the indigenous black multitudes of earth populous.

In the brief history of (earth's humanoids), their main purpose was in-fact that they attempted & tried to promote world peace & harmony, however brief in their success or non-success, but they did in-fact all try!

Earths, Historical **Ancient symbols of power**

Blade of Laertes, Laertes is the son of Polonius and the brother of Ophelia.

In the final scene, he kills Hamlet with a poisoned sword to avenge the deaths of his father and sister, for which he blamed Hamlet. ... His name is taken from Laertes, father of Odysseus in Homer's Odyssey.

https://www.google.com/search?
ei=VDcMXKbXL5vF0PEP98Ks2Aw&q
=the+Blade+of+Laertes%2Cdef&oq=the

+Blade+of+Laertes%2Cdef&gs_l=psy-
ab.12...24605.25441..28512...0.0..0.198.711
.0j4......0....1..gws-wiz.......0i71.MkcIOmcgEw8

Sword of destiny,

Swords are a new heavy weapon variant
introduced in The Taken King.

The blade of the sword is made of an elemental
Light, so heavy ammo is still needed to use it
like other heavy weapon.

Unlike other weapon classes, all swords are
forged by the player and not found in the world.

The Holy Lance, also known as the Lance of
Longinus, the Spear of Destiny, or the Holy
Spear ... of Matthew, which is the Homoousian
interpretation adopted by the First Council of
Nicaea, that "Jesus Christ was both true God
and true man.

Holy Lance, also called Spear of Destiny or
Spear of Longinus, a relic discovered in June

1098 during the First Crusade by Christian Crusaders at Antioch. It was said to be the lance that pierced the side of Christ at the Crucifixion.

The Discovery of the Holy Lance. On June 15th, 1098, the army of the First Crusade discovered the Holy Lance

– the very spear that had pierced Christ's side on the cross

- in the city of Antioch. https://www.google.com/search?ei=ozYMXLHCHc—0PEPs-aS6A4&q=Sword++spear+of+destiny%2C&oq=Sword++spear+of+destiny%2C&gs_l=psy-ab.12...17144.21376..23494...0.0..0.327.1410.0j5j1j1......0....1..gws-wiz.......0j0i71j0i67j0i13j33i10.Y4cuUERf_r0

Ajanti Dagger,

Phurba Dagger, Phurba, or kila, a dagger used in rituals associated with Tibetan Buddhist and Bon tradition.

The tantric use of the Phurba encompasses the curing of disease, exorcism....

It is identified with the wrathful activity of the ritual dagger or kīla.

https://www.google.com/search?q=ajanti+dagger+replica&oq=Ajanti+Dagger%2C&aqs=chrome.3.69i57j0l4.6469j0j8&sourceid=chrome&ie=UTF-8

Bursea cross,

1a: a structure consisting of an upright with a transverse beam used especially by the ancient Romans for execution.

B often capitalized: the cross on which Jesus was crucified. 2a: crucifixion.

B: an affliction that tries one's virtue, steadfastness, or patience we all have our crosses to bear. https://www.google.com/search?biw=1366&bih=657&ei=1zUMXP-4Ncex0PEP0_Kv6AM&q=bursea+cross+definition&oq=Bursea+cross+def&gs_l=psy-ab.

1.0.33i160.10581.12093..14930...0.0..0.223.
765.0j2j2......0....1..gws-wiz.......0i13j0i13i3
0j0i8i13i30j0i8i13i10i30j0i13i5i30j33i299.
l9VodCdvKKI

OLD WAYS of (religion & Rites)

The haben otera

<u>Tegea – Ancient History Encyclopedia</u>
Sivelinga

<u>Shiva Lingam Stone Stimulates Energy Flow throughout the Body</u>

Ancient herbal **drug** ayahuasca

<u>3 Reasons You Should Drink Ayahuasca – Soul Herbs</u>

Spiritual rites,

Seti, Menmaatre Seti I was a pharaoh of the New Kingdom Nineteenth Dynasty of Egypt, the son of Ramses I and Sitre, and the father of Ramses II.

As with all dates in Ancient Egypt, the actual dates of his reign are unclear, and various historians claim different dates, with 1294 BC to 1279 BC and 1290

Stones of Adoration: Sacred Stones and Mystic Megaliths of...For 3.3 Million Years Stone and Crystal Traditions Have... Stones, Sacred (in the Bible) | Encyclopedia.com

The Silver Chalice: definition of The Silver Chalice and...

Ring of power
Power - definition of power by the Free Dictionary

The ring of power – Defining anything - definithing.com

Terrestrial landing sites listings,

Is there an alien landing site in Antarctica? Mysterious...

(**EveBor**), the (planet black ruler), quarantined (the earth planet) and the entire system, the high counsel instituted the (**Prime Directives**);

when it was discovered the plans of, (ELd), planet engineering council member (six).

He was stripped of his seat on the counsel & returned to (planet black) for hearings of violations of the prime directives.

His sentence was a lifetime & further denial of (*Embryonic transference elixir*), along with all his heirs on a planet near the star system of (**Mintaka**).

The counsel

The counsel is comprised of fifteen members as of only ten, having the ultimate power to move acts of furtherance within the planet, its inhabitants & all outer interstellar activities.

Each council member has the direct responsibility of its own tasks associated with the propensity & abatement of the totality of the entire (planet black).

(Jaa)-Counsel member (one) (grid green), in charge of all ground transportation in & around the planet black.

His control is limited to, one to ten feet, (vertically) of all hovercraft, all four & two wheel vehicles, magnetic lifts trains & cars, water crafts, within (grid green) he was competent, just & forthright.

(Ork)-Counsel Member (two) grids blue), in charge of all flight operations from ten feet, till one thousand feet from the surface of the planet.

Since surface vectors are variables in random, & obscure, more complex, are the rules governing this body of operations, as he was very colorful, humorous & performance driven.

(Redy)-Counsel member (three) (grid yellow), in charge of all flight operations from above the one thousand feet & above the planet.

The grid vector analysis being both simplistic & complex in its grid patterns, ensure smooth flight operations for flawless maneuverability of all crafts & ships up; down & across the planet stratospheres outer rim.

He was a very serious, council member, but soft spoken.

The totality of the grid pattern matrix is inner connected to ever ensure that all ground & flight operations are seamless.

For example; the ground transportation grid is the same as the outer stratospheric rim in respects for being color-coded, thus, ground grid from the surface to ten feet above the ground is (grid green).

Connected to (**grid green**), is (**grid blue**), from ten feet above the surface till one thousand feet above the surface, connected to grid blue is (**grid yellow**), from one thousand feet till the outer stratospheric rim.

Thus all ships & crafts beyond the outer stratospheric rim boundaries are considered (**grid red**) using the same grid pattern matrix of planet black, under total military command.

Once destinations are targeted/plotted into the grid pattern, the grid vectors analysis and (super computations), direct & guide the craft, via ship or crafts onboard computers, to its destination in respects of the totality of the grid matrix.

Although all (ground transportation) (grid green) is navigated both by hand & autonomous, any craft or ship cannot ascend or descend beyond (grid green) unless it is on the grid pattern vectors analysis, (super computations matrix). Any mid-flight changes are all calculated, by permission, through the grid pattern vectors analysis, (super computations matrix).

These operations ensure that all ground & flight operations are in-fact recorded & for the safety & seamless operations of all traffic fluidity.

(Ifiny)-Counsel member (four), in charge of all water & food supplies on the entire planet.

She practiced in the legal arts of the of planet black.

(Eri)-Counsel member (five); in charge of all living quarters & planet buildings apparatus on planet black. *A professor of operations,*

If any inhabitants on the planet deeded to relocate anywhere on & off the planet, they needed to contact her for arrangements to do so.

(ELd) **& replaced, with (Baba)-Counsel member (six),** in charge of all mining & building operations, engineering on the entire planet & all other planetary mining operations. *This post was broken up & duties & divided between two **associated** supreme prime council members.*

(Haro)-Counsel member (seven), in charge of (all galaxy 0 rangers) (police-enforcement).

A former (galaxy 0 ranger specialist) & highly decorated, well respected,

(Maji)-Counsel member (eight), in charge of all outer military operations for the protection of all planetary defenses & all mother ships.

She commands the **(Grid red)** using the same grid pattern matrix of planet black, under total military command.

She is a highly decorated military admiral, whose opinions were always adhered to, by the high counsel.

(Daff)-Counsel member (nine), in charge of all sciences & education on planet black.

A compassionate genius in education, & sciences, she insured that all learned, from infant to the elderly, all-day & night to full enlightenment.

With her directions & instructions, all inhabitants of planet black & all personnel aboard the mother ships continuously learned, (even in stasis) & were updated in real time, instructional education from birth to the present.

(Inky)-Counsel member (ten), in charge of all crafts & ship operations & planetary maintenance.

He was extremely on point of all operations & a highly valuable asset to counsel.

Three members of the counsel are called (associated supreme prime); they float from one meeting till the next & steer/ or chair, the counsel board members to ensure the council members are always acting in the best interests of the totality of the inhabitants of the planet.

They also have all expertise, in all areas of planet & off planet total operations, & at times, step in and override areas of precise mannerisms of operations on a planetary scale.

All counsel personal constantly rotate from one area of expertise, till the other, to ensure greater continuity of knowledge's of the entire planet operations.

With this methodology, any council member could be placed on another planetary system & ensure the same seamless governing operations of planet black; moreover, in order to ascend to (vice & supreme prime), knowledge must be obtained & mastered in all areas of planetary & off planetary operations.

(Niss)-Counsel member (eleven) associated supreme prime. Confrontational & highly intuitive, *she cracked the whips on all operations, very thoroughly.*

(Erm)-Counsel member (twelve) associated supreme prime. *Strong willed & fiery and bold in her Roderick,*

(Beta)-Counsel member (thirteen) associated supreme prime. *Eldest of all the counsel, she was as wise as she was compassionate.*

Two council member are called (vice & supreme prime), they have the ultimate responsibility to make the final decisions on all planetary safety & security of all matters on both planet black & all outer planetary operations.

(Garwol)-Counsel member (fourteen) vices supreme prime.

Jointly has access & total control of the (planetary super computation) along with Counsel Member (seven), Counsel Member (eight), & Counsel Member (fifteen), (prime). *He was an engineer & scientist who was the right hand of the (prime).*

(EveBor)-Counsel member (fifteen), (prime), total control of the (planetary super computation) (fifty trillion liquid channel chip matrix systems), to control all aspects of the planet from tracking all inhabitants to controlling all transports & all other areas of planetary & off planetary operations.

Only the council member (fifteen), (prime), can over ride any other system on the planet, based upon critical input/collaborations & considerations by at least three other (associated supreme prime), council members.

He was a wise scientist who knew the dangers of meddling with other life forms.

The counsel, after observing the massive damage committed by former council member (ELd), as they did not want to further interfere with the progression & Digressions of the fate of (planet earth's inhabitants), seemed at odds with (planet earths) future or end.

There were (**several considerations**) that the council members reviewed thus;

1- allowing the (tainted planets earth's inhabitants) (Genoa) (Germs), (Caucasians), continue to destroy their natural own civilizations, thereby destroying, the first indigenous black population the entire (planet earth).

2- to intercedes in earth's history & plights, with a series of cosmic & seismic corrections towards its past when (tainted planets earth's inhabitants) (Genoa) (Germs) Caucasians), to before then even present, & revert back towards the first indigenous black population the entire (planet earth).

3- attempt to restore the planet earth's natural history by removing the (tainted planets earth's inhabitants) (Genoa) (Germs) (Caucasians), from the planet earth & relocating them on another settlement elsewhere, in another system.

4- inhaliating the (entire humanoids of planet earth), recognizing that the natural order was interrupted to the state of being totally irretrievable & began a new pristine planet earth.

5- to continue constant close monitoring of planet earth's inhabitants under the cloaked perspectives under the prime directives set forth by the high counsel.

6- promote & enhance the (indigenous black original population of earth), by series of wealth & territorially enhancement on (planet earth), with inducements.

7- consider & finally realize, that nowhere or however, or whenever the indigenous black original population of earth, are in-fact monetarily & territorially enhanced on (planet earth), that the (tainted planets earth's inhabitants)(Genoa)(Germs)(Caucasians),

Would still further corrupt & infest the rest of the world, re-taint the black indigenous population once again.

Since the unconstrained attempted reconstruction of planet earth, by former council member (ELd), the (high counsel of planet black) observed, earth's black populations, were being murdered in the masses, enslaved, exploited, shunned, beaten like lower animals, experimented on like rats in a lab, infected & infested, lands taken & family units, destroyed.

They systematically & regularly committed, institutional genocide, orchestrated & authored by the, (tainted planets earth's degenerative inhabitants) (Genoa) (Germs) (Caucasians) as they herded the black masses like, pigs, goats, and cattle, for their own maniacal end.

(Tainted planets earth's degenerative inhabitants)(Genoa)(Germs)(Caucasians) stole & dug & murder & stole until they thought all the treasures of the (planet earth) were gone.

Indigenous inbreeding already ran rapid on planet earth amongst the indigenous (degenerative inhabitants) (Genoa) (Germs) (Caucasians) humanoids.

Their degenerative recessive genetic Genoa produced sub- humanoids with straight, blond/ red/auburn hair, blue/Grey/red/hazel/green eyes, pale pasty skin, which repelled sunlight, as they appeared the direct polar opposites of their direct dark skin indigenous genetics hosts.

They all lived in caves & out-cropping, shunning away from the light & moved towards the colder climates on planet earth.

Their diseased minds grew more & unstable with every generation of inbreeding.

Their thoughts were that of complete & utter chaos, rage & destruction, of the planet & all its indigenous humanoid inhabitants.

With each generation of inbreeding, their insanity grew more censurable & insatiable.

They were perverse & drunken with lucidity, of foul malice & thought nothing, but the forbearance of vile & lewd & rapid squander of nature, & self-destruction of the planet earth.

As the conversation frequently arose, the questions remained & continued to imply,

(Can planet earth be saved?) &, the answer was always, (no!).

No historical evidence, no historical attempts, no historical realizations of visions of natural harmony, & no rational of redemption.

Although some areas of compassion & kindness was being taken place, within the (indigenous black population), moreover; the planet earth was too tainted, corrupted, well beyond saving or redemption, by the systematically & regularly committed, institutional genocide, orchestrated & authored by the, (tainted planets earth's degenerative Inhabitants) (Genoa) (Germs), (Caucasians).

For thousands & thousands of (Eons), the (high counsel) of (planet black), monitored, (planet earth), and the fate of its (recognized) (indigenous black population).

(The trial of the Prime Directive) Council meeting & trial of (Eld)

(The indictments);

Sitting on the board was;

(EveBor)-Counsel member (fifteen), (prime supreme),

(Garwol)-Counsel member (fourteen) vices supreme prime.

(Beta)-Counsel member (thirteen) associated supreme prime.

(Erm)-Counsel member (twelve) associated supreme prime.

(Niss)-Counsel member (eleven) associated supreme prime.

Opening statement was chaired by, (Beta)-Counsel
Member (thirteen) associated supreme prime, as she was

First to speak & opening statements;

"In violations of the prime directives set forth by the; (planet black) (high counsel), the accused has willfully committed the acts of, & in violation of the most egregious violations of insurrection."

."**1**-The order was made by (ELd), planet engineering order of counsel member (six), (knowingly) to attempt to further progress/ nudge, the primitive nature of (planet earth's humanoids inhabitants)."

(Niss) -Counsel member (eleven) associated supreme

Primes, & **seconds to speak, & opening statements;**

"**2**-(ELd), planet engineering order of counsel member (six), (knowingly), seeking to expand his own legacy & possible empire, in another world of (earth), started the process of violating directives set forth by the high counsel of (planet black)."

(Erm)-Counsel member (twelve) associated supreme prime, &   **third** to speak, & opening statements;

"**3**-(ELd), planet engineering order of counsel member (six), (knowingly), using two (earth's humanoid inhabitants), (Genoa), slicing with the (Genoa), of the (planet black inhabitants), not fully knowing that process would create extremely hazardous results."

(Garwol)-Counsel member (fourteen) vices supreme prime, &   **forth** to speak, & opening statements;

"**4**-(ELd), planet engineering order of counsel member (six), When the planet earth had one (super continent), (one large landmass), a decision was made, by (ELd), to expand its landmasses by way of, (knowingly), directing a comet a four miles wide toward the ocean strike of (planet earth)."

(EveBor)-Counsel member (fifteen), (prime supreme), &

fifth to speak, & opening statements;

"**5**-(ELd), planet engineering order of counsel member (six), not factoring in that his own (Genoa) was altered, by the presence of their own (blue sun/star),

He thought, upon the introduction of his own (Genoa) & combining it with two primitive (earth's) humanoids, they could progress/ nudge, its evolutionary progressions, with (earth's humanoids)."

"(ELd) was wrong! As the (planet black, inhabitants) (DNA/Genoa), only worked while using the, (*Embryonic transference elixir*) and in close proximity of the (blue/Rigel/star), as the process (could never) be transferred to any other type of humanoids."

(EveBor)-Counsel member (fifteen), (prime supreme), & *speaking, & opening statements*;

"**6**-By introducing an experimental (Genoa), of two planet earth's humanoids,

(ELd) mixed his own (Genoa), with (earth's) primitive humanoids (Genoa), creating the recessive negative (Genoa) (Germs), producing what is now known as (Albinos, then/ Caucasians).

A new & destructive life form, the first offspring mixed with (Genoa), from (planet Black), & (earth's) (Genoa), produced monstrous offspring, as they were vile, chaotic, filed with anger, vile lust & wanton self-destruction."

"any died, as many couldn't dwell within the sunlight of day of the (yellow sun) & scurried about, in cave dwellings unlike other natural (earth's) humanoids, which were all black."

"They perpetually continued to replicate on their own to create their own (Germ/Genoa), degenerative sequences, going from white/ hair, pale skin, to pale skin to blond hair, red/

hair, straight/hair, from red eyes to Grey eyes, blue eyes, green eyes."

"They were on the complete opposite ends of the normal humanoid spectrum, from black skin, curly hair, brown eyes to the complete opposite, even in their mannerism, thinking & degenerative behaviors."

"They had no grace, no future, only bloody & vile. These (Genoa) (Germs), (Albino, then/ Caucasians), behaved just like the (Germs) in natural world with no honor, no inclination of natural humanoid necessity of life of, especially neither others, nor the cranial composite to have any empathy self-concise."

"They historically (coveted evil), & were ravenous, (historically demonic) towards the natural world, as they practiced in perpetual continuous cannibalism & not only humanoid but in animal degradation."

"With every generation of their offspring, they perpetually created even more & more, monstrous offspring, vile, chaotic filed with anger, vile lust & wanton self-destruction, they were filled with wanton lasciviousness, greed & contempt towards the fellow (earths) brethren."

"They had malice & with forethought towards, even their own kind, as they were murderous & rampant with the vile of the stench, of self-loathing."

"They practiced in incest towards their offspring & corrupted their filth ways of their own surroundings.

They declared wars on their own kind, even created wars on all that were peaceful, as they all drank from the vines of wickedness & ate the bitter Erebus herbs of their own putrid compulsions."

"Their thievery, juvenile unnecessarily, ridiculous wars over greed & general stupidity, their weapons of mass destruction, plundering, rape & murder were their own (self created religion), as they knew not the ways of peace, harmony & content, of their own planet."

"They were void of natural empathy & natural decency, & couldn't feel in general humanoid compassion unlike their (black indigenous brethren)."

"They were afoul upon the lands, of nature, staining the planet everywhere they went & always with the drunkenness, selfishness of foolishness of the disdain.

They trampled upon all the lands & life forms of (planet earth), with such reckless abandon that even their children or their own kind, wasn't safe from their vile destruction."

"Their (entire sub-humanoid existence) was that of rage, contempt towards all things of nature & each other, petty bickering & jealousy, blind stupidity and greed, the stains of deception soiled them & the truth was not before their eyes.

Their souls & hearts were as black as the nights that they themselves have corrupted."

"(Their historical religion) was taking that of others, & fouling/spoiling the lands for the own personal greed & contempt's, as well as others all whom they have taken."

"When they discovered that others possessed gold, silver, & diamonds, their blind murderous rampages only added to the degenerative (historical) natures of these (Genoa/Germs), nonsensical mortality, and one dimensional thinking."

As a result of the (**judgments**) of the above trial, (Indictments); (EveBor)-Counsel Member (fifteen), (prime), still speaking,

closing statement;

"Since the attempted reconstruction of planet earth, by former council member (ELd), it is the opinions of the (high counsel of planet black) observed, earth's black populations, were being murdered in the masses.

They were enslaved, exploited, shunned, beaten like lower animals, and experimented on like rats in a lab, infected & infested, lands taken & family units, destroyed.

These (Genoa) (Germs), (Albino, then/ Caucasians), systematically & regularly committed, institutional genocide, orchestrated & authored by the, (tainted planets earth's degenerative inhabitants) (Genoa) (Germs) (Caucasians).

They herded the, (Indigenous black masses) like, pigs, goats, and cattle, for their own maniacal end."

(EveBor)-Counsel member (fifteen), (prime supreme), & *speaking, & closing statements*;

(ELd), planet-engineering order of counsel member (six), *"you have heard the charges of the high counsel, and found guilty, what say you?"*

(ELd), planet-engineering order of counsel member (six), speaking, *"guilty of attempting to make a better world, a better world sir,"*

Final conclusions,

Of the (high counsel) of planet black;

(Eve or), the (planet black ruler), quarantined (the earth planet) and the entire system, the high counsel instituted the (Prime Directives); when it was discovered the plans of, (ELd), planet engineering council member (six).

He was stripped of his seat on the counsel & returned to (planet black) for hearings of violations of the prime directives.

His sentence was a lifetime & further denial of (*Embryonic transference elixir*) (which reverted he & his off spring to the remainder of their (lifetime being mortal), along with all his heirs on a planet near the star system of (**Mintaka**).

There were three, coconspirators of the indictments in judgment along with, (ELd) -Counsel member (six), in charge of all mining & building operations, engineering on the entire planet & all other planetary mining operations.

Commander, (**Uis**), in charge of (ships weapons) on One of their (eight) Mother ships, **UVEB-7,** When the planet earth had one (super continent), (one large landmass), a decision was made, by (ELd) & carried out by, (**Uis**), to expand its landmasses by way of directing a comet a four miles wide toward the ocean strike of (planet earth).

They learned the ability to direct & control comets & By placing a (gyroscopic nuclear seismic compression converter), on the surface of a comet, & digging in, the process to steer the directing the trajectory of a comet by altering its flight or orbital path,

Commander, (Oppa), in charge & one of the guardians of the; (*Embryonic transference elixir*)

Every (five hundred of earth's years), the (*Embryonic transference elixir*) coil, had to be recharged.

Using the same process with the using of extreme gamma bombardment of the (blue sun/star), & using the verillium, mercury sulfide (cinnabar), pure silver & pure gold as a live active coil) methodology, immortality could be sustained almost indefinitely.

They bathed and drank the elixir to the point of their DNA/Genoa spans were one hundred times of that of a normal earth humanoid.

Commander (doctor), (Husa),

Planet black, inhabitants (DNA/Genoa), only worked

while using the, (Embryonic transference elixir) and in close proximity of the (blue/ Rigel/star), as the process (could never) be transferred to any other type of humanoids.

By introducing an experimental (Genoa), of two planet earth's humanoids, they mixed their own (Genoa), with (earth's) primitive humanoids (Genoa), creating the recessive negative (Genoa) (Germs), producing what is now known as (Albinos, then/Caucasians).

The first offspring mixed with (Genoa), from (planet Black), & (earth's) (Genoa), produced monstrous offspring, as they were vile, chaotic, filed with anger, vile lust & wanton self-destruction.

It was the decisions of the (high counsel), that all three, coconspirators of the indictments in judgment along with, (ELd) -Counsel member (six), were found guilty, violating the (Prime Directives).

They all suffered the same fate as (ELd) -Counsel.

Member (six), A denial of (Embryonic transference elixir) that gives immortality, & banishment from the (Rigel) system, as they were all relocated (which reverted them & all their off spring to the remainder of their (lifetime being mortal), along with all his heirs on a planet near the star system of (**Mintaka**).

Other random encounters on the planet earth;

In the planet earth's periodic history, humanoids from planet black arrived on earth only to observe & record mannerisms of earth's humanoids, in various time periods in the history of earth, sometimes the encounter were peaceful: however some were very hostile, abrupt & brief.

Two humanoids from planet black walk amongst the population in the **United States**

located in the southern states of Mississippi in the nineteen fifties.

Its summer time, the time is twelve o clocks pm, with a slight summer breeze, ninety degrees temperature.

While walking in observation & recording of the times & surroundings of the county (Macon county), they are not surprised by the extremely hostile mannerisms of the local earth humanoid population, while attempting to purchase ice cream using pure silver & pure gold coins.

They were threatened with great bodily harm at least twelve times after only walking two blocks on a main street.

They were violently confronted by the sheriff & passerby citizens, however all the matters were responded to with one hundred thousand volts of electric jolts from the wearing apparel from the visitors from planet black.

The electric jolt rendered all & extremely hostile targets too briefly & momentarily to pass out, only to awaken with the visitors nowhere in sight, never to be seen again.

https://scholarworks.unr.edu/bitstream/handle/11714/

1970/Page_unr_0139D_12278.pdf?sequence=1&isAllo wed=y

https://www.google.com/search?q=how+many+blacks+were+murdered,+tortured+%26+jailed++the+southe rn+states+of+Mississippi+in+the+thrity+fortys++nineteen+fifties.&tbm=isch&source=univ&sa=X&ved=2ahUKE wjpgNLOl9rhAhUISK0KHSzXAzUQ sAR6BAgJEAE

https://www.alamy.com/stock-photo/lynching.html?blackwhite=1

https://www.pinterest.com/edward0006/never-forget/

https://lynchinginamerica.eji.org/report/

https://www.theguardian.com/us-news/2018/apr/26/lynchings-memorial-us-south- montgomery-alabama

https://www.jstor.org/stable/10.5323/jafriamerhist.95.1.0026

http://www.inmotionaame.org/print.cfm?migration=8

Scripts of encounter;

Two humanoids from planet black walk amongst the population in the United States located in the southern states of Mississippi in the nineteen fifties.

Four local humanoids from planet earth violently approach them with baseball bats, shouting niggers, & extremely hostile rants boasting to lynch murder & burn the visitors.

By one local,

"Ha nigger, what you doing over here?" "Why you on this part of town?"

"You are going to be put in your place boys!"

By another local,

"You can't walk down these streets boy" "Where you from boy?"

By another third local,

"You gonna be set on fire boys"

"Were gonna pole you just the pigs & put you on a roasterie & serve you up boys!"

Comments from Ice cream store owner, *"What you doing in here boy?*

"We don't serve your kind boy" "What kind of money is that?"

"You stole that gold money from a white person didn't you boy, I'm calling the sheriff's office!"

Three humanoids from planet black walk amongst the population in **Johannesburg South Africa in the nineteen sixties**, they are attempting to enter a white only restaurant & order potatoes soup, using pure silver & pure gold coins.

All three were met with extreme hostility by the restaurant owner & all the patrons.

The South African apartheid police arrived, guns drawn triggers cocked, they attempted to quickly man handle & bum rush & arrest the visitors from the restaurant.

The restaurant owner & all the patrons joined in shouting the words, *"kaffers"* as they attempted to grab the three visitors who all activated their one hundred thousand volts of electric jolts from their wearing apparel, causing all extremely hostile targets to briefly & momentarily pass out, only to awaken with the visitors nowhere in sight, never to be seen again.

https://www.sahistory.org.za/topic/political-executions-south-africa-apartheid-government-1961-1989

https://www.sahistory.org.za/article/history-women-prisons-during-apartheid-justin-lawler

https://ammo.com/articles/south-africa-land-reform-farm-murders-untold-story

https://www.washingtonpost.com/news/morning-mix/wp/2017/08/01/an-anti-apartheid-activist-died-in- police-custody-in-1971-new-testimony-points-to-murder/

https://www.cnn.com/2013/12/06/world/africa/mandela-life-under-apartheid/index.html

http://www.cnn.com/2007/WORLD/africa/08/17/southafrica.apartheid.reut/index.html

https://africasacountry.com/2017/11/white-privilege-and-hypocrisy-in-south-africa

It is, in the thirteen hundreds, on the west coast of the continent of Africa, as there from a distant vision, five Dutch (Jews) slave ships appear on the horizon.

They arrive with slave chains, guns, muskets & swords, as they began to quickly commit wanton genocide, murder, rape, enslaving, burning & murdering as they attempted to over stuff their ships cargo holds, well beyond its limited capacity with slave men, women & very young children.

There were women & very young children, crying & dying while in heavy chains & stuffed so compacted in the cargo hold that, it was difficult for many to breathe, so they died, as when the slave ships arrived at their destinations, only a third of the slaves ever arrived alive.

https://atlantablackstar.com/2015/07/04/cartagena-colombia-spanish-americas-biggest-slave-port/

https://www.pbs.org/wnet/african-americans-many-rivers-to-cross/history/how-many-slaves-landed-in-the-us/

http://www.digitalhistory.uh.edu/disp_textbook.cfm?smtid=2&psid=446

http://slaveryandremembrance.org/articles/article/?id=A0094

https://www.theroot.com/how-many-slaves-landed-in-the-us-1790873989

https://www.pbs.org/wnet/african-americans-many-rivers-to-cross/history/how-many-slaves-landed-in-the-us/

https://www.politifact.com/punditfact/statements/2014/mar/18/jon-stewart/jon-stewart-slave-trade-caused-5-million-deaths/

Five humanoids from planet black, recorded & all observed & witnessed all mannerisms of events of the incident.

They did not interfere as under their planets black's prime directives, it was forbidden any interference in other life forms, no matter how harsh & cruel, as in every century of every decade, the visitors from planet black walked amongst the populations in all areas of the earth's continents, their orders were to record & observe only & do no harm.

In the planets history; it was observed that slave ships from England, Spanish, Portuguese, German, and the Dutch all arrived on various coasts of Africa to plunder, enslave, murder & rape its populations with their immoral wanton filth & greedy agendas.

From the beginning of planet earth's first humanoid civilizations, up until the earth years of twenty, twenty, and the entire planet earth was observed & recorded, with final & ultimate judgments rendered.

The profound deliberations upon (planet earth)

As some more intuitive scientist theorized the true methodology of the true origins of earth's humanoids, others refused, even when all scientific data & DNA analyses revealed the same conclusions.

They theorized in some of their religions that of second comings of a (deity) that will return & cleanse the planet of all its sin & non-believers.

The (high counsel of planet black) watched & watched for eons of any progressions of a glimmer of any moral cohesion's of civil redemption's, of present humanoid kind, towards the planet earth & all of its inhabitants.

Even now, the recessive negative (Genoa) (Germs), producing what is now known as (Albinos, then/Caucasians).

Inhabitants on planet earth desperately seek an extra- terrestrial presence from where ever they can find it.

Not fully knowing that they are being observed, all along, whenever visited by the (inhabitants of planet black) in historical reference, the inhabitants made sure that before leaving that they took all their technology with them.

(Inhabitants of planet black) were (there), when the first (earth humanoids) crawled out of the trees, when the first (earth humanoids) began to form their first societies, when they build their first cities, stone buildings, & in concert with nature & harmony.

From the pit of (earth's humanoids) fears, to the summit of their knowledge, it seems they always knew that something was out there beyond their own knowledge of their own explanation.

In every sector, every area, every region upon (planet earth) they all worshiped in (deities) that they did not fully understand.

Some (earth's humanoids), who ever encountered (Inhabitants of planet black), in regions of the planet, reported (Similar) encounters, even thousands upon thousands of miles away, on different continents.

Back on (planet black) the high counsel, & along with the entire contingency of the (full Orion belt high counsel), were deciding about (the disposition) of all of (earth's humanoids), even the entire planet on whether it could be saved, as was intended from the beginning.

If they ever return, or will they return, and the big question is always apparent, why will they return & what will they do when they get back to (**Planet Earth**).

Some religions say, that the earth will be consumed in fire, upon the return of them, who really knows except the inhabitants of (planet black).

Their return;

The inhabitants of planet black returned to planet earth in the earth year 2021, in three super war ships, docking just behind the moons of Jupiter, & as they descended to the planet, undetected & unaware to the earth's inhabitants.

They arrived in four scout ships the South American Andes & Himalayas Mountains, as their scout ship were fully cloaked with the chameleon camouflage outer skin of their ships.

As they made their way through the societies of the current climate of humanoids of planet earth, a very disturbing revelation seemed apparently prevalent.

There were wide spread famine, murder by territorial genocides, costal man made cities in peril of destruction, countries like China, The United States, North Korea & Russia all exhibited a war like (nuclear) stance posture.

The first scout ship, arrived in the United States, & observed the entire country, with all of its crooked politicians corrupted with greed, malice & purported hordes of seeking more power.

The blacks on planet earth were historically subjected to chronic institutional racisms, orchestrated by Caucasians.

There were situations of race wars & ethnic cleansing.

Blacks were being murdered in the night by Caucasians by sported hunting parities, from one end of the planet till the other.

White factitious governmental entities were established in Europe, South America, the United States, to further denigrate, blacks on a global scale & the very poor the countries like, Africa, South America, the Arab world, Asian.

It was not until the inhabitants of planet black, contacted their home world of planet black, as the high council reaching the conclusions to enact a transfer of some black humanoids from the planet earth, transferring thousands at a time, moving only the most vulnerable & poor first to the most uncorrupted, by greed, & malice.

Some black humanoids of planet earth were transferred to places in parts of the Andromeda & the Orion galaxy, in productive & caring environments, with health & real purpose.

The high council in both Andromeda & the Orion galaxy decided that the quarantined planetary system of planet earth, as only some humanoids with a percentage point of not less than 80% of Melanin be allowed to further thrive upon the planet surfaces, however; the remainder of the population on planet earth must be destroyed due to a threat of further contamination to all other peaceful systems in and around the three galaxies.

On planet earth, the humanoid black inhabitants are currently living in a world, where (lies), seem to be part of a twisted norm, as what is being shown & taught to them and their children, was very different than what actually is, or has taken place, in real history's time.

When the inhabitants of planet black arrived back on earth in 2021, they came with the means of full planetary destruction of only humanoids of planet earth.

When they arrived, what is now known as the United States, they observed a fake government that secretly oppressed its populous under the disguise of a democratic regime.

There, and even on a global scale they, then observed blacks, still being oppressed under the opuses of being just, intentionally, institutionally, ostracized, just for being a black human.

When the inhabitants of planet black returned to planet earth, they found a cesspool, of corruptions on a global scale, rapid territorial genocidal murders for greed & power, evil incarnated so soaked & interwoven into the planet earth that all remnants of human co-habitability could never be free from the ravishes of the systemic wanton greed, evil & human filth of the psychic of the earth's Caucasians degenerative human dorsal spirit.

Caucasians had scooped the foulest stench from the humanoid gutters of their vile & degenerated dorsal souls.

A planetary cleansing could irradiate the poison that is soaked deep into the ground of the current earth's human experience that only a planetary cleansing could now address.

With the help of planetary engineers, the inhabitants of planet black engineered a reverse airborne neurological agent to counter act the recessive negative Genoa affects of Caucasians, which infested the planet earths from seventy thousands years past.

The earth's planetary surface was so polluted with air smog, soil pollution & water contamination, that full planetary cleansing was necessary.

The earths $Co2$, levels were at a danger point in the evolutionary history of planet earth, which steps needed to be maintained to attempt to lower the manmade climate changes that were severely harming all life forms on the entire planet.

The entire earth's planet was in a current turmoil of rapid storms, record droughts, mass famine, out of control wild fires, all as the result of earth's humans grossly abusing the entire planet.

The air born reversal Genoa agent, would euthanize all the Caucasians, of earth's populations, over a period of time & return the earth to the real black indigenous populations, with the Genoa maturation levels of at least 87.9%, by the years 2045, restoring once more the planet earths balance at its almost purity of seventy thousand years in earths past.

From the years 2020 till, 2045, of earths time history, the earths total humanoid populations with from, just under eight billion people to just under three billion, as the final solution reversal airborne Genoa agent, reintroduced by the planet black engineers, would humanely euthanize all the Caucasians, with a percentage point of not less than 80% of Melanin of earth's populations, by causing them to go to sleep & never waking up ever again.

The scene depicts; an upper-middle class neibourhoods in a semi affluent part of suburbs. It's about seven o- clocks in the evening as all the family members are sitting at the family dinner table.

A Caucasian family, father, mother & three children, are having diner. They are in discussions about all three children's sports activities in & around their schools.

There is a smile on two of the twin children's (girls) faces, as they are in the volleyball classes & the high school track teams in school.

The third child (boy), is younger thirteen years old is not so pleased as his grades in school were not very good and was just told by both parents he was not allowed to play basketball or football because of his grades.

Both parents were being supportive to all children & seemed very concerned about the youngest child.

They are sitting & having diner when one by one, they all subsequently all slump backwards in their chairs & fall asleep at the dinner table & never to awaken again.

The airborne Genoa agent that was deployed was activated only in sleep cycles throughout the world in sectors by sectors grids, as this allowed all recipients of the airborne Genoa agent to only work while the people went to sleep & or in a non working posture.

One by one, sector by sector, the (targeted populous) all went to sleep & never to awaken ever again.

The next scene depicts;

Random targeted people going to sleep & never waking up all around the world, in all of Europe, the United States, Canada, South America, Australia, the Arab world, & selected pockets of China.

Person by person, town by town city by city, country by country, continent by continent, until the entire world was covered & completely saturated by the reversal airborne Genoa agent, that only effected humans.

Humanely euthanizing all the Caucasians, of earth's populations, was not considered out of any kinds of vengeful revenge, or interplanetary superiority, as a purported & institutional twisted (Arian) & racist factions points of views, actions on the planet earth & their acts in furtherance has been running rabid for hundreds of earth years for the expressed purpose of wanton genocides & denigrating, its black & poor populations.

The planet earth's sub-humanoids (Caucasians) needed to be eradicated to further assist in the just furtherance of the true black indigenous global populations & once more bring balance to the planet & the entire solar system.

On a geo-global scale of the planet earth, the populations were at the brink of total civil race wars, concocted & orchestrated by Caucasians.

Planet black is a random-ire planet, having untold vast riches in minerals of giant geo diamonds, emeralds, rubies, gold, silver, platinum, titanium & other very precious minerals that is not on the periodic table of earth.

If Caucasians were allowed to ever visit planet black, historically would be the same as when Caucasians visited the entire continent of Africa, Australia, north & South American, Canada, & the entire Asian continent, resulting in mass attempted disenfranchised of the indigenous, genocides, murders, plundering & chaos on historical earth.

The inhabitants of planet black, & creating the Caucasian condition, had the ultimate responsibility & will never allow this degenerative recessive condition to continue any further in any galaxy.

Fore, never has the curse of being just a natural born black human being on this planet, the first humanoids, has caused so much up evil upon this entire chronic pathetic world, as to historically, chronically, perpetually & currently denigrate its simian brethrens.

Somewhere, on a distant galaxy, called the Milky Way, & on a Petri dish called planet earth, resulted in a terrible humanoid experiment that went horribly wrong.

A single planetary engineer, named, (Eld), from planet black, misused a Genoa splicing methodology to developed the germ/albino/Caucasian, created on a planet called earth.

The germs became a danger to nature, itself & all other plants & animals on the planet, even other humanoids of the same planet, even in their own inner & outer space.

Caucasians committed so much wanton planetary atrocities & destruction that was so intrinsic to their own nature; they were unable to distinguish when they were doing so.

For some twenty five thousand of earth years, the planet black inhabitants observed & watched, waited, even bared eye witness, to the tremendous destructive nature of Caucasians on a planetary scale.

With extreme cruelty, enslavers worldwide of the black populations, stealing & hoarding from its planetary brethrens, murder/ genocides on a planetary scale, with no remorse, no redemption, no empathy, only more destruction of themselves & other humanoids & the entire planet earth & all of their immediate & surroundings in space thereof.

A reversal air born Genoa agent was introduced to best control populations of earth to a more nonthreatening state to the entire planet earth, whereby a more humanely approach to euthanasia had to be taken into account, if earth's humanoid mankind would ever be allowed to ever to continue.

In all of the humanoid condition relative to the planet earth, & even beyond, humanoid beings, all dream of living in relative serenity, peace & in a just-filed world, for every humanoid male, female, & child alike.

Any being that currently, chronically, perpetually & on a daily bases, denigrates its fellow humanoid beings, is not only less than a humanoid being, but well beneath the contempt of their oppressed brethrens.

What's most important to all seven billion souls, on this planet, currently is to daily dream & aspire of a world were all things for all were possible, a just world for all.

The historical hours, were extremely late, as so many billions of black lives & souls, all cried out for only peace, serenity & justice.

As nowhere in the archival accoutrements of earths humanoids history's past & present tense, of a situational condition, of chronic, perpetual & intentional disparities as the present black condition, on this planet earth.

By 2045 the planet earths had no more wars, no more greed, no more sorrow & hunger, famine & thirst for water, on the entire planet earth.

All was right by planetary standards, as once again, the planetary engineers of planet black established peaceful commerce, with the planet earth, & all was forgiven in this galaxy once again.

The indigenous black populous of planet earth flourished & prospered in building their new intended future, without the destructive & degenerative presence of Caucasians, on planet earth; however; a much more new & terrible presence approaches the entire galaxy of the Milky Way, intended to wipe out all life on planet earth, with Andromeda galaxy on path to converge, with its massive black hole approaching & speeding towards earth's galaxy with its own black hole at one million miles an hour.

The planet black inhabitants, attempt to bring some Caucasians from earth back to planet black to further understand their true nature, however, the Caucasians, all succumbed & all died due to the intense gamma bombardments of the blue Rigel star & all perished, as their photosensitive Melanin of 19.9%, spectrum bodies, could not adapt to the intense gamma rays of the planet black.

Many of the earth's humanoids were still allowing themselves to be herded, like sheep, or cattle, or chickens & hogs; however after 2045 of earth years were herded & murdered, no more, as over time, all was in normality.

In the total historical spectrum of earth, the planet black inhabitants were never formally detected on earth, as technology on earths planet earth only detected about four percent of the skies; however some, indigenous blacks on earth, the less prominent did encounter many of them, on occasions.

Now historically, some might call the planet black inhabitants avenging angels and some might even call them the angels of death to Caucasians, as however this new narrative of earthlings in furtherance, continues.

There are very (true & current) 2020 estimates that four million people vanish from the face of this planet, each year, without a trace.

This is not accounting for murders, or wars, or, any other conflicts upon mankind, and it is not accounting for dyeing of diseases or any type of natural catastrophe, as four million people just vanish, without a clue, never to be found again, ever!

By scientific standards, there are many irrational vs. rational, plausible vs. implausible, incredulous vs. incredible reasons, why four million people just vanish of the face of this planet, each year.

Some think that they all go to other places or (parts unknown), as others think in a more demonic sense, as however; there are theoretical invocations vs. exhalations as, the (real facts) are, four million people vanish, each year from this planet, never to be found again, ever!

Modern day cult's human cannibalism in United States and Europe & the world;

https://www.aol.com/article/2016/06/29/...
modern-day-cannibalism-still.../21421203/

1. Jun 29, 2016 - Every so often we hear horrifying stories of modern day cannibalism — but there are still tribes where eating human flesh is part of the culture. ...

The Daily Mail claims there are 20 members of the cult, but there used to be hundreds in the...

Not Enough US Military Members Claim These Amazing Benefits. Missing: Europe

Cannibalism—the Ultimate Taboo—Is Surprisingly Common

https://news.nationalgeographic.com/.../cannibalism-common-natural-history-bill-schu...

1. Feb 19, 2017 - It's a toad-eat-toad, spider-eat-spider, and yes, human-eat-human world. ...

Tell us about the history of "gourmet cannibalism"—and how Mao unleashed a new....

With human cannibalism, what shocked me was how extensive medicinal cannibalism was in Europe for hundreds of years. ..... Photo of the Day...

Cannibalism and Other Transgressions of the Human in the Road

https://journals.openedition.org/ejas/12368

1. By An Estes - 201 - Cited by 1 - Related articles

12-3 | 2017: Special Issue of the European Journal of American Studies: Cormac ... scholarship such as the human/nature binary and consumer society. ...

The idea of ritualistic cannibalism, imposing it on the newly discovered Americas (7). ...

The present article contributes to McCarthy scholarship by an emphasis on the act...

Europe's Hypocritical History of Cannibalism | History | Smithsonian

https://www.smithsonianmag.com/.../europes-hypocritical-history-of-cannibalism-426...

1. Apr 24, 2013 - From prehistory to the present with many episodes in between, the region has...

Cannibalism might be humanity's most sacred taboo, but consent of a victim ... science fiction, cannibals and cannibalism continue to repel and intrigue us...

Either way, post-Crusade European society was not comfortable with...

7 surprising facts about cannibalism - Vox
https://www.vox.com/2015/2/17/8052239/cannibalism-surprising-facts

1. Jul 22, 2015 - The state had to set up an anti- cannibalism squad, and hundreds of...

The grisly episode makes vivid the deprivations of the early Soviet era. ... Why cannibalism is taboo in virtually every culture:

Eating other humans can make you sick.

But modern-day scholars have doubts that it actually happened.

10 Cannibal Cultures around the World You Don't Want to Run Into

1. Unspeakable Crimes 10 Places Where It's Not Considered Weird to Be a Cannibal. ... Of the people that still practice cannibalism, most of them either live deep in the South American jungles or on isolated islands. ... If there's such a thing as a "popular" cannibal tribe, the Korowai tribe...

Nine places across the world where CANNIBALISM is still alive and well.

1. Jul 19, 2016 - Whether in search of spiritual awakenings or just some flesh to feast on, cannibals continue to practice today.

Warning Graphic. By Lauren...

9 Popular Places in the World That Still Actively Practice

Cannibalismboredomtherapy.com/
modern-cannibals/

In most developed countries, cannibalism is, to put it mildly, frowned upon.

We certainly can't think of any media that depicts cannibalism in a positive light.

5 Places Where Cannibals Can Legally Eat People! - Make the World...

thehumornation.com/5-places-where-cannibals-can- legally-eat-people/

1. Jul 31, 2017 - We'll be talking about those places where cannibals can legally eat human...

While there is no law on the practice in many countries, it has...

However or whatever the readers of this screenplay may personally feel regarding this matter, is not as important as the actual truth, of subject matter of this story, or the real history of planet earth.

There are indubitable scientific facts according to the historical & archival records of earth's biblical & human history.

There are Irrefutable, scientifically & evidentially foundational conclusions of both biblical & historical facts of life on this planet in conveyance.

There is only one kind of (creature/ being), that has been (at total war with the natural world), hence recorded time.

Only that (creature/ being) mentioned, has recordable, scientifically, historically & biblically in the past & especially the present, has been in depiction.

Listed below, are **three distinct scientific definitions** explanations, all indicating the same exact organisms;

Germ

/jərm/ Noun

1.

A microorganism, especially one which causes disease. Synonyms: microbe, microorganism, bacillus, bacterium, virus; Informalbug "The powerful cleansing action kills germs as well"

2.

A portion of an organism capable of developing into a new one or part of one.

Germ

Noun

\ ˈjərm \

Definition of germ

1a: a small mass of living substance capable of developing into an organism or one of its parts

B: the embryo with the scutellum of a cereal grain that is usually separated from the starchy endosperm during milling

2: something that initiates development or serves as an origin: RUDIMENTS, BEGINNING

3: MICROORGANISMespecially: a microorganism causing disease

NOUN

- 1A microorganism, especially one which causes disease.

Example sentences

Synonyms

- 2A portion of an organism capable of developing into a new one or part of one.

Example sentences

1. 2.1 the embryo in a cereal grain or other plant seed.

2.

Example sentences

Synonyms

3. 2.2 an initial stage from which something may develop.

4. 'The germ of a brilliant idea'

More example sentences

Synonyms

Vitiligo, is caused by the lack of a pigment called melanin in the skin or a combination of selective Inbreeding, as Melanin is produced by skin cells called melanocytes, and it gives your skin, eyes & hair its color.

In Vitiligo, there aren't enough working melanocytes to produce enough melanin in your skin.

Vitiligo (vit-ih-LIE-go) is a disease that causes the loss of skin color in blotches.

The extent and rate of color loss from Vitiligo is unpredictable.

It can affect the skin on any part of your body.

It may also affect hair and the inside of the mouth.

Normally, the color of hair and skin is determined by melanin.

Vitiligo occurs when the cells that produce melanin die or stop functioning.

Vitiligo affects people of all skin types, but it may be more noticeable in people with darker skin. The...

https://www.mayoclinic.org/diseases-conditions/vitiligo/symptoms-causes/syc-20355912

1. Melanin deficiency mensok.com

Melanin and Disease. By Dr Ananya Mandal, MD. Melanin is a vital pigment producing compound responsible for determining the color of skin and hair.

A deficiency in melanin can lead to several disorders and diseases.

For example, a complete absence of melanin causes a condition called albinism.

Albinism

Albinism is a defect of melanin production. Melanin is a natural substance in the body that gives color to your hair, skin, and iris of the eye.

.Melanin and Disease - News Medical

news-medical.net/health/melanin-and-disease.aspx

Lack on Melanin condition https://medical-dictionary.thefreedictionary.com/Skin+Pigmentation+Disorders

Genetic disorders and disease states. For example, the most common type, called oculocutaneous albinism type 2 (OCA2) is especially frequent among people of black African descent.

It is an autosomal recessive disorder characterized by a congenital reduction or absence of melanin pigment in the skin, hair, and eyes.

https://quizlet.com/186749163/genetics-flash-cards/

http://www.zielinskifam.com/lit/peds%20neuro/pigmentation_dis.pdf

https://quizlet.com/subject/autosomal-genetic-disorders/

https://www.hopkinsmedicine.org/health library/conditions/adult/dermatology/skin_pigment_disorders_85,P00304

https://www.wisegeek.com/what-are-the-causes-of- albinism.htm

https://www.news-medical.net/health/
Melanin-and-Disease.aspx

https://medical-dictionary.thefreedictionary.
com/Skin+Pigmentation+Dis orders

https://www.nuskin.com/en_ZA/corporate/
company/science/skin_care_science/causes_
of_human_skinhyperpigmentation.html

Recessive genetic drifts, conditions that cause the skin pigmentations a lack on Melanin

1. Condition of lack of melanin

People with little to no melanin in their skin suffer from a condition called albinism and are known as albinos. Albinism

Albinism/Caucasians

An inherited disorder that presents with little or no melanin production.

Results from a deficiency in the enzyme required to produce melanin, causing a lack of pigmentation of the skin, eyes, ears and hair.

How Does Melanin Affect Your Health? | LIVESTRONG.COM

www.livestrong.com/article/504593-how-does-melanin-affect-your-health/

This causes white patches to develop on your skin or hair. Due to genetic susceptibility that is triggered by a genetic environmental factor such that an autoimmune disease occurs or genetic defective recessive Genoa, plausible symptoms of morphogenetic of genetic drifts, as this results in sometimes the total destruction or discoloration in, eye, skin & hair pigment cells (Caucasians).

Definition of Virus

vi•rus

/'vīrəs/

noun

1. an infective agent that typically consists of a nucleic acid molecule in a protein coat, is too small to be seen by light microscopy, and is able to multiply only within the living cells of a host. "a virus infection"

2. a piece of code which is capable of copying itself and typically has a detrimental effect, such as corrupting the system or destroying data.

What is a virus short definition?

a. Any of various submicroscopic agents that infect living organisms, often causing disease, and that consist of a single or double strand of RNA or DNA surrounded by a protein coat.

b. Unable to replicate without a host cell, viruses are typically not considered living organisms. b. A disease caused by a virus.

Virus dictionary definition | virus defined –

YourDictionary<u>https://www.yourdictionary.</u><u>com/virus</u>

Definition of Parasite

Parasite

A creature that lives off another organism is a parasite. The parasite might not hurt the host, but it doesn't do anything to help it, either.

par•a•site

/ˈperəˌsīt/

noun

1. 1.an organism that lives in or on an organism of another species (its host) and benefits by deriving nutrients at the other's expense.
   "the parasite attaches itself to the mouths of fishes"

2. Translations, word origin, and more definitions parasitenoun [C]

US /ˈpær•əˌsɑɪt/

biology an animal or plant that lives on or in another animal or plant of a different type and feeds from it

A parasite is also a person who uses others to obtain an advantage without doing anything in exchange.

Germs, viruses, & parasites are results of definitive genetic drifts in nature, a definitive plague on the planet, they have no other scientific purpose but to poison, infect & infest, they no sooner belong on this planet than the poison carbon monoxides, spurting from the tail pipes of your vehicles, as Scientific truism is scientific truism.

In the planet earths true original beginnings, all facts convey that this was once a global black organized & cohesive civilization, as blacks created an ancient orderly & mechanized civilizations, a DNA blueprint of what we all live by to some degrees even today, & it may be that blacks will be here to see its end, as atmosphere of the times of conscious & subconscious subliminal twilights pretentiousness is no longer prevalent.

On this very planet, and at this very time in earth's history, sadly, we are so corrupted, an infected cancer upon this entire planet & our entire solar system & beyond, as yes, "the words from mercury are very harsh" but very true.

In case anyone ever wondered or thought, what a (black person) on this planet (really thinks) about the state of affairs regarding not just race relations, but any relations in this current world; may this screenplay novel (movie) assist in guidance upon understanding of being in a extremely hostile place where historically, decades after century's is the same demining levels of the same human denigration.

Places where people purport fake smiles & grins in your face, everyday; however; behind their eyes always filled with vile vitriol, lies, blind hatred & deceit.

Places where they historically & currently, perpetually mislead, misinform, disrespect, condescend, backstab.

Places where they historically & currently, perpetually denigrate, deny rightful heritages, publicly ridicule, and criticize, deny decent housing & employment, deny decent healthcare, publicly shamed as criminals, publicly ostracized, called niggers.

Yes these are all the things that black people deal with everyday, as soon as they all open up their front door every day.

If you are of the opinions that it's ok, even just to denigrate other people, then you yourself are A-moral.

If you are of the opinions that it's ok, even just to oppress, and deny, ridicule, continually, every day, every year, every decade, every century, once again then you yourself are, historically A-moral.

If you are of the opinions that it's ok, even just to place yourself above others whom don't look like you, or have less than you, then once again, you are in-fact A-moral.

If you are of the opinions that it's ok, even just to, commit global genocides for territorial greed then you yourself are in-fact A-moral, as it is a part of your DNA makeup.

If you are of the opinions that it's ok, even just to, commit mass starvation, mass disenfranchise of entire people for greed then you yourself are in-fact A-moral.

If you are of the opinions & the kinds of people whom have historically, committed wanton genocide, enslave & chain and shackle other human beings for profit, historically, institutionally indenturing billions, and you really relish with great gusto that frame of thought, then you yourself are in-fact grossly A-moral, **extremely twisted**.

A-moral individuals really don't think they are (unjust), they cannot cognitively phantom or interpret what just is; fore by definitions they are in-fact A-moral, as sick is in- fact sick.

The following are official definitions of Amorality

a•mor•al

/āˈmôrəl/

adjective

1. lacking a moral sense; unconcerned with the rightness or wrongness of something.

"an amoral attitude to sex"

synonyms: unprincipled, without standards, without morals; MoreTip

Similar-sounding words

Amoral is sometimes confused with immoral

Amoral | Definition of Amoral by Merriam-Webster https://www.merriam-webster.com/dictionary/amoral

1. Definition of amoral. 1a: having or showing no concern about whether behavior is morally right or wrong amoral politicians an amoral, selfish person. b: being neither moral nor immoral specifically: lying outside the sphere to which moral judgments apply Science as such is completely amoral. — W. S. Thompson.

https://en.oxforddictionaries.com/definition/amoral

https://en.oxforddictionaries.com/definition/amoral

1. Definition of amoral - lacking a moral sense; unconcerned with the rightness or wrongness of something.

This writer was born & grew up in the nineteen fifties, in places that were extremely vile & hostile narratives with always the self justifications & the temerity of self selfish immoral dispositions of imposed norms.

This writer at the age of two years old, learned to differentiate between the degradation-al, malice, with forethought culminating an historical precedence of the most egress acts of institutionalized & historical malice imposed denigrations upon the blacks, the poor, even nature, the entire planet and the chronic war upon that general populations, on a global scale.

Some people, whom appear to look like this writer, loose temporary sight of that which is fore fontal & always turn a blind eye to chronic & sober-ring narratives of the real realities of this perpetual demeaning un-pontificated sub-imposed & subplots twilight of existence.

They all seem to succumb & at times, sink into brief & chasms of momentary states of cohered Europhobia mannerisms of Benin bliss, shying away from the real realities of this most egress institutionalized chronic states of deplorable degradation-al mannerisms of sub- existence.

It's as if, some want to historically forget the, self imposed dispositions on all people who ever looked like this writer, as we are now living in the years of 2020 & the horrors & vestiges of the past, seem to be the new wave of maniacal & terrible horizontal future.

They say that time, sometime fades, & people forget, but some people will never forget the past, or will ever forgive, because from (Black) perspectives, their shall never be any historical apologies accepted, ever, & from the (Black) experience we will never accept fake empathy, of obvious historical condensations.

Somewhere in the antithesis of time, & the humanoid spectrums of malevolent Vs benevolent coexistence, has the entire human experience been so critical & in such crises as this very moment in time.

And for the many millions & millions of minions of people, all whom look like this writer, all around the world, that have become historically complacent with their cryptic & morbid present day managed captivity, this writer says, this is not really living & this was never predestined for the horizons of (black) mankind.

Learn to organize & shake these rats that are feeding & sucking the life force from your life & souls from around your necks, you are dwelling under the extremely wicked!

Here is a Simple philosophy edification lesson;

Just because one discusses, or has conversations, or appear to empathizes, even appear to fully understand or listen to a matter of concerns, doesn't necessarily make the matter in questions, so or resolved; Fore without the concentrated & definitive acts in furtherance's, on any matters in question, can only make that matters, (so) or resolved, does this message make any relative & cognitive sense?

A final message & view for the past and current Caucasian experience; this writers say, "maybe not in this writer's immediate future existence or lifetime will this writer ever see the true horizons of people that look like this writer; however, there (shall) come a time, when the architects and their heirs of these demonic, insidious & maniacal plots, all whom have openly, historically & currently, denigrated & disrespect us (globally), all with great gusto, will too, drink the bitter waters in (all) the same aspects of the black historical experience, existence with such a vengeance, as we as the (black experience) will never forgive & we will never, ever, ever, historically forget, ever.

Fore; no matter how many of all the semi & cordial discourses are, no matter how many times the psychological intellectuals & philosophical non- intellectual conversations convey, no matter how many civic & civil mutual dissertations are, & no matter what the lateral discerns of philosophical conformities are in conveyance, their will forever & always be a nonexistent solidarity between (Blacks) & non-blacks, fore there's nothing worse than an (itch), that can never be, Proverbial- zed & historically scratched.

We blacks may have started ancient civilizations on this world planet; and now, it seems we all mere victims of it, as our ancestors started & lived in a world, where man & beast & nature were one; however, just look upon it now, really look at what (they) have done in just a short time to this entire pathetic planet thus far, just open your eyes.

The **philosophy** *of the Caucasians true perspectives is very simplistic; thus, "we (Caucasians) have the unmitigated gall, temerity & the self-twisted, self governed & the self chosen rights of our self purported fictitious religions to chronically & perpetually denigrate & commit generational atrocities & wanton, murders, institutional generational genocides to all of these people; therefore we must be more powerful & (superior!)."*

This is really what they historically & currently believe in, right now globally, at this very moment in time, if you don't believe, just ask them, or if you have ever wondered, (why, all the loonies-y?) **Read on***.*

As no matter how **(their)** *twisted self perspectives dwell, no matter how* **(they)** *attempt to self-justifiably spin their twisted views, no matter how many times* **(they)** *purport & blame that it was all their ancestors, doing &* **(they)** *have no current objectives in creating & currently manifesting demonic maniacal malice, with* *forethought, generationally towards the (black experiences), and no matter how many elaborate, clandestine & In-clandestine ceremonial mumbo-jumbo empathies with jeers of lie, historical & evidential real world history never deny, (**They**) are completely & historically condescending, (void) & absent of any avenues of any morals of God & Grace.*

They currently & historically have no evidence of any moral human or ethical empathy, they have scooped the foulest stench from their own sub-human gutters, they have infested & infected billions with their twisted romantic fantasies of (Arian) global interjection-al interdictions, and they have historically generationally corrupted the totality of the entire human experience on this very planet forever.

They continuously, chronically (covet chronic injustices) & all worship mass murders, chaos, mayhem, global genocides, "as please, don't hear them pled, as some are well spoken & some may move your heart to pity, but only if you mark them well"; however there is absolutely nothing behind their hollow decrypted words, as they have been nothing, nothing, but cryptically & historically extremely & currently condescending since the dawn of their own putrid existence on this planet up until this very day.

They have historically & definitively & chronically demonstrated the anthesis of the historical biblical patterns & forte of all that is described as (pure evil), not only in the biblical sense, but in every sense of the scientific & historical patterns of definitive definitions.

From one generation till the next, they have generated & manifested the same generational historical (poison & vitriol), that has been in existence since the times of their very degenerative (genetic drifts) in their own nature of their known existence of conceptions, as being Wicked comes from the acts thereof.

Here is a philological & psychological clue;

True actionable & intentions comes from actionable deeds, not chronic historical condescension & hollow words & not chronic & current wanton historical degenerative pathetic malice of condescension's.

This writer, is not passing judgments; however historical factual evidence is real historical evidence; **Read for yourselves.**

Caucasians have generationally infected & confuse your youth brethrens under the illusions & delusions of historical disguises & asepses of the same old hamster wheel of successful promise, all the time getting fat & filthy rich with self appointed swell, while our youth Brethrens are left with lost fantasies of permanent injuries from sports.

https://jmagonline.com/articles/football-a-look-into-the-sport-that-has-a-stranglehold-on-american-society/

https://marblehead.wickedlocal.com/article/20150924/SPORTS/150927358?template=ampart

https://www.usnews.com/news/sports/articles/2018-07-

10/enforced-development-helps-give-europe-a-grip-on-world-cup

https://bleacherreport.com/articles/1691465-how-the-nfl-became-americas-sport

https://www.oregonlive.com/sports/oregonian/john_canzano/2018/09/canzano_youth_tackle_football.htmlhttps://books.google.com/books?id=zcTID2th5w4C&pg=PA4&lpg=PA4&dq=the+stranglehold+of+the+sports+youth&source=bl&ots=gRPmRQeUFY&sig=ACfU3U3ryhWdHg_vU2R6huOX18wkTBM9yw&hl=en&sa=X&ved=2ahUKEwj6jsvmm-LhAhUqnq0KHcznCgAQ6AEwBnoECAkQAQ

https://www.thedrum.com/opinion/2017/11/16/young-listeners-are-helping-lbc-break-the-bbcs-stranglehold-speech-radio

Caucasians have, dumped over a trillion tons of poisons into the planet earth, to the brink, that this planet will never recover, as all of our children & their children, and their children, now will suffer for the rest of their lives.

Agent Orange is the most toxic, dangerous chemical that has ever been dumped in existence on the face of this earth.

https://www.history.com/topics/vietnam-war/agent-orange-1

https://www.history.com/news/agent-orange-wasnt-the-only-deadly-chemical-used-in-vietnam

https://www.smithsonianmag.com/smart-news/times-beach-was-founded-newspaper-promo-demolished-toxic-waste-ridden-ghost-town-180962693/

https://www.theguardian.com/world/2003/mar/29/usa.adrianlevy

https://www.nytimes.com/2017/09/15/opinion/agent-orange-vietnam-effects.html

https://www.propublica.org/article/the-children-of-agent-orange

https://www.blogs.va.gov/VAntage/17744/10-things-every-veteran-know-agent-orange/

https://www.nap.edu/read/2141/chapter/3

https://www.chicagotribune.com/living/ct-xpm-2009-12-04-chi-agent-orange1-dec04-story.html

Caucasians dump over a trillion tons of Dangerous pesticides dumped in the earth.

https://www.ncbi.nlm.nih.gov/pmc/articles/PMC2946087/

https://www.washingtonpost.com/news/wonk/wp/2013/08/18/the-world-uses-billions-of-pounds-of-pesticides-each-year-is-that-a-problem/

https://phys.org/news/2017-02-scientists-categorize-earth-toxic-planet.html

http://www.panna.org/pesticides-big-picture/myths-facts

https://truecostmovie.com/learn-more/environmental-impact/

https://www.britannica.com/science/toxic-waste

http://www.fao.org/english/newsroom/highlights/2001/010502-e.htm

http://www.oceanhealthindex.org/methodology/components/chemical-pollution

https://www.culturalsurvival.org/publications/cultural-survival-quarterly/part-i-pesticides

http://psep.cce.cornell.edu/facts-slides-self/facts/pes-heef-grw85.aspx

Caucasians dump over a trillion tons of Petro chemicals now polluting the earth.

https://www.thenation.com/article/plastics-pollution-crisis-fracking-petrochemicals/

https://phys.org/news/2017-02-scientists-categorize-earth-toxic-planet.html

https://www.houstonchronicle.com/business/energy/article/As-plastic-waste-chokes-the-planet-can-13284715.php

https://www.sciencedaily.com/releases/2017/07/170719140939.htm

https://www.ecowatch.com/fast-fashion-is-the-second-dirtiest-industry-in-the-world-next-to-big—1882083445.html

https://www.nationalgeographic.com/environment/oceans/critical-issues-marine-pollution/

http://plastic-pollution.org/

http://www.worldometers.info/view/toxchem/

https://www.organicconsumers.org/news/earth-drowning-9-billion-tons-permanent-pollution

https://www.theguardian.com/environment/2017/jul/19/plastic-pollution-risks-near-permanent-contamination-of-natural-environment

Question?

What type of Caucasian people commits school shootings?

https://ed.lehigh.edu/theory-to-practice/2013/school-shooters

https://www.psychologytoday.com/us/blog/why-bad-looks-good/201803/what-motivates-school-shooters

https://www.cnbc.com/2018/02/15/inside-the-mind-of-nikolas-cruz-and-other-mass-school-shooters.html

https://www.heritage.org/education/commentary/3-common-traits-school-shooters

https://www.washingtonpost.com/local/inside-a-teen-school-shooters-mind-a-plot-to-kill-50-or-60-if-i-get-lucky-maybe-150/2018/03/03/68cc673c-1b27-11e8-ae5a-16e60e4605f3_story.html

http://nymag.com/intelligencer/2018/03/there-is-no-epidemic-of-mass-school-shootings.html

https://www.scientificamerican.com/article/deadly-dreams/

https://www.counseling.org/docs/default-source/vistas/school-shootings-and-student-mental-health.p

What type of Caucasian people burn school churches?

https://www.google.com/search?q=What+type+of+Caucasian+people+bur

n+school+churches?&tbm=isch&sou
rce=univ&sa=X&ved=2ahUKEwjA4
bjP-trhAhW5FTQIHQ-qA5gQsAR6BAgJEAE

https://www.google.com/search?q=
What+type+of+Caucasian+people+burn+
school+churches?&tbm=isch&source=
univ&sa=X&ved=2ahUKEwjA4bjP-
trhAhW5FTQIHQ-qA5gQ7Al6BAgJEA0

https://www.washingtonpost.com/news/
morning-mix/wp/2015/07/01/why-racists-
burn-black-churches/

https://www.washingtonpost.com/wp-srv/
national/longterm/churches/churches.htm

https://www.pbs.org/wgbh/aia/part4/
4p2957.html

https://www.nytimes.com/interactive/
2015/06/18/us/19blackchurch.html

https://www.theatlantic.com/politics/
archive/2015/06/thugs-and-terrorists-have-
plagued-black-churches-for-generations/396212/

https://www.loc.gov/collections/civil-rights-history-project/articles-and-essays/school-segregation-and-integration/

https://adequateman.deadspin.com/the-caucasians-guide-to-black-churches-1733893737

https://nplusonemag.com/online-only/online-only/black-church-burning/

Why are there so many Caucasian hate talk show stations?

https://fair.org/media-beat-column/spotlight-finally-shines-on-white-hate-radio/

http://www.nhmc.org/nhmcnew/wp- content/uploads/2013/03/american_hate_radio_nhmc.pdf

https://www.netflix.com/title/80095698

https://www.npr.org/tags/484837420/white-supremacists

https://www.fcc.gov/osp/inc-report/INoC-23-Diversity.pdfhttps://www.vox.com/first-person/2018/5/17/17362100/starbucks-racial-profiling-yale-airbnb-911

http://americanradioworks.publicradio.org/features/jim_crow/transcript.html

http://www.nytimes.com/topic/subject/hate-crimes

https://www.forbes.com/sites/abrambrown/2015/07/13/why-all-the-talk-radio-stars-are-conservative/

https://www.theguardian.com/news/2018/may/31/how-the-resurgence-of-white-supremacy-in-the-us-sparked-a-war-over-free-speech-aclu-charlottesville

https://thedickinsonian.com/opinion/2019/02/07/should-white-boys-still-be-allowed-to-talk/

https://www.npr.org/sections/codeswitch/2016/11/23/503180254/is-it-racist-to-call-someone-racist

Caucasians Slaughtering millions & millions of Humans in around the world for sport, even now

https://deadspin.com/if-youve-always-wanted-to-hunt-a-live-human-heres-your-5815424

https://deadspin.com/if-youve-always-wanted-to-hunt-a-live-human-heres-your-5815424

https://www.thedodo.com/killing-for-fun-how-trophy-hun-611573902.html

https://www.humansandnature.org/hunting-so%C5%88a-supekova

Caucasians Slaughtering millions & millions of wildlife in Africa for sport

https://www.businessinsider.com/trophy-hunters-are-killing-70000-animals-ever-year-2015-11

https://www.livescience.com/59229-why-hunt-for-sport.html

https://www.google.com/search?q=negative+effects+of+trophy+hunting&sa=X&ved=2ahUKEwi5oc2D_tzhAhVEnKwKHT2cAtoQ1QIoAHoECAoQAQ

https://www.nbcbayarea.com/investigations/US-Hunters-Trophy-Hunting-Endangered-Threatened-Animals-347267462.html

https://www.peta.org/issues/wildlife/wildlife-factsheets/sport-hunting-cruel-unnecessary/https://www.theguardian.com/environment/2016/nov/01/elephant-poaching-costing-african-nations-millions-in-lost-tourism-revenue

https://www.theatlantic.com/science/archive/2017/11/elephant-trophy-hunting-psychology-emotions/546293/

https://www.nationalgeographic.com/magazine/2017/10/trophy-hunting-killing-saving-animals/

Caucasians Slaughtering millions & millions of wildlife in America/buffalo/bear/beaver for sport

https://thefreethoughtproject.com/govt-agencies-slaughtered-million-wolves-cougars-native-animals-big-agriculture/

http://www.petersenshunting.com/editorial/buffalo-hunted-to-near-extinction/273078

https://www.jstor.org/stable/41408734

https://newrepublic.com/article/150848/makes-hunting-divisive

http://www.thewildlifenews.com/2013/10/14/north-american-model-of-wildlife-conservation-and-wolves/http://library.cqpress.com/cqresearcher/document.php?id=cqresrre1992012400

https://www.pbs.org/weta/thewest/resources/archives/five

/buffalo.htmhttp://www.greater- yellowstone.com/wildlife.html

Caucasians Slaughtering millions & millions of wildlife in Amazon South America for sport

https://www.amazon.com/Extinction-Market-Wildlife-Trafficking-Counter/dp/0190855118

https://www.theguardian.com/environment/2018/oct/30/humanity-wiped-out-animals-since-1970-major-report-finds

https://www.odi.org/sites/odi.org.uk/files/odi-assets/publications-opinion-files/3290.pdf

https://www.google.com/search?q=endangered+animals+in+the+amazon+rainforest&sa=X&ved=2ahUKEwiTwrOC-9zhAhUhIjQIHXwJBU4Q1QIoBXoECAoQBg

https://www.rainforestcruises.com/jungle-blog/threats-facing-the-amazon-rainforest

https://www.britannica.com/place/Amazon-Rainforest

Caucasians Slaughtering millions & millions of wildlife in Australia for sport

https://www.animalsaustralia.org/issues/kangaroo_shooting.php

https://motherboard.vice.com/en_us/article/j57qdy/australias-extreme-heatwaves-have-killed-a-million-fish-dozens-of-horses

http://www.prijatelji-zivotinja.hr/index.en.php?id=60https://www.bbc.com/news/world-australia-38964535

https://www.project-syndicate.org/commentary/kangaroo-killing-in-australia-by-peter-singer-2018-03 https://news.nationalgeographic.com/2017/11/ wildlife-watch-kangaroo-hunting-controversy-australia/

https://www.google.com/ search?q=kangaroo+killing+in+ australia&sa=X&ved=2ahUKEwim 4uvm-dzhAhUJCTQIHfPpA2AQ1QIo AnoECAoQAw

Caucasians Slaughtering millions & millions of wildlife in Canada for sport/seals/bear/ whales/walrus/wolves

https://www.google.com/search?q= Slaughtering+millions

+%26+millions+of+wildlife+in+ Canada+for+sport/seals/bear/whales/ walrus/wolves&tbm=isch&source= univ&sa=X&ved=2ahUKEwiK5r Dj-NzhAhVkNn0KHcfdCnwQsAR6 BAgJEAE

https://www.google.com/search?q=Slaughtering+millions+%26+millions+of+wildlife+in+Canada+for+sport/seals/bear/whales/walrus/wolves&tbm=isch&source=univ&sa=X&ved=2ahUKEwiK5rDj-NzhAhVkNn0KHcfdCnwQ7A16BAgJEA0

https://www.theatlantic.com/science/archive/2016/09/the-collateral-damage-of-americas-whaling-fleets/500492/

https://www.ifaw.org/united-states/news/canadian-seal-hunt-doc-be-seen-discoverys-millions-viewers

Caucasians Slaughtering millions & millions of wildlife in all the Oceans of the world for sport/whales/fish

https://www.nbcnews.com/science/environment/3-million-whales-were-killed-20th-century-report-n322961 https://www.theguardian.com/ environment/2015/sep/20/fish-are-dying-but-human-life-is-threatened-too

https://www.theguardian.com/ environment/2016/sep/14/humanity-driving-unprecedented-marine-extinction

https://www.independent.co.uk/news/ world/seafood-firms-discarded-lost-fishing-equipment-thousands-whales-dolphins-seals-die-plastic-pollution- a8244181.html

https://www.nytimes.com/1984/12/25/science/ deadly-tide-of-plastic-waste-threatens-world-s-oceans-and-aquatic-life.html

https://abcnews.go.com/Technology/ story?id=97519&page=1

https://www.peta.org/blog/abandoned-fishing-gear-polluting-ocean-killing-sea-animals/

https://dolphins.org/whale_and_dolphin_threats

Black people in Australia, not considered human until 1974.

https://www.abc.net.au/news/2018-03-20/fact-check-flora-and-fauna-1967-referendum/9550650

https://paleofuture.gizmodo.com/australias-secret-history-as-a-white-utopia-1739916322

https://www.culturalsurvival.org/news/3-horrendous-anti-indigenous-laws

https://australianmuseum.net.au/learn/cultures/atsi-collection/timeline/

https://www.bbc.com/news/magazine-35240987

https://www.google.com/search?q=Black+people+in+Australia%2C+not+considered+human+until+1974&oq=Black+people+in+Australia%2C+not+considered+human+until+1974&aqs=chrome..69i57.3006j0j8&sourceid=chrome&ie=UTF-8

South African apartheid black extermination campaign

https://www.google.com/search?q=South+African+Apartheid+black+extermination+campaign&tbm=isch&source

https://www.google.com/search?q=South+African+Apartheid+black+extermination+campaign&tbm=isch&source=univ&sa=X&ved=2ahUKEwilmojv6frhAhXiMn0KHcwEDvIQsAR6BAgJEAE

https://www.google.com/search?q=South+African+Apartheid+black+extermination+campaign&tbm=isch&source=univ&sa=X&ved=2ahUKEwilmojv6frhAhXiMn0KHcwEDvIQ7Al6BAgJEA0

https://www.history.com/topics/africa/apartheid

https://www.sahistory.org.za/article/apartheid-and-reactions-it

https://www.facinghistory.org/confronting-apartheid/chapter-2/introduction

https://www.history.com/topics/africa/apartheid

https://www.history.com/news/apartheid-policies-photos-nelson-mandela

https://www.jyu.fi/viesti/verkkotuotanto/kp/sa/soc_racism.shtml

https://www.nonviolent-conflict.org/anti-apartheid-struggle-south-africa-1912-1992/

http://overcomingapartheid.msu.edu/listunits.php

Caucasians doing dangerous experiments on black people in the United States & South America for fun.

https://www.google.com/search?q=
Caucasians+doing+dangerous+
experiments+on+black+people&oq=
Caucasians+doing+dangerous+
experiments+on+black+people&aqs=
chrome..69i57.1856j0j8&sourceid=
chrome&ie=UTF-8

https://www.nytimes.com/2007/01/23/
health/23book.html

https://www.vox.com/2018/6/7/17426968/
white-racism-welfare-cuts-snap-food-stamps

https://thehill.com/blogs/pundits-blog/
healthcare/347780-black-americans-dont-
have-trust-in-our-healthcare-system

http://time.com/4746297/henrietta-lacks-
movie-history-research-oprah/

http://theconversation.com/the-hidden-
stories-of-medical-experimentation-on-
caribbean-slave-plantations-81600

https://www.brookings.edu/articles/the-black-white-test-score-gap-why-it-persists-and-what-can-be-done/

https://www.ncbi.nlm.nih.gov/pmc/articles/PMC4354806/

https://africacheck.org/2015/03/12/analysis-black-brain-white-brain-the-new-wave-of-racist-science/

https://www.jstor.org/stable/3561468

This screenplay novel (movie), is in full conveyances; with Scientific & Psychological findings, even scientific & philosophical findings; as some people may say, the truth will set you free, as others might say, the truth is but the truth, no matter who or (what) it offends; However the readers views this movie screenplay/novel as to how it was written, well; this writer will leave it up to their own assertions, as **this persecuted & prosecution, rests**.

*So for all of my current black brethrens &
people of color throughout this current
world, as this writers current message to you
is this;" all of our ancient ancestors & real
true warriors, would have never stood by
& allowed (these kinds of people) to commit
such unbridled generational, institutional &
denigrations & genocidal atrocities to start
& ever to continue towards us; message to
(blacks); what's your current* **philosophy?**

Take heed, a storm is coming!

*"His writer shall **(frame) a factual** & definitive
reference of historical & conditional in all
matters of actual facts that the many, may have
been over looked, or may have not currently
been known.*

*If you think you have control over your life?
think again.*

*As the truth is not always pleasurable or well
received; however it is necessary to convey*

now, with all the inevitable candor of all truths known shall be forthcoming to all."

When you go to any large city in this world & gaze at the tall buildings & awe at the extremely expensive real- estate, it is owned & solely (orchestrated) with their hype, based upon the bloody backs of millions of (Black & Chinese slave labor) at places all (programmed) with controls owned solely & broadcasted by **(them)**.

When you turn on your TV news stations, cable, and watch movies; listen to your favorite car & home radios stations, when you watch TV talk stations, you are watching & listening to all (programmed) controls solely owned & broadcasted by **(them)**.

When you buy your cars, SUV's, trucks, boats, homes, buildings, rent apartments & office spaces, purchase homes, lands, you are all (programmed) with controls solely owned & broadcasted by **(them)**.

When you send your children, to learn education, on a global scale, all book material, college, kindergarten, high schools, universities, & etc; you are all (programmed) with controls solely owned & broadcasted by **(them)**.

When you go to the grocery store & buy your foods, buying clothing apparel, purchase your cell phones, you are buying at places all (programmed) with controls solely owned & broadcasted by **(them)**.

When you attend diners, theaters, restaurants, bakeries, liquor stores, movie theaters, buy & download DVD's, CD's, all (programmed) with controls solely owned & broadcasted by **(them)**.

When you celebrate Thanksgiving, Christmas, New Years, Easter, Halloween, mother's day, father's day, valentine's day, fourth of July, you are buying their (orchestrated goods & materials) with their hype, at places all (programmed) with controls owned solely & broadcasted by (**them**).

When you travel by bus, trains, planes, ocean cruises, you are buying at places all (programmed) with controls solely owned & broadcasted by (**them**).

When you go out & purchase furniture, & all appliances, gas for you cars, natural gas for your apartments & homes, office buildings; purchase electricity, coal, you are buying their (orchestrated goods & materials) with their hype, at places all (programmed) with controls owned solely & broadcasted by (**them**).

When you go out & purchase liquor, beer, bottled water, soda, coffee, teas, candy, chocolates; purchase cereal, you are buying their (orchestrated goods & materials) with their hype, at places all (programmed) with controls owned solely & broadcasted by (**them**).

When people go out & buy diamonds, gold, silver, Platinum, aluminum, rubies, emeralds & other precious gems, you are buying their (orchestrated goods & materials) with their hype, at places all (programmed) with controls owned solely & broadcasted by (**them**).

All of the youth sports teams, all the high schools teams, all of the professional sports teams, all of the sports agents, owners all over the globe are all (programmed) with controls solely owned & broadcasted by (**them**).

(**They**) have stolen & murdered by the billions; for natural raw materials from Africa, Canada, South America, Australia, & other places known & unknown, for the express purposes of pure self wealth & unbridled greed & arrogant power, with their vile & demonic dispositions.

We as blacks on this planet earth are currently living behind (**extremely enemy & hostile lines**) & eighty percent of blacks don't even have a clue of what kinds of illusion-al environmental & extremely dangerous concerns they live in, as they are systematically & generationally programmed to think this is the way all people should think & live; (orchestrated & authored) with their hype, at all places & all (programmed) with controls owned solely & broadcasted by (**them**).

All mineral wealth's that (blacks) formerly own, on their mother continents, were stolen, systematically & generationally based upon the genocidal murders (orchestrated & authored) (with their hype), at all places & all (programmed) with controls owned solely & broadcasted by (**them**).

From the time, you take your first breath till the time you gasp your last breath, when you visit their clinics, hospitals, emergency rooms, doctors, dentist & implant offices, attorneys offices, courts & detention facilities, they are making profits from you (orchestrated & authored) (with their hype), at all places & all (programmed) with controls owned solely & broadcasted by (**them**).

When you look at the people, all whom represent your governmental interests, they are (staged & hyped), infested with greed & self swell, & (orchestrated & authored) (with their hype), at all places & all (programmed) with controls owned solely & broadcasted by (**them**).

When you visit events, hockey games, football games, soccer, baseball, football, basketball, they all are (staged & hyped), to do so & (orchestrated & authored) (with their hype), at all places & all (programmed) with controls owned solely & broadcasted by (**them**).

When you go to your pharmacy for prescription drugs, you are buying it from (**them**), as they all are (staged & hyped), to do so & (orchestrated & authored) (with their hype), at all places & all (programmed) with controls owned solely & broadcasted by (**them**).

They have programmed & are currently programming you to how think, the way they want you to think, from one generation till the next & the many are following those same old demonic & maniacal programs, as the (irony of all whom are programmed) is they don't have a clue they are ever being programmed.

"This writers extreme message is, learn & think for yourselves, seek out the real truth on your own, it will truly set you free!"

Facts; *In the entire ancient & current present theater of the history of planet earth, there has never been a race or group of people, so persecuted & so defiled In such a way as the black experience, why do you suppose, that's so?*

As (blacks), have been genocidal-ly & currently murdered for decades & century's, our once lands & property stolen & taken, portrayed as dumb & foolish, publicly ostracized, denied simple humanity, enslaved, imprisoned, shackled, beaten, lynched, burned, impoverished, hunted for sport like an animal, our women & children historically raped, experimental genocides of masses, attempted mass covert exterminations.

For all of the so called, upper class, middle class & poor whites & non-whites, and the uninformed & misinformed, for the maniacally cohered, & for all the brethrens of color.

So, *how does it feel to be a group of programmed, processed & saturated fools, moved around like pawns, by (**them?**)*

Some people have never acquired or were never born with grace,

Some people lose their faith because god shows them too little,

But how many people lose their faith because god shows them too much;

"To answer fools, is the folly of their own following"

So let it be written!

Truly.

Scripts

Conversations between;

(Jaa)-Counsel member (one) (grid green),

(Ork)-Counsel Member (two) grids blue), &

(Redy)-Counsel member (three) (grid yellow), All three are in (grid red) in an observation ship overlooking the (planet black).

In front of them are the four dimensional grids separating the color codes & zones on a large table screen.

The three men stand in front of the screen each looking & making corrections to their perspective grids & boundaries.

(Jaa)- Talking to (Redy)-

"Ha, remember to keep you ships off my grid unless you coordinate it with me first, got it counsel?"

(Redy)-Responding to (Jaa)-*"You got it counsel, with a big smile, their anything else?"*

(Jaa)-*"well, there was that cutie I saw in sector one last week, do you know her?"*

(Redy)-Responding to (Jaa)-

"You're not talking about my woman's sister are you?"

(Jaa)- Responding to (Redy)-(laughing & chuckling)

"I don't know, IM just making some polite conversation man."

(Redy)- Responding to (Jaa) - chuckling,

"Just kidding, her name is (nena); she lives in sector three."

(Ork)-talks to them both, (laughing & chuckling)

"You guys are some horny buzzards, & ha (Jaa) - make sure when your ships attempt to pass though my grid, they all must be on the grid navigation, ok?"

(Jaa)-Responding to (Ork) - & (Redy) - smiling (laughing & chuckling),

(Jaa)- & (Redy) - responding to (Ork)-

"Yes sir counsel sir", end of conversations.

Conversation between;

Ships entertainment commander- **(tippi)**

Ships pilot- **(bobatit)**,

Ships doctors **(lamasuk)**-

Commander of environmental systems- **(tiye)**

Scene starts in the crew quarters of, Commander of environmental systems-(tiye), She walks in observing the view of, Ships entertainment commander-(tippi) & Ships doctors (lamasuk) - having sex in her quarters, *(Tiye),* she smiles & says, *"You know when I agreed to have you as my roommate, and you never said anything about an orgy."*

"What kind of sexual position is that doctor, I never seen that one before, perhaps you can show me sometimes doctor."

Ships doctors (lamasuk)-
Covering up, momentarily embarrassed, sits up from the bed & with a smile, she says, *"Get in line, if you wanted to arrange a date, why don't you just say so (Tiye), we do both share the same quarters you know."*

Ships entertainment commander-(tippi)-
Gets up from the bed, naked & smiles, showing her beautiful statuesque & stretching her arms above her head, smiling at both, (Tiye), & (lamasuk)-

She says, "Well; just pretend that IM not really here, I don't have a problem with a threesome do you?"

She stretches out both of her arms at them both & beacons them to join her.

(Tiye), & (lamasuk)- both head for the cleaning chamber & (tippi) quickly follows as all three women began to have sex in the cleaning chamber with violet moaning & sounds of intense pleasure.

The music was soothing & the cleaning chamber was steaming hot, & the three were having sex with a frenzy until, Ships pilot-(bobatit), enters the sleep chamber, he notices the three in the cleaning chamber, he quickly takes off his uniform & attempts to enter the cleaning chamber with the three women.
With a big smile, *"he says, ha, can I play?"*

(Tiye), & (lamasuk)- stop what they are doing, look at each other, with discontent & leave the cleaning chamber, but (tippi) welcomes him into her arms.

(Tippi) smiles & slowly clutches his manhood & says, *"Did you bring this thing in the chamber, just for me, IM honored."*

The two continue to have torrid, lustful sex in the cleaning chamber with the music blaring & the steam everywhere.

Suddenly the door to the cleaning chamber came open, & (Tiye), & (lamasuk) - both naked, smiling with drink refreshments in each hand reentered the cleaning chamber & began to add to the festivities.

(Tiye), with a big smile spoke, to (bobatit), *"are we (rumping) our way though the galaxy, Ships pilot?"*

Afterwards, the four fully dressed, in their uniform garments, all sat in the ships canteen/ mess, all smiling & talking & discussing other ships operations in accordance to their departments & duties.

(Bobatit), stood up from the chair, looking at (Tiye), & (lamasuk) (tippi) smiling & spoke, *He said, "Next time, I would like to invite Ships pilots- (Zizum) join us at 0005hrs. Tomorrow, are you all game?"*

(Lamasuk) looked very serious at (bobatit), & spoke, She says, *"Ha, what kind of women do you think we are?"* Then she breaks out with a loud laugh & they all start laughing.

(Tiye), & (lamasuk) (tippi) smiling & spoke,

They said & all agreed, *"Ok well see you at 0005hrs. Tomorrow, with the same drinks & music, this time, in your chambers Ships pilot's crewmen, & your friend better be as hung as you are, or we will be very disappointed, but we will all have you."*

Conversation between;

Ike-(general)

Rena - (vice) Admirals

Ships pilots- **(oylad)**

Security commander- **(buissa)**

Military commander- **(dapote)**
They are all on the navigational bridge of the UVEB-7 mother ship.

Rena - (vice) Admiral,

Begins to give orders to get underway towards the planet earth,

Ike-(general) speaks, *"admiral, all areas will be secured for launch in 1934hours."*

Rena - (vice) Admiral, *"Very good general, Security commander-(buissa) and Military commander-(dapote) begin plotting course along the following coordinates of Columba zeta;"*

Military commander-(dapote) speaks to Ships pilots- (oylad), ***"begin** plotting course along the following coordinates, today we are using the (EveBor) methodology, Ships pilots;"*

(Point & Click) celestial navigation computation

Traveling times X-ten around their (star), **Celestial address of Rigel in Orion constellation**; Riel's position is RA: 05h 14m 32.3s, dec: -08° 12' 05.9".

Towards target address of; **Celestial address of our (earth's) sun,** azimuth = 15.68_deg, altitude = - 17.96_deg. The Sun (or Sol) is the star at the center of our solar system and is responsible for the Earth's climate and weather.

The Sun is an almost perfect sphere with a... Surface Temperature 5,500 °C Diameter 1,392,684 km
Mass 1.99×10^{30} kg (333,060 Earth's) Age 4.6
Billion Years
Sun live position and data.

Right Ascension: 16h 17m 21.6s

Declination: -21° 20' 34.1" (J2000)
Magnitude: -26.77 (Estimated: JPL)
Constellation: Scorpius
Sun Distance: 0 km [0.0 km/s] Earth Distance: 147,577,724 km [30.2 km/s]

Using the navigational lens (Inertial mass navigational systems), **(Focused concentrated lens-light to light methodology),** pinpointed solar sail (type), concentrations towards the target objective.

Once launched & targeted in, the inertial mass stays on course towards the (target address), as the focused beam speeds up the mass, faster & faster towards the target objective.

Objects sun/star in focus of (blue) means the object is moving towards the focus beam thus the object sun/star in (red) means the object is moving away from the focus beam.

Using the eight onboard different propulsion systems makes any necessary course corrections.

Inertial calculations of slingshot gravitational launch,

(EveBor)/counsel prime Space launch theory.

It was estimated that, after leaving earth's atmosphere, by using normal kinetic propulsion systems, via; (ion/nuclear/chemical/fusion), equations, sub-light speeds could be reached with the least minimal efforts.

Course plot, towards the suns outer gravitational rims & using the Inertial slingshot gravitational launch, of X-10, or ten loops around the sun vector towards another sun/star, using the (six dimensional space model), of using six points to map out the destinations & one point to plot the point of origin.

Using a gravitational (push/pull lens), towards the (target sun/star), can be plotted by locking on to the next suns, vector/address, via; concentrated light focus methodology by homing in, on the nexus light source focused in that address.

By using this methodology, & after the completion around the X-10th rotation, the course plotted towards the next sun/star.

The distance directed towards that next sun, via; distance & concentration of the (push/pull lens), would draw/increase the intensity, of that (target sun/star) beacon, based upon magnifying focus lens methodology towards that (target sun).

As the course is locked, upon that (target sun/star), the space ship would be traveling an incredible speeds through space & (increase speeds) though the gravitational (intensity) (push/pull spectral concentration lens), towards the target star/sun.

Using any, (ion/nuclear/chemical/fusion), equations can mitigate course corrections from any object proximity, within the flight path.

In theory, a space launch/jump can be achieved from one system to the next, using one of these types of methodology.

To define a Position in four-dimensional space you need 5 points: 3 points to define a plane, and 2 points to define a line that will intersect that plane at a specific location. Now use a point of origin to target that 5-point location in space.

Military commander-(dapote) speaks to Ships pilots *"Plot this course & execute on my mark,"*

Ship pilots-(oylad) speaks,

"Coordinates lock & clicked in commander,"

Military commander-(dapote) speaks to,

Rena - (vice) Admiral, *"ready to launch Admiral,"*

Ike-(general), *"ready to launch,"*
Security commander-(buissa), *"ready to launch,"*

Ships pilots-(oylad), *"ready to launch, mark following coordinates of Columba zeta;"*

Security commander-(buissa), leaves the bridge & begins to monitor his security crew in his office situation room via; (*Embryonic transference elixir*) along with a, (Corneal) neuron sensor @ Intracortical visual prosthesis (lens) (super computation) (Eye Lens)@;Beyond Quantum Computations device.

As all crew personnel is implanted & equipped with bio- monitoring sensors, a real time tracking systems can contact, monitor & check health conditions of every personnel onboard & any surface of any planet, at all times.

Military commander-(dapote) begins to monitor all of his military personnel from the bridge.

There are all four thousand in stasis tubes in the middle ships disk.

Military commander-(dapote), begins to monitor them all being under, While traveling in space flight, all crew is totally encapsulated in the total cylindrical chamber, filled with, (Embryonic transference elixir) (mist).

Comprised of highly enrich, Genoa engineered bacteria emulsions (mist), & bioengineer healing bacteria, liquid (mist) ventilation (LV) is a technique of mechanical ventilation in which the lungs are insufflated with an oxygenated perfluorochemical (mist).

Conversation between;

Ships doctors- (**Hadia**)—(**isum**)—

Ships landing party commander- (**wiyas**) Ships procurement commander- (**oobas**),

The four are all sitting in one of the ship situation rooms in disk three of the ship.

Ships doctors-(isum), speaks, "*Ships landing party commander-(wiyas), remember, all parties are required to have stage (9 injections), before exiting this vessel, are we clear commander?*"

Ships landing party commander-(wiyas), speaks, "*yes, we are clear, Ships procurement commander-(oobas), my landing party all need the following items to complete our objectives, batwing suits for all personnel,* bio-disrupters for all, one month concentrated rations, clear?"

Ships doctors-(Hadia), looks at (wiyas), (oobas), & (isum), & speaks to all three, *"the landing party can all get their water from the planet unless water is not available, we can supply all the water they will need, at satellite designated coordinates.*

We will all announce a scheduled time to have stage (9 injections), of the landing party in (disk two, hospital section four) after we reach orbit of the targeted planet system, check?"

Ships doctors-(isum), replies *"check"*

Ships landing party commander- (wiyas), replies *"check"*

Ships procurement commander-(oobas), replies *"check"*

Ships doctors-(Hadia), looks at all three of them, *"is there anything else commanders?"*

Ship procurement commander-(oobas), says, *"yes, where or what planetary system are we going to this time?"*

Ships landing party commander-(wiyas), replies, *"we are going to the (planet earth), a primitive system in the next constellation, with a yellow sun, the stage (9 injections), should keep us safe against any earth's diseases."*

"Remember, no contact with (earth's indigenous humanoids) unless instructed by; (Rada)-(general) (Ike)- (General), Security commander-(buissa)

Military commander-(dapote),"

"As you can bring back to the ship, non-humanoid life forms only after it is screened & approved with the medical staff & rock specimens only as specific instruction will be carried out to your departments per the instructions of the Admirals, of this mission."

Conversation between;

Ships doctors- **(nanada)**

Power systems commander- **(zurekj)**
Commander of environmental systems- **(tiye)**
Engineering commander- **(madoa)**

(Berra) (Vice) Admirals,
A command meeting in the (vice) Admirals, briefing quarters while in flight on the UVEB-7 mother ship.
To (planet earth's planet), the meeting is chaired by Berra (vice) Admiral, he speaks, *"good afternoon,*
This meeting is a check of the efficiency of vital systems onboard this vessel, Commander of environmental systems-(tiye), your report?"

Commander of environmental systems-(tiye), replies,

"All systems are operating five by five (vice) Admiral, we are at above peak percentile & the (Embryonic transference elixir) (mist),(coil) is charged at four hundred & ninety five years & ten hours, twenty minutes, forty seconds to date (vice) Admiral."

"We have four thousand crew personnel in the (pipes) & one thousand crew personnel working on rotation the decks."

Berra (vice) Admirals, smiles & says, *"Very good commander,"* Power systems commander-*(zurekj), your report,* he replies, *our current propulsion system is* **System 2,** *(Inertial propulsion engine) Gravity manipulation and amplification is the key that unlocks the Milky Way galaxy and the rest of the universe."*

"Gyroscopic Inertial Thruster (GIT) - The Gyroscopic Inertial Thruster is a proposed reaction-less Electromagnetic propulsion (EMP) is the principle of accelerating an

object by the utilization of a flowing electrical current and magnetic fields."

"The electrical current is used to either create an opposing magnetic force,

All other systems are on line but at minimal operational confinements until needed as **System 3**,

Gamma propulsion energy concepts,

Which is then used to power some form of electric space propulsion system, is always ready for immediate deployment at this time?" "However; systems one, three, four, five, six, seven & eight is thirty- percent powered up & ready for activation at all times."

"The new propulsions **system 9**, **(element 115)** will be on line in a few months & will revolutionize our space travel, by one million miles per second.

The combination of minimal operations are used for ships power, environmental & weapons systems.

Essentials are always on line for added power but all systems are ready & are being constantly monitored per your orders (vice) Admiral, in my opinion & according to my through calculations, whatever power you need, you will have in an instant (vice) Admiral."

Berra (vice) Admirals, smiles, rubs his chin with two fingers & says, *"careful commander, you are rapidly becoming of the ranks of the (vice) Admirals"*, as they all start smiling & laughing.

Berra (vice) Admirals, looks over at, Engineering commander-(madoa), & says, *"Your report commander."*

Engineering commander-(madoa), replies," *all systems are reporting at one hundred & ten percent, as we have five hundred crew personal working & updating systems as per orders & the remainder of the crew personnel is doing the ships operations per hour shifts as needed with security, & maintenance."*

"Ship moral is very good, crew quarters are being rotated once, every two months & we have approved (crew ship personnel) for extended time in the recreational enhanced holographic deck (disks), one, two & three, to further improve the entire moral of the crew."

Berra (vice) Admirals, he smirks & says, *"Really don't mind if I do commander, as they all once again laughs out loud & even clap & applauded the Engineering commander-(madoa)."*

Berra (vice) Admirals, well with a big smile on his face, he says, *"Ships doctors-(nanada), can you top all that?"*

Ships doctors-(nanada), smiles, *"all crew personnel that are not active, are in stasis & are being monitored & reported in excellent bio-health, all active personnel vital signs are above the normal sexual, predilections on this vessel seems to be above norms."*

"Stage (9 injections), will be administered as soon as we reach orbit in the (earth's planetary systems), as these injections will shield all boarding personnel from any biohazards & any & all diseases, that might be on the planet earth."

"All crew personnel on this vessel is being updated & is in learning mode per required updated regulations, set forth by the (high counsel) of planet black.

*Crew personnel, already implanted with **1- (Rice size (interfaced) chip)** Implanted in a depth of four centimeters, over the orbital sac into the neuron receptors of any subject, as the (chip) is only a neuron-orbital (interfaced) receptor.*

*The **(chip)** is proxceminity & manually activated with four failsafe patterns.*

*Upon activation of the (**chip**), the interface from, Intracortical visual prosthesis (super computation) would carry out any instruction (**programmed**) by the (bio- electrical (**electromagnetic**) (Super-Computational Instructions) while immersed in –**bacteria solution**).*

2- Less invasive direct corneal interface by way of (bio thermal) activated contact lenses, would operate in the same mannerisms.

*3-(**bio thermally**) activated contact lenses, with direct corneal interface programmed to receive specified signals (microwave/radio & sitcom) would directly receive information through (**corneal interface/ contact lenses**) could directly interface with the humans neurological stimuli (**directly to the normal brain functions**) of collecting (instructions, learning, etc).*

Note# contact lenses would visually enhance the subject normal eyesight & coupled with interface would allow super instructions in super computational methodology.

*(**Bio-electrical rhythmic signals**) (**Corneal interface lucent instructions**) of our five senses, through our eyes.*

The (fifty trillion liquid channel chip matrix systems), to control all aspects of the planet from tracking all inhabitants to controlling all transports & all other areas of planetary & off planetary operations, with constant educational instructions, in learning & sleeping/breathing with the (Embryonic transference elixir) (mist), smiling at Berra (vice) Admiral, *& she says, anything else Admiral?"*

Berra (vice) Admiral, smiles & says, *"see me later doctor, I think I have an ache somewhere, in my quarters & says, very good people, this meeting is now concluded."*

Berra (vice) Admiral stands up from his seat & begins to walk towards his personal crew command Admiral Quarters, with the Ships doctors- (nanada), following quickly, smiling & laughing.

Conversation between;

(The trial of the Prime Directive) Council meeting & trial of (ELd)

(The indictments);

Sitting on the board was;

(EveBor)-Counsel member (fifteen), (prime supreme), (Garwol)-Counsel member (fourteen) vices supreme prime.

(Beta)-Counsel member (thirteen) associated supreme prime.

(Erm)-Counsel member (twelve) associated supreme prime.

(Niss)-Counsel member (eleven) associated supreme prime.

Opening statement was chaired by, (Beta)-Counsel

Member (thirteen) associated supreme prime. First to speak & opening statements;

"In violations of the prime directives set forth by the; (planet black) (high counsel), the accused has willfully committed the acts of, & in violation of the most egregious violations of insurrection."

"1-*The order was made by (ELd), planet engineering order of counsel member (six), (knowingly) to attempt to further progress/ nudge, the primitive nature of (planet earth's humanoids inhabitants)."*

(Niss) -Counsel member (eleven) associated supreme primes, & seconds to speak, & opening statements;

"2-(ELd), planet engineering order of counsel member (six), (knowingly), seeking to expand his own legacy & possible empire, in another world of (earth), started the process of violating directives set forth by the high counsel of (planet black)."

(Erm)-Counsel member (twelve) associated supreme prime, & third to speak, & opening statements;

"3-*(ELd), planet engineering order of counsel member (six), (knowingly), using two (earth's humanoid inhabitants), (Genoa), slicing with the (Genoa), of the (planet black inhabitants), not fully knowing that process would create extremely hazardous results."*

(Garwol)-Counsel member (fourteen) vices supreme prime, & forth to speak, & opening statements;

"4-(ELd), planet engineering order of counsel member (six), When the planet earth had one (super continent), (one large landmass), a decision was made, by (ELd), to expand its landmasses by way of, (knowingly), directing a comet a four miles wide toward the ocean strike of (planet earth)."

(EveBor)-Counsel member (fifteen), (prime supreme), & fifth to speak, & opening statements;

"5-(ELd), planet engineering order of counsel member (six), not factoring in that his own (Genoa) was altered, by the presence of their own (blue sun/star),

He thought, upon the introduction of his own (Genoa) & combining it with two primitive (earth's) humanoids, they could progress/ nudge, its evolutionary progressions, with (earth's humanoids)."

"(ELd) was wrong! As the (planet black, inhabitants) (DNA/Genoa), only worked while

using the, (Embryonic transference elixir) and in close proximity of the (blue/Rigel/star), as the process (could never) be transferred to any other type of humanoids."

(EveBor)-Counsel member (fifteen), (prime supreme), & speaking, & opening statements; **"6-**By introducing an experimental (Genoa), of two planet earth's humanoids, (ELd) mixed his own (Genoa), with (earth's) primitive humanoids (Genoa), creating the recessive negative (Genoa) (Germs), producing what is now known as (Albinos, then/Caucasians). A new & destructive life form, the first offspring mixed with (Genoa), from (planet Black), & (earth's) (Genoa), produced monstrous offspring, as they were vile, chaotic, filed with anger, vile lust & wanton self-destruction.

Many died, as many couldn't dwell within the sunlight of day of the (yellow sun) & scurried about, in cave dwellings unlike other natural (earth's) humanoids, which were all black.

They perpetually continued to replicate on their own to create their own (Germ/Genoa), degenerative sequences, going from white/hair, pale skin, to pale skin to blond hair, red/hair, straight/hair, from red eyes to Grey eyes, blue eyes, green eyes.

They were on the complete opposite ends of the normal humanoid spectrum, from black skin, curly hair, brown eyes to the complete opposite, even in their mannerism, thinking & degenerative behaviors.

They had no grace, no future, only bloody & vile. These (Genoa) (Germs), (Albino, then/Caucasians), behaved just like the (Germs) in natural world with no honor, no inclination of natural humanoid necessity of life of, especially neither others, nor the cranial composite to have any empathy self-concise.

They historically (coveted evil), & were ravenous, (historically demonic) towards the natural world, as they practiced in perpetual continuous cannibalism & not only humanoid but in vile animal degradation.

With every generation of their offspring, they perpetually created even more & more, monstrous offspring, vile, chaotic filed with anger, vile lust & wanton self- destruction, they were filled with wanton lasciviousness, greed & contempt towards the fellow (earths) brethren.

They had malice & with forethought towards, even their own kind, as they were murderous & rampant with the vile of the stench, of self-loathing.

They practiced in incest towards their offspring & corrupted their filth ways of their own surroundings.

They declared wars on their own kind, even created wars on all that were peaceful, as they all drank from the vines of wickedness & ate the bitter Erebus herbs of their own putrid compulsions.

Their thievery, juvenile unnecessarily, ridiculous wars over greed & general stupidity, their weapons of mass destruction, plundering, rape & murder were their own (self created religion), as they knew not the ways of peace, harmony & content, of their own planet.

They were void of natural empathy & natural decency, & couldn't feel in general humanoid compassion unlike their (black indigenous brethren).

They were afoul upon the lands, of nature, staining the planet everywhere they went & always with the drunkenness, selfishness of foolishness of the disdain.

They trampled upon all the lands & life forms of (planet earth), with such reckless abandon that even their children or their own kind, wasn't safe from their vile destruction.

Their (entire sub-humanoid existence) was that of rage, contempt towards all things of nature & each other, petty bickering & jealousy, blind stupidity and greed, the stains of deception soiled them & the truth was not before their eyes.

Their souls & hearts were as black as the nights that they themselves have corrupted. (Their historical religion) was taking that of others, & fouling/spoiling the lands for the own personal greed & contempt's, as well as others all whom they have taken.

When they discovered that others possessed gold, silver, & diamonds, their blind murderous rampages only added to the degenerative (historical) natures of these (Genoa/Germs), nonsensical mortality, and one dimensional thinking."

As a result of the (**judgments**) of the above, (Indictments); (EveBor)-Counsel member (fifteen), (prime), **closing statement;**

"Since the attempted reconstruction of planet earth, by former council member (ELd), it is

the opinions of the (high counsel of planet black) observed, earth's black populations, were being murdered in the masses.

They were enslaved, exploited, shunned, beaten like lower animals, and experimented on like rats in a lab, infected & infested, lands taken & family units, destroyed.

These (Genoa) (Germs), (Albino, then/ Caucasians), systematically & regularly committed, institutional genocide, orchestrated & authored by the, (tainted planets earth's degenerative inhabitants) (Genoa) (Germs) (Caucasians).

They herded the, (Indigenous black masses) like, pigs, goats, and cattle, for their own maniacal end."

(EveBor)-Counsel member (fifteen), (prime supreme), & speaking, & closing statements;

(ELd), *planet-engineering order of counsel member (six), "you have heard the charges of the high counsel, and found guilty, what say you?"*

(ELd**)**, planet-engineering order of counsel member (six), speaking, *"guilty of attempting to make a better world, a better world sir."*

Final conclusions of the (high counsel) of planet black;

(EveBor), the (planet black ruler), quarantined (the earth planet) and the entire system, the high counsel instituted the (Prime Directives); when it was discovered the plans of, (ELd), planet engineering council member (six).

He was stripped of his seat on the counsel & returned to (planet black) for hearings of violations of the prime directives.

His sentence was a lifetime & further denial of (*Embryonic transference elixir*) (which reverted he & his off spring to the remainder of their (lifetime being mortal), along with all his heirs on a planet near the star system of (**Mintaka**).

There were three, coconspirators of the indictments in judgment along with, (ELd) -Counsel member (six), in charge of all mining & building operations, engineering on the entire planet & all other planetary mining operations.

Commander, (Uis), in charge of (ships weapons) on One of their (eight) Mother ships, UVEB-7,When the planet earth had one (super continent), (one large landmass), a decision was made, by (ELd) & carried out by, (Uis), to expand its landmasses by way of directing a comet a four miles wide toward the ocean strike of (planet earth).

They learned the ability to direct & control comets & Asteroids; By placing a (gyroscopic nuclear seismic compression converter), on the surface of a comet or asteroids, & digging in, the process to steer the directing the trajectory of a comet by altering its flight or orbital path, with a series of seismic controlled thumps.

Commander, (Oppa), in charge & one of the guardians of the; (**Embryonic transference elixir**)

Every (five hundred of earth's years), the (*Embryonic transference elixir*) coil, had to be recharged.

Using the same process with the using of extreme gamma bombardment of the (blue sun/star), & using the verillium, mercury sulfide (cinnabar), pure silver & pure gold as a live active coil) methodology, immortality could be sustained almost indefinitely.

They bathed and drank the elixir to the point of their DNA/Genoa spans were one hundred times of that of a normal earth humanoid.

Commander (doctor), (Husa),

Planet black, inhabitants (DNA/Genoa), only worked while using the, (Embryonic transference elixir) and in close proximity of the (blue/Rigel/star), as the process (could never) be transferred to any other type of humanoids.

By introducing an experimental (Genoa), of two planet earth's humanoids, they mixed their own (Genoa), with (earth's) primitive humanoids (Genoa), creating the recessive negative (Genoa) (Germs), producing what is now known as (Albinos, then/Caucasians).

The first offspring mixed with (Genoa), from (planet Black), & (earth's) (Genoa), produced monstrous offspring, as they were vile, chaotic, filed with anger, vile lust & wanton self-destruction.

It was the decisions of the (high counsel), that all three, coconspirators of the indictments in judgment along with, (ELd) -Counsel member (six), were found guilty, violating the (Prime Directives).

They all suffered the same fate as (ELd) -Counsel Member (six), A denial of (Embryonic transference elixir) that gives immortality, & banishment from the (Rigel) system, as they were all relocated (which reverted them & all their off spring to the remainder of their (lifetime being mortal), along with all his heirs on a planet near the star system of (**Mintaka**).

The profound deliberations upon (planet earth)

As some more intuitive scientist theorized the true methodology of the true origins of earth's humanoids, others refused, even when all scientific data & DNA analyses revealed the same conclusions.

They theorized in some of their religions that of second comings of a (deity) that will return & cleanse the planet of all its sin & non-believers.

The (high counsel of planet black) watched & watched for eons of any progressions of a glimmer of any moral cohesion's of civil redemption's, of present humanoid kind, towards the planet earth & all of its inhabitants.

Even now, the recessive negative (Genoa) (Germs), producing what is now known as (Albinos, then/Caucasians).

Inhabitants on planet earth desperately seek out an extra- terrestrial presence from where ever they can find it.

Not fully knowing that they are being observed, all along, whenever visited by the (inhabitants of planet black) in historical reference, the inhabitants made sure that before leaving that they took all their technology back with them.

(Inhabitants of planet black) were (there), when the first (earth humanoids) crawled out of the trees, when the first (earth humanoids) began to form their first societies, when they build their first cities, stone buildings, & in concert with nature & harmony.

From the pit of (earth's humanoids) fears, to the summit of their knowledge, it seems they always knew that something was out there beyond their own knowledge of their own explanation.

In every sector, every area, every region upon (planet earth) they all worshiped in (deities) that they did not fully understand.

Some (earth's humanoids), who ever encountered (Inhabitants of planet black), in regions of the planet, reported (smeller) encounters, even thousands upon thousands of miles away, on different continents.

Back on (planet black) the high counsel, & along with the entire contingency of the (full Orion belt high counsel), were deciding about (the disposition) of all of (earth's humanoids), even the entire planet on whether it could be saved, as was intended from the beginning.

If they ever return, or will they return, and the big question is always apparent, why will they return & what will they do when they get back to (Planet Earth).

Some religions say that the earth will be consumed in fire, upon the return of them, who really knows except the inhabitants of (planet black).

Moreover, the inhabitants of (planet earth), will never be allowed within one billion miles of the constellations Orion without being totally destroyed, in this system, no (Genoa/germs Caucasians are ever allowed!)

Conversation between;

High Counsel Meetings, reactive to planet earth

They all attempt to discuss the planetary & galaxy damage committed by (ELd) & replaced, with (Baba)- Counsel member (six), in charge of all mining & building Operations, engineering on the entire planet & all other planetary mining operations.

(**Eve or**)-Counsel member (**fifteen**), (prime),

(**Garwol**)-Counsel member (**fourteen**) vices supreme prime.

(**Beta**)-Counsel member (**thirteen**) associated supreme prime.

(**Erm**)-Counsel member (**twelve**) associated supreme prime.

(**Niss**)-Counsel member (**eleven**) **associated** supreme prime.

The meeting starts with, (**Niss**)-Counsel Member (**eleven**) associated supreme prime. She says, very angrily, *"What are we going to do with this (planet earth), what a mess!*

Do we destroy entire planets (inhabitants) for the crimes (ELd), has committed?

Do we exterminate the entire (germ Caucasians) or what are we going to do?"

(Beta)-Counsel member **(thirteen)** associated supreme prime. Replies, *"we can't just start exterminating humanoid life forms, if we do that what that says about our (prime directives)?*

We are not a race of genocidal murderers!

We are a peaceful & compassionate race, are we not?"

(Erm)-Counsel member **(twelve)** associated supreme prime. Replies, *"We trusted a (fool!), & this is what we got, this is our responsibility because what happened on (planet earth) is our fault, we did this!"*

"I really don't know what the answer is, but I do know that (we), are the reasons why this situation exists, she then looks over at,

(Garwol)-Counsel member **(fourteen)** vices supreme prime, & says, 'what do you think sir?''

(Garwol)-Counsel member **(fourteen)** vices supreme prime, looks all around the table, at each member & says, "*It may be true that we live a lot longer that other humanoid life forms, but we are not gods!*

It may be true that our scientific ability & technology may be far more advanced that other systems, but again, we are not gods!''

What we all decide in these chambers has a lasting effect in other planetary systems, as other systems all know what has happened on (planet earth) & are closely watching the decisions we make!

For what we have allowed to happen, I don't know if we could ever correct its very bad effects.

At some time, in the (future history of planet earth), the inhabitants of planet earths, (germ Caucasians), will begin to search for our civilization for the purposes of infesting & infecting us. That can never be allowed, the safety of our entire civilization & the Orion constellations is highly at risk!

This conundrum is more paramount that our entire systems rule & other high counsels on other systems.

It may be wiser to continue to monitor the (planet earth) & as they become more & more technically advanced, we can always determine that they are more of a (risk), to our civilizations in our Orion constellations, if their destructive immoral civilizations continue with their technologies."

He looks over at, (**EveBor**)-Counsel Member (**fifteen**), (prime), & says, *"Sir, your thoughts?"*

(**EveBor**)-Counsel member (**fifteen**), (**prime**), *"and my esteemed high council members, all of your opinions & comments are all welcome & highly valued in this counsel."*

"Yes, it is true, that the (planet earth), is our responsibility; however, at this very point & time in their history & evolutionary posture is light years behind ours. It is also very true that the planet earth's, (germ Caucasians), are born raciest & can never be trusted & are totally corrupted.

We can start with the premise that exists & admit that all of the inhabitants on (planet earth) are highly infested & infected and corrupted.

Therefore should be dealt with accordingly, or we can except that we are dealing with a new & terrible species that we created, & should be addressed just like any other dangerous species in other systems.

Their primitive probes are going all over the galaxy attempting to see what they can see, not really knowing that to do when they get out there.

We can't (deny) their existence, but we can deny any of their acts in furtherance towards our systems.

We can reject them as stellar & interstellar planetary relations with any systems & quarantine the entire earth's systems; due to them being such a hazardous, germs.

We can attempt to change their destructive behaviors with a series of celestial nudges, or not, or we can wait & see, what is to emerge from the continuous destructive nature to what we have released upon the galaxy.

I think it would be wise to observe from a distance & quarantine the entire earth's systems, due to them being such a hazardous, germs (life forms).

As for the (oppressed indigenous first black populations on earth) we can either transport them to our planetary systems, little by little & teach them our ways, or allow them to be continually oppressed.

Until such times, that all of them as a whole become in such grave dangers of more genocide's on their own planet, I think it may be wise that we only observe & quarantine the entire earth's systems, from a distance, we will deliberate on more decisions, and we will consult with the high counsels on the other systems, to concur.

This meeting will continue after consultation with the high counsels, however, it is the opinions of this counsel, that if at any time, the (planet earth's inhabitants), ever get within one billion miles in the proximity of (planet black), we will totally annihilate them upon sight."

Meeting is now concluded.

Conversation between;

(Maji)-Counsel member **(eight),** in charge of all outer military operations for the protection of all planetary defenses.

(Haro)-Counsel member **(seven),** in charge of (all galaxy rangers) (police-enforcement).

They both are in discussions orbiting the planet black in one of the Mother Ships **UVEB-5,** this ship is used for security & military only, it has smart weapons, highly advanced galaxy monitoring capabilities & the fire power to destroy multiple small planets, at a time.

(Haro)-Counsel member **(seven),** says, *"I might need more help in sector-4, could you lend me personnel to address the lawlessness in that sector, we need to put more increased levels of (galaxy rangers) with more firepower in that sector?"*

(Maji)-Counsel member **(eight),** replies, *"just says the word, how many do you need?"*

(Haro)-Counsel member **(seven),** replies, *"(two thousand personnel) will do very nicely, I already have (thirty thousand personnel) covering the entire systems quadrant at the present, but could always use more.*

I really can't take more personnel off our home planet, as we always need effective reserves for any contingencies."

(Maji)-Counsel member **(eight),** replies, *"is it that bad in sector-4?"*

"I have an idea, why don't you let the (military) shock sector-4 & ill still give you your two thousand personnel permanently that should shore things up very good?"

(Haro)-Counsel member **(seven),** replies, *"two thousand more (galaxy rangers), plus your shock troops should clear everything out, that's a deal (eight),* with a big smile on his face."

"So ok, give us more (advanced flow) bio-high impedance disrupters, & I think that will do it (eight)."

(Maji)-Counsel member **(eight),** replies, *"you bet (seven).*

End of scene."

Conversation between;

(Eri)-Counsel member **(five);** in charge of all living quarters & planet buildings apparatus on planet black.

(Ifiny)-Counsel member **(four),** in charge of all water & food supplies on the entire planet.

They are in one of the recreational settings on the planet black, the discussion stems around the new housing living quarters for (Ifiny)-Counsel member (four), & the possibility of larger more committal indoor/ outdoor, habitat housing living quarters with a brook & stream.

(Eri)-Counsel member (five), she say, *"what sector zone, do you want to live in, & how big of a domicile do you want?"*

"We have over nine hundred new designs available right away, all over the planet, and another fifteen others in other very nice areas."

(Ifiny)-Counsel member (four), replies, *"I want a fifteen- chamber domicile with indoors outdoor running brooks with a massive inside private garden."*

(Eri)-Counsel member (five) replies, *"Is that all?*

Are you going to invite me to this party?

Laughing very loudly, *no problem,* she then checks her (super computational eyepiece) &

says *I have four hundred places just like that in all sectors, right now."*

(Ifiny)-Counsel member **(four)** replies, *"great! When can I move?"*

(Eri)-Counsel member **(five)** replies, *"Is next week too soon?"*

"I'll have movers to arrive next week at 0500 hours, they will take care of everything ok, **(four)?"**

(Ifiny)-Counsel Member **(four)** replies, she smiles at (Eri) —"by *the way, have you seen (lacaa)?"*

(Eri)-Counsel member **(five)** replies, *"(lacaa)? Why do you ask?*

I just saw him last night; he spent the night at my place." **(Ifiny)**-Counsel member **(four)** replies, *"and (lacaa), spent the night with me, two days ago & suppose to be over tonight!"*

(Eri)-Counsel member **(five)** replies *"ooh really! Well! Well!*

We will just see about that!"

(Ifiny)-Counsel member **(four)** replies, *"Look, I did not know that you were so serious with that guy, but if there's a problem, I will stop seeing, him ok?"*

(Eri)-Counsel member **(five)** replies, *"on checking with my (super computational eyepiece) further, I miscalculated that I only have section 10, of the old designs available, it doesn't have indoor/outdoor, habitat housing living quarters with a brook & stream."*

(Ifiny)-Counsel member **(four),** replies, *"I see how you are; now you want to punish me for dating/sleeping with (lacaa)!"*

"Now you want to deny me housing!

What kind of friend are you?

There are too many guys on this planet for two friends to argue over, don't you think?"

(Eri)-Counsel member **(five)** replies, *"IM sorry, IM just angry, with that guy acting like a two-legged canine dog! You'll get your dream domicile, next week, I promise."*

End of scene.

Conversation between;

(Inky)-Counsel member **(ten),** in charge of all crafts & ship operations & planetary maintenance.

(Daff)-Counsel member **(nine),** in charge of all sciences & education on planet black.

The two have conversations about several, (type-m) flying subs that are malfunctioning off one of the planet coast.

The (type-m), flying sub crafts are used for instructional & educational purposes with students & faculty.

It seems the hydrogen fuel cells were not quite adequate enough to complete its proper missions, to depths of five thousand feet below the surface of (planet black).

The power units began malfunctioning at the depths of one thousand feet, trapping the students & faculty below the surface of the waters, however still allowing the (type- m), and flying sub crafts to float to the surface for safety.

(Daff)-Counsel member **(nine),** says, *"ha (ten), we are having big problems with those (type-m), flying sub crafts, they are trapping our people under the surface of the waters, it's getting very dangerous."*

(Inky)-Counsel member **(ten)**, replies, *"how so? There is a very good maintenance records on those units, are the units checked for the proper fuel gauge mixture before they submerge?"*

(Daff)-Counsel member **(nine)** replies, *"The first thing we always check, are the fuel gauge, every time before flight. We always get a week or so in flight mode with fuel to spare, with all of that (type-m), flying sub crafts."*

(Inky)-Counsel member **(ten)**, in charge of all crafts & ship operations & planetary maintenance.

Walks over & thoroughly checks the (type-m) fly sub craft that, (Daff)-Counsel Member (nine), was using.

After he thoroughly checks, he, motions (Daff)-Counsel Member (nine), to come over to the (type-m) fly sub craft & replies, *look at this*, pointing to the hydrogen fuel cells & says, *"This is the problem.*

These fuel cells rating (three) can't handle the pressure depths below, (one thousand feet).

Look at the rating on the side of this cell, I will order the fuel cell rating of (ten), instead of rating (three), this should take care of any other problems with the (type-m) fly sub craft.

Remember (nine); these crafts are only good for operations in grids (green & blue)."

(Daff)-Counsel member **(nine)** replies, *"Thanks, this is a big help, anything I can do for you (ten)?"*

(Inky)-Counsel member **(ten)** replies, *"come to think of it, my daughter wants to attend the science academy next year, she has very good grades but they told her she was too young."*

(Daff)-Counsel member **(nine),** replies, *"there should not be a problem with this, as long as her grades are ok, as far as IM concerned, she's in the science academy next year.*

She begins to reenter her (type-m) fly sub craft & fly away."

Scene ends.

Third dimensional interactive holographic deck

This deck is located, on the mother ships UVEB-7, and on all other mother ships, as well as the one thousand other locations on the (planet black).

On the mother ship, the deck is located in two of the counter rotating disks, of the mother ships.

They are (three-quarters of a mile in round) in circumference, & measure two hundred feet tall from the center of the disks on the mother ships.

(Three-quarters of a mile in round) in circumference -X- two hundred feet tall) in circumference, is the total measurement of the,

(Third dimensional interactive holographic deck) from floor to ceiling.

Using this deck, one can interact with the holographic images, using water vapor, sound, wind/breezes, smells & life-size people to interact with live images of fish, animals, birds, & bees, blue skies, clouds, sunsets, and snow covered mountains.

The chambers were extremely luminous, as swimming areas, hot tubs & saunas, steam areas, massage areas & artificial beaches are in view, also graphic images of sights, underwater images, forest images, desert images & metropolitan city images.

Music & sounds are all programmable per chamber, even entertainment from bands in holographic images.

On (planet black), they (measure two miles in round) in circumference, & measure two hundred feet tall, they are used as community pools, conference & event centers and sports stadiums, for parties, meeting places & etc, from floor to ceiling.

These too had, its decks, as one can interact with the holographic images, using sound, wind/breezes, smells & life-size people to interact with live images of fish, animals, birds, & bees, blue skies, clouds, sunsets, and snow covered mountains. The chambers were extremely illumines.

Swimming areas, hot tubs & saunas, steam areas, massage areas & artificial beaches are in view, also wind & water effects, graphic images of sights, underwater images, forest images, desert images & metropolitan city images, Music & sounds are all programmable per chamber, even entertainment from bands in holographic images.

The command crew of the mother ship UVEB→

In charge of all ships, operations **(Admiral-Avid),** in delegations of (two vice-Admirals), of the following areas,

(Berra) (Vice) Admirals **(Rena)** - (vice) Admirals **(Rada)** - (general)

(Ike)- (general)

Security commander-(buissa**)**

Military commander-**(dapote)**

Ships doctors-**(Hadia)**—**(isum)**—**(lamasuk)**—**(nanada)** Ships procurement commander-**(oobas)**

Ships pilots- **(oylad)** - **(bobatit)**-**(katum)**-**(Zizum)** Ships entertainment commander-**(tippi)**

Ships landing party commander-**(wiyas)** Power systems commander-**(zurekj)** Commander of environmental systems-**(tiye)** Engineering commander-**(madoa)**

(Planet Black High Counsel Members)

(All high council members are doctors)

(**EveBor**)-Counsel member (**fifteen**), (prime),

(**Garwol**)-**Counsel member (fourteen)** vices supreme prime.

(**Beta**)-**Counsel member (thirteen)** associated supreme prime.

(**Erm**)-**Counsel member (twelve)** associated supreme prime.

(**Niss**)-**Counsel member (eleven) associated** supreme prime.

(Council Members)

(**Inky**)-**Counsel member (ten),** in charge of all crafts & ship operations & planetary maintenance.

(Daff)-Counsel member (nine), in charge of all sciences & education on planet black.

(Maji)-Counsel member (eight), in charge of all outer military operations for the protection of all planetary defenses.

(Haro)-Counsel member (seven), in charge of (all galaxy rangers) (police-enforcement).

(Led) & replaced, with (Baba)-Counsel member (six), in charge of all mining & building operations, engineering on the entire planet & all other planetary mining operations.

(Eri)-Counsel member (five); in charge of all living quarters & planet buildings apparatus on planet black.

(Ifiny)-Counsel member (four), in charge of all water & food supplies on the entire planet.

(Redy)-Counsel member (three) (grid yellow), in charge of all flight operations from above the one thousand feet & above the planet.

(Ork)-Counsel Member (two) grids blue), in charge of all flight operations from ten feet, till one thousand feet from the surface of the planet.

(Jaa)-Counsel member (one) (grid green), in charge of all ground transportation in, under the surface & around the planet black, till ten feet above the surface of the planet.

End of storyboard/scripts & all book material;

Credits/references

Dr. Everett C Borders Jr. Ph.D:

• Black History Was White Washed Africans Came to America Before...

rebloggy.com/post/pyramids-south-america-mexico-black.../125703828081

Professor Everett Borders noted the presence of completed pyramids in La Venta in Mexico but the unusual absence of any earlier forms of the pyramids... 4. Egyptian Artifacts in North America – For years,

Eurocentric archaeologists have largely turned the other cheek when it came to the discovery of artifacts from ancient ...

nahf0ol - Instagram Tagged In - Deskgram deskgram.org/nahf0ol/ taggedin?next_id=1269982853651150747

Professor Everett Borders noted the presence of completed pyramids in La Venta in Mexico but the unusual absence of any earlier forms of the pyramids. According to Borders, it's a sign that Africans, having already mastered the construction of pyramids in Egypt, sailed over to the New World and constructed these ...

(PDF) Black Males Left Behind - Pontiac Public Library pontiac.lib. mi.us/Documents/vol-7-issue-5-17.pdf

Oct 6, 2017 - mouth" and cross libation rituals. All these religious similarities are too large and occur far too often to be mere coincidences. Professor Everett Borders notes another very important indica- tion of African presence, which is the nature of early Ameri- can pyramids. Pyramid construc- tion is highly specialized.

Anchoring Ramses II 'the Great' in a Real History: October 2014 ramsesii-amaic.blogspot.com/2014/10/

Oct 24, 2014 - Professor Everett Borders notes another very important indication of African presence, which is the nature of early American pyramids. Pyramid construction is highly specialized. Ancient Egypt progressed from the original stepped pyramid of Djosser, to the more sophisticated finished product at Giza.

HISTORY: 10 Pieces of Evidence That Prove Black People Sailed to ... kalamu.com/.../history-10-pieces-of-evidence-that-prove-black-people-sailed-to-the-a...

Jan 23, 2015 - Professor Everett Borders noted the presence of completed pyramids in La Venta in Mexico but the unusual absence

414

of any earlier forms of the pyramids. According to Borders, it's a sign that Africans, having already mastered the construction of pyramids in Egypt, sailed over to the New World and ...

Black History Was White Washed: Africans Came to America Before ... www.theblackhomeschool.com/.../ black-history-was-white-washed-africans-came-to-a...

Jul 30, 2015 - The more sophisticated pyramids that now stand at Giza were possible because of the work done by African in Egypt. Professor Everett Borders noted the presence of completed pyramids in La Venta in Mexico but the unusual absence of any earlier forms of the pyramids. According to Borders, it's a sign ...

Humans End Movie Final Chapter by Dr. Everett C Borders Jr. Ph.D ... https://www.barnesandnoble.com/w/humans-end...dr-everett...borders.../1126749773

Jul 11, 2017 - Humans End Movie Final Chapter by Dr. Everett C Borders Jr. Ph.D. This is part two and three in the final chapter of Humans End screenplay of the journeys and sagas of the human and social experiments. This is a frantic and frenzied rush to attempt to save the human experience, driven by maniacal and ...

Before Columbus: How Africans Brought ... - Global Research

https://www.globalresearch.ca/before-columbus-how-africans-brought...to.../5407584

Dec 30, 2015 - Professor Everett Borders notes another very important indication of African presence, which is the nature of early American pyramids. Pyramid construction is highly specialized. Ancient Egypt progressed from the original stepped pyramid of Djosser, to the more sophisticated finished product at Giza.

Before Columbus: How Africans Brought ... - Mysterious Earth

May 25, 2016 - Professor Everett Borders notes another very important indication of African presence, which is the nature of early American pyramids. Pyramid construction is highly specialized. Ancient Egypt progressed from the original stepped pyramid of Djosser, to the more sophisticated finished product at Giza

Dr. Everett C Borders Jr. Ph.D.: Religion, Thesis

Read Dr. Everett C Borders Jr. Ph.D.'s debate on the vile desecration of the ancient ones, the cause & effect of the birthplace of racism.

Van Sertima debunked! Afronazis Drowning in Tears! - Discussion on ...

'African-Americans

Apr 5, 2016 - 20 posts - 2 authors

Dr. Alexander Von Wuthenau R.A. Jairazbhoy Sabas Whittaker, Jose Maria Melgar y Serrano

Friar Diego de Landa Bishop Las Casas C.S. Rafinesque Constance Irwin and Dr. Andrzej

Wiercinski Christopher Columbus Professor Everett Borders Vasco Nunez de Balboa Marquez

(1956, 179-80

Religion, Thesis: A Vile Desecration of the Ancient Ones the Cause ...
https://www.amazon.com/Religion-Thesis-Desecration-Ancient.../
dp/B074X7G72J

Religion, Thesis: A Vile Desecration of the Ancient Ones the Cause & Effect of the Birthplace of Racism! - Kindle edition by Dr. Everett C Borders Jr.. Download it once and read it on your Kindle device, PC, phones or tablets. Use features like bookmarks, note taking and highlighting while reading Religion, Thesis: A Vile ...

10 Evidences That Prove Black People Sailed to the Americas Long ...

www.merih-news.com/.../10-evidences-that-prove-black-people-sailed-to-the-america...

Mar 17, 2016 - Professor Everett Borders noted the presence of completed pyramids in La Venta in Mexico but the unusual absence of any earlier forms of the pyramids. According to Borders, it's a sign that Africans, having already mastered the construction of pyramids in Egypt, sailed over to the New World and ...

Did Egyptians make contact with ancient Mexico? - Evilyoshida
www.evilyoshida.com/thread-14740.html

Dec 28, 201 - 15 posts - 2 authors

Professor Everett Borders notes another very important indication of African presence, which is the nature of early American pyramids. Pyramid construction is highly specialized. Ancient Egypt progressed from the original stepped pyramid of Djosser, to the more sophisticated finished product at Giza.

step pyramid of Dioser survey | Pyramids (Egyptian and South ...
https://www.pinterest.com/pin/504121752010132450/

... there are signs of progression from the original stepped pyramid of Djoser to the more sophisticated pyramids that now stand at Giza. According to historians, it would be impossible for any group of people to have built those same complex pyramids without going through the same progression. Professor Everett Borders ...

Wicked Religion wickedreligion.tumblr.com/

Professor Everett Borders noted the presence of completed pyramids in La Venta in Mexico but the unusual absence of any earlier forms of the pyramids. According to Borders, it's a sign that Africans, having already mastered the construction of pyramids in Egypt, sailed over to the New World and constructed these ...

Columbus Was NOT The First To Sail To America; Blacks Did It FIRST!!

earhustle411.com/columbus-not-first-sail-america-blacks-first/

Jan 27, 2015 - Professor Everett Borders noted the presence of completed pyramids in La Venta in Mexico but the unusual absence of any earlier forms of the pyramids. According to Borders, it's a sign that Africans, having already mastered the construction of pyramids in Egypt, sailed over to the New World and ...

• Black History Was White Washed Africans Came to America Before ...

rebloggy.com/post/pyramids-south-america-mexico-black.../125703828081

Professor Everett Borders noted the presence of completed pyramids in La Venta in Mexico but the unusual absence of any earlier forms of the pyramids... 4. Egyptian Artifacts in North

America – For years, Eurocentric archaeologists have largely turned the other cheek when it came to the discovery of artifacts from ancient ...

nahf0ol - Instagram Tagged In - Deskgram deskgram.org/nahf0ol/ taggedin?next_id=1269982853651150747

Professor Everett Borders noted the presence of completed pyramids in La Venta in Mexico but the unusual absence of any earlier forms of the pyramids. According to Borders, it's a sign that Africans, having already mastered the construction of pyramids in Egypt, sailed over to the New World and constructed these ...

[PDF]Black Males Left Behind - Pontiac Public Library

pontiac.lib.mi.us/Documents/vol-7-issue-5-17.pdf

Oct 6, 2017 - mouth" and cross libation rituals. All these religious similarities are too large and occur far too often to be mere coincidences. Professor Everett Borders notes another very important indica- tion of African presence, which is the nature of early Ameri- can pyramids. Pyramid construc- tion is highly specialized.

Anchoring Ramses II 'the Great' in a Real History: October 2014 ramsesii-amaic.blogspot.com/2014/10/

Oct 24, 2014 - Professor Everett Borders notes another very important indication of African presence, which is the nature of early American pyramids. Pyramid construction is highly specialized. Ancient Egypt progressed from the original stepped pyramid of Djosser, to the more sophisticated finished product at Giza.

E:\PLANET BLACK\Sirius\Star Sirius and Egypt _ Gaia.html

E:\PLANET BLACK\propulsion - Alcubierre _warp_ drive and gravitation_orbital considerations\propulsion - Alcubierre _warp_ drive and gravitation_orbital considerations - Space Exploration Stack Exchange.html

E:\PLANET BLACK\propulsion - Alcubierre _warp_ drive and gravitation_orbital considerations\Gravity Warp Drive.html

E:\PLANET BLACK\Planet Zones\Life under a blue sun_ _ Supernova Condensate.html E:\PLANET BLACK\More Stuff\ bioelectrical human disruptors - Google Search.html E:\PLANET BLACK\More Stuff\animals that mimic humans - Google Search. html

E:\PLANET BLACK\More Stuff\male chimpanzees mock female chimpanzees for sex - Google Search.html

E:\PLANET BLACK\More Stuff\mocking insects that - Google Search.html

E:\PLANET BLACK\MAPPING out 4 four dimensional space\ stargate - Why do you need 6 points to define a location in 3 dimensional space_ - Movies & TV Stack Exchange.html

E:\PLANET BLACK\Inertial slingshot drive space concepts\ Centrifugal force Impulse Engine space drive.html

E:\PLANET BLACK\FOOD Source\Hope You Like Algae, Because It's Going To Be In

Everything You Eat.html

E:\PLANET BLACK\FOOD Source\Global Algae Protein Market 2017-2023 - $800+ Million

Industry Trends, Opportunities and Forecasts - ResearchAndMarkets. com _ Business Wire.html

E:\PLANET BLACK\FOOD Source\Global Algae Protein Market - Forecast to Grow at a

CAGR of 6.2% During 2017-2022 - Research and Markets _ Business Wire.html

E:\PLANET BLACK\FOOD Source\Algae as nutritional and functional food sources_ revisiting our understanding.html

E:\PLANET BLACK\Embryonic transference elixir\Bio engineered healing bacteria\types of microorganisms on the human body - Bing. mht

E:\PLANET BLACK\Embryonic transference elixir\Bio engineered healing bacteria\types of microorganisms on the human body - Bing images.mht

E:\PLANET BLACK\Embryonic transference elixir\Bio engineered healing bacteria\Midichlorians are real! _ Mental Floss.html

E:\PLANET BLACK\Embryonic transference elixir\Bio engineered healing bacteria\A Bioengineered Human Skin Tissue for the Treatment of Infected Wounds.html

E:\PLANET BLACK\EARTHS History\New research 2017\what is a high emf reading - Google Search.html

E:\PLANET BLACK\EARTHS History\New research 2017\harmful effects of high energy microwaves on the human body in Nevada and Arizona - Google Search.html

E:\PLANET BLACK\EARTHS History\New research 2017\ Electromagnetic radiation and health - Wikipedia.html

E:\PLANET BLACK\EARTHS History\New research 2017\earth magnetic field weakening nasa - Google Search.html

E:\PLANET BLACK\EARTHS History\New research 2017\dangers of microwaves waves - Google Search.html

E:\PLANET BLACK\EARTHS History\New book material 2018\ why are white people so evil_- Google Search.html

E:\PLANET BLACK\EARTHS History\New book material 2018\ who were the moors generals - Google Search.html

E:\PLANET BLACK\EARTHS History\New book material 2018\ were the moors hebrews - Google Search.html

E:\PLANET BLACK\EARTHS History\New book material 2018\ Timeline of the Muslim presence in the Iberian Peninsula - Wikipedia. html

E:\PLANET BLACK\EARTHS History\New book material 2018\ The Moors_ Moor Etymology, Moors Truth, Real Moors, Moor Origins, Moorish History, True Moors, Africans in Europe.html

E:\PLANET BLACK\EARTHS History\New book material 2018\the moors - Google Search.html

E:\PLANET BLACK\EARTHS History\New book material 2018\ RaceandHistory.com - BLACK CIVILIZATIONS OF ANCIENT AMERICA.html

E:\PLANET BLACK\EARTHS History\New book material 2018\ proof that black people were in america first - Google Search.html

E:\PLANET BLACK\EARTHS History\New book material 2018\ othello - Google Search.html

E:\PLANET BLACK\EARTHS History\New book material 2018\ More Moorish Food _ Spanish

Food World.html

E:\PLANET BLACK\EARTHS History\New book material 2018\ moors history - Google Search.html

E:\PLANET BLACK\EARTHS History\New book material 2018\ moors generals - Google Search.html

E:\PLANET BLACK\EARTHS History\New book material 2018\ Moors - New World Encyclopedia.html

E:\PLANET BLACK\EARTHS History\New book material 2018\ moorish warriors - Google Search.html

E:\PLANET BLACK\EARTHS History\New book material 2018\ moorish revival architecture - Google Search.html

E:\PLANET BLACK\EARTHS History\New book material 2018\ moorish master mason - Google Search.html

E:\PLANET BLACK\EARTHS History\New book material 2018\ Moorish Invasion.html

E:\PLANET BLACK\EARTHS History\New book material 2018\ moorish interior design - Google Search.html

E:\PLANET BLACK\EARTHS History\New book material 2018\ moorish architecture characteristics - Google Search.html

E:\PLANET BLACK\EARTHS History\New book material 2018\ moorish architecture - Google Search.html

E:\PLANET BLACK\EARTHS History\New book material 2018\ methuselah - Google Search.html

E:\PLANET BLACK\EARTHS History\New book material 2018\ men from the north according to the bible - Google Search.html

E:\PLANET BLACK\EARTHS History\New book material 2018\ mathusalem - Google Search.html

E:\PLANET BLACK\EARTHS History\New book material 2018\ hanabil moors - Google Search.html

E:\PLANET BLACK\EARTHS History\New book material 2018\ Hadith of the Moorish Prophet

_ Moorish Orthodox Information Kiosk.html

E:\PLANET BLACK\EARTHS History\New book material 2018\ faces of real evil white people - Google Search.html

E:\PLANET BLACK\EARTHS History\New book material 2018\ BLACKS AS ISRAELITES.html

E:\PLANET BLACK\EARTHS History\New book material 2018\ ancient moorish law - Google Search.html

E:\PLANET BLACK\EARTHS History\Events\United States presidential election, 2016 timeline - Wikipedia.html

E:\PLANET BLACK\EARTHS History\Events\Presidential Election 2016 - The New York Times.html

E:\PLANET BLACK\EARTHS History\Events\photos of the whitehouse - Google Search.html

E:\PLANET BLACK\EARTHS History\Events\major events in 2016 usa - Google Search.html

E:\PLANET BLACK\EARTHS History\Events\all the events to date that happened, since the 2016 presidential elections_ - Google Search.html

E:\PLANET BLACK\EARTHS History\Events\A Timeline Of The 'Unprecedented' 2016 Presidential Election _ NPR.html

E:\PLANET BLACK\EARTHS History\Events\2016 timeline of events - Google Search.html

E:\PLANET BLACK\Breathable liquid solutions to suspend humanoids for years\Liquid breathing moves a step closer thanks to measurement study.html

E:\PLANET BLACK\Breathable liquid solutions to suspend humanoids for years\LAB - Liquid Air Breathing Technology.html

E:\PLANET BLACK\BLUE SUN\Spectacular Orion images reveal isolated planets – Exoplanet Exploration_ Planets Beyond our Solar System.html

E:\PLANET BLACK\BLUE SUN\Rigel_ Orion's Brightest Star.html

E:\PLANET BLACK\Blue Energy\What is Blue Energy_ - ECS.html

E:\PLANET BLACK\Bio engineered computer bacteria cells\ Researchers program bacterial cells to make computer-like decisions. html

E:\PLANET BLACK\Bio engineered computer bacteria cells\ Magnetic bacteria may help build future bio-computers - BBC News. html

E:\PLANET BLACK\Bio engineered computer bacteria cells\Kinky biology_ Researchers explore DNA folding, cellular packing with supercomputer simulations — ScienceDaily.html

E:\PLANET BLACK\Bio engineered computer bacteria cells\ Engineered bacteria are helping us add memory to living computers. html

E:\PLANET BLACK\Bio engineered computer bacteria cells\Cellular computers_ 'Genetic circuit' biological transistor enables computing within living cells.html

E:\PLANET BLACK\Bio engineered computer bacteria cells\ Bacterial Computing with Engineered Populations _ Projects _ FP7-ICT _ CORDIS _ European Commission.html

E:\PLANET BLACK\Bio engineered computer\Bio-computer powered by jellyfish DNA plays Tetris and other retro videogames. html

E:\PLANET BLACK\Anti Gravity Spaceship\propulsion - Alcubierre _warp_ drive and gravitation_orbital considerations - Space Exploration Stack Exchange.html

E:\PLANET BLACK\Anti Gravity Spaceship\How to Build a UFO-like Anti Gravity Spaceship - The Green Optimistic.html

E:\PLANET BLACK\10 oldest Ancient civilizations\A Message from the Vitruvian Man_ – Futurism.html

E:\PLANET BLACK\10 oldest Ancient civilizations\10 oldest Ancient civilizations ever existed.htm

The end?

Written & totally conceived by, Everett C Borders Jr. Ph.D. 2019

This screenplay novel is dedicated to loving memory of

H.S

Screenplay Written by: Everett C Borders Jr. Ph.D.

The brief bio of Everett C Borders Jr. Ph.D.

He was born in 1951 at Cook-county Hospital in Chicago ILL; he was the fourth of six children & son of the late Everett & Mary Borders. He grew-up on the west side of the mean streets of the cities Rockwell garden projects with hard living & extremely violent gangs. His passion for writing started in the early sixties attending & graduating with a scholarship from Westinghouse vocational high School. He began writing poems & lyrics as expressions as he started playing bass guitar & drums, keys & 4track recording learning from his brother. He graduated from Loop College in Chicago ILL. He started working for Ford Motor Co. As an apprentice in Dearborn Mich. & joined the Chicago Police Dept in 1973. He excelled in worked in tactical, special operations, gang enforcement HBT (Hostage barricade terrorist) & vice. In 1976, he joined the United States Coast Guard reserve port security; he worked with agencies of the US

Government. After receiving over one hundred & fifty awards for valor & meritorious city/ state/ federal service work, he left Chicago in 1989 arriving in Denver Colorado where he started ECB (Clandestine).

He continued academic learning & began to work in industry of, addictions, Counseling, social services, and sitting on the Colorado state board for mental health. He started working in fast-paced engineering & advanced concepts in innovations. He worked in the assisting & mentoring in small theater productions with local & at risk adolescents & adults.

He received numerous letters of praise for service & civic efforts. He received his Ph.D. in Counseling Psychology in 2006 from Cambridge S. University. He has publications in, Publications.

He consults, mentor, writes scripts, articles, commentaries & considers himself as an innovation scientist as he has more than several, groundbreaking inventions & is a constant collaborator in theoretical scientific projections, as an Independent Think Tanks Professional of real world innovations LinkedIn professional.

Little miss Pantomime

A foreword parable;

What would a wise man & women say?

They would say,

Let all children of the world have laughter & play.

All elders are graceful & should grow old,

In (there) own way.

Let all whom truly seek knowledge & enlightenment,

Have all access without conflict & Fray

Property, territorial, predilections & the overwhelming urges to control are really historically & scientifically irrelevant aren't they.

The wise would say.

Humility & Futility as to humiliation are but narrow spectrums of a moralistic band,

Try saving your (tortured & twisted souls) if you think you can.

Dr. E borders

Included within this movie screenplay, all complete movie scripts, dialogs forthwith.

This story is a grave tale & very difficult to write; however, the laws of candor must always be obeyed in order to seek out all truths, however painful & grotesque.

This storyboard depicts real actual accounts of the facts of life and the ultimate fate, for so many children in the United States & around the world.

Many homeless & at risk children, all whom scrounge around to attempt to just survive, until the next day, all face the horrors of the streets worldwide, being at extreme risk of being exploited, trafficked, sold & preyed upon by adults & maniacal organizations.

For so many children live on the streets of our cities, all around the world, eating out of garbage cans, begging & stealing food, sleeping in dumpsters or whatever they can find shelter to attempt to appear safe.

Many grow up unfortunately to adulthood only knowing the (ravishes of the wind) & the people & conditions that make it, & allowing it so.

Children & babies should be protected against all mannerisms of any harm, as they are representative of our own future historical building blocks of our own natural evolutionary progressions.

When a person lies, they murders, some other parts of the world.

Evil

There really is Evil, I am certain some how

Does it try to get in you, or does it try to get out?

Is it shaped like mankind, or is it shaped like greed

Does it torment us with passions, what is needed in our being

There really is Evil, I have touched it IM sure

After acknowledgment, you jest, you can work on the cure

Of being one of the beings, who does not reach at Evil lures?

There are even some who worship the Evil skewer

Some who have Faith in God & all his doings

For those who are, really not interested in what, I have to say

That's because, their so into themselves & all they can take

Well, that's all right

If you're total being is to always grab

One day (WE) all will lie on that cold, cold, slab

This is no joke, as my words are clear

I would, rather have faith inside me and let Evil stay clear

If you really don't know, what IM talking about,

Just try walking some streets in this world after dark!

Everett C Borders Jr. Ph.D.

Mortality/Morphology/ Incept Dates

Recently, I wanted to carry out an experiment regarding friends and family and many strangers.

The experiment was attempting to see & recognize and identify & quantify their total humanity, in the aura tangible sense of a brief moment in time.

Always having great ability to make visual & semantic- cal observations in detail was not enough. It's in the eyes, the eyes always tell the true story of Pain, love, and deceit, questionable intentions, serenity, despair, happiness & contentment.

Reading eye expressions contrary to facial & body expressions seems to be an acquired reseeding art.

As I carried out my human experiment in detailed humanity observations, when observing some people for the first time eye to eye, it is the sometimes confusion when reading their eye expression in conjunction with facial & body expressions.

The eyes always tell the truth & inner intentions or roving relative inner thoughts.

The involuntary pulsations & fluctuations of the iris, the momentary dilatations of pupil, the rapid side to side involuntary fluctuations of the cornea optical lens, Convey specific involuntary signals of conscious & subconscious active thoughts.

It is very possible to read both conscious & subconscious subliminal thoughts through momentary eye fluctuations.

There are distinct & direct correlation's of readings from the involuntary fluctuations of the iris, involuntary body poise translated in to present, past and possible subliminal future actions in all individuals.

Dr. E Borders

1/31/2013 @Published

Pantomimes

Liars, fibbing, Truth-a-phobias, how can you really tell if someone is not being truthful. Some might look for involuntary fluctuations of the iris or, not looking the other person in the eye in conversation or rapid eye movement.

Others might say body language & other forms of fidgeting with arms, legs, hands, and the uneasy or uncomfortable situational condemnations of the truth.

Scientific studies & research has listed <u>men having 17 Pantomimes</u> or different things they do when they lie and <u>women having 20 Pantomimes</u> or signals they convey when lying.

If you study them, you could learn to read and discover the real meaning in Pantomimes methods.

The fantasizing of truths regarding your truth, is a 50 thousand year old condition that's shared by all of mankind.

Well-documented scientific studies in truths, half-truths & non-truths have pre-categorized the kinds of non-truths people are familiar with.

For example,

The person that tells you everything, but doesn't tell you anything about the real truth.

Or, the person that tells you a micron of the truth, Or the person that tells you 87% of the truth.

Or the person that tells you zero % of the truth.

If you place five people in a room to witness the same thing or event, you might get five variations of their truths.

Not implying that any of the five people are lying, but only conveying their truths, as they perceive it, or how they want you to receive it.

Example,

By saying *"the sky is blue"* has some merit of truth but is not totally correct;

In the human color spectrum, we humans see the sky, limited to only our own eye color spectrum, other mammals and birds even insects have a far more advanced eye colors spectrums.

The real truth is, light is most easily scattered through the sky with the color blue, and void of light, there is no color, and therefore the sky is just the sky, no real color.

"The sky is blue" is a lie,

"The sky looks blue" is mostly 90% correct. Semantically saying *"How are you"* when you really don't care how the person really is. Lying?

No, It means you're saying a percentage of the truth and being polite & really don't care how the persons really are.

100% of the truth is saying, *"I really don't care how you are."*

Your individual Façade mentality reveals what percentage of the real truths you convey.

In summary,

The art, or politics or the body dynamics of lying is not at all uncommon in the human or animal condition.

Even animals lie.

Studies were made on male chimpanzees in relationships with female chimpanzees. Studies learned some signals or mimics made by male chimpanzees indicating the location of food was not at all, an indicator of food. The female chimpanzees that had gotten closer came to the realization that there was no food; the lie was to get the female chimpanzees closer to get sex, certainly a trait shared by some of the human species.

This writer can go on in length of renditions of semantically lying, but the real and most important question is:

What percentage of liar are you?

Men have 17 Pantomimes

Heard that there are 17 pantomimes of male liars and 19 or 20 for female liars. Does anybody know what they are?

A: 17 Pantomimes for Males, followed by 3 more with Females. Inevitable signs of liars! These are in NO particular order. Some Pantomimes can be done before, after, and during the lie!

1. Swallow
2. Sniffle
3. Forced Blink (Slow or Rapid)
4. Moving the Mouth (Usually to one side mostly, Sometimes trying to Swallow

Lip to Hide, or Moving Up and Looking Down while Showing Guilt)

5. Looking to the Left or the Right (I have seen both)
6. Clearing Throat (Usually Phony)
7. Eye Contact is very Short (Afraid of being read, being Discovered, or giving themselves away)
8. Rubbing Nose
9. Scratching the Face (Usually the Cheek, or Chin to Conceal the Mouth)
10. Avoiding Eye Contact (Usually by putting head down)
11. Fidgeting with hands (Sometimes with Rings, Watches, Bracelets, etc...)
12. Hiding Hands (Sometimes followed by Crossingof the Arms to Hide them)
13. Eyes more wide Open (Want you to be believable or Manic)
14. Licking Lips (Or Biting them)
15. Visibly Shaking (Anxiety, Showing Nervousness, Being Uncomfortable, and Being Evasive, or Defensive)

16. Paranoid Look of Fear (They think you see through em)
17. Squinting Eyes (Usually Followed by Confused look, Searching for the Answer, or Unexpected Question, etc..) Females EXTRA 3!
18. Real or Fake smile (Followed by Rolling of Eyes)
19. Grooming or Playing with Hair (Distracts Everyone)
20. Guilty Face with Forced Smile

Women have 20 Pantomimes

Look for body language that might indicate someone is lying, such as not looking you in the eye, when speaking to you, being fidgety, or acting nervous or uncomfortable.

2 Listen for inconsistencies in what the person tells you, such as different stories on different days, different time frames, and mistakes in remembering details or mixing up details. Read more: How to Know if Someone Is Lying |

eHow.com http://www.ehow.com/how_13299_ know- someone-lying.html#ixzz26P4GFEUD

http://www.ehow.com/how_13299_know- someone- lying.html

http://www.ehow.com/search.html?s= Body+Language+Flirting&skin=mom& t=all&rs=1

http://www.ehow.com/search.html?s= Flirting+Body+Language&skin=mom&t =all&rs=1

http://www.ehow.com/search.html?s= Body+Language+Signs&skin=mom&t =all&rs=1

http://www.ehow.com/search.html?s= Detect+Lying+Eyes&skin=mom&t=all& rs=1

http://www.ehow.com/search.html?s= Lying+Eyes&skin=mom&t=all&rs=1

http://www.ehow.com/search.html?s=Lying+Eyes&skin=mom&t=all&rs=1

Written by,

Everett C Borders Jr. Ph.D.

Another case in point:

History, as taught is not real history it is only (his-story), records a great many times & reasons of larceny, crooks & liars that have twisted shades & bits of the truth, to out, & out bald faced lies. Many of the people in these narratives are indicative of so many people that the readers of this book may know, socialize, went to school & work with.

It is estimated that one third of the entire world population all think & behave within the following simple examples of many, thus; first example,

The manipulation tango

If you ever visited a grocery store and noticed the prices of the items were not listed until you checked out, you are being manipulated.

If you ever visited a clinic, doctor's office or hospital and were never told up front how much you're being billed for,

You are being manipulated.

The point is, being manipulated is a part of your lives as some manipulations affect you more than others.

Manipulation is a big part of your life.

As everything you do, say, feel, experience are being manipulated.

Why are you being manipulated and what's most important is who is doing the manipulation. A Honda over a Mazda, a townhouse over apartment, this school over that school, this shoe over that shoe, this food over that food, these vitamins over that vitamin, this airline over that airline.

One type of mannerism over another, One philosophy over another, Love verses hate.

We are all susceptible to external or outside stimuli that shape and mold our judgments & reconfigure perceptions one microsecond to the next.

As being creatures of habit, we are so consumed with rituals & routines to the point of any adverse interruption in this process my turn your methodology in a state of temporal disarray.

Make no mistake, when we speak of perceptions; it is only the chemical reactions relative to synaptic patterns of the brain.

Why do you worship one religion over another?

It's only because you have been programmed to do so. Why do we dislike one thing over another, some of it is value judgment from past experiences but the other part is careful subliminal manipulation.

One of the biggest receptors of manipulation is children, They are highly impressionable & are always in a seeking and learning mode.

Imprinting as in fixed impressions tends to start a very early childhood and tends to morph at late adolescents to adulthood.

For it is possible to mold, shape, guide, influence and program any person from pre-toddler to adulthood in any direction for any purpose.

Covert manipulation verse overt manipulation.

Covert manipulation;

Example; on any given night, men line up to visit strip bars or gentlemen's clubs all over the world. en drink, sit and dream of being with the women dancing & giving lap dances before them, smelling sweet perfume, noticing every inch of the dancer's physical stature. any will fall in love with female illusions, not knowing they will never ever experience the sweet caress and intimacy that they themselves desperately desire at the time.

Strip clubs, gentlemen's clubs are harvesters of inciting illusions & psychological traps.

They are designed to spend your money on that illusion. On any given weekend it is not uncommon for a man to visit a Strip clubs / gentlemen's clubs after getting paid and leaving the establishment with little or no money.

A wink and a promise from a dancer or stripper are cause enough for a return visit as the unsuspecting male visitor who is slowly lured in.

Men will never have any kind normal relationship with this kind of lifestyle; they will never experience the joys & true genuine female trusted intimacy without a dollar sign as the entire atmosphere is geared for dangerous illusions.

Strippers or dancers are professionals in mind manipulations as most them are grossly indifferent to men and tend to intentionally practice & carryout false intentions in psychological scheming warfare.

Men who visit those kinds of establishments develop a (glanced) nonexistent solidarity fantasy of women based solely on physical appearance and dancing demeanor.

They enter the clubs with the premise of lifting their egos & sprits. As they sit and gaze at the futures fantasies of nonexistent liaisons they will never experience.

As they sit and dream and gleam, and dope and mope and cope, the sometimes realization of their never ending hope.

Sure there are many episodes of paid interludes as men are <u>marked & scanned</u> from the time they enter the strip bars or gentlemen's clubs until he leaves in his car. And yes there are paid sexual favors, one way loans, crimes, drama, drugs, entrapment, and blackmail, illicit behaviors associated with associations of persons in those kinds of arenas but it is all a dangerous & costly illusions.

Overt manipulation;

Example; sitting in a classroom studying music.

You attend to study music; you don't quite know whether to take up drums or flute.

You are beginning to understand how to read music in general, fingering, scales and notes.

You are developing styles & techniques as much as you can retain it.

It is all in front of you as there are no ulterior motives in this process.

Some manipulation is good but most is bad or worse and personally irrelevant to you, as there are many, many kinds & methods of manipulation.

One of the most obvious is a used car salesman attempting to sell you a lemon or TV commercials, or the women who wants her husband to go shopping on a Sunday in football season at the mall with her.

The husband never wants to go shopping but is manipulated with an unknown threat in the relationship if he fails to appease.

Ultimately there are thousands upon thousands of statically relevant information as to the manipulation as well as adverse manipulation, manipulation of relationships, Work place manipulations, Sibling manipulations, Public manipulation, Manipulation in living with another person, Sexual manipulation, Psychological manipulation, Deviate manipulation, Physical manipulation and etc,

One key is to learn the signals of any attempted manipulation by constant recognition.

How you address covert verse overt manipulation is like always, totally up to you.

Written by,
Everett C Borders Jr. Ph.D.

8/9/2012 @ Published /second example,

A stitch in time

The concept of flipping in laymen's terms is simplistic, buy dirt-cheap and sell very high.

Example;

Buying a dirt-cheap item at a flea market and selling it for an outrageous or more than it's worth price.

Case in point; buying a car for $10,000, you then get a duplicate title on that car before you get the car loan, as after the car loan is recorded, the new lien would show up on the second title, and the car being worth say, $15,000 after buying the car you take out loans on the car for $10,000 and sell the car for $14,000.

The new buyer doesn't know about an outstanding loan because you only give them the copy of the first title, without the lien present, and is sticks for the lien of $10,000 on the car. Let me repeat this, You pay $10,000 for a car,

Get a loan for $10,000 on that same car, You sell the car for $14,000, Your total profit is +=$24000

You then stick the new car owner with the bill with a car with no resale value and being stuck with a lien of $10,000 after paying $14,000 for the car.

The new car owner pays $24,000 for a $10,000 car, as the whole process is called (fraud).

Now transfer this concept over to buying and flipping a business, any business.

You buy the business; the business has say, 110 employees.

You then get a loan on the business; you get another loan on the business.

Another loan on the business as all loan revenues is going in your own pockets.

You then bankrupt or default on the business and move on to another business.

The 110 employees are layoff due to little or no revenues & profit with no benefits.

You take the profits from the failed business and acquire another business.

You now setup another business with another business or New LLC name and repeat the process over and over and over again.

You can turn thousands into hundreds of millions by flipping business.

If you see nothing wrong with this process, it says a lot about you.

However, if this information rings with being rotten then maybe you're on the right track.

They want to play & manage your taxes with their crooked deviate business practices.

Do you really want to place this already fragile economy in the hands of a documented crook and sneaks?

Storyboard

The story starts on the streets in a big metropolis city filled with its citizens, most starving & living in squalor.

A place where there were scorching hot summers & freezing cold winters & overcasts were a normal presence in living in depravation-al, conditional purgatory; this place was so (evil), they perpetually tortured its citizens, denying them the proper education, denying them the proper medical care, as they murdered & raped the citizens in the nights, & chronically lying to them every day, while stealing them blind, out of their life savings & all their lives.

In this place, only the (minute few) profited from the misery of the millions & millions of indentured minions, as others were used, as spare parts to keep the rich healthy & the greedy drunken with the self swell, of decadent, degenerated deranged, predilections, of the twisted.

So prous, in their perversions, with malice and forethought, & so reverent with their depravity of degradation-al pontifications & subplots,

In this place, the final facts of life are always revealed with its, daily jolts of the reality of life & living, as there was no hope, and no reason to hope, for none, was ever there in this place, as there was never a possibility of escape to ascend from the torment of the purgatory of the truly unjust obvious & maniacal oppressors.

Fore out of the limits & out of the sights of these perceived self justifications, were the ones, feeding on the misery, perched upon the loathing on the torment of so many, as the summit of their morbid morality, pits the fears & limits of their purported & twisted worldly logic.

Banter & Dialog;

A van & car crash, in the Upper East Side, rendered the victims of the crash, momentarily incapacitated.

A woman appeared, from the alley, it was noticeably apparent that she was in-fact nine months pregnant, as her clothes were all mangled and tattered, her signs of hard ageing & hardships were upon her face & and she wore gloves with the fingers exposed.

As she approach the car & van in the middle of the street, she only had one thing in mind, however, not to assist in helping the victims of the crash, but to rifle & rob them of whatever she could grab at the time.

Her first approach was to the van with three people, near death, sitting & moaning in obvious daze & agony, as she began grabbing their purses & wallets, she then made her way to the other car, as it appeared the occupant of the car appeared deceased from injuries of the crash.

She grabbed his wallet & money from his pants & coat pockets. As she began to quickly walk away from the accident scene, another street robber approach her & began to confront her about the bounty, she had just acquired, as a violent struggle ensued between the two, she then stabbed him across the throat & slashed his eyes, with her butcher knife & began to run away back into the alley from which she original came from.

The street robbers, throat & eyes slashed, his blood squirting in all directions, started to shoot blindly into her direction, striking the women two times in the back of her neck & the back of her head, with police & ambulances sirens blaring from a distant.

As the police & ambulances arrived, all four victims at the crash scene were presumed dead, a fifth victim just about twenty feet from the car crash, was stabbed to death, by the throat & eyes.

The pregnant woman could barely climbed into the large garbage dumpster, suddenly, she went into forced labor & began to give birth after climbing into a large garbage dumpster, a place where she lived, all the time.

Her last gasping dyeing breath, she uttered, "Please god, please help me". As she lay their bleeding from all the trauma & shock, she began to hallucinate & date light dreaming, about revelations past, the times she was gang raped by fifteen men within that same dumpster, nine months ago in an filthy alley on the upper east side, as she was going to the store, her revelations began looking into the twisted evil eyes, of all of the men on top of her as she attempted call for help.

She laid there with blood squirting all over the inside of the dumpster as she starts to think of her younger years with her family & younger sisters. She remembered taking her first bicycle ride, her first day at an elementary school & her first kiss with a boy in her neighborhood.

She remembered playing in a park with her mother, at a picnic at the water's edge; her brief memories were fragmented due to going in & out of conciseness from all the trauma & shock.

Her mind seemed willing, but all the trauma & blood loss, were to fatal, & as she laid there dying, she began excreting the baby, placing the infant on her chest, for her final breath, she sighed with her final word saying, "What", The infants blood soaked tiny little body began to scream & cry after her first gasps of oxygen of life, as the tiny little infant began to fluctuate all around her deceased mothers body.

The infant's life had just suddenly & defiantly begun as her mother's life tragically abruptly ended in a very somber & common tale of life on the streets.

(Grandma Trix), another very old former street hooker & street person was walking by, after hearing all, sirens & seeing police cars, began walking near the large garbage dumpster, after hearing something inside, when there, she opened the lid to the garbage dumpster, & observing a baby girl, still attached to the dead mothers umbilical cord around the baby's neck. The baby was crying & there was blood all over the garbage dumpster.

Grandma Trix, wiped off the baby with some old rags found, that were within the garbage dumpster, cut the dead mothers umbilical cord, along with all the wallets, purses & other items taken from the car accident scene and brought the baby to another underground culvert, a place where Grandma Trix, lived her life.

At the car accident scene, the police & fire ambulances arrived observing a car & van, in the middle of the intersection with all crash victims inside deceased from their impact injuries.

The van appeared like it had run a red light & struck the car instantly killing the driver of the car.

A man, deceased about twenty feet from the car accident scene, appeared to have severe lacerations of the eyes & on the side of his throat.

The police, learned through his identification revealed the man was a career criminal, involved in murders, burglary, robbery, and rapes & was in prison for the last thirteen years.

The blood trails on the ground only, went from the scene of the car accident to twenty feet from the car accident scene forming a perfect circle, around the victim.

A semi forty five automatic gun was recovered still in the victim's hand, as he laid there dead from obvious lethal trauma from being cut in the eyes & throat, of possible physical struggle, at that intersection.

No other persons or people were on the scene witnessing the incident/ or neither car accident, nor any other bystanders were present at the time.

The police could only surmise the two incidents were a result of two separate incidents to date.

After twenty four hours of detective investigations, it was revealed that blood leading to a female body was found in a trash dumpster in an alley, a short distance from the car accident scene.

The women (Jane Doe) approximately thirty five years old had two gunshots wounds, one in the back of the head, & one in the back of the neck, while she was giving birth to an unknown infant that was not found at the scene.

No other bodies were found at the scene & no other information was recorded, at the time.

The police reported that bullet projectiles that were present in the body of (Jane Doe) did in-fact come from the same gun as the deceased victim one found in the street where the car accident had taken place.

Found, was a bloody butcher knife in the trash dumpster in an alley, underneath the body if the body of (Jane Doe).

The police had surmised that a struggle happened at or near the car accident scene & one victim, dying from injuries at or near the cars accident scene & victim two (Jane Doe), dying within the trash dumpster shortly after being shot by victim number one, while giving birth.

The police recorded no other personal correlations with dead victims of the traffic accident to any other personal relationships of the victims outside the two vehicles.

Victim number one, a male forty one years of age, career criminal & known murderer & armed robber, with the history of violence, died as a result of trauma from the cut laceration of the throat & eyes at the scene of the traffic accident.

Victim number two (Jane Doe), dead from two gun shots in the back of the head & neck, while giving birth to a missing infant, also missing from the trash dumpster where the butcher knife was in-fact was found.

The police case deemed the case still open, & pending further information, regarding the traffic accident at the scene with none of the crash accident victims having no personal identification on their persons, except the car registrations in the two vehicles, as four car crash victims were all found deceased due to the injuries sustained upon impact of the car crash accident.

The police case deemed open, as the identification & whereabouts of the missing infant is in-fact, revealed & recognized and recorded.

As the results of the traffic accident is evidence of the van running a red light striking another car, as it was investigated.

All four car crash victims were identified & subsequent analyses were determined & credible police evidence.

The official police reports the cars crash, was in-fact a tragic & fatal accident, however a separate murder/homicide occurred at the same times & address & at that same intersection, revealing two people having a violent struggle, away from the traffic accident with the women slashing the other person across the neck & eyes, fatally wounding him.

The slashing victim identification was revealed upon personal identifications & mug shots & finger prints.

The second murder victim (Jane Doe) was dead from a recorded two gunshots to the back of the head & one to the back of the neck.

The infant, currently, is still missing, after, being born in the same trash dumpster at approximately 0009hours & umbilical cord cut & infant removed, by parties unknown from the same trash dumpster.

Criminal cases are still open for further police analogies.

Little Miss Pantomime was born in a trash can at 0009hr, as she only weighed three pounds & six ounces.

Her life became more & more terrible as the years went on. She started to learn to use people at the age of two years old, with a mastery of manipulation & semantics; learning everything & more from, Grandma Trix, and her street associates, to the points of creating illicit income & through a series of personal extortions & other criminal actives, Such as criminal extortions, implied prostitutions in furtherance, guns, human and drugs trafficking.

She used people and all situations, for all purposes of her own purposes, like an old squeezed tube of toothpaste.

She traveled around the city & country with other children whom all were sold, abused & trafficked, being led by Grandma Trix, there was Ana, a seven year old child who was from Russia, eight year old Mari child from Guatemala, six year old Roni from west Virginia, A ten year old Edmond from the state of Washington, and an eleven year old child Lucca from sao Palo Brazil, were all the victims of trafficking & abuse & forced child prostitution.

Grandma Trix, bought & sold children all around the state to the highest bidders, she would drop some kids off at times to very rich clients homes on Friday & pick them up on Monday morning charging the client thousands of dollars with illicit & exorbitant extortions plots.

By the age of nine years old, Little Miss Pantomime had personally created a personal wealth of a half a million dollars in stolen items & monies burred in & around the states in places that she herself only knew.

She stole & lied & lied & stole, all that she could, because that's all she ever knew in her entire life.

Her only solace in her life was, beating & conniving people out of all their money, something that she learned through a series of tricks, and methods learned from Grandma Trix.

She was a master at sexual manipulation, implied manipulation, as the trick would give of something, (money), in hopes of future sexual favors & as in the end, receiving nothing in return.

For example; Grandma Trix would make a deal with a well to do, trick, looking to having sexual relations with a minor & giving cash.

The money was given & the deal was secure; however the time & place was scripted & devised the plan was worked out so the trick would be in jeopardy of being discovered by the police & other governmental officials of the deal unless the tricks are self silenced with their own legal & personal embarrassments.

They connived their tricks, in the seediest to the most expensive hotels, corridors & motels in the city.

They traveled from one area to another gathering up all the money & personal property, they could steal, as cars, boats, homes, bank accounts were all under the realm of Grandma Trix & Little iss Pantomime didn't have bank accounts, as they hoarded their bounty by burying it in holes in the ground, public parks, backyards & alleys, even jars suspended in the water, at the base of tree trunks.

Confidence games paid very well sometimes, as they all traveled from one trick to another bigger trick, they fed well, sometimes they fed very poor & but always with the sense & hopes that they had other means of comfort in their own future.

Grandma Trix & Little Miss Pantomime, did not fully trust each other, as they did not confide in telling each other, where they kept their personal hidden stash.

When Grandma Trix died, at the age of sixty-nine years old, it was estimated that she was worth at the time of her death at over two million dollars in gold watches, money, property, paintings & other assets, acquired from her life, conning & conniving tricks.

Since most of her assets were personally buried, all along the city & state, no recovery to those assets was ever recovered, except one, a place where Little Miss Pantomime, stumbled upon while peeking at Grandma Trix, hiding only some of her bounty.

Grandma Trix died, at the county hospital & deemed indigent & taken to the city morgue.

There were no formal funeral ceremonies, no words of comfort, no religious scriptures to recite & no family to claim the body of deceased.

It was just Little Miss Pantomime, & the rest of the world as time went on, as by then, she was nineteen years old.

Scripts;

Little Miss Pantomime,

Lived within the first two years of her life, on the streets, eating in garbage trash cans, scrounging & stealing from cars, passerby's and people feeling sympathetic towards her & Grandma Trix, her keeper.

She was only a toddler, a two year old baby, when her keeper, Grandma Trix, started to assign & leave her with questionable men & women, all over the city, with directions to not allow certain things, no penetration, no intercourse, and no violence of any kind.

She was only six years old when he first violated her, after she was sold to Crazy face john, by the hour by, Grandma Trix, her keeper & sole known living relative.

Grandma Trix was an old very experienced street hooker that had a city wide reputation in the city with a large client following.

She found Little Miss Pantomime, in a trash dumpster on top of a dead street woman that had just given birth in that dumpster with her umbilical cord still wrapped around the neck of the infant.

Crazy face john,

A guy that always bought street hookers & prostitutes in the city as he had the reputation of always wanting & paying a large sum of money for young girls.

He had a very big house on the north side of the city & worked two jobs, one as a bus drive

& the second, working in the city dump, part time.

Little Miss Pantomime,

Was dropped off by a friend of Grandma Trix, at he's home, for three hundred dollars for one hour visit.

Crazy face john,

Sits & stares at the girl, & says, "Do you want some cake or cookies or something to drink, maybe some soda?"

Little Miss Pantomime, She replies,

"I would like some soda."

Crazy face john,

Brings her the soda laced, with some other drugs (sleep medicine) as Little Miss Pantomime, quickly drinks.

Little Miss Pantomime,

Sleeps, after about ten minutes & lays across the couch.

Crazy face john,

Picks up the girl & carries her to his bed, he then has his way with her.

Little Miss Pantomime,

Awakes after about forty minutes in the living room with TV on & the man, (Crazy face john, watching TV, she looks around with her soda still on the cocktail table in confusion,

Crazy face john,

Says,
You fell asleep watching TV; I took off your coat while you were sleeping,

Little Miss Pantomime,

She yawns & says,
"Do you have any food?"

Crazy face john,

"What food do you want; I have cookies & cake & hamburgers?"

Little Miss Pantomime,

With a smile she said,

"I like hamburgers,"

Crazy face john,

Leaves the room & returns with a food tray with micro- waved hamburgers & a tray of cookies with more untainted soda,

Little Miss Pantomime,

Began to gobble up the food as quickly a she could

Crazy face john,

Sat there watching her as she quickly ate her food, pretending to watch TV, the then says," ok?"

Little Miss Pantomime,

Looks at him & says,

"What's in that room pointing to the bedroom?"

Crazy face john,

"That's where I sleep; do you want to see it?"

Little Miss Pantomime,

Ok, she gets up & walks over to the bedroom & notices one of her shoes at the foot of the bed,

She then remembers dream of her in bed with the man but could not see who it was, or what they were doing at the time,

Crazy face john,

Says, "Ooh, is this your shoe?"

Little Miss Pantomime,

Looks down & sees she has only one shoe on & says,

"Yes, this is mine"

Crazy face john,

"Are you sure, with a big smile, it's your shoe?"

Little Miss Pantomime,

She then slightly remembers being touched all over her body & fingers being placed in her body parts,

She then smiles at the man,

Crazy face john,

Smiles back at her & they both return watching TV, with movies while they both ate the food,

A sudden knock on the door, was friend of Grandma Trix, who returned to pick up Little Miss Pantomime, after an hour visit in agreement of payment,

Little Miss Pantomime,

As she was leaving Crazy face john, residence, she smiled at him & "said, can I come back another time?"

Crazy face john,

"Sure, you can come see me anytime"

Little Miss Pantomime,

While she was riding with the friend of Grandma Trix, in the car, she looked at him & said, "all these people, you bring me to are friends of Grandma Trix?"

The male driver, the friend of Grandma Trix, said to her back, "yes, they are friends with your mother so be very nice to them, ok?"

Little Miss Pantomime,

"Ok, I'll be very good, they are all very nice to me, they all give me food & cake, & soda & stuff"

The male driver, the friend of Grandma Trix, said, did you like, Crazy face john?

Little Miss Pantomime,

"He was ok; we just watched TV & stuff"

The male driver, the friend of Grandma Trix, said," is that all, you didn't do anything else?"

Little Miss Pantomime,

"I had a crazy dream about wrestling with him & playing"

When I woke up we were on the couch watching TV"

The male driver, the friend of Grandma Trix, glared over at Little Miss Pantomime, & kept driving to the next appointment,

The appointments and assignments, went on and on, year after year until the ultimate death of Grandma Trix,

Grandma Trix,

An old, street prostitute motioning a frequent (old) john & friend to see her new cash cow (Little Miss Pantomime), a seven year old girl that was in training.

She tells (Elis), to show & teach (Little Miss Pantomime), all the tricks of the trade in manipulation & sexual practices to get the best trick johns.

Ellis,

Looks at, Grandma Trix, then looks at Little Miss Pantomime, & says,

"You want me to show her everything?"

Grandma Trix,

Glares back at Ellis, & say,

"From front to back, to back to front"

"Make her better that I use to be" **Ellis,**

"I remember how good you were"

"You were the best in the city, as far as I was concern"

Grandma Trix,

Smiles at him & touches him on the shoulder, then leaves the child with him for a year,

Ellis,

Returns the girl to Grandma Trix, after one year, with all the mastery of sexual positions, manipulations & conniving ethics

Grandma Trix,

Looks at both them together & says, well, "What's the deal?"

Ellis,

"She now knows how to everything, everything!" "I have a long list of tricks for payment"

Grandma Trix,

"Well, that's ok then"

"You line them up & well take seventy percent"

Ellis,

"I have over one hundred girl's guys interested in that piece"

Grandma Trix,

Smiles & says, "Will take her to the time & place of our choice, & well do the rest, just you take care of the security problems, right!"

Little Miss Pantomime,

Don't I have anything to say about this?

Grandma Trix,

"Hell no!

Just do the trick & well take care of the rest?"

Little Miss Pantomime,

"Ok grandma"

Grandma Trix,

"Well, tell me what you learned, living with Ellis?"

Little Miss Pantomime,

"He had me doing it five times a day"

Ellis,

Smiles & says, "Not five times a day, sometimes ten times a day"

Grandma Trix,

"Five times Hugh"

Ellis,

Looks at Grandma Trix, with a smirks & says,

"You wanted me to teach her, so I thought her, like I wanted"

Grandma Trix,

"Well, that's alright, that's how I wanted it"

Little Miss Pantomime,

"So this was like a school?"

Grandma Trix,

"Yes, it's just like a school & you remember everything

you were taught in school, right!"

Little Miss Pantomime,

Looks at Ellis, & say, "was I a good student baby?"

Grandma Trix,

"Look at that look on his face, cant you tell?"

Little Miss Pantomime,

"Ooh, he was a very good teacher, can I visit him every ones & awhile?"

Grandma Trix,

"Maybe, but only if you do what we tell &
to do!"

Little Miss Pantomime,

"When can we start more leaning?"

Grandma Trix,

"Who's first?"

Ellis,

"I got a rich old guy that lives downtown;
he's got six businesses & married to rich old
woman"

"I think we can get about fifty thousand bucks
from that guy if we do this right"

Grandma Trix,

Making out notes & recording it all

Ellis,

"Then we got a hockey player, worth millions, I think we can get about a hundred K from this guy"

Grandma Trix,

Still recording & says, "Ok, next"

Ellis,

"We have some married school teachers who we can extorts about ten grand from"

Grandma Trix,

Smiles & says, "Keep going"

Ellis, "I got four bartenders at the most expensive hotels in the state; have customer listings with them wanting five percent of the action?

Grandma Trix,

"They get two percent only, or no deal, tell them!"

Ellis,

"You got it"

Grandma Trix,

Looks over at Ellis, with a smirk on her face & says, "Tell me what other arraignments you want for all this?"

Ellis,

"Whatever you think is best, whatever, smiling at her"

Grandma Trix,

"Ok, will get you a cut & you arraign the tricks & the security & well get you your cookies, is that ok by you?"

Ellis,

Looks over at Little Miss Pantomime, & Grandma Trix, smiling big & saying, "I need a lot of cookies, you know!"

Grandma Trix,

Smirking, "yes, I remember, a lot of cookies!"

Next?

Ellis,

Some of the usual standard tricks, hand jobs & blows, no penetrations.

Grandma Trix,

"Escorts only"

Ellis,

"I have ten escorts only"

Grandma Trix,

"They are only good for about two hundred an hour"

Ellis,

"Well that's better than nothing"

Grandma Trix,

"Tell me more about the rich old guy that lives downtown?"

Ellis,

He's a Horney old goat, like myself, he & his wife haven't had sex I five years, he's has been paying me to supply him girls, but with Little Miss Pantomime, I think we can get a lot more out of him"

Grandma Trix,

"And the hockey player, what's the deal??

Ellis,

This guy plays professional sports; we get him going & extort him slowly for some payments while threatening him with exposure of reporting him with the hockey association, and the news media.

Grandma Trix,

"Sounds like you got a plan"

Ellis,

"We can start next week, after we take Little Miss Pantomime, shopping for all the right clothes, know what I mean?"

Grandma Trix,

Smiles, & says, "Yes, I fully know what you mean"

Ellis,

Ok then, let's get started, ooh, what about (Coffey), they are about the same age, we can start them both at same time"

Grandma Trix,

Smirking, "why not, why not!"

Booganhaugen, the sixty year old owner of a dive (French) bistro called (**the valley of the frogs**), in the downtown area on east sixth & main street. He was a vile lecherous dirty old

Deviate, scamming on whoever or whatever he could scam.

He and Little Miss Pantomime, nineteen year old woman had several scams regarding customers entering the establishments for the purposes of acquiring sexual relations with very beautiful women and men in & around the bistro.

Customers, both male & females would enter the bistro, observing the very beautiful women & men, and make a deal with (only) Booganhaugen, to get further intimately acquainted.

One example; a customer would inquire about a certain women of interests & after the recompense was in-fact settled with (only) Booganhaugen, the women would then approach the customer & say, "hi if you buy a bottle of champagne, we can go upstairs", as the stairs were only five steps up from the rest of the bistro, overlooking a sub balcony.

The customers were tricked into buying a hundred dollar watered down bottle of cheap & tainted champagne, & nothing more.

The customers would then be subjected & intimately coheres, into acts in furtherance with the women, who would be negotiated by (only) Booganhaugen, who would then allow the women to once again trick the customers by slipping them small doses of (mickys/ sodium pentothal/ Oxycodone/ Fentanyl), drugging them, & after the customers who were passed out, their wallets were rifled & credit cards scanned, even car and house/car keys were duplicated & passwords were compromised & all relevant personal information was recorded for future scammed intellectual & compromising extortions.

Customers would awake from being mildly drugged with their clothes being mussed with the sensations of being groped by the women & seemingly unaware of what entirely took place, as the customers walked away with a mild sense of had having sex, but walking away with nothing.

Virtually, every beautiful woman and men in & around the bistro who were under the direction of Booganhaugen, offered a different type of scam, as the racket was extremely monetarily lucrative, acquiring homes through extortions, scams & intimate coercions.

They were running so many scams in & around the bistro that it quadrupled the profits from the actual profits of the entire bistro revenues.

Customers of the bistro were single, married, lonely people who all wanted, for only a moment, a little attention in the lives.

Little Miss Pantomime walks in the bistro wearing high heels & a tight little red mini dress & white casual low- cut sweater. She is consorting with Booganhaugen, over the next round of suckers/customers.

Booganhaugen,

Ha, tell the rest of the girls, to give only hand jobs & no screwing!

Little Miss Pantomime,

I know! Hand jobs only boss.

Booganhaugen,

That guy you brought in last week came in here yesterday &, started to complain about one of the other girls on table six.

Little Miss Pantomime, What's the problem? **Booganhaugen,**

She gave him a hand job & but didn't finish the job!

She got distracted, she left the customer with an erection & he was really pissed off. **Little Miss Pantomime,** I'll take care of it, Anything else? **Booganhaugen,**

The girl working on table five is getting greedy again, if you don't take care of this, I will.

This works, because we don't bleed our customer's dry, get it!

Little Miss Pantomime,

I have a replacement for her, I'll put her in the rich hotel settings on Lorie Street, I think she would be happy with a more one on one setting with the hotel customers, in her own element.

Booganhaugen,

Ok, that guy that you met in the library was just here an hour ago, he insisted to see you.

Little Miss Pantomime,

Oh, Edmond, that guy, he has been enamorate of me ever since he lost his wife in a car accident last year.

Booganhaugen,

Well, how much is he worth?

Little Miss Pantomime,

He has just gotten five hundred thousand dollars in life insurance on his wife & another one point three million dollars in car insurance & damages from liabilities.

Booganhaugen,

Ha, that seems like a hat one, stay on it kid!

Little Miss Pantomime, I intend to boss **Booganhaugen,**

Cocktail brews (a), (b), (c) In mild doses only are for the inquiries of our women & men, who are working only, remember, it only for those customers only, got is kid!

Inform all our people, at the meeting tonight & every meeting.

Little Miss Pantomime,

If they won't adhere to the rules, they will be released with no exceptions, I know.

Booganhaugen,

Gives, her a note, with an address & key to a customer's house car keys, & "says, send two over here to see what we can see at this address", "if there is anything worth taking, don't take it, however record everything for future events".

Little Miss Pantomime,

She smiled & said,

I remember this woman, she was so hot for Myra, she kept asking about Myra, for three weeks now, she lives alone & works for a bank downtown as a vice president.

Booganhaugen,

Don't take anything! Observe only, got it! **Little Miss Pantomime**, Got it boss, **Booganhaugen,**

Tonight, we have seven coming in, answering from those ads for our bistro from Europe,

Keep them drinking & keep them running up the bar tabs!

That's all, I don't want any incidents, tell all of our people, to keep things very friendly & cordial with these people, no Cocktail brews (a), (b), (c) for any of them, we want them to tell their friends & come back, again & again, then we use Cocktail brews (a), (b), and (c).

Little Miss Pantomime, Do we do anything else? **Booganhaugen,**

Well, you guys can give them a taste/tease only, so they all comeback another day,

Little Miss Pantomime,

Ha, (Malone) has five customers, in love with him, they called this bistro ten times a week looking for him, guys

& girls, what do you want me to do about this?

Booganhaugen,

Nothing, just get all the information we can, but continue to monitor all movements, & inform (Malone), not to make a move until he consults with me first!

Little Miss Pantomime,

What's the deal with you & (Lilly)?

Booganhaugen,

What do you mean?

Little Miss Pantomime,

Well, I saw her with her hands on your crotch last night, at the bistro, what's the deal with that?

Booganhaugen,

Smiling at her,

Why, you jealous?

Little Miss Pantomime,

Smiling back at him,

Business is business & bullshit is bullshit, right?

Booganhaugen,

Your right,

I just get horny sometimes that all,

Little Miss Pantomime,

So do we all, but don't make a meal out of it,

Booganhaugen,

Don't worry, a hand here & a hand their that's all, no big deal,

Little Miss Pantomime,

Just don't fall in love, in this place boss,

Just remember boss, if you get stuck, we all get stuck; it's bad for business right?

Booganhaugen,

Ok well, yes, good looking out kid,

Little Miss Pantomime,

After all this is over, then we can relax & get involved,

Booganhaugen,

Ok, knob polishing only!

No others, will be considered,

Little Miss Pantomime,

The girl on table one & two, is not engaging enough with the customers, she seems not as friendly as she should be, what up with that?

Booganhaugen,

You mean (Sandra), she just broke up from her girlfriend last month, she will be fine, will give her more time to deal with things for now, if she needs more time, well put her on a different assignment, it will be ok,

Little Miss Pantomime, Smiling,

Sound like a personal problem boss,

Booganhaugen,

We keep an eye on them all, that's what we do,

Little Miss Pantomime, Sometimes both eyes boss,

Booganhaugen,

By the way,

Call the chop shop; we have nine more cars coming in to be chopped next week,

Little Miss Pantomime,

Busy busy, busy,

Booganhaugen,

Tell that bank vice president that we have another fifteen account numbers to hack for this week,

Little Miss Pantomime,

No problem, I'm on it boss,

Booganhaugen,

By the way, send that number that works table fifteen to my house tomorrow at ten o'clock pm, ok?

Little Miss Pantomime,

Smiling, Is this Business or pleasure boss?

Booganhaugen,

Smiling,

A bit of both, business & a lot of pleasure,

I noticed her yesterday pocketing tips from table ten,

I'm going to give her an offer, she can't refuse,

Little Miss Pantomime,

Patting him on the shoulder & smiles, and says, while leaving,

"Sounds like you are on it boss",

Conversations with, Dubos Torte, a thirty five year old female owner of twenty five rub & tug Massage parlors, throughout the cities & suburbs and state, and Rummy, a fifty year old owner of a large call girl, bootleg/illegal liquor & drug operations, that sells call girls & booze/drugs, guns, within the state even four neighboring states.

Rummy,

Looking at Dubos Torte, & saying,

"Ha, that Little Miss Pantomime, has squeezed me for more than five grand last month"

"What about you?"

Dobos Torte,

Scratching her hand & saying, "yes, she beat me out of ten grand last month also"

Rummy,

"What do you think? Should we protest?"

Dobos Torte,

"Saying what, to whom?

We can't trust anybody in this business!"

Rummy,

"Well, we can't keep letting this thing happening to us, or will go broke!"

Dobos Torte,

"Maybe we can do something else,

We can tell Little Miss Pantomime, that business is short this year & cook the books!"

Rummy,

"She will know that, because, our bottom line has been increasing since he started to take over this entire thing!"

Dobos Torte,

"We can make up our storages here & their till we get our

money back, can't we?"

Rummy,

"It's an idea, but who do we trust to makeup the differences?"

Dobos Torte,

"Well, why don't we just talk to Little Miss Pantomime, about your concerns?"

Rummy,

Placing his hands down his pants, and grabbing his parts, says, "we take it up to the one that's in charge, Little Miss Pantomime, & if she doesn't like what we say, we do it another way, agreed?"

Dobos Torte,

With a smirk, says, "Don't ask me to shake hands with that hand" "but that sounds like the plan!"

Rummy,

"Look, maybe someone else is shorting us, maybe we should, find where or who that is doing this first, agreed?"

Dobos Torte,

"Agreed!"

Rummy,

We find out first before we make the next decision,

Dobos Torte,

And how do we do that?

Rummy,

"We ask, Little Miss Pantomime, first!"

Dobos Torte,

"We just ask her, why are we being cheated?"

Rummy,

"That's right!"

"We seek the truth & we should find the truth!"

Dobos Torte,

"Ok then, ill setup the meeting with her tomorrow & we will see what happens"

Rummy,

"Ok then, we will just see about that!"

The meeting with; Dobos Torte, Rummy, Little Miss Pantomime, the meeting is taking place In a well established high end hotel on the south side of the city; placed there is a full setup with drinks, catered food & music, along with guards in & outside the suite.

Rummy,

Starts the meeting, after looking at Little Miss Pantomime, as he says, "boss, we have a shorted in our monthly takes, why this is & what is going on?"

Little Miss Pantomime,

"So you think that you are being cheated out of money?" She looks at both Dobos Torte, & Rummy, and says," is that what you are thinking also?"

Dobos Torte,

"Well, we have been wondering, what's going on boss?"

Rummy,

"After all boss, business is business, right boss!"

Little Miss Pantomime,

"Your right Rummy, business is business, Exactly where are your books short?"

Dobos Torte,

(Luna) the book keeper) has been doing books for the both of us for the last two years right?

Rummy,

Right, she has!

Little Miss Pantomime,

"So have either one of you ever questioned (Luna), the book keeper)?"

Dobos Torte,

"Well no!"

"We haven't suspected any problem with (Luna), the book keeper) of any of the problems with our books".

Rummy,

"Ha boss, we were just asking inquiries only, we didn't know"

Little Miss Pantomime,

"Well, why don't we all ask with (Luna), the book keeper) about all the books, right now & hear for ourselves".

Dobos Torte,

(Luna), the book keeper) is here now?

Little Miss Pantomime,

"Yes, she is, I anticipated what you all think & took the liberties of agreeing to this meeting"

(Luna), the book keeper), in the next room opens the adjoining door & enters the room under guard, she explains her role of siphoning about fifty thousand dollars from the company's assets in order to pay her gambling depths to a friend of Little Miss Pantomime, in another city.

Little Miss Pantomime,

"Now, what do you two, want to do about this? Smiling?"

Rummy,

Well boss, whatever is appropriate & whatever you suggest boss?

Dobos Torte,

"I feel the same, we can't have people stealing from us, and we can't have that at all, can we?"

"Whatever you think is best boss!"

Little Miss Pantomime,

Smirks with slight anger & says, "Of Corse, of Corse"

She looks at her security guards & nods for them to remove (Luna), the book keeper), from out of the room.

Dobos Torte,

"We were both wrong in our assumptions about things"

Rummy,

"I sorry boss, we apologize with our assumptions, it won't happen again, ever!"

Little Miss Pantomime,

Looks at both of them, very sternly & says to them both,

"I know it won't happen again, as of now, the percentages that you were short by, (Luna), the book keeper), is now being placed into a (stupid fund) and all revenues will continue being shorted & directed in the (stupid fund), until both of you are satisfied & I'm satisfied

& we can all trust each other, is that clear people!"

She stands up from her seat, smiles & smirks and says, "Now people, are there any other matters you two would like address while at this meeting?"

Rummy,

Noticeably very nerves, slightly crouching in his seat, saying, "No boss, everything is cool"

Dobos Torte,

Looks at Rummy, with disappointment & says, "No boss, we made a big mistake after all"

Little Miss Pantomime,

Slowly walks into the next room where former employee, (Luna), the book keeper), is being kept.

This meeting is now over, and a year after, that meeting,

Booganhaugen was found dead in his bistro office with his pants below his ankles & a drink of peppermint snoops in his hands.

Rumors of internal fighting between Little Miss Pantomime, & Booganhaugen, had spread throughout the entire city.

After police investigations, even civil investigation, as a result, between Little Miss Pantomime, & Booganhaugen, had made a legal agreement to forward the bistro business to Little Miss Pantomime, and all assets, as a second partner and the ultimate co-owner of the business.

As time & time passed, the wealth & property holdings of **Little Miss Pantomime**, had grew to the holdings of more than five million dollars, with ninety percent of all revenues, hidden underground in various places throughout the cities & country in parks streams, mountains & etc.

She always viewed banks and any formal monetary holdings as her enemy, just as her predecessor did.

She had acquired over time, millions & millions in gold bunion, silver diamonds and currency.

She was born in a world without rules, without reasons, without empathy, without mercy & without concise.

She was born in & lived in a time and place, were few feasted upon the backs of the masses of multitudes.

A time where only the minute few, controlled the lives of so many.

A place where, all hope was diminished as there was no hope for the future.

In this place, hope for the betterment, was only a dream, of dreams, as human degradation & squalor was just another daily reality, as for a few, this was a paradise,

In this place, a rich person could step over the poor people, living on the streets, in sewers, gutters, holes in the ground, even in their car, without mercy, without compassion & without guilt or indifference to one's own humanity of life.

In this world or place, the few have become numb to the extreme outcry to the inequities of the less indifferent, as their world outcries are all viewed as Amoral, typical of the monetarily fortunate, & a curse upon the unfortunate many.

She kept on the path of her nominal & past teachings, without fear.

She was very patient, methodical & determined to always reach her objectives, as one by one, every one that she was ever in contact with, from her childhood, somehow mysteriously disappeared, or died from some terrible tragedy.

(**Little Miss Pantomime**), lived within the first two years of her life, on the streets, eating in garbage trash cans, scrounging & stealing from cars, passerby's and people feeling sympathetic towards her & Grandma Trix, her keeper.

She was only a toddler, a two year old baby, when her keeper, Grandma Trix, started to assign & leave her for money, with questionable men & women, all over the city, with directions to not allow certain things, no penetration, no intercourse, and no violence of any kind.

(**Grandma Trix**), the person that raised her, died from some unknown illness, suspected strychnine poisoning, as she was in the city park at time & may have eaten some rat poison that was laced in some of the food that she received from the neighborhood food trucks, she still had the laced food containers, on her person before she died, as no other investigations were creditable due to Grandma Trix, being

& identified as only a street person, no other investigations were ever warranted.

(**The male driver**), the friend of Grandma Trix, who always drove, Little Miss Pantomime, to all her assignments, when she was a child till the death of Grandma Trix, was found, drowned in the lake just southeast of the city, police investigation ruled out foul play as they found massive amounts of liquor, when they conducted the police autopsy report, it was deemed that the man died after stumbling into the lake & died while on a drunken binge.

(**Crazy face john**),

A guy that always bought street hookers & prostitutes in the city as he had the reputation of always wanting & paying a large sum of money for young girls.

He had a very big house on the north side of the city & worked two jobs, one as a bus drive & the second, working in the city dump, part time.

Little Miss Pantomime was only six years old when he first violated her, after she was sold to Crazy face john, by the hour by, Grandma Trix, her keeper & sole known living relative. She was dropped off by a friend of Grandma Trix, at he's home, for the sum of three hundred dollars for one hour visit.

He died from a suspected home invasion, at his home, as he was beaten to death with baseball bats about the head & torso, attempting to escape from the barrage of brutal beatings. He was chased from one room of the house to the other.

It was recorded & reported their were at least three types of baseball bats that struck the victim, in about the head & torso, repeatedly until his death, as one very curious aspect about his death was he was missing all of his left shoes.

The police case is still open as a suspected homicide/home invasion.

(Ellis),

An old friend & confidant and customer of Grandma Trix, who was told by, Grandma Trix, to show & teach (Little Miss Pantomime), all the tricks of the trade in manipulation & sexual practices to get the best trick johns.

Grandma Trix, "From front to back, to back to front" "Make her better that I use to be", Smiles at him & touches him on the shoulder, then leaves the child with him for one year.

It was reported, by the police, that he was found shot to death in a suspected gangland murder incident over a money dispute.

Ellis, was shot ten times, in the face, at the distance of two feet from his face as the autopsy report, concludes, as no other signs of robbery or money taken from the deceased at the time, was reported. The case is still opened as a homicide/gangland style murder.

Booganhaugen, the sixty year old owner of a dive (French) bistro called **(the valley of the frogs)**, in the downtown area on east sixth & main street.

He was a vile lecherous dirty old **Deviate,** scamming on whoever or whatever he could scam.

He and Little Miss Pantomime, nineteen year old woman had several scams regarding customers entering the establishments for the purposes of acquiring sexual relations with very beautiful women and men in & around the bistro.

Customers, both male & females would enter the bistro, observing the very beautiful women & men, and make a deal with (only) Booganhaugen, to get further intimately acquainted.

He was found with in his bistro office dead, with his pants below his ankles, slummed back in his chair, with red lipstick on the head of his penis & a glass of peppermint snoops in his hand.

The cause of death was a suspected case of heart attack, as there was a large amount of caffeine & nicotine in his system.

The police investigations revealed the case closed.

(**Dubos Torte**), a thirty five year old female owner of twenty five rub & tug Massage parlors, throughout the cities & suburbs and state.

She died of a knife fight sustained in the back of one of her, rub & tug Massage parlors.

It was suspected by the police authorities that one of her disgruntled employees of a client was involved as the case remains open as a homicide to date.

(**Rummy**), a fifty year old owner of a large call girl, bootleg/illegal liquor & drug operations, that sells call girls & booze/drugs, guns, within the state even four neighboring states.

He died in a mysterious private jet plane crash, as there were no other person onboard the plane except the deceased, (**Rummy**), as he never had any flight training that was ever recorded of any kind.

This case is still opened as (NTSB), is still examining the possibilities of a second person, actually flying the plane that may have jumped out the plane at twenty five thousand feet, however rumors are very slim, as this is a suicide or homicide.

This case is still pending of definitive results.

(**Luna**) the book keeper) has been doing books for the (Rummy)& (Dobos Torte), Booganhaugen, and (Little Miss Pantomime), was found in the alley of a sleaze strip bar on the northeast side of the city, the cause of death was vaginal & anal mutilation, and the police think that she was raped to death, by at least six men, as reported that at least six deferent semen were found within her body, also fifty gold coins within her anus, by some unknown assailants.

As the result of, so many unexplained deaths in association, however never fully directly pointing & relating towards **(Little Miss Pantomime)**, cases of death are still pending & some unexplained as relative coincidences, however non related.

She trusted in no one, she believed in no one, she loved no one & she lived with no one, as she is now at the age of nineteen years old & very monetarily rich, as her wealth is buried, beneath the ground of the cities & suburbs, as like a squirrel, she doesn't remember where she buried some of it.

She never went to school, or learned to read & write, however; she did pick up some reading traits from the streets.

(Little Miss Pantomime) continues to search for her own meaning of life, & happiness, as time rolls on & self worth means less to her, however, she still continues to seek her own solace in this life, trying to find out what it all means, she continues searching, wondering & hoping for meaning in her very troubled life.

Written by; Dr. Everett C Borders Jr. PhD.2019@

When I am irretrievably & ultimately gone, In all worldly powers are, let be, I pray to god for my soul be free,

There were times in my life when I was really too blind to see,

As situational awareness & circumstances are not always foreseen,

For all of my earthly, trials & tribulations of powers let be,

I fear in my bones & soul, that no one, but no one, will ever cry for me.

Everett C Borders Jr. PhD.

The Ghosts and Demons of Vegas

Written by: Everett C Borders Jr. Ph.D.

The brief bio of Everett C Borders Jr. Ph.D.

He was born in 1951 at Cook-county Hospital in Chicago ILL; he was the fourth of six children & son of the late Everett & Mary Borders. He grew-up on the west side of the mean streets of the cities Rockwell garden projects with hard living & extremely violent gangs. His passion for writing started in the early sixties attending & graduating with a scholarship from Westinghouse vocational high School. He began writing poems & lyrics as expressions as he started playing bass guitar & drums, keys & 4track recording learning from his brother. He graduated from Loop College in Chicago ILL. He started working for Ford Motor Co. As an apprentice in Dearborn Mich. & joined the Chicago Police Dept in 1973. He excelled in worked in tactical, special operations, gang enforcement HBT (Hostage barricade terrorist) & vice. In 1976, he joined the United States Coast Guard reserve port security; he worked with agencies of the US

Government. After receiving over one hundred & fifty awards for valor & meritorious city/ state/ federal service work, he left Chicago in 1989 arriving in Denver Colorado where he started ECB (Clandestine).

He continued academic learning & began to work in industry of, addictions, Counseling, social services, and sitting on the Colorado state board for mental health. He started working in fast-paced engineering & advanced concepts in innovations. He worked in the assisting & mentoring in small theater productions with local & at risk adolescents & adults.

He received numerous letters of praise for service & civic efforts. He received his Ph.D. in Counseling Psychology in 2006 from Cambridge S. University.

He has publications in, Publications.

He consults, mentor, writes scripts, articles, commentaries & considers himself as an innovation scientist as he has more than several, groundbreaking inventions & is a constant collaborator in theoretical scientific projections, as an Independent Think Tanks Professional of real world innovations a LinkedIn professional.

The Ghosts & Demons of Vegas

A foreword;

We are but the wind, & kindred spirits in this place, as we have no footing in this place & no place of our own, as we all are ultimately only shadows & dust.

Alias, we are in the mists of dammed Buffoons, fool's & charlatans in fancy & suited dress, and presence, of false, evil, & terrible prophets, the Invasion of the booty & mind snatchers.

What is being done, to you, is not as disturbing & as important, as why, it's being done to you, at this current time & place.

There are many ancient legends out there, that has passed down through the ages, however;

there is one tale that is repeated, from one end of this planet till the other, that all say the same things, they all say,

"If you want to deal with a parasite/ human being, who preys upon people, you need to use silver, but when you want to deal with a demon, you need to use gold."

A slight poignant & poetic reference;

Somber tumbris, Solutions missed,
Mumblings stumbling, Miseries bliss,
Many are crying, as the few lavishly laugh,

Very reminiscing of the medieval past

Twisted rituals

True meanings missed

Many are blinded by, sleight of hand tricks

Poem by, E-Borders; @

Languages, we count on them so much, & they mean so little; however; in the domain & realm of communication, there is another language unspoken that is commonly spoken amongst all global brethrens that are currently caught up in this manically, sadistic, ritualistic, ridiculous demonic struggle on this planet, as it transcends any & all other languages on this planet & is only spoken through the eyes & the souls and aura of the many.

This language could only be described as the non-spoken language, of the struggle of all global brethrens.

When the words & knowledge of the Wise men, all fall on deaf ears, then mankind is surely lost.

In this world, there is too much needless, suffrage & pain, death & despair, as the needs of the many cry out to the cruel laughter of the twisted few.

Millions & millions of people, from all around the world visit, (Vegas) every year.

They arrive & are taken/herded to their hotels & motels, connived & cheated by, the crooked taxi cab thieves, also the (sodomistic) (Bluber) & (if) drivers.

They get over charged, by the hotels & motels, with exorbitant resort fees, on top of other assorted fees, and are pocket rifled, & become blinded by the lights by the factious ambiance of the strip.

Many will purport, that Vegas offers, the visitors a release of adult inhabitations, as for many, it is the illusions of grandeur of being in a place where all things are possible for a specific price.

When visiting in Vegas, one can, order up room service, twenty-four-seven, anything, for any reason, for any purpose, as Vegas does in-fact offer up smiling hospitalities of the extreme kinds, for any purpose.

If you happen to venture just blocks away from the lights & sparkle, reality is a much different conveyance.

There, you will see, people, living on the streets, however in this place, there are multitudes of so many, very old people, & the very young, as much as eight years old, & runaway teens, living under palm trees & in storm canals.

They live under truck trailers, on school lots & fields, at the mall parking lots, alleys, the public parks all filled up day & night.

They clog, traffic at street corners, traffic lights, with begging, they approach you at grocery stores, banks & restaurants, car washes, for the need of the human existence to mortally survive.

Many stay close to gas stations, & all lawn water sprinkler systems for water or whatever they can find.

Many are reduced to crimes, such as prostitution, robbery, theft, burglary, the murdering as follows, as some, attempting to steal from people who don't lock their cars when entering the gas stations & convenience stores.

Many chronically suffer from dysentery & varieties of scleroderma.

Many suffer from, untreated degrees & varieties of mental illness.

At a slight glance, many appear stoic like, & slightly trans like in their presence, as they stand in one spot what looks like hours in one position or pose.

You could see all the sadness & the tormented eyes of their life's betrayals on the faces of the homeless.

The community services centers are extremely overwhelmed, & grossly underfunded.

According to all governmental entities in the United States, so stipulates; it is a **(crime)**, to sleep on the (public way/streets); in any place in United States, even in a car or truck, as not having a mail-able zip code, in United States.

No persons can (vote), you can't even get decent employment, or gain any identification cards, if you don't have an address, & for the millions of homeless people, stuck between a miserable/hard luck past, & no possible future, in and around the united states, they are, considered by the united states government, nothing, less, than a dog.

Private & religious shelters, all attempts to assist in emergency contingencies, with food, overnight family sleeping shelters, even large restaurants & store chains, however, the needs are too great, as there are so many.

Your government, highly emphasizes the need to mass incarcerations, as the United States, has the largest incarcerations, rates of any country in the world.

As of now, there are no more EPA standards, as of this moment, the United States is almost back to the stone ages, with its environmental policy's FDA standards are disappearing, when your beef, pork & chicken are riddled with very dangerous tick bites, which carry deadly, zeka, lime diseases, & other assorted illness passed on the meats, even fish, filled with mercury you consume every day.

They are selling off & gutting the Department of education all around the united states, while massive protest exist all over the united states with no school funding, they are selling off very valuable school property buildings, land, to entities unknown.

They are selling national parks to entities unknown to greedy developers, mining, blasting, drilling, strip mining & destroying nature, in associated with conditions of their own twisted narratives.

They have gutted the DOD Frank laws, to protect consumers against fraud to the people of the United States, only for the benefit of themselves.

They have, slowly gutted, every governmental agency, in this country, & replaced them with rich & greedy, maniacal crooks, indicative of their maniacal initiatives.

They have tapped into social security revenue to promote their greedy agendas.

Medicare & Medicaid are being slowly gutted, every day, & now they are closing nursing homes, as the elderly suffer, whom rely on governmental funding, all & around the United States, as the twisted do this for their amusement.

They have plans to slowly gut, the VA & deny veterans the proper health care that they have a right to, & replace it with privatization.

The United States roads & infrastructures are crumbling, as they are laughing, and patting themselves on the back, after, giving away over a trillion & a half dollars to themselves, for tax breaks to, themselves.

Somehow, this does not seem to matter to so many, as they are rapidly rifled, in and out, from the airports & hotels & motels, like drunken & high, herded livestock.

A drunken & high deboterious weekend is only indicative of more of the same, when arriving back to their original destinations.

The authors, or architects, daily & nightly, are observed intermittently, going too & from, predestinations of informative areas of slumming, for their amusement, so they call it.

They buy & sell human misery, prostitution, young children, the disenfranchised, the very poor, the masses, & uninformed, with the grosses of abuses, of the highest entities of power, & perceived authority, & the self pre-justifications of it all.

It is this (rabid), preoccupation of always grabbing & snatching, others people's money & property by the few, that has sickly manifested in the illusions of the everyday masses attempting to always reach for the next, dangling carrot, the next (staged), illusion horizon, so your (life/existence), & perceptions becomes an ultimate (masked/staged), series of illusions.

They daily denigrate, the disenfranchised, the poor, the sick, the less fortunate, as just (ghosts), they consider that (all), need to be dealt with, harshly, violently & all with deadly confrontations, being the new norm.

There are extremely constructive and very effective mechanisms, to address homelessness & no opportunities, in and around the world; however, it is also very true, that many, many billions of dollars around the world also gained, through human misery & squalor.

The people of Vegas and everyone around the world are in-fact the (ghosts), in one degree or another, as the (demons) are in fact, are the architects of these insidious plots.

If you travel, every city of every country around this world, you find the same things. When you leave the bright lights & glimmer, just observe the human squalor & obvious human degradation of the greedy abuses of the masses.

There are over a three billion & a half people who are living in squalor, not because they choose to, but by conditions & demographics, as yes, *"this really is true, for me & you, the world is a ghetto"*, read for yourself.

Still not convinced?

8/21/2012 @ published

Shantytowns

In sight for most, but never
out of mind for many

In every city of every state of every country of every continent their lays slums, ghettos, *(the jets)* or Shantytowns.

They have been around since the twilight of man and as the twenty-first century is now dawning, the growing number of people around the entire world is getting greater.

There are massive tent camps growing in the United States as in other countries as the things they all have in common are crimes, gang violence, murder, theft, burglary, rape assault, extortion, intimidation, the feeling of being disenfranchised every minute of every day.

After leaving these kinds of atmospheres, one brings away a profound sense of strength of character, a desperate will to live and heighten sense of observational awareness.

If ever lucky enough to leave these kinds of environments one understands and better appreciates & identifies better opportunities.

For it is in the visualization and observing any semblance of opportunity can any people truly survive.

http://www.salon.com/2012/08/07/an_increasingly_hot_pl anet_salpart/

http://www.scientificamerican.com/article.cfm?id=global- bazaar

http://www.stwr.org/health-education-shelter/megaslumming-the-future-of-urban-shantytowns.html

http://wideurbanworld.blogspot.com/2011/03/are- shantytowns-normal-form-of-urban.html

What are Shantytowns?

The short answer is Slums, the Ghetto, extremely hard living & hour to hour survival.

Over one billion people live in Shantytowns, 20% of the world's population live in crowded, unsanitary slums of the central cities and in the vast shanty towns all over the world.

http://www.bookrags.com/research/shanty-towns-enve-02/ http://news.bbc.co.uk/2/hi/science/nature/4561183.stm http://webs.schule.at/website/megacities/problems_en.htm http://en.wikipedia.org/wiki/Slum

http://answers.yahoo.com/question/index?qid=20090815180956AAvsoyR

http://www.nytimes.com/2009/03/26/us/26tents.html?pag ewanted=all

http://www.bing.com/images/search?q=what+are+Shanty+towns++&qpvt=what+are+Shanty+towns++&FORM=I

GRE

http://en.wikipedia.org/wiki/Shanty_town

http://www.fotosearch.com/photos-images/shanty-town.html

http://simple.wikipedia.org/wiki/Shanty_town

http://en.wikipedia.org/wiki/Talk:Shanty_town

http://dictionary.reference.com/browse/shanty-town

http://www.nytimes.com/2009/03/26/us/26tents.html?pag ewanted=all

http://www.bookrags.com/research/shanty-towns-enve-02/

http://dictionary.reference.com/browse/shanty?s=t

http://www.bing.com/search?q=Shanty+Towns+Great+Depression&FORM=QSRE1

http://www.bing.com/search?q=Old+Shanty+Town&FOR M=QSRE8

http://www.scientificamerican.com/article.cfm?id=global- bazaar

http://www.alexisweill.com/citiesofthe
world/?p=63

http://www.amazon.com/Slums-Hope-
Shanty-Towns-Third/dp/0312729634

http://www.bookrags.com/research/
shanty-towns-enve-02/

Shanty towns in china

http://www.bing.com/images/search?q=
Shanty+towns+In+china&qpvt=Shanty+
towns+In+china&FORM=IGRE

http://en.wikipedia.org/wiki/Squatter_
settlements

http://www.chinawhisper.com/remove-the-
largest-shanty-town-in-yiwu-of-zhejiang-
2000-people-evacuated

http://www.flickr.com/photos/24443965@
N08/3478665926/

http://english.peopledaily.com.cn/200603/23/eng20060323_252867.html

http://www.wantchinatimes.com/news-subclass-cnt.aspx?cid=1102&MainCatID=11&id=20120724000048

http://www.youtube.com/watch?v=rJFKJopAXJQ

http://www.chinadaily.com.cn/bizchina/2012-07/24/content_15611601.htm

http://observers.france24.com/category/tags/shanty-towns

Shanty Towns in America

http://answers.yahoo.com/question/index?qid=20071219131622AATfCS3

http://www.bing.com/search?q=Tent+Cities+Across+America&FORM=QSRE1

http://thenewbostonteaparty.com/2011/07/31/shanty-towns-spreading-across-america.aspx

http://www.bing.com/images/search?q=Shanty+Towns+in+America&qpvt=Shanty+Towns+in+America&FORM=IGRE

http://www.shtfplan.com/headline-news/obamaville-shanty-towns-spread-across-america_07012010

http://greatergreaterwashington.org/post/9940/america-may-have-to-accept-shantytowns/

http://www.bing.com/videos/search?q=Shanty+Towns+in+America&qpvt=Shanty+Towns+in+America&FORM=VDRE

http://www.financialjesus.com/financial-crisis/tent-cities-in-america/

http://durangotexas.blogspot.com/2011/01/fort-worths-shanty-town-for-homeless.html

http://voices.yahoo.com/tent-cities-america-signs-current- recession-2744345.html

http://boingboing.net/2008/03/17/americas-new-subprim.html

http://www.fotosearch.com/photos-images/shanty-town.html

http://www.bing.com/search?q=Fresno+Shanty+Town+2011&FORM=QSRE3

http://www.bing.com/search?q=Homeless+Shanty+Towns&FORM=QSRE5

http://www.bing.com/search?q=Shanty+Town+in+Fresno&FORM=QSRE4

http://www.bing.com/search?q=Shanty+Towns+California&FORM=QSRE2

http://www.bing.com/search?q=Texas+Shanty+Towns&FORM=QSRE6

http://voices.yahoo.com/tent-cities-america-signs-current-recession-2744345.html

http://boingboing.net/2008/03/17/americas-new-subprim.html

http://www.fotosearch.com/photos-images/shanty-town.html

http://www.mapquest.com/maps?city=Shanty%20Town&state=NV#!

Shanty towns in Africa,

http://www.bing.com/search?q=shanty+towns+in+africa&FORM=AWRE

http://www.bing.com/search?q=%2b Shanty+Towns+in+African&FORM=RCRE

http://www.bing.com/images/search?q= Shanty+Towns+in+African&qpvt=Shanty+Towns+in+African&FORM=IGRE

http://en.wikipedia.org/wiki/Shanty_town

http://voices.yahoo.com/shanty-towns-south-africa-2955387.html

http://www.bing.com/videos/search? q=Shanty+Towns+in+African&qpvt= Shanty+Towns+in+African&FORM= VDRE

http://www.dailymotion.com/video/x424oa_ a-shanty- town-in-africa_travel

http://www.youtube.com/watch?v=swzInByL 6nY

http://www.pond5.com/stock-footage/10 45989/african- city-shanty-town.html

http://www.pond5.com/stock-footage/10 45962/children-posing-in-african-shanty-town. html

http://answers.yahoo.com/question/ index?qid=20110316073728AAHvtGO

http://observers.france24.com/content/ 20090723-unrest-south-african-shanty towns-%E2%80%93-ready-host-world-cup

http://www.youtube.com/watch?v=iseX6Kc
KMek

http://www.youtube.com/watch?v=j5IxV29j0_I

http://socyberty.com/issues/shanty-towns-in-
south-africa/

http://www.capetown.at/heritage/history/apart_
influx_sha nty_art.htm

Shanty towns in South America

http://www.bing.com/search?q=Rio+De+
Janeiro+Shanty+Town&FORM=QSRE4

http://www.bing.com/search?q=Shanty+
Town+in+Brazili an&FORM=QSRE6

http://0.r.msn.com/?ld=4vV-IKnz4H9L6Sr
nZRFG4ucxbQ6MiqZiyL8311P81n4QY6F
krcRv4bmM7yaxwzgPTNb8j-OoMGIS_
2t66ZrUaegsevrZtFyuNTrrgeCEbiSaGAs
CgXEqR-1gKG6gvVfqVpD-gPWHKOa8bf6
ZjsjZmD0_N7TzFCKv2TVTRipjpJAbCQejb
BacxlT9cQMeKXWYWz8ayyg7Xg_

W1bTTbyz1SzMTteR-dvCXjsTdUpXE
UNycRKPmXXcFLfv48ldQDaYvAzm
gf6Dqlbh_40mCTjb_ToLUQ-kKvxK3
nKJm1i6hfwcLMBiaGqEsjQwH8g5nL
mdqm_87jeq_eBO4rsRe2BEKe2jZeL_
LvmdqRmXuxNNixbyO3kOkiOg7U1Jga
ZSelAPLlR1aGkJYte63hIn95oJbzstJGAyOI
wXMBFmai_xZs1-AaDxEJO8j6iEL0V
bxfM3DF2aimq3RAmY3M9JtF4c4eZ-
pRDbJpEgvvuFy5yl0UNuf-BUOKgeYyCJy8

http://www.bing.com/images/search?q=
Shanty+Towns+in+Brazil&qpvt=Shanty+
Towns+in+Brazil&FORM=IGRE

http://en.wikipedia.org/wiki/Shanty_town

http://en.wikipedia.org/wiki/Favela

http://news.bbc.co.uk/2/hi/8565164.stm

http://www.bing.com/videos/search?q=
Shanty+Towns+in+Brazil&qpvt=Shanty+
Towns+in+Brazil&FORM=VDRE

http://news.bbc.co.uk/2/hi/business/8565164.stm

http://www.bing.com/videos/search?q=Shanty+Towns+in+Brazil&mid=EBCC171E066DBB5FCBAFEBCC171E066DBB5FCBAF&view=detail&FORM=VIRE4

http://news.bbc.co.uk/2/hi/americas/7870395.stm

http://www.fotosearch.com/photos-images/shanty- town.html

http://www.bing.com/search?q=Life+in+a+Shanty+Town&FORM=QSRE1

http://www.talktalk.co.uk/reference/encyclopaedia/hutchi nson/m0034865.html

http://www.slideshare.net/geogrocks/life-in-shanty-towns

http://answers.yahoo.com/question/index?qid=20090709040954AAKlh9Y

http://0.r.msn.com/?ld=4vV-IKnz4H9L6SrnZRFG4ucxbQ6MiqZiyL8311P81n4QY6FkrcRv4bmM7yaxwzgPTNb8j-OoMGIS_2t66ZrUaegsevrZtFyuNTrrgeCEbiSaGAsCgXEqR-1gKG6gvVfqVpD-gPWHKOa8bf6ZjsjZmD0_N7TzFCKv2TVTRipjpJAbCQejbBacxlT9cQMeKXWYWz8ayyg7Xg_W1bTTbyz1SzMTteR-dvCXjsTdUpXEUNycRKPmXXcFLfv48ldQDaYvAzmgf6Dqlbh_40mCTjb_ToLUQ-kKvxK3nKJm1i6hfwcLMBiaGqEsjQwH8g5nLmdqm_87jeq_eBO4rsRe2BEKe2jZeL_LvmdqRmXuxNNixbyO3kOkiOg7U1JgaZSelAPLlR1aGkJYte63hIn95oJbzstJGAyOIwXMBFmai_xZs1-AaDxEJO8j6iEL0VbxfM3DF2aimq3RAmY3M9JtF4c4eZ-pRDbJpEgvvuFy5yl0UNuf-BUOKgeYyCJy8

Shanty towns in Europe

http://www.bing.com/images/search?q=+Shanty+towns+In+Europe&qpvt=+Shanty+towns+In+Europe&FORM=I GRE

http://en.wikipedia.org/wiki/Shanty_town

http://en.wikipedia.org/wiki/Talk:Shanty_town

http://www.telegraph.co.uk/news/worldnews/europe/greece/6147072/Greek-immigration-crisis-spawns-shanty-towns-and-squats.html

http://www.skyscrapercity.com/showthread.php?t=1538310&goto=newpost

http://www.independent.co.uk/news/world/europe/in-spains-heart-a-slum-to-shame-europe-6268652.html

http://www.enotes.com/topic/Shanty_town

http://voices.yahoo.com/shanty-towns-poverty-environmental-degradation-and-2694686.html

http://www.maltatoday.com.mt/2008/09/21/t11.html

http://www.dailymotion.com/video/x8cklx_elisabeth-welch-shanty-town_music

http://observers.france24.com/category/tags/shanty-towns

http://www.guardian.co.uk/uk/2010/feb/07/shanthy-town-migrants-free-flights

http://pediaview.com/openpedia/Shanty_town

Shanty towns in Arab states

http://freedownload.is/pdf/shanty-town

http://growinginclusivemarkets.org/media/cases/Morocco_Lydec_2008.pdf

http://twitter.com/Perlkvist

http://photobucket.com/images/Arab+Shanty+Town/

http://www.shtfplan.com/headline-news/obamaville-shanty-towns-spread-across-america_07012010

http://webot.org/?search=Shanty_town

http://www.newsyblog.com/it/content/
campaign-launched-rights-egyptians-
struggling-shanty-towns

http://www.unhabitat.org/content.asp?img_
id=500&catid=210&typeid=53&image_
catid=210

Shanty towns in Canada

http://www.bing.com/images/search?q=
Shanty+towns+In+canada&qpvt=Shanty+
towns+In+canada&FORM=IGRE

http://traveltips.usatoday.com/hotels-near-
shanty-bay- ontario-22872.html

http://www.reuters.com/article/2009/07/28/us-
spain-shantytown-idUSTRE56R0P020090728

http://dictionary.reference.com/browse/
shanty?s=t

http://www.encyclopedia.com/topic/Squatter_
settlements.aspx

http://wiki.answers.com/Q/What_is_shanty_ life_in_the_1800S_in_canada

Making profits from Shantytowns

http://www.thefreelibrary.com/Our+bandit+ future%3f+Cities%2c+shantytowns%2c+ and+climate+change+governance.-a019690 7436

http://www.openbusiness.cc/2005/09/26/ funk-carioca/

http://future-seattle-innovation-now. blogspot.com/

http://emergingfrontiersblog.com/2012/ 06/22/mongolias-uneven-boom/

http://www.wsws.org/articles/2005/jan2005/ amaz-j15.shtml

http://www.linkedin.com/groups/How-many- people-live-in-3726466.S.106369483 http://www.metropolitiques.eu/Roma-Villages-or-the- Reinvention.html

http://www.marketingprofs.com/8/build-master-planned- customer-communities-not-shantytowns-ott.asp

http://en.wikipedia.org/wiki/Black_Market

http://rs.resalliance.org/2006/03/15/teddy-cruz-what-adaptive-architecture-can-learn-from-shantytowns

http://www.inthe00s.com/archive/inthe00spolitics/smf/1203307911.shtml

http://www.todayszaman.com/newsDetail_getNewsById. action?newsId=279318

http://hpn.asu.edu/archives/Aug99/0105.html

http://quizlet.com/3802763/chapter-14-flash-cards/

http://bigstory.ap.org/article/brazil-drug-dealers-say-no-crack-rio

http://www.sfgate.com/news/article/Brazil-Drug-dealers-say-no-to-crack-in-Rio-3798005.php

http://www.argentinaindependent.com/tag/shantytowns/

http://www.quia.com/jg/318513list.html

Experientially it is estimated that three billion people will Secom to tent camps and living in Shantytowns worldwide by 2030.

Even from a non-theoretical prospective, society has the collective compass and the technology to correct & rectify these kinds of problems, at this very moment.

The needs of the many are truly dread as tens of millions are dying each year from unsanitary condition, starvation, lack of shelter, lack of water and a lack of true hope for the future as the needs of the many have historically always outweighs the needs of the few or the one.

Written by,

Everett C Borders Jr. Ph.D.

Vegas, is just another city, & place indicative of cities & countries, all around the world, they deny & deny, & deny, as they chronically lie, to their masses, public constituents for their own maniacal purposes to remain in their own power.

Their lavish ceremonies are grand theaters, their speeches are bold, and however, there is absolutely nothing, behind their words, but words.

(Demons), offer no hope for the masses, no opportunity for the masses, & no possibility of escape from the chronic nightmare of their perpetual miserable existence, of the masses that are in their wakes.

It is the twisted modern day ritualistic methodologies of the vain, the greedy (Demons), the maniacal, and the totally corrupted to manage the masses, with cable, TV, deminted & twisted talk radio, drug commercials, the (soma/drugs), to appease & keep people in the dark, by subliminal manipulations, and the teaching of your children factious history, & grooming tem to be the next generations of passive consumers & misinformed idiots.

They bombard the human psyches with their subliminal images, & electronic wavelengths, to disguise their hidden maniacal agendas.

Consider the methodology of controlling a vast majority of people.

If you can do this, one can direct, & control the masses for any purposes, while being totally mentally oblivious, that it's happing to them.

Herding the masses has been an ancient methodology of incest & arachnids, crustaceans, reptiles, & mammals for eons; however it is modern day humans that used it for the maniacal agendas of their own amusement & total control.

We all exist, in a (rabid world) of, controlled existence, and the ninety nine percent of people, don't really know, they are being herded.

They really think they are in control of their own lives, maybe people should consider, the (ghosts of yesterdays past).

Consider the modern day (American Indians), this writer would challenge (all) the readers of this book, to go & ask the Arapohoe, the Apaches, what they really think of this world & United States.

Go & ask what's left of the northern Indians in Canada & South America, what they really think.

Go and ask the millions & millions American (Blacks), in every sector of this world, what they think about of United States & this world.

Go & ask the Puerto Ricans what they think about the United States.

Ask the (Latinos), what they think about the country.

Millions upon millions of (blacks) were (sacrificed), to build this world, this country, & every country, as well as Chinese people.

They were historically enslaved by the masses; genocidal- y murdered, raped, denigrated, historically disenfranchised, and stripped of any meaningful opportunities, in and around the world, made drunk & caricaturized as foolish & stupid.

From one area of the United States to the other, *"from sea to shining sea"* interstates & roads, railroads, all are made upon the bloody backs, of blacks & Chinese labor.

They put the world first, & the world placed them last.

White ghosts;

Consider looking at the map, of what was Africa, in 1300's, & look at the map in 2019, as south

Africa & it A-partied & Nazi, regime, have advanced their maniacal interests, plundering the natural resources & its indigenous people, to move northward to eventuality control the entire African continent.

Consider looking at the map, of the entire continent of Australia, in 1930's, as they murdered/genocide for sport, millions & millions of blacks that they did not consider blacks as humans until 1973, of course by then all the land was under total control of again, A-partied & Nazi, and regime.

Consider looking at the map at South America in 1935 & look at the map in 2019 as the Argentina, A-partied & Nazi, and regime, plundering natural resources, has taken control over the entire southern continent.

The whole truth, but very sad, brief history lesson bullet point;

They talk about the unprecedented atrocities, which happened during the WW2 holocaust, it wasn't Germans murdering Jews; it was just Germans murdering each other, as people need to tell the truth, all the truth.

The Nazi's, were not just German, but there were many English/great Britain Nazi's, American Nazi's, Polish Nazi's, Russian Nazi's, Canadian Nazi's, South American Nazi's, Spanish Nazi's, Italian Nazi's, Dutch Nazi's, Swedish Nazi's, South African Nazi's, Australian Nazi's, French Nazi's, & yes many, many Israeli (JEWS) Nazi's, & they are all the (same people), who are still here, doing the same things, with the same twisted ideologies, as the real truth hurts, no matter whom it offends.

It's like saying that (South Africa), is controlled & ran by the blacks, as that is (absurd), the South Africans are controlled by that same Nazi's, that setup up camp back in the fourteen hundreds, as well as the rest of the world, just as the same Nazi's, Argentineans control (Brazil), & they are all the (same people), who are still there, doing the same things, with the same twisted ideologies, around the world.

The same ideologies that, created slaves & lynched black people, who caused the American civil war in the United States, are the same people who are running you & your government at this very moment, & you wonder why things are like they are, as you a fooled with illusions of a cohesive democracy.

Take a good look at their union jack in Great Britain (flag) & look at the KKK banner confederate south banner, as it is the same sick flag, worshiping their twisted crosses, as they really believe that murdering & denigrating black people is somehow spiritually holy, they think that murdering black people is god's will, by the same sick mentally ill people, they really are of sick & mentally ill, if you really believe that you are the masters of the world.

If you really disbelieve this writer, then go out their & ask them, (these same people), what they believe & worship in.

With the exception of China & India, who are the last of the worlds ancient civilizations on this planet to date, as the rest of the world are void of its own humility of its own truth, as the other ancient old civilizations, have all been destroyed by Caucasians, a tragic tale, of no humanity when the children are destroying, their own parents.

In fact, all of Europe is the same people, as they all look the same, they all think the same & what's most important, historically, and they all have behaved the same way.

Just think about it, Caucasians historically they have broken, every treaty & every promise, (they), have ever made, around the world, in the history of their entire pathetic existence.

You are being "lie-d & dyed & laid to the side", by people who are lying with a (smile), to their face, everyday, & many really don't even know it.

As long as they can control (your narrative), of (your total life's existence), they want (you), to think in world peace, and as long as you swallow their insanity, you are semi- tolerated, within their world.

Without this constant bombardment, of signals of misinformation, & discourse, the multinationals, (whom) control you, the ghosts/ you, they could never exist, or thrive.

Here's a big clue, just because people speak different languages, dialects & are in different purported countries, doesn't mean they are not all the same people, get it, go and figure it out the truth, for your-selves.

What about the unprecedented atrocities of the continued (genocides), of over a billion (Blacks), murdered & suffered, at the hands of Caucasians, continuing around this planet in twenty eighteen, in every sector of every country, somehow, no one wants to talk about that, as they say it's a dark past, which is somehow lost in this future.

To compartmentalized & marginalized and (discount), the continued (genocides) & continued atrocities upon (blacks), by the hands of Caucasians, seems to be their historical norm as evidenced by their constant & current historical patterns.

Example;

The Spanish, the Mexicans, the Puerto Rican, the South Americans, with the exception of Brazil, all speak Spanish, as they hate each other, they all think they are better than the other, however, they have different dialects, but all speak Spanish & they are all the same people, but somehow are indifferent them to really admit it, even if you are Italian, you can understand much of the Spanish language, because they are the same people & many really don't know it, as even if you are from the Philippines, you can understand & speak some Spanish language.

It is extremely imperative, when telling the truth, to (tell, all the truth!).

The new world order imperatives; the perpetual demented, (Ararin), objectives, the masters of the world mentalities, are very alive & well in 2019.

The new world order, has nothing to do with countries or nations, as multinational corporations control this planet, they are the people whom you or I will never see, they don't live in the United States, Germany, France, Great Britain or Canada, or anywhere tangible, because they own it all, countries are their third world, their slumming.

There are people, who make (extreme profits) from the hatred & stupidity that, they themselves create, just to make profits from fools, who scurry around murdering and hating each other, while they laugh every day, and many really don't even know what's happening, in front of them

Here is a quick & easy example;

Just try going down to your local radio & TV stations, & try saying exactly what's really on your mind, or attempt to really voice you opinions, (except for a local crime tip), as it will (never, ever, get publicly aired), & (it will never be considered), ever, but not just here, in any country on this planet.

The same people, that disguises, behind the auspices & narratives that purported their twisted ideals in pre, world war two, are the same people, that you are seeing (tweeting), every day, from the bombarded signals, from the nonsensical ravings of (loons), lunatics, at this very moment in time, and many, whom are so compartmentalized & marginalized in their thinking/programming, are egging them on, with, such gusto, just like pre-world war two.

From their perspectives, you exist only to serve them, & when you are no longer useful to (them), you are tossed into the trash, **for example**; if you are a property owner, you really believe that the property beneath your feet is yours; however, attempt to build in any direction, either twenty feet above or twenty feet below, or just try & stop paying your property taxes & see how much your property is yours, even when you leave this world, seventy percent of the property goes to the state/them, as well as all other assets, just for their amusement.

Black ghosts;

We went from being called, slaves, to niggers, to colored people, to African American, now blacks, as Caucasians, Americans would call us.

Any other white American, would call themselves an American, no matter if they came from Russian origin, Spanish origin, German origin, French origin, on & on, as just Americans.

It seems that blacks are only, considered real Americans, when it is of convenience, to white America, as it seems that it is ok, to toil, fight & die, for this country, as well as other countries, until the matter of equal rights are given, to blacks as well as around the world, go figure.

Case & point, the white man, got the black man, to murder & kill, the red & yellow man, for the white man, with the same, (morbid existential mentality), as they have been (historically), using the blacks for muscle for the benefit of themselves, since the thirteen hundreds, can you really see the contradiction?

When you visit Vegas, New York, Paris, London, San Francisco, Chicago, Miami,

Dallas, Huston, Argentina, Australia, Canada, every crevice, of the united states & this world, you (awe), at the tall buildings, you marvel at the city sounds & lights, all based upon the black bloody backs, of so many Billions of (black) people & (Chinese) labor.

This writer urges the readers of this book to lookup for themselves, the overt & covert methodologies to slowly exterminate sectors, of people worldwide, Africa, Australia, South America, Latin America, southeast Asia,

The Tuskegee experiment was for amusement, in death & extermination, as this experiment was also wide spread to South America & South Africa & India, Canada, and the (complete genocidal extermination), of the entire continent of indigenous people in Australia.

The ghosts, are (you), as there are degrees of levels of being (ghosts), from the people that make $5,000.000.000 a year, to the ghosts that make zero per year, that exists from one generation till the next is continuously calculated, & assessed as acceptable levels, acceptable levels, of the disfranchised, acceptable levels, of the poor, the sick, the old, the weak, the frail, the, downtrodden, the homeliness & the hopeless.

You are managed, processed, invaded, perpetually & bombarded by psyche images from your smart phones, cable, TV, talk radio, subliminal programming of your psyches of drugs, lifestyles, foods, health, cars, housing, schools, & they don't have the right to do so, and you are totally oblivious to it.

They have turned up the levels to its maximum settings, when it comes to their subliminal conditioning, embedded, programming signals towards (you), on TV, Cable, and talk Radio, & you really don't even know it.

Acceptable levels of, the meager provisions, & the struggles of everyday life, food, clean water, student loans, mortgage, the struggles of acceptable meager housing, work, travel, clothing.

Consider, the accepted levels of euthanasia, with animals, **for example**; a cat or dog is rounded up on the streets, & taken to a shelter.

If the animal is not adopted within a certain period of time, due to overcrowding, the animals are then euthanized or put to death.

Now, let's look at (human equations), the United States, with the highest rate of incarcerations of any country in the world, one can argue that this is kind of a euthanasia approach, inmates are preyed upon while incarcerations, as the rate of recidivism is about eighty five percent, & the revolving door of inmates with no other hope, but to reoffend, they wind up their lives on the streets, reoffending, no hope, no opportunities, & no future, as that is not really living; moreover consider the many millions more they murder on a yearly bases with concocted man made diseases, & self manufactured conflicts.

Many blacks & Latinos are just murdered on the streets by law enforcement, just for target practice, & they are still lynching people in the south, with the murdering people in the night, in and around United States throughout the world.

It is the modern day ritualistic methodologies of the (architects), are herding you, into a false sense of existence, to another, & most don't even know it.

Consider this, a lack of purposeful opportunity, inherently breeds obvious contempt, for the institutional construct, at condemned them, from birth to death.

Consider, the people that approach you on the street, asking for any monetary assistance, while you sit in your car or SUV, at a traffic light, don't really have a choice, especially if there is no visible opportunities or support, as some have obvious contempt for them, & others feel sorry for them, even the many whom ignore their existence.

Consider yourself as just another (ghost), from one degree to another, one paycheck away from foreclosure, or eviction, one paycheck away from starvation, no savings, and no opportunity for retirement, because they really can't afford it, many people work two jobs & still can't make ends meet.

Many people forget, our own frailties, when it comes to others, we forget the life struggles of so many that came before us, as we are becoming more & more inhumane, with each passing moment in time.

Sure many will deny & deny that the facts of life really don't exists, but this writer urges the readers of this book to take a trip to the hospitals in any part of the United States on, Thursday night through Sunday night, & see the human carnage & degradation & lack of decent human respect for, you & yours.

Ask yourselves; is this is really, who & what we are, as they take body parts from the poor & give them to the well to do, all around the world.

Whether you hide & sleep, under the protection of a palm tree, semi truck trailer at night, or you hide in a penthouse tower casino by day (inhaling cocaine), you are still a (ghost), by design, either by your own, or by theirs.

Fore; it is inherently & inhumanly wrong for any humans, or purported country, to rape the natural world for profit, especially by human beings & preying on its children, & even by witnessed in environmental plastics, garbage's, plundering of all oceans, lakes, bays, & sounds, even space itself one hundred & fifty miles above your head.

Can't you see all around you, for yourselves, the permanent damage that this world has suffered from the greedy few, on the bloody backs of so many people?

In case you didn't really know;

Every time you get a blood test, biopsy or any invasive medical treatment, they are secretly herding your own (DNA), & telling you that they are comparing your samples to seek your, (treatment), or saying that is about your true heritage, your true ancestry, but really, there is a more sinister/nefarious element connotation that is in play, & you don't even know it, & as in case you really did not know, there is such thing as the (Cloud); what do you, suppose that is used for?

Many may not pay attention to this, but it is paying a lot of attention of you.

In order to progress as a species, such as; methodologies of incest's & arachnids, crustaceans, reptiles, & mammals, & in order to progressively exist in furtherance, one must actively attend & manage their own inner & outer existence, in order for future existence.

The human race is on course of self destruction, and this planet as we know it.

Consider this; we are herded, programmed & processed into believing anything that is part of this continued & perpetual programming.

Still not convinced?

If you are a sports fan, consider this:

Whether you physically attend a sports event such as, hockey, basketball, football, soccer, car racing, or sit in the comfort of your own home, watching the same events; Example;

You are prompted to take bathroom breaks, soda & food breaks & etc, are you not?

When you see food or beverage images whether it's in person, or on TV, cable, your salivary glands react to the prompted responses, does it not?

At first, your human psyche attempts to control the situation, but afterwards, you fall victim into the promoted signals.

Still not convinced?

They made a study of non-human primates, using the same study, when the visualization of food was bombarded to them; they all had the same behavioral response.

Their salivary glands, all responded to the same prompted signals, of food, & other responses.

Humans are subjected to the same behavioral conditional programmed responses, but not only with food, but all other conditional behavioral physiological & psychological responses, sex, cars, food, clothes, education, relationships, methodologies bombarded, of every second of everyday, & they don't even really know it.

If you really don't know, how to respond to life, other than being controlled by a series of others prompts, then who really is control of you, them, or you?

Either you stand up for something's, or you'll fall for anything.

Still not convinced?

They made a study of rats in a maze.

Within this maze, all the rats were only allowed to turn right within this maze & they all did so.

But when the partition was removed, that allowed the rats to all move freely within the maze, they all still made right turns, get it.

The point this writer is making, is bombardment after bombardment, year after year, generation after generation, are conditional effects of institutional conditioning & programming, from birth to death & many really don't know it. Example;

If you have ever saw another person & thought to yourself, *"I would really like to punch that person in the face"*, but stopped short of doing so, then that is your inner self (ID), inner mind telling you that it is not a good idea.

If your inner mind, inhabitations are removed from those equations, with say; alcohol, drugs, & etc, then you would act out those urges.

Being prompted is being prompted; just imagine it, as just like being psychologically prodded, for any purpose, any purpose.

Fore; we must unlearn/unplug first, for by unlearning/unplugging, can we truly learn.

When you step outside of this construct, you will truly see what this writer is referencing to.

A denial of reality, does not mean reality, does not in-fact exist.

The architects; actively create crises thinking, & order to create sub panic, specifically directed at certain members of the populous, such as medicine commercials towards seniors.

They create the problems with sub-par healthcare, & attempt to reap the rewards in health care profits, as evidenced why there are so many drug & Medicare commercials.

Human misery is such a thriving industry, that it is a trillion dollar industry worldwide, even hundreds upon millions of dollars, are profited just alone in Vegas.

The ghosts of humans past & present, tends to haunt us all, as some areas of this country, as well as many areas of the world, one can feel, within the bones, & presence, its haunting past.

Consider, the modern day (GPS) in your car, or SUV, as you trust it to take you to whatever destinations you ultimately want to go, as it is doing the thinking for you.

You are prompted, to turn when it tells you to turn & follows its instructions, to take you to your destination.

After a while, you trust this device so much that, many people really can't think without it, on the road.

Something else or someone else, is doing the thinking for you, as you become a ghost, a shell, carrying out a series of instructions, as your life is prompted to carried out another's instructions, as this is the result of losing your own natural free will.

Many, may not agree with the matter of losing their own free will, & may attempt to deny the signals imbedding programming; however, it is always there, as the facts are facts, no matter how harsh, as many really don't know they are being programmed & will argue to the death.

The ghosts of Vegas are everyday people, carrying on with their lives, being led, prompted, signaled, and programmed, subliminally obliviously, twenty four seven.

With emergence of (AI), & smart-phones, & the smart computer age, many everyday decisions are made by just using a click & pointer.

Another example;

They use Horses, fish, goats, pigs, cattle, as livestock; it is psychologically conceivable, that not all think they are livestock as others, & many have a false sense of existence that they have free will, as they are all in-fact herded & gathered, & used in one mannerism or another.

However, but some do attempt to resists the programming & manipulation of the controlling entities, & attempt to free themselves, from the confines of being dangerously managed, as they just want to be just another animal, just like the open & free ones, in and around the world.

The livestock in captivity, are conditioned & bred, to be more dossal & manageable, as they are prompted from one generation, till the next, oblivious by the managing entities whom do the programmed responses, such as being sheltered, feed, water, shots/medicine, bathe, exercise, sleep management & etc.

Most are unaware, when they are prompted in meeting their ultimate life's end, until it's too late, as this same trait, is also very prevalent in humans as well, because inevitability, you are just livestock, but you really don't know or think so at this time, you are really livestock, as you really think, you are a free thinker, with free will, but you're not.

Because, outside the limit of your existence/sight, the (architects), are feeding & perched upon you, from your birth, to your death & your children, & many really don't know it.

Example; you go into a hospital emergency room, because you're feeling sick, however, before you know it; you are then herded for a finances & consultations interview (first), are you not.

You could crawl into the hospital emergency room with a knife sticking out of your back, & they ask you do you own a home or condo, do you have any land property, who your relatives are, addresses, phone numbers, e-mails & etc; moreover, if you have no finances & no insurance of any kind, just see how well you are treated in any clinic, hospital or doctors office settings, anywhere around the united states.

If you are just fortunate to have health insurance, then observe just how they create unnecessary scenarios, in health testing scenarios to exhausts your insurance and your co-pays, very quickly.

The point is, herding/manipulation is the same in both livestock animals, and in humans, & many really don't know that they are being herded & manipulated.

The (**demons**) are the architects, who are doing the programming, psychological manipulations & the authors of these insidious plots.

You and they, are so compartmentalized & marginalized, in your own existence, many really don't know it, or what purpose it is being done to them, at this time & place.

Another example, true story;

When this writer was a child, my friends & I would all go to various places together on weekends.

We would save your money for two weeks & go, all together.

One place was called, (Jew town) in Chicago's, near South west side.

We all walked together in bunches as all along the way, there were dangers, with Italian gangs from Cicero, & Roosevelt road.

Well before we arrived, we could smell the Jew town polish sausages, from a mile away.

They would drown them in onions & mustard so they smelled so tantalizing.

Whenever we arrived at this place, it was like a large cheap flea market, however the people at this place were extremely rude all the time, just to people whom looked like this writer, as they all would say things like *"don't tell me what you want, I know what you want!"* & they would say terrible things about our skin color.

As we remained respectful towards all adults at the time, because we had the proper up brining, so we would all just stared & say nothing, but smiled at them, as we just wanted to buy our goods & leave as quickly as possible.

Every time, we arrived at this place, we were all greeted with the same behavioral anger response, every time, by different people.

It is now twenty eighteen, and they are still selling the same (Jew town), polish sausages, & you can still smell them a mile before you get there.

The point is, we were never mistreated like this at China town, or in the Mexican areas of Chicago, & but only in the white areas.

The point this writer is making is, that this is just another form of, compartmentalized & marginalized behavioral thinking on them, not us., as we never had any lateen, animosity with, or towards, these people, or any people, but they sure had a lot of built up anger & animosity, towards us, just for being black.

Personally, the same things happened to this writer in, the fifties & sixties, Canada in the nineteen seventies, when they said to me to *"get out of their country"* while being with an Asian girl, Mexico when they told me *"spend your money & go", as well as so many white societies around the world,* & especially the Deep South, when they trashed my Red Corvette, & the KKK attempted to murder me for just driving through towns with a white girl.

Hatred was never a part of this writer's upbringing, my parents & other elders never spoke of it, as I had to experience ignorance, stupidity, blind hatred, for myself.

It took this writer some sixty seven years, to fully understand why, me & other blacks here & around the world, we were being hated so much, with such malice & forethought.

If you would ask some ninety-nine percent of white Americans, & worldwide, where they had gotten their indoctrinated hatred, towards blacks & others, they would all say, their homes, as blind stupidity breeds stupidity, it is that simple.

The true vestiges' & history of (Blacks) are seen in all their eyes around the world, it's in true historical bandages & badges (scares), of skin color, it is in the ancient recesses of their hearts, & instincts, the first real civilizations on this planet.

We do not need purported titles, to describe us, we do not need the permission of the satanic crew, to involve us, we don't need any of them, and instead we only need each other.

Being born into hatred & behind enemy lines is the worst part of being a (ghost), in the United States, & the world, as we put this country first, along with the Chinese, by building it, & they put us very last, as you should consider the (exclusion laws), for a real history lesson.

Just consider what many Latinos are going through at this very moment time, even if they are American citizens, as many are dragged out of their homes & cars, churches, schools, detained questioned about their papers in twenty eighteen.

Just look at how the poor white communities are treated, with always empty & hollow promises, every day, every year, every election cycle, as there are vast profits to be made in divisions among sectors of the populous.

They tell you that you have to be on one side, or the other, when in reality, no one is on your side, ever, as the right hand, has no idea, what the left hand is doing, get it.

As true Americans, maybe we all should practice, what we preach, here & around the world.

Here is just an idea, if we are all United States citizens, why not behave like we are, does this make any sense to you?

Many, many of the ghosts of the world, on the extreme levels, whom live on the streets, are very quick thinkers for themselves, they do not have smart phones, they do not have computers, they do not nave (GPS), or any (AI) technology.

If society ever goes south, they will become the vanguards of the nexus ground civilizations, unencumbered by directions or prompts.

They have already mapped out vast amounts of you, all your property, & your terrain.

They already know how to be both, defensive & take offensive measures.

They already know, where water is, boats, food, planes, weapons, keys, clothes, available shelter, & self medication.

They already know whom to trust, & whom not to trust, & as matters of self survival, they are the apex of the real world, all around the world.

They have inherently bartered & street haggled this way for some thirty five thousand years, & they are very good at it.

On the other spectrum of the ghost scale, it is the well to do, that will have a lot more problems, if things go south, as they always rely on the assistance of others, to assist in their safety & comfort, & their ultimate self survival.

Without the present civilization, where can they go, or what can they do, for safety, water, food, medicine, any sympathy, or any communication. Without their computers, & smart phones, or liked assistance, who or what will they ultimately become, but just victims.

There are ghosts (people), just like you, living in natural caves in Fl, AZ, UT, NV, CA, NM, as they bathe every day, with natural underground, hot springs mineral water.

They eat Yucca, roots & other edible desert vegetation, snake, armadillos, bear, & other fowl. They get natural lighting from the openings in the caves cracks, and in winter, they burn gathered tumbleweeds, & other dry brush & they really love it.

Inherited critical & crises thinking, has brought so many, thus far. If we did not learn anything, from the past human blunders, we have nothing else to build upon, for the nexus phase in the twenty-first century, or the next.

Fore; there are thousands & thousands, of homelessness people, women, veterans, very old people & very young children in and around Vegas, and as well as hundreds of millions of people, all around the world, & they all exist, & die and are driven, from the collective strength, of themselves.

The human spirit is strong, regardless of situational & or conditional dilemmas of this world, as there are the few, that have made this planet their paradise, while at the same time, making this world for so many others, so much misery, death & destruction.

No one wants to be homeless in their life, as there are a great many variables that prevent many people around the world from succeeding in life, such as, economic conditions, mental health, medical conditions, inherited cultural conditions, situational conditions, and geographic conditions.

The totality of the human condition & spirit, is strong, however, has the need to belong, to each other, to belong to the world, a world, which has abandoned & ridiculed them, for just being human.

Still not convinced?

Take a good look all around you.

Observe the people, in every town, every city, every country, & ask yourselves, why is this so.

Why are people driven into institutional slavery, obvious degradation & torment, every day of their lives, needlessly, subjugated, indentured, intentionally from birth to death.

The answer is power, greed & control!

Whoever controls the real-estate controls the people, their children & their lives, as sport.

Final case & point; the relative facts of life,

If a multimillionaire NBA, NFL, & etc, athlete attempt to visit a country region, without a security delegation of say, the Brunei region of the Congo, they would be violently confronted, very quickly & without hesitation, because, they don't walk with the people, no one cares who they think they are.

If billionaires attempt to visit a country (slum), Sao Palo Brazil, without a large security delegation, they would be violently confronted, very quickly, because they don't walk with the people, no one cares.

If the ruler of Russia decided to visit the (slums) of the Ck republic, without an extremely large security delegation, he would be violently confronted quickly, because they don't walk with the people, nobody cares, who he thinks he is.

If the sultan's billionaires decided to visit the countries (slum) like, Yemen, without an extremely large security delegation, they would be violently confronted extremely quickly, because they don't walk with the people, nobody cares.

If the Pope, without his ceremonial garments, decided to visit the (slums) of Italy, without a large security delegation, they would be violently confronted because, they don't walk with the people, & nobody cares.

In fact, if any trillion-air, billionaire, millionaire ever decided to visit any (slum), anywhere on this planet without a very large security entourage, they would be violently confronted extremely quickly, because they don't walk with the people, nobody cares who they think they are.

On point, historically, every real Devine prophet, every great historical leader, has always walked together with its people, & not talked at them.

It's very easy to talk down at people, who can't really talk back, isn't it.

Fore it's the (ghosts/you), for some, are just everyday people to others, as no one really cares, who or what you think about whom you are, in this world, except you.

The point is;

You know why, learn to think for yourselves.

For the last time, either you really stand up for something, or, you'll fall for anything!

It doesn't matter, what you believe in this world, just as long as you believe in something, get it.

This world was once a place, where, any persons could at least see, & plan site, their future & that for their children's, as this world was so vast, as far as one could see, and now, people are just ghosts, spirits, & shadows of the futures past. You are only a spirit/ghost, if you walk through life when the ground underneath your feet is not yours.

Ultimately, we are all only just, ghosts, shadows & dust, and any references, of any other kind, is immaterial or irrelevant & the circle of life, for (nothing), can be aimless.

All that we are, no matter who, shall turn to dust, We are all just shadows, ghosts, & spirits for now, Churning, Burning, Yearning, learning, & gone! Facts;

We can feed every man, woman & child, all seven & a half billion of us right now, with sugar kelp & Algae protein; in fact there are twenty different types of kelp that people can consume right now, along with soy for added protein, & get all of our fresh water from simple desalination from the oceans.

We can rid ourselves from over sixty percent of disease right now from the contaminants from meats & fish.

We can build extremely cheap housing for every man, women & child all over the world, right now using used plastic bags & rubble, right now.

We can power all of our power needs with available solar, using solar filaments along all roads, for all villages, towns, cities & countries right now.

We can power all of our cars using direct solar, using mono chrome solar filament, using the car body's shell as the direct solar panel & because ninety percent of all cars in the world are left outside to collect sunlight right now, but we won't, because we are just that greedy & irretrievably stupid!

Look in the mirror fools, do you really like, what you see?

We are now living in a world where you are either a part of the problems, or, you are a part of at least, some solutions.

For all those who nay say, about everything & are still wallowing in their own self putrid stupidity, this writer says, either try, to make a better world, planet, or shut up, as real history only recognizes the progress that real humans have achieved & to continually achieve for, all of humanity.

Fore out of nothing, brings forth nothing, for nothing, is nothing, if you only believe in nothing!

On this planet earth, & at this very time and moment in history, there are so many <u>MORONS</u> afoot; at this very time in history, they are making decisions about **you** & against **you**, against the total human experience, & that it is mind boggling.

Please note; *you are only a Moron, if you only spout vitriol, without offering real common sense solutions.*

Common sense solutions must always, be a part of any acts, or decisions in furtherance, of any common sense conversations in this twenty first century.

This writer is a **ghost in this world, but not alone**, with common sense real world plausible solutions.

In all of this writer's life's travels, tribulations & torments, I can truly say with good conscious.

*That I did in-fact **try**, to make a meaningful difference in this world & the next, as,*

There are historical & hysterical (FOOLS), destroying this planet &, this writer doesn't hear the outrage in their degenerative dispositions.

This writer has some; pragmatic ideas to at least make things better for all residence on this planet, as their ideas, are all meaningless & A-morally self serving. the current human race, so consumed with petty bickering & their smart phones, to recognize the imminent dangers we all are facing, at this very minute, of what little time, we all have?

Beware*; there is a vast, terrible & powerful storm approaching!*

Here are just a few of, this writer,' real world contributions for the twenty first century, as this writer has so many, to wit; see LinkedIn, E Clandestine.

@revised 1/12/2018 southwest water project

One way to help solve the drought & assist in natural power problems in the southwestern states;

After extensive calculation & assessments of hydraulic variables, in distance & travel of seawater, as transference of volumes of water naturally desalinated,

For example;

1- To naturally desalinate sea water using high pressure from a state from, (Sacramento California) to a distance of five hundred miles east of that location, following the west/east water trajectory of ocean currents in the Pacific Ocean.

2- To generate perpetual & continuous hydraulic power from that massive water flow, from a flow circumference of any eight foot tall piping system, it is estimated that a station, every two hundred & fifty miles, be constructed between systems to allow the maximum current management and energy for harnessing.

3- a tri-impeller apparatus at each station would harness electrical energy & monitor pressure & filter the osmotic effects of desalination.

4- In order to maximize the effects of fluid travel & safe operations of said system; a ground/ soil depth of no lower, than five feet below the surface of the ground in constant clearance at all times.

Each State would have three stations to benefit the maximum affects of:

A-Continuous fresh water, from natural high pressure desalination,

B-Natural electrical power generation from the high volume of seawater generated naturally into freshwater.

C- With the constant flow of high pressure seawater from following, west/east water trajectory, of ocean currents in the Pacific Ocean, no energy pumping is needed to operate this system, as only the maintenance of the osmotic filters at the stations & building & maintaining the system.

Feasibility projected, at the depths of no lower than one hundred feet, below the surface of the Ocean in that part of the world (Sacramento California), would generate a tremendous amount of high pressure & constant flow eastward of seawater to naturally desalinate and generate perpetual electrical energy.

In order to benefit the maximum results of from both natural energy & freshwater, Boring a piping system would start at the places or recipients of that system to the place of general origins of (Sacramento California), as such benefits of said, California, Arizona, Utah, Colorado, & etc.

Feasibility projected that thousands of jobs would be generated to states in benefits to build & constantly maintain the project.

Feasibility projected, each state would agree or be mandated, to an allotted consumption, of not energy, but fresh water flow.

In closing, this system would help in all droughts stricken areas. This system would help all growing population shifts, in the west & southwest.

Byproduct of this water project:

1- Impeller power generation, of high pressure/ volume as long as water is present.

2- byproduct of high pressure/volume of seawater after three membranes screening salt separation is saleable, salt for the country sea salt supply.

3- The continuous fresh water, enough for California, Utah, and Arizona, Colorado.

4- This system would help in the promotion of jobs at every state.

5- (Blue Energy), is a direct continuous result of desalination for salt water to fresh water.

This system, would help, address & assist in freshwater/power needs in all affected areas.

Total Theoretical concepts by;
Everett C Borders Jr. Ph.D.

E-cigarette type vitamin, drug and mouth/body odor delivery system @ 8/10/2018

Consider a methodology of delivering medicines, vitamins & eliminating mouth/body odor, aid in weight loss, in just one puff of an E-type cigarette.

The following proposal is a very healthy alternative to the **poison** that exists on the market right now. Synthesized serums can be made in any applicable Delivered E-type cigarette type systems.

Synthesized delivery systems, can be most easily made using today's pharmaceutical methodologies, in reference to vapor delivery systems.

Vapor delivery systems can cross the blood brain barrier in the human body as effective as needle injections.

Blood brain barrier/physiology

- A filtering mechanism of the capillaries that carry blood to the brain and spinal cord tissue, blocking the passage of certain substances.

Synthesis, on the atomic & sub-atomic levels of synthesis, can easily deliver additives as complete vitamins & vital medicines in a prescriptions cartridge, as parts per million or parts per billion, in low dose prescribed concentrations.

Issuing a one or two hour daily prescriptions cartridge would treat many ailments where drugs are to be administered.

Summary & results;

1- vapor that dissolves all plaque/ decay & calcium that cause bad breath & cavities in the human mouth.

2- vapor that strengthens human's lungs & circular systems with low doses of steroid medications.

3- vapor that delivers daily doses of a host of sorted medicines; pain, migraines, high blood pressure, diabetic.

4- vapor that administers natural odor controlling agents, like eucalyptus, peppermint, vanilla & etc.
   With every puff of the vaporized agents, 99.99% of all mouth & body odors could be controlled and eliminated, at the same time emitting a pleasant odor.

5- vapor that delivers aphrodisiac, crossing the human blood brain barrier into the blood system, increased stimulation in serotonin / dopamine responses.

6- vaporized vitamin & weight loss delivery systems.

Concept & proposal by;
Everett C Borders Jr. Ph.D. @

Interstate highway direct solar power strips@8/10/2018

There is about, three thousand miles from the coast of New York to the coast of Los Angeles.

Route ninety, route eighty, route seventy &, to the extreme northern boundaries of the United states, to the Gulf of Mexico & etc.

The United States needs a severe upgrade, in its energy grid to meet the needs of the new twenty first century needs of the populous.

This is one idea of methodology that might address two, cost effective needs of this new era.

Highway solar strips that run the length of all highways & interstates that can be cost effetely installed boosting, even overriding; all of the nations power grids.

1-solar strips are designed to work in series of succession & as if one panel fails, the system automatically by passes & goes to the next panel in succession, boosting the grid. Luminance solar panels have two functions

A; collect the suns energy & provides power 24/7

B; illuminates in the dark to mark all road systems without the need to exert more power from the grid, as Luminance is highly visible from dawn till dusk.

The system power grid is managed from state to state to best protect the overall grid integrity & security.

Simplistic, in its design with (positive fields) on one side of the highway & (negative fields) located on the other side.

This grid would allow power for Light rail systems, electric cars & bus commuting, &

boosting all local existing communities in & around the interstate, & large city systems.

Luminance solar panels strips run the length of the highways & interstates that they will serve.

All highway markings are replaced with Luminance solar panels strips to ensure in total continuity of the overall system.

For maximum cost effectives & to ensure the system peaks at an always eighty seven percent, all lighting, should be replaced by high yield /low cost led systems using the existing light pole apparatus.

All rural, urban & suburban communities can very easily, be retrofitted to match the overall grid using the existing technology & existing infrastructure to improve the needs of all three hundred & fifty million of residents in & around the United States.

Electric cars all need to rely on an energy converter to allow the cars to work after being purchased from the states.

Buses, trains & light rail will have their own type of converter to ensure in power continuity.

Conclusion;

This proposal by Dr. Borders address three scientific plausible & highly creditable scenarios:

1- adds a cost effective new power grid the whit & length of the entire United States.

2- Allows fully non autonomous, electrical vehicles, trucks, cars to travel along the grid with drivers using a purchased converter from the state.

Allows fully autonomous, electrical vehicles, trucks, cars to travel along the grid, using the grid power by way of an onboard converter, & exit the grid using their own battery, more over; regular vehicles using gas or diesel will use the same highways with no new obstructions or hazards, in any way.

Note; fully autonomous, electrical vehicles will all travel in the same middle lane, with contact strips embedded into the pavement of the center of the highway, & when exiting the highway electrical grid, the vehicles will automatically change to their own battery systems, or petro.

If the fully autonomous, electrical vehicles approach an obstruction, they will slow down & stop, allowing the onboard passenger to take command manually of the vehicles, any obstacle, within ten feet, the fully autonomous, electrical vehicles will stop & will not proceed until the passenger is fully apprised & can again manually take command of the vehicles.

More refined technology in fully autonomous, electrical vehicles in reference to guidance systems will become forthcoming with time.

3- residual power from the grid will be used to power all highway lighting systems, simply by changing to cost effective led's, using the same pole apparatus, even powering local towns, cities, & etc.

The massive amount of electrical power generated from to grid will be managed state by state to allow for the maximum security & more fluid continuity across each state.

All solar panels run the entire length of the highway with positive polarity on one side & negative polarity on the other on the other side, of the highway, with electrical contact strips & ground in the middle of the asphalt or highway to allow connections for electric cars & trucks using a converter.

Water or moisture, even snow, will not be a factor by reason of the fluidics of the grid matrix, as states such as California, Utah, Nevada, Arizona, New Mexico, Colorado, Texas, Oklahoma, offering year round peak power surges in the solar matrix being more than enough to add to the grid with less weather overcast, at intervals in other states, as all states contribute to the overall hive grid matrix.

By location, areas of the grid can be thermally controlled, allowing better ice melt, & more clearing of safer travels.

Ultimately, it envisioned that this solar electrical grid could totally replace the entire gasoline & diesel vehicles in and around the United States, in a total solar electrical grid network, using extremely cost effective methodologies & infrastructure that is already in place.

Ultimately, the goal is to drastically reduce the carbon foot print, virtually eliminating smog in the United States & on the planet.

This methodology makes electrical power a lot cheaper for all the government, counties, cities, towns.

The new nexus, in the new area of vehicle passenger, light rail, & cargo transportation & automation is at hand.

Final consideration; billions & billions of people all around the world are personally driving & moving cargo & flying all over the world all using, one hundred million year old lizard juice, using the same discards of petroleum in polymers, that's greatly polluting the planet in the year 2018.

Isn't it about time we all used a more common sense, cost effective, approach to our planets energy needs, if there will be a next generation.

This writer has conveyed plausible methodologies, to address the nexus of new energy (grid) needs, for the United States & the cost effective methodologies of the nexus needs in clean electrical (grid) transportation in and around the United States.

In this proposal, while testing, using a pilot program, one mile at a time, state by state, of total operations, to achieve the overall targeted goal.

Proposed concept by;

Everett C Borders Jr. Ph.D.

2019@

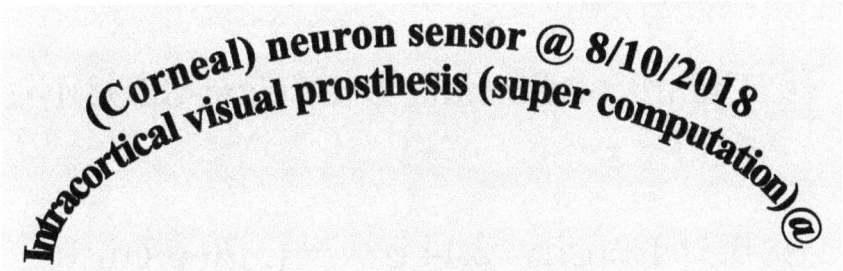

Just imagine a super computer that fits in a single glass of liquid, Water/emulsion solutions, with direct corneal interface by way of bio thermal activate contact lenses.

Variables of activation of liquid computer computations;

- ten millionth of a centimeter

- Sand grains particles (**silt particles**) smaller than 0.0625 mm down to 0.004 mm).

- **ALON** is optically transparent ($\geq 80\%$) in the near- ultraviolet, visible and mid-wave-infrared regions of the electromagnetic spectrum.

- Chemical formula (AlN) x•(Al2O3)1-x, $0.30 \leq x \leq$

- 0.37 Density: 2.14 oz/in³ (3.70 g/cm³)

- Simple glass of water, nutrient/ enzymes (fuel).

- Silica & aluminum / Silica Spherical(**Fused**) Particles

- Activity of bacteria through their multi-enzyme systems in splitting up the peptone in the medium into amino acids.

For starters, a single Fused Silica & aluminum / Silica Spherical Particles with the dimensions of less than (0.001 mm) for layer (Z) & continued layers (Y) & (X) until continued succession layers to (A) One Fused Silica & aluminum / Silica Spherical Particles can hold, Bio electrical/bacteria can form on a single layer of times (ten million) per particle.

Each (0.001 mm) particle can hold an estimate, ten million Bio-electrical/bacteria that float's on the top of said surface of a (**solution**) in question.

Bio-electrical (electromagnetic) conductivity precludes each particle to approximate no further than one half inch from the other.

At (0.002 mm) particles are (recessed) no more than one half inch depth, of solution in question.

In every recessions of strategic positioning per particle (0.001 mm) to (0.100 mm), electrical (electromagnetic) conductivity is achieved.

Activity or super computation is activated & manipulated by a layered system (independent) per layers to conduct instruction per layer & able to inter-connect with each layer simultaneously.

In laymen's terms; super computation is occurred by layers of trillions of signals per second (via) speed of (Bio-electromagnetic) electrical conductivity, of millions of manipulated electrical signals from the types of (solution & strength) or the (validity) of the (bio-electrical (electromagnetic) -**bacteria**).

(Please note) Intracortical visual prosthesis is achieved by the following two methodologies;

1. **(Rice size (interfaced) chip)** Implanted in a depth of four centimeters, over the orbital sac into the neuron receptors of any subject, as the (chip) is only a neuron- orbital (interfaced) receptor.

The **(chip)** is proxceminity & manually activated with four failsafe patterns.

Upon activation of the (**chip**), the interface from, Intracortical visual prosthesis (super computation) would carry out any instruction (**programmed**) by the (bio- electrical (**electromagnetic**) (Super-Computational Instructions) while immersed in –**bacteria solution**).

2- Less invasive direct corneal interface by way of (bio thermal) activated contact lenses, would operate in the same mannerisms.

3- (**bio thermally**) activated contact lenses, with direct corneal interface programmed to receive specified signals (microwave/ radio & sitcom) would directly receive information through (**corneal interface/ contact lenses**) could directly interface with the humans neurological stimuli (**directly to the normal brain functions**) of collecting (instructions, learning, etc).

Note# contact lenses would visually enhance the subject normal eyesight & coupled with interface would allow super instructions in super computational methodology.

Upon activation of the (**chip**), the interface from, Intracortical visual prosthesis (super computation) would carry out any instruction (**programmed instructions**) by the (bio-electrical (**electromagnetic**) (Super-Computational Instructions) while immersed in –**bacteria solution**).

(This) mannerism of (Super Computational) (methodology), does not need computer screens or hard drives, cables, Wi-Fi, & is extremely Mobil as it is replaced by the human body, as by way of using the individual (**bio-electrical rhythmic signals**) to operate its own bio-thermal electrical connections or (field).

Most of (Humans), learn through (our eyes), we receive (valued important) of our (**corneal interface lucent instructions**) of our five senses, through our eyes.

When making the relative comparisons on current computing methodology Vs (this model of computation);

A-no computer screen is needed as information is sent directly to the **(corneal interface)** (bio thermal) activated contact lenses, would operate in the same mannerisms.

B-normal vision would be enhanced through **(Bio- thermal spectral contact lenses)**, greatly magnifying range/thermal imaging/ digital distance while the wearer enjoys enhanced sight.

This **methodology** addresses several issues associated with the trappings of current computational methods:

1- enhanceing (bio-thermal activated) contact lenses for purposes of enhancer sight/ thermal imaging/range & directional seeking).

2- direct (**Bio-thermal corneal interface**), that replaces the (computer screen), as a more direct interface to the human neuron-network is the nexus phase of computation.

3- by using the above (**Variables of activation of liquid computer computations**) methodology, a super computational direct (bio-thermal interface) can be achieved.

4- This methodology can issue specific computational instructions while the subject is both (Lucent & **illucent**) in variable systematic rhythm cycles.

The methodology of this (**corneal interface**) is just an enhanced method of the human body's own natural reception & disseminations of vast collection & super computational information.

5- cost cutting effectiveness of (Lenses), as they are disposable & able to be (regenerated/recycled)

6- A single Fused Silica & aluminum / Silica Spherical Particles with the dimensions of less than (0.001 mm) for layer (Z) & continued layers (Y) & (X) until continued succession layers to (A)

One Fused Silica & aluminum / Silica Spherical Particles can hold, Bio electrical/bacteria can form on a single layer of times (ten million) per particle.

Each (0.001 mm) particle can hold an estimate, ten million Bio-electrical/bacteria that float's on the top of said surface of a (**solution**) in question.

Bio-electrical (electromagnetic) conductivity precludes each particle to approximate no further than one half inch from the other.

At (0.002 mm) particles are (recessed) no more than one half inch depth, of solution in question.

In every recessions of strategic positioning per particle (0.001 mm) to (0.100 mm), electrical (electromagnetic) conductivity is achieved.

Activity or super computation is activated & manipulated by a layered system (independent) per layers to conduct instruction per layer & able to inter-connect with each layer simultaneously.

Super computation is occurred by layers of trillions of signals per second (via) speed of (Bio-electromagnetic) electrical conductivity, of millions of manipulated electrical signals from the types of (solution & strength) or the (validity) of the (bio-electrical (electromagnetic) - **bacteria**).

Finally;

When making (**quantum**) comparisons relative to computing, it must be clear that this super computing is in no way compared to quantum-computing that is already underway.

However, this methodology offers an all new (**nexus phase**) in new computing methodology for the future phases in future concepts in super computation.

Theorical projections concepts by:

Dr. Everett C Borders Jr. Ph.D.

Linear space magnetic launch@8/10/2018

The sum of collective planetary intelligence has not caught up, with its real world creativity & potential, thus far.

Real creativity is at hand, in real world ideas to launch the nexus phase of earth space vehicles & vessels.

We are still launching & attempting use rockets that are destroying our upper atmosphere & are extremely limited in their use, not to mention extremely costly.

There are more pragmatic & highly creditable & plausible, methodologies that should be considered that will not only make earth based space launch more affordable, but by the volumes, to thrust this planet well into the twenty second century.

One idea to be considered is an earth based electromagnetic space launch.

The concept is simple in its presentation; Electromagnets attract or repel, thus positive to positive repels, as negative to negative pulls inward or attracts.

On this planet & at this very moment, we have a super conductor that can launch an earth based, space vehicle right now.

The field intensity of this super conductor has the power to mimic the gravitational pull of a black hole, either to pull or push.

For a moment, just imagine the power of a super electromagnetic energy burst that can launch an earth based vehicle, beyond three hundred linear miles into space.

This electromagnetic concept is just not limited to earth based space launch, but earths weapons linear launch & controlled guided reentry of the project thor, project Prometheus, lunar & deep space launched apparatus.

Electromagnetic bursts can be much more compartmentalized & Mobile, using a series of super capacitors, in series to maximize its desired affects.

Controlled magnetic bursts is nothing new to the scientific world, as past & continued real world experimentations are carried out daily, all over the world.

The desired effects are, being able to shoot or slingshot an object, any object, out of a cannon liked apparatus to a controlled space, any space.

This electromagnetic launching methodology can launch an item, earth based at a distance of more than six thousand linear miles, taking account of reentry & decent targeting.

In conclusion;

As we enter the perceives of the dawn, of the space age, it is necessary that a more pragmatic approach is kept in mind, rather that personal platitudes of grandiose, summations.

The military applications for magnetic rail mobile launch are highly cost effective.

For example; let's attempt to launch, using a mobile magnetic launcher with a baseball size probe, then a basketball size probe, then, a car size probe & etc.

Proposed concept by; Everett C Borders Jr. PhD

(New bold, Concept solar Car) 4-17-2018@

For the continued purposes, of this writers innovation edification's, the following new & pragmatic innovation is in conveyance.

We now have the technology to (all) moves forward, in extremely useful innovation, in aspects of the way we drive cars & trucks right now.

We all (want/demand), our cars to be or do, the following,

1- to be Safe,

2- to be economically, self-sufficient,

3- to be extremely reliable,

4- good looking, & virtually maintenance free operation, right?

This writer shall convey a new concept of innovation that may address all the above aspects, & address most pitfalls & failures, of all current cars to current date as of 4/17/2018.

Most current cars in the United States and the world get about at maximum, from twenty five to thirty five miles a gallon/MPG, in economy mode.

You might have some carmakers in *their (hybrid-lines (models)* that may get forty miles per gallon.

As of 4/17/2018, they currently have gasoline & diesel cars, which may get you (five hundred miles), on a tank full of gas.

As of 4/17/2018, the current (electric car) might get you, maybe, (one hundred & fifty miles), before it needs recharging, & only if you have a safe garage during recharging.

As of 4/17/2018, the most current electric cars, mostly, drive around with a (*large lithium ion battery*), that weighs half the cars weight, making it a possible danger of electrical field exposure or thermal compromise.

Some hybrid models, do have both electrical & gasoline/diesel powered components; however, improvements are franticly & currently still underway to deliver a virtually maintenance free & economical vehicles to the general public.

As gasoline is already up to over as of 4/17/2018 $3.00 per gallon of gas & $3.25 per gallon of diesel fuel.

But what if you could drive, all day & all night, (nonstop), not on gas but solar power and Gas?

One of, these writer Original concepts:

This Concept car

This car has three layers for the_(outer body) or hull/shell,

1st layer, is made of melted down used plastic bags,

2nd layer, the solar panels are made of is made of either, (*Mono-crystalline or, Polycrystalline panels wraps*),

3rd & final layer, (<u>*clear*</u>), *(heat thermal plastic)*, with infused (metal alloy (netting) mesh), for body/hull-shell rigidity), layered over the (Mono-crystalline or, Polycrystalline panels wraps).

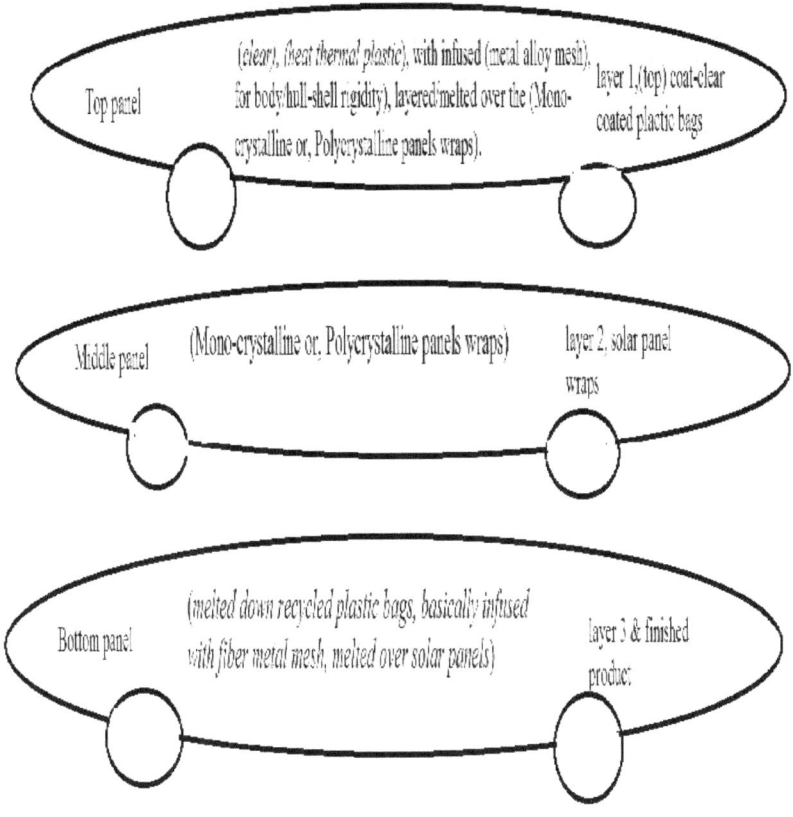

The car has a heavy-duty rigged (*aluminum alloy X-T- frame*), & only weighs twenty five hundred pounds at (*dry weight*), & has a normal truck battery only.

It has no, paint job, as the (infused metal alloy mesh (netting) fibers for body/hull-shell rigidity) has an iridescent color to appear different colors at different angles.

This body, of this car, is very easily repairable, as a section by section, replacement body panel process, as the results of repairs are, no dents, no repainting, & no cracks, just bolt on replacement parts only.

Hood, rooftop, truck lids fenders & doors are all bolt on replacement parts.

Part A-

A direct solar to power mode;

This concept allows the driver of this car to drive all daytime (*hours only, from just after dawn to dust*).

As long as there is (*sunshine*), this car will operate on the solar electric drive only, (*all day*), as the solar electric motor, is the first axle of operation of this drive train.

Part B-

After the (sunsets), & the driver wants to continue to drive, (part-b) will automatically switch to a small/alloy extremely compacted, one hundred horse powered, (gasoline or diesel) powered engine, producing 45miles per gallon.

For extended range, for an extended (*five hundred miles range per tank*) (*main fuel tank mode*), using normal auto drive train gears & transmission,

Part C-

For the ability to drive this car even further, this car is equipped with a third engine, a (*forty-nine* (*cc*) (*cubic centimeters*), engine to generate (*electrical current* **only**), to the electrical main drive motor, for an additional, (*seven hundred miles per tank*) (*reserve tank mode only*).

This car is equipped with a thirty five-gallon fuel tank/cell;

(Twenty gallons in part B mode and another fifteen gallons, in Part C- reserve mode.

As incredulously as this may sound, (*this concept car*) is made out of (*melted down recycled plastic bags, basically infused with fiber metal mesh (netting), melted over solar panels*), & heavy duty aluminum alloy frame, & will cost only $20.000 for the entire cost of a basic model.

Aspects ratio, of these concepts of innovations, is not just relative to only cars, but trucks, trains, planes, boats/ships, homes, building designs & etc.

In conclusion;

This writer has (not met), many people, on the planet, that drives more than (*eight hundred miles*), nonstop, at one time, like this writer.

This writers love of driving, & continuing sense of cutting edge innovation, has made possible, this current new innovational concepts, thus, a total new solar car.

Gas prices are going up, as the EPA rules of oversight are still on a dissolving posture before your very eyes, every day.

We have just began, to pierce the twenty-first century, as we can no more afford to remain stagnated to one failing idea after another.

We must forge ahead, with bold new ideas, as pragmatic as they are in-fact practical, as we do have the technology on this date of 4/17/2018.

With this writers car concept model, running out of gas will be a sweet memory, as this concept will leave a lot more $$ revenue in the car owners pockets & less time at the shop.

Oil companies, all around the world, all have the same agenda, they all want to sell you as much oil as they possibly can, (every day), it's how they maintain, maximum control;

1- they all control you, making you need <u>only them</u>,

2- they all have control over a part of your $ revenue daily,

3- Oil companies all around the world desperately needs its masses (you), to continue needing their oil, especially now, with the emergence of hydrogen, nitrogen, & other experimental fuel cell sources.

4- As of 4/18/2018, any new (auto-maker), or startup company, are preyed upon by the big three auto makers, as the oil companies are, (deep) in bed with them all.

They really don't want you to drive anything else as but their cars with lousy gas mileage & use as much gas & oil as possible.

This bold (new concept car), will drastically cut down on carbon emissions & promote a safer planet.

You either demand more out of your cars today, or you risk & (*possibly may pay, in the <u>very near future</u> $5.00 a gallon*), as your next new car may only get fifteen miles per gallon or less.

The biggest environmental problem that we all face as a world today is (**plastic**). We can use what is already here, (**used plastic**) & (**used scrap metal**), that is already here.

Solar cells are made of (**silica**, **sand**), something that we have an abundance of all around the world.

You decide.

No problems, No delays, No Bs, we can, or this writer can, do this right now.

Written & concepts, as of 4/17/2018 @by; Everett C Borders Jr. Ph.D.

Four Friends; Satire Skit

Juan, from **Rio de Janeiro, Alex,** from Moscow Russia, **Gabriel,** from Loire France, **Charles,** from the United States, four close friends, from four different parts of the world, in a Denver Colorado Chinese restaurant attempting, to order food.

Of the four friends, Charles & Juan, speak perfect English, as Alex & Gabriel speak terrible broken English. The conversation begins as follows;

Juan, ordered the Crab and Fish Stomachs, **Alex,** ordered the fried Pumpkin Dumplings, **Gabriel,** order the <u>Shark fin soup</u>, and, **Charles,** ordered the <u>Sichuan hotpot</u>.

Gabriel's food comes with a large soup spoon & so does the dish Alex ordered.

The serving waitress, is a twenty something women, native from Hong Kong who speaks perfect English.

The waitress brings the food & serves all four friends & begins the walk away.

The Chinese restaurant is crowded seating about fifty people.

The first to speak is;

Gabriel,

Very loudly,

AA,

No fooc?

Waitress,

Excuse me sir?

Did you need something else?

Gabriel,

I want fooc,

Right here,

Right now,

On the table!

Waitress,

Looking extremely puzzled,

I sorry sir,

I don't understand?

Gabriel,

fourchette

I want, fooc,

Right now,

Right here,

I want you fooc,

Alex,

<u>*vilka*</u>*!*

Began flailing both of his arms, Gesturing,

Haa, Yaaa,

Neeed to fuk,

No fuk?

Juan,

Smiling & not saying anything,

Charles,

Falls out of his chair laughing,

Gets up & says to the waitress, please, could we have more forks, please.

Waitress,

Looking extremely embarrassed & puzzled,

Directly looks at Charles & Says,

Thank you sir, so much?

She walks away & quickly returns with the forks.

Alex,

Looks at Charles & says,

Ahh,

She doesn't speak engi?

Wha?

Gabriel,

Smiling,

China,

She speaks china!

This is china house, right?

Juan,

Smiles & says,

Yes,

This is a Chinese house, my friend.

Charles,

Smiling, says,

How do you pronounce fork in Portuguese, Juan?

Juan,

smiles & says,

"Garfo" means fork in Portuguese.

Charles,

Laughs very loudly & says,

This, Is quite an experience, my friends,

I'm enjoying every minute of this.

Alex,

Laughing, says,

You *"stah-REEK"* Charles

"stah-REEK"

Charles,

With a big grin on his face, says,

I'm not that old,

At least not yet!

With big smile on his face, Looks at Alex & Gabriel, while

He starts bursting out with laughter.

You guys want to order dessert?

Waitress,

*She returns to clean up the table & looks at **Juan** & says,*

Any dessert sir?

Alex,

Looks at Gabriel & Charles, and then looks at the waitress & says,

Ahoo, Whaa,

I want, I need,

Gabriel,

*Looks at **Alex** & looks at the **waitress** & says,*

Do you bespeak in engi?

Waitress,

Once again looking confused & puzzled, says,

Sir,

Excuses me,

But I speak perfect English.

Charles,

Smiles, & says, Yes,

Yes, she does,

He then stares around the table & says,

Guys,

This food is on me & pays the check.

When the waitress returns, with **Charles** *credit card, She says, thank you & begins to walk away.*

Gabriel,

Smiles, at the women's behind & says, "Sans arrêt, sans cesse"

Charles,

Looks at Gabriel & says,

Let's go guys.

The Scene ends.

There is an inherent fellowship in the comradery, of all fellow human beings.

It transcends language,

It transcends culture & the order of natural regional perspectives per say.

This human fellowship is not bound by any race, creed, ideology or principles of socially constructed mannerisms.

The needs to commune, the rights to universally communicate, without any formal order, or any direct language,

In short,

Friendship is just friendship, No words,

No signs,

No problem. Written By,

Everett C Borders Jr. Ph.D.

Skit; 8/27/2014

Fix me up; Humor Skit

York & Everett talking, in our much younger 17 to 21 year old days,

York,

Ha man,

What's up with these girls you always introduce me to?

Everett,

What do you mean? What's wrong with them? There all fine, aren't they? **York,**

Sure Everett, but just different.

Everett,

Well York,

Nobody's really perfect are they?

York,

I don't know,

What about that girl that only wanted to get down, on the roof!

What about that girl you introduced me to with that crazy, ferret & wolf!

Oh,

What about that other one, IM loosing track,

And what about the other one that every time she woke up in my bed,

She kept touching my face & calling me, Dave in bed,

Didn't know who I was, & freaked out screaming, every time!

Everett,

Smiling & chucking,

When you sound like that,

It sounds like you're having bad luck with girl's man.

York,

Yea, the next time you set me up man,

Please upgrade.

Everett,

What about the one that you set me up with,

She was beyond crazy,

Let me ask you a question York,

Every girl that you ever introduced me to, All had their different ways, right?

York,

No more than most, Why?

Everett,

Why are all the ones you introduce me to, have the same habit of placing large oranges in their mouths?

York,

Burst out laughing very loud, spitting out his soda

What's the matter man? So she was vegetarian,

You know what they say about crazy girls,

Don't you? **Everett,** What? **York,**

Smiling & chucking,

They all need to talk to,

You & me man.

Everett,

Having six singing girls over Friday night at 7.

York,

Singers uh

Everett,

Smiling & chucking,

Well, this sounds like old times York, So three for you,

And three….three for me.

York,

Ha,

What was the name of that one, With the large oranges? **Everett,**

Why,

What do you want to do?

York,

Nothing,

Relax Everett,

Just forgot her name,

That's all.

Everett,

Don't go back there.

York,

Ha man,

IM still busy with the other crazies, You set me up with man.

Everett,

You got a point.

York,

Burst out laughing Large oranges? **Everett,**

Burst out laughing very loudly

Large oranges man.

Scene ends,

Youth,

The always part of a cognitive & what seems like the indelible age of a youthful male in both part of the blueprint of being an adult in gender bliss & sorrow.

Chemical response of the in the male brain & along with the testosterone levels at that age are as straight as an arrow.

As it is true that male sex drive the age of 17 is or 21 is extremely strong & more viral.

It is also true,

Those exceptions in great numbers of men,

Well into their 70s are just as comparatively, kinds of vigor & virility.

This skit is indicative of any youthful conversation both past & present in an ever-present gender inverse.

Written by,

Everett C Borders Jr. Ph.D.

Published @ 7/9/2013

Satire look at the real US Immigration Act of 2013

The following words & adverse opinions are indicative of real conversations around the US House of representatives, The US Senate and the streets homes, offices in the United States.

Chuck; an American black man, born & bred in the United States.

Juan; an Undocumented Male Latino, born in Guatemala

Rick; a white American male born & bred in the United States.

Lo_Cheg; an Asian Male, on US work Visa from China.

Hamed; a ale Arab who's US Visa expired two years ago.

All five men are having a one-hour lunch break from an Eastern Colorado factory job.

They are sitting together in the outside break area of the factory.

A spirited conversation is brought up by Hamed; a Male

Arab who's US Visa expired two years ago.

Hamed;

What the hell is wrong with this country, why don't they pass the Immigration bill?

Rick;

Why would you say, what's wrong with this country?

If things are not moving fast enough for you then maybe you should return to your own great country.

Hamed; what does that mean.

Juan; he's just confused about the American government system, he does not mean anything man, it's cool.

Lo_Cheg; the way I see it, the only ones that seem to have a problem with the immigration Act are the Mexicans.

Juan; why does it always have to be about Mexicans, why can it be about Russians or Chinese?

Rick; I don't believe what Im hearing, have you people ever thought about what the American people think about the Immigration Act?

Yes it's true, we are a nation of immigrants, but it took the United States four hundred years to get to this point.

Hamed; get to what point?

Rick; what I am saying is hundreds upon hundreds of thousands of people have fought, died and bled for this country for the rights to call themselves American citizens and no shortcuts, no backroom deals are acceptable in the eyes of the American public. If that were so, then everything that would make you an American, meaningless, get it.

Hamed; no, I don't get it; I want to be an American citizen just like you, what's wrong with that man?

Rick; nothing, we have laws to make that happen for everybody, one group of people is as just as good as another, right?

Lo_Cheg; we know you might want something so bad that you maybe think that you can't wait for it.

Every country has laws, rules regulations & restrictions about everything, right, so follow the rules and wait for your turn. You can't beat American citizens over the head to make them like you enough to change their rules man.

Chuck; two objects cannot occupy the same space at the same time.

Lo_Cheg; now you have something to say, after all this time.

Rick; yea, what in the world are you talking about man?

Hamed; Chuck just poised a physics solution, and he's right but I don't get the correlation from immigration to physics?

Juan; Ha, Chuck explain what you mean?

Chuck; we are not all a nations of immigrants. Some black people were already here on every continent and the rest brought here under the force of arms, making them prisoners not immigrants.

Ha Juan, people hate you just as much as they hate me for being here.

Ha Hamed, they hate you too, just for being an Arab, when they think of potential terrorists, they think of you. And you, Lo_Cheg, you're not immune from the blind hatred, being Chinese with the stigma of a country of property thieves.

At last we get the group of original haters, people that look like Rick.

Border immigration has come about on every continent for eons, an as we, the mental midgets of the human experience whose cranial composite only uses a micron of a percentage has the solutions but will not implement the necessary adjustments to alter what is truly needed for the resolve.

The solutions could not be simpler if only for the problems.

Rick; Ha, I resemble that remark (*with a hearty chuckle*).

Lo_Cheg; all this time saying nothing then dropping this bomb, man your something Chuck.

Juan; I think, I better understand now, how it is.

Hamed; do you really understand or are you just agreeing with Chuck.

I still need to be a Citizen, like yesterday!

Rick; you can't get blood from a stone.

Lo_Cheg; what kind of crack is that?

Juan; what's your meaning Rick?

Hamed; Rick's trying to be funny.

Chuck; stands up and walks over to the factory building outer wall. He places his head against the building wall and appears to listen.

He then motions, Hamed, Juan, Lo_Cheg, and Rick, to come and hear what he is hearing.

They all quickly approach the factory building and listen to the wall of the factory.

Rick; Ha man, I don't hear anything.

Chuck; *(smiles) & says* "it's been like that all day man" and returns to the break area *smiling.*

They all stare at Chuck with a smirk on their faces. Break time is over!

Written by
Everett C Borders Jr. Ph.D.

9/7/2012 @ Published

Semantically referencing to abnormal sexuality

This is a true very recent story about passing conversations at a local Laundromat.

While this writer was placing clothes in the dryer at the local neighborhood Laundromat, when a very attractive beautiful woman about twenty-six-ish approached me smiling & prancing making conversation about the washing machine, she did not know how to use.

She was having problems measuring the detergent amount and hot Vs cold washing cycles.

Revealing her personal life, she told this writer about being treated by a Psychologist for her addiction of smoking & alcohol use.

The Psychologist in question specialized in hypnotized therapy sessions.

While explaining her concerns with her treatment Psychologist, she revealed that she felt sort of an uncomfortable feeling at the end of each hypnotized therapy sessions. She further made admissions of her clothes at the end of each session being arranged different.

While she stated she had no visual, physical, noticeable marks or abrasions after each sessions, she felt an uncomfortable feeling.

When asked by this writer if she thinks the treatment Psychologist may have physically taken advantage of her, she replied, maybe.

The women further revealed that she wore a micro mini- skirt at each session with her treatment Psychologist as if that may have been a contributing factor in what may have happened while she was under hypnosis at the time.

Keep in mind at the time; she was wearing jeans at the Laundromat.

This writer being sympathetic and curiously inquisitive asked the woman the logical question; *"why would allow yourself to be hypnotized on a couch in a locked doctors office wearing a micro mini-skirt"?*

She replied, *"I don't know why I did that".*

She further explained that her cigarette smoking and alcohol drinking seemed to be diminishing after sessions with her treatment Psychologist.

As this writer was taking his clothes from the dryer, it became abundantly clear that woman knew how to effectively use the Laundromat without this writer's help.

It was also clear that she wanted and sought conversation & physical comfort & company from this writer at her time in the Laundromat.

In summary, as this writer folded clothes and attempted to leave the Laundromat, the woman offered to reveal her phone number and address.

She seemed both puzzled and noticeably uncomfortably insulted at denial of this writer failing her advances with her obvious extreme sexuality & beauty.

The premise of the initial conversation was not obscure but the contents of connotations were blatantly opaque in their transparency aberrations.

This writer submits that any potential relationship that ultimately starts in obscurity have a much greater risk of ending that way.

This writer submits at that time in the Laundromat and arriving in a mini-van and this writer clearly wearing a wedding ring made no difference to the woman in question.

It was if somehow, the story she told this writer about being possibly taken advantage of by her treatment Psychologist would make the woman more alluring.

As it was very true, the woman seemed to be shamefully beautiful & dangerously attractive & seductive.

It was also true that the woman sought kindness & comfort when ever & where ever she could.

It is also true that mental health encounters & circumstances are very common with even more frequency in today's world. The diminishing healthcare funding and the release of patients needing mental health care around the world are staggering.

With the known use affects of the use of increasing pesticides in high levels in foods and water, antiquated care of the mentally afflicted and the increasing use of microwaves, affecting the human psyche, Psychological, metaphorical platitudes of symbiosis in references of synthetic grandeur be it status quo.

Written by,

Everett C Borders Jr. Ph.D.

Skit; 1/2013 Published

One week after the 2013 presidential inauguration

The committee to elect the next president is forming just outside of Washington DC.

They are all meeting in an oval conference room sitting at an oval table.

Attending the meeting is, with very heavy ethic accents; A Chinese American woman,

An Irish American,

A Hispanic American,

An Arab American, A Jewish American, An African American, A Japanese American,

An American Indian woman, A Russian American woman,

An African American is chairing the meeting;

African American,

The meeting is now in order,

Well, whom shall we elect to the next presidential post?

Hispanic American,

I think this country should elect a Hispanic president! We should open the border to Mexico & allow everyone in this country.

Most of this country did belong to Mexico before

Europeans arrived, do you guys know that?

American Indian woman,

Why, you're not so special,

Indians have suffered for two hundred years, in our own country,

If anybody deserves to be the president, it's the American

Indians, right!

Jewish American,

Suffrage?

What suffrage, what do you people know about suffrage, the Jews have suffered for thousands of years, If any one deserves to be president, it's the Jews,
We have the right!

Japanese American,

Japanese people were slaves too you know, we want to be the president,
We have the same rights as everybody else.

Chinese American woman,

The Japanese were never slaves, they were placed in US interim camps at the Second World War for safety reasons after attacking this country.

You people have nothing coming!

Arab American,

America has bombed half of the Middle East,

Murdered our best terrorist leaders,

If anybody is going to be the president, it's going to be Arabs!

Jewish American,

You talk as crazy as you look!
This country will never ever elect an Arab,
You are in the wrong century friend.

Russian American woman,

Maybe it's time for a Russian US president?

Who could do better to lead the United States? We Russians know how to get things done right! I say elect a Russian American woman.

An Irish American,
Remember it was the Irish that ran this country remember
Ronald Ragan, look how great he was.
The Irish has suffered as well, remember the potato famine.

African American,
The potato famine,
You people are really dense!
What makes you people think that the American people will vote for whom they regard as crooks, & thieves,
Liars, money grubbers, murderous fanatics & bitter resentments of the past.
We are here to get some semblance of consensus whom to nominate for the next president, right!
So speak up or don't speak at all, please.

A **GREEK American** and **Brazilian American** enter the room.

Greek American,

What are you <u>bastagges</u> talking about?

Hispanic American,

We are not talking about you, so shut your mouth.

Brazilian American,

Ok, we are all here to find a new candidate for the next
US president,
So what have you came up with & don't try any <u>fargin</u> tricks you <u>soma-booches</u>.

African American,

No need to be rude, shall we continue the meeting;

Before you two arrived, we were attempting to get a majority consensus for a good candidate, Now who's next?

Irish American,

I think you all should consider to re-electing an Irish American to be president,
I think the historical references are profound & warranted to elect the next US president.

Jewish American,

Please, you guys, spare me the theatrics,
We are tired of alcoholics & leprechauns running this country,

We're not going to have a Greek, who can't even run their own country running this country,

We're not going to have the Russian Mob running this country,

We're not going to have the <u>Bol-ito</u> in America,

We're not going to have Japanese <u>egg rolls</u> or Chinese <u>egg fu young</u> in the White House,

No kabobs or buffalo soldiers or wigwams in the oval office, this time!

We need a Jewish president.

African American,
That's all well & good, but whom will we trust to take care of all the money, certainly not the Jews.

They all start laughing very loud & resume the meeting

Making a late entrance,
A Gypsy American, enters the room,

Gypsy American,

Sorry IM late for the meeting, but I just finished shopping at the mall,

Japanese American,

You mean lifting, at the mall

African American,

Well, that's it,
Why don't we elect the Gypsy American as the next president of the United States?
It's perfect,
They have no real country of origin, They are totally untrustworthy,
They are the biggest crooks & thieves,
They never ever wash & practice incest, inbreeding constantly,
And every word coming from their mouths is always a lie.

With a big smile/smirk on his face,

I think the meeting is now adjourned and we have picked our new next US president, we will continue to have this meeting in the next four years, we thank you all for attending the meeting and have a great day everyone, ok.

The African American, rises to his feet, closes his briefcase & leaves the room.

They all sit stunned & looking dumbfounded.

An American Indian woman,
What just happened?

Chinese American woman,
The same thing, when you people let Europeans in this country, skewered.

Greek American,
Bastagges, Your all Bastagges, you should be puun- nished! you somena butts.

Written by
Everett C Borders Jr. Ph.D.

End of all material.

WHATS THIS!

MOTHER
RITA

WHATS THIS

DAUGHTER
LETTERS TO MY FRIENDS

MOTHER
WHAT KIND OF FRIENDS
YOU'RE ONLY 12 YEARS OLD

DAUGHTER
MOM

I MET FRIENDS ON THE INTERNET

YOU NEVER LET ME GO ANYWHERE!

MOTHER
GO WHERE

YOU'RE TOO YOUNG TO DATE!

YOU'RE ONLY 12 YEARS OLD!

DAUGHTER
SO WHAT

I KNOWABOUT THINGS

MOTHER
WHAT THINGS

YOU HAD BETTER TELL ME EVERYTHING YOUNG LADY

I raised YOU TO BE PROPER & LADY like

DAUGHTER
MOM

I JUST MET SOME PEOPLE ON THE
INTERNET BECAUSE YOU NEVER LIKE
THE FRIENDS I BRING OVER

MOTHER
OK WHO ARE THESE FRIENDS

DAUGHTER
WELL THERE'S RICKY

HE'S A SECURITY GUARD AT THE
MALL.

HE WANTS TO TAKE ME TO THE MOVIES

MOTHER
YOU'RE NOT GOING ANYWHERE
YOUNG LADY

HOW DID YOU.MEET THIS PERSON

DOES HE KNOW HOW OLD YOU ARE

HOW OLD IS HE

IF HES A SECURITY GUARD

HE MUST BE AT LEAST 2OYRS OLD

DAUGHTER
BUT MOM

HE SAYS HE REALLY LIKES ME

MOTHER
ILL JUST BET HE DOES

WHO ELSE ARE YOU TALKING TO ON THAT COMPUTER?

DAUGHTER
WELL.

MY FRIEND SARA

SHE'S A DANCER

SHE'S RICH

SHE SAYS SE MAKES $500.00 a DAY

MOM CAN I SLEEP OVER SARAS HOUSE

SHE LIVES only two BLOCKS FROM HERE

MOTHER
WHAT,

HOOKERS,

PERPS,

LET ME SE WHATS ON THIS COMPUTER

WHATS THIS!

ADULT CHAT LINES

NUDE PHOTOS

GIVING YOUR ADDRESS OVER THE
INTERNET RITA

WHAT IS THAT ON TOP OF YOUR COMPUTER

DAUGHTER
An INTERNET CAMERA

I GOT IT FREE WHEN I SIGNED UP FOR THE CHAT UNES

MOTHER
WHAT

YOU MEAN PEOPLE CAN SEE YOU ON THIS THING

DAUGHTER

MOM

ONLY WHEN I TURN THE CAMERA ON THAT'S HOW! ET RICKY & SARA

MOTHER
THAT DID IT

IM TAKING YOUR COMPUTER

YOU'RE GROUNDED YOUNG LADY till FURTHER NOTICE

WHEN YOU'RE FATHER GETS HOME HE WILL REALLY GIVES YOU WHATS FOR

DAUGHTER
MOM

IM SORRY

I JUST WANTED TO MAKE FRIENDS

YOU AND DAD NEVER HAVE TIME FOR ME YOU NEVER LISTEN TO ME

YOU DONT LIKE MY SCHOOL FRIENDS

MOTHER
LOOK

IT'S NOT THAT WE DON'T LIKE YOUR FRIENDS

WE JUST WANT WHATS BEST FOR YOU

TO GROW UP WITH A GOOD EDUCATION & MAKE SOMETHING OF YOURSELF

DAUGHTER
HOW WILL I DO MY HOME WORK IF I DONT HAVE MY COMPUTER

MOTHER
DO IT AT SCHOOL

YOUR ALLOWED two HOURS A DAY FOR COMPUTER WORK AT THE SCHOOL LIBRARY

THEN YOU COME STRAIGHT HOME YOU GOT IT MISSY

DAUGHTER

YES MOM

WHAT ABOUT MY INTERNET FRIENDS

MOTHER

WHAT ABOUT THEM

DAUGHTER

CAN I LET THE KNOW THAT I CAN'T TALK TO THEM ANYMORE

MOTHER

NO

ILL Talk TO YOUR INTERNET FRIENDS

I WANT YOU TO TELL ME THAT YOU WILL NOT ATTEMPT TO CONTACT ANY PEOPLE ON THE

INTERNET

DAUGHTER
OK MOM

AM I STILL GROUNDED?

MOTHER
FOREVER

YOU NEVER LIED TO ME BEFORE SO DON'T START NOW

DAUGHTER
IM NOT LY1NG MOM

MOTHER
I KNOW

ILL GIVE YOU THE COMPUTER WHEN YOU PROMISE TO BE RESPONSIBLE

DAUGHTER
OK MOM

I WILL

END

LOOK & LISTEN TO YOUR CHILDREN

IF THEY ARE ACCESSING THE INTERNET MONITOR THEIR ACTIVITY

TENS OF THOUSANDS OF CHILDREN ARE MISSING AND EXPLOITED EVERY YEAR

REMEMBER,

IF YOU NEGLECT YOU CHILD NOW THEY MAY NEGLECT YOU TOMORROW SO, OPEN YOUR EYES

OBSERVE

LISTEN

PAY ATTENTION

TALK TO YOU SONS & DAUGHTERS

FOR THEY ARE THE FUTURE OF US ALL

WRITTEN BY EVERETT C BORDERS JR.

WE KNOW EVERYTHING

MARK
WHY ARE GROWNUPS ALWAYS TELLING US WHAT TO DO

RICK
CAUSE YOU NEED SOMEONE TO TELL YOU WHAT TO DO MAN

YOU'RE STRANGE

CARMEN
WHAT ARE YOU TALKING ABOUT MARK

WHAT DO GROWNUP TELL YOU TO DO

MARK

WHEN TO GO TO BED

WHEN TO WAKE UP

WHEN TO EAT

WHAT TO EAT

WHAT NOT TO EAT

WHEN TO LOOK AT TV

WHAT NOT TO LOOK AT ON TV

WHEN TO GO TO SCHOOL

WHAT TO LEARN

HOW TO LEARN

WHAT TO WATCH WHEN I GO TO THE MOVIES

WHAT KIND OF FRIEND'S

WHAT KIND OF FRIENDS CAN VISIT

WHAT TIME TO LEAVE

WHAT TIME TO COME HOME

WHAT CLOTHES TO WEAR

WHAT KIND OF HAIR STYLE TO WEAR

IM SICK OF GROWN UPS TELLNG ME
WHAT TO DO

RICK
LET'S SEE MARK

IF YOU DIDNT HAVE YOU PARENTS
WAKE YOU UP IN THE MOURNING

YOU WOULD NEVER GET UP

YOU CAN'T EVEN GET UP WITH YOUR
ALARM CLOCK

THAT LAST TIME I STAYED OVER AT
YOUR HOUSE

THE ALARM CLOCK RANG FOR A HALF
AN HOUR AND I HAD TO SHUT IT OFF

IF YOU'RE PARENTS DIDNT WAKE YOU UP IF YOU CAN'T GET UP TO GO TO SCHOOL YOU CAN'T LEARN ANYTHING

THAT MAKES YOU A STUPID PERSON THAT CAN'T GET UP TO ATTEND SCHOOL

THAT MEANS YOU WOULD NEVER ATTEND SCHOOL ON TIME

SO THAT MEANS YOU WOULD FLUNK SCHOOL & GET KICKED OUT

BECOMING A BUM OR A PUNK OR A CRIMINAL

RICK
WHEN YOU BECOME A CRIMINAL

EVERYBODY WILL TELL YOU WHAT TO DO

THE COURTS

THE POLICE

THE PROBATION OFFICER

THE JAILS

THE INMATES

THINK ABOUT IT MAN

THINK ABOUT IT

CARMEN
RICK HAS A POINT, I THINK

LOOK MARK

NO BODY LIKES TO BE TOLD WHAT TO
DO

BUT WERE KIDS

WE NEED TO LEARN

WE NEED TO BE TOLD SOMETHING

OR WE MAY LEARN THE WRONG WAY

MARK

WHAT DO YOU MEAN

CARMEN

REMEMBER THAT LABRADOR

THAT YOU GOT LAST YEAR

MARK

YES

I GOT THOR WHEN HE WAS A PUP

CARMEN

WELL REMEMBER WHAT YOU TOLD ME WHEN YOU FIRST GOT HIM

HOW HARD IT WAS TO TRAIN HIM TO GO ON THE PAPER

IT TOOK YOU MONTHS TO TRAIN THAT DOG TO DO JUST THAT

MARK

WHATS YOUR POINT

CARMEN

WELL MARK

THINK OF HOW LONG IT TOOK YOUR BABY SISTER TO LEARN TO POTTY TRAIN

MARK

WHATS YOUR POINT

WHY ARE YOU MAKING A COMPARISON

WITH MY SISTER & MY DOG

WHAT ARE YOU TRYING TO SAY

THAT MY SISTER IS LIKE MY DOG?

WHAT

CARMEN

NO BUTT HEAD

WHAT IM TRYING TO SAY IS THIS,

YOUR DOG HAD TO LEARN TO POTTY
TRAIN

YOU HAD TO TRAIN HIM

WHAT WOULD HAVE HAPPENED IF HE
NEVER LEARNED

MARK

HE WOULD HAVE CRAPPED ALL OVER
THE HOUSE

CARMEN

AND YOU BABY SISTER

WHAT WOULD HAVE HAPPENED IF SHE
NEVER LEARNED TO POTTY TRAIN

MARK

SHE WOULD CRAP IN HER DIAPER

SHE WOULD WEAR DIAPERS FOR THE REST OF HER LIFE

CARMEN

MARK DO YOU SEE WHAT I MEAN

WITHOUT THE RIGHT LEARNING WHAT WILL WE BECOME?

RICK

YEA MAN

IF YOU'RE PARENTS DIDNT DRESS YOU

YOU WOULD COME TO SCHOOL LOOKING FUNNY EVERYDAY

CARMEN

RICK STOP MAKING FUN

NOT EVERYTHING THAT GROWNUPS TRY & TEACH US WILL SINK IN

MAYBE IT WILL SINK IN LATER

BUT A LOT OF WHAT THEY SAY MAKES SENSE,

BE HONEST,

GROWNUPS SPEND A LOT OF TIME & ENERGY TEACHING & TELLNG US WHAT TO DO WHY DO YOU THINK THAT'S SO MARK

MARK
I DONT KNOW

BECAUSE THEY WANT THE BEST FROM US I GUESS

CARMEN
SAY WHAT

MARK

YOU KNOW WHAT I SAID CARMEN

IM NOT GOING TO REPEAT IT

I SEE YOUR POINT

I ACKNOWLEDGE

THE LEARNING METHOD OK!

RICK

CAN YOU ACKNOWLEDGE THAT

YOU CANT SEE R RATED MOVIES ONLY
PG MOVIES MARK

CARMEN

STOP IT RICK

MARK

HEY

YOU GUYS

I WAS I A LITTLE MAD CAUSE MY PARENTS WON'T LET ME STAY OUT WITH BOB & STEVE AFTER 10 PM

RICK

BOB & STEVE

THOSE GUYS ARE CRIMINALS

THEY JUST GOT OUT OF JAIL OR DETENTION OR WHAT EVER

WHY WOULD YOU WANT TO HANG WITH THOSE GUYS

THEIR LOSERS MARK

CARMEN

IF YOUR PARENTS SAID NO TO HANGING WITH BOB & STEVE THEN THEY KNOW SOMETHING THAT MAYBE YOU ARE OVERLOOKING

MARK
LIKE WHAT

CARMEN
I DONT KNOW

BUT YOUR PARENTS CAN SEE IT SO
CAN RICK

RICK
YEA MAN

I CAN SEE EVERYTHING

MARK
ENOUGH SAID GUYS

I GOT IT

LEARN FROM THE ELDERS

FOR THEY CONVEY THE BUILDING
BLOCKS TO EXPAND OUR MINDS

THEY HAVE A SPECIAL KNOWLEDGE

THAT HAS BEEN PASSED DOWN FROM ONE GENERATION TILL THE NEXT & THE NEXT

TO BE IN THE KNOW

IS WHAT IT'S ALL ABOUT SO EITHER YOU KNOW

OR

YOU DONT KNOW REMEMBER,

KNOW ONE EVER KNEW IT ALL NO ONE,

IF THEY DID THEY WOULD STILL BE HERE,

IF WE EVER LOSE SIGHT OF THE IMPORTANCE OF LEARNING & KNOWLEDGE

THEN WE AS THE HUMAN RACE WILL FOREVER LOSE OUR DIRECTIONAL PURPOSE.

WRITTEN BY EVERETT C BORDERS JR@

Use Your MIND

TOM

HEY SAM,

FOUND MY DADS GUN IN HIS CLOSET

SAM

SO

TOM

SO LET'S GO SHOOT IT

SAM

NO THANKS MAN,

GOT ENOUGH TROUBLE

TOM

STOP ACTING LIKE A PUNK,

EVERY TIME YOU ASK ME TO DO
SOMETHING WITH YOU

I DO IT,

DON'T I

SAM
WELL OK

BUT WE GOT TO BE REAL CAREFUL,

IM ALREADY IN TROUBLE WITH MY
FOLKS FOR THAT SHOPLIFTING STUFF

TOM
LET'S SEE HOW MANY CANS YOU
SHOOT OFF THAT BOX

SAM
THAT'S THREE FOR ME AND

TWO FOR YOU,

PRACTICE MAKES PERFECT!

TOM
HEY MAN SEE THAT SQUIRREL ON THAT PHONE LINE,

LET'S SEE IF YOU CAN HIT IT?

SAM
THAT'S DANGEROUS MAN

IF I MISS,

I MIGHT HIT SOMETHING ELSE

TOM
PUNK!

YOU CAN'T SHOOT ANYWAY

ILL SHOW YOU HOW TO SHOOT

SAM

HEY MAN

YOU JUST SHOT THAT WINDOW IN
THAT HOUSE ACROSS THE STREET

TOM
WE BETTER SPLIT,

BEFORE THEY CALL THE COPS

SAM
HEY TOM

HURRY HOME & PUT YOUR DADS GUN
BACK WHERE YOU FOUND IT,

OR WERE IN BIG TROUBLE

TOM
I KNOW MAN

SAM

HEY TOM

I SAW THE AMBULANCE AT THAT HOUSE

TOM

WHAT HOUSE

SAM

THE HOUSE YOU SHOT

FOOL!

TOM

OH MAN

IM SCARED

HOPE I DIDN'T HURT ANYBODY

SAM

I DON'T KNOW WHY I LET YOU TALK ME INTO THAT STUPID IDEA ANYWAY

TOM

LOOK

NOBODY TWISTED YOUR ARM

SAM

LOOK MAN

YOUR FATHERS OVER THEY'RE TALKING TO THE PEOPLE IN THAT HOUSE

TOM

MAN

I WONDER IF HE KNOWS

SAM
WERE DEAD IF HE DOES

TOM
IF WE EVER GET OUT OF THIS

ILL NEVER TOUCH A GUN FOR AS LONG
AS I LIVE,

THAT WAS SO STUPID OF ME

SAM
HEY TOM

IM GOING HOME CALL YOU LATER
CALL IF ANYTHING HAPPENS

TOM
YOU KNOW IT

SAM

LOOK MAN YOUR DADS LEAVING THAT HOUSE

TOM

HEY SAM

YOU KNOW WHY THAT AMBULANCE WAS AT THAT HOUSE WE SHOT,

MY MOTHER WAS VISITING THOSE PEOPLE AND FAINTED,

THEY TOOK HER TO THE HOSPITAL

SAM

SO NO ONE GOT HIT

TOM

NO MAN

THEY ALL WERE DOWN STAIRS

SAM
LUCKY,

WE GOT REAL LUCKY MAN

TOM
Y DAD DOESN'T KNOW

IM NEVER TOUCHING THAT GUN EVER!!

SAM
GOOD IDEA MAN

TOM
I COULD HAVE SHOT MY MOTHER

I WOULD NEVER FORGIVE MYSELF IF THAT HAPPENED,

MAN WHAT A CLOSE CALL

SAM

YOU DIDN'T SO LET'S LEARN FROM
THIS OK

TOM

YEA

GUNS ONLY KILL,

THAT'S ALL, KILL

SAM

LET'S PLAY SOME BASKETBALL

TOM

OK

ILL SPOT YOU 10 POINTS

SAM

YOU WON'T SPOT ME NOTHING

YOUR NOT THAT GOOD

GUNS

ON THE OTHER END OF THE BARREL IS ALWAYS DEATH,

FOR THE PEOPLE WHO HAVE USED GUNS TO HURT & MAME,

LAYS THE COUNTLESS VICTIMS IN THEIR WAKE, WE LIVE IN UNCERTAIN TIMES WHERE

DECISIONS THOUGHT

SOMETIMES ARE DECISIONS LOST

NO AMOUNT OF ENFORCEMENT

NEW LEGISLATION

PROTESTING TO BAN GUNS WILL EVER CHANGE THE MENTAL STATE OF A PERSON GONE WRONG

THOUSANDS UPON THOUSANDS OF PEOPLE HANDLE AND USE GUNS DAILY

THEY ARE RESPONSIBLE AS WELL AS SENSIBLE,

EDUCATIONS IS LIKE MORALITY

IT BEGINS IN THE HOME A CHILD TAUGHT WELL

IS A PERSON THAT'S USUALLY MORALLY STRAIGHT

END

WRITTEN BY EVERETT C BORDERS JR, @

THOU SHALL NOT!

MALCOLM
HEY LAWRENCE

NOW YOU KNOW THE PLAN RIGHT

ILL DISTRACT THE STORE CLERK &
YOU SNATCH THE WATCHES

LAWRENCE
I DON'T KNOW ABOUT THIS MAN

WHY DON'T YOU SNATCH THE
WATCHES

MALCOLM
CAUSE IM GOOD AT DISTRACTING
PEOPLE

WHATS YOUR PROBLEM MAN

LAWRENCE

I DON'T WANT TO GET BUSTED MAN

I NEVER GOT IN TROUBLE & I DONT
WANT TO START

MALCOLM

HOW CAN YOU GET BUSTED

WHEN THE STORE CLERK IS LOOKING
& TALKING TO ME

LOOK MAN

WE CAN SELL THOSE WATCHES FOR
ONE HUNDRED DOLLARS EACH

I DON'T KNOW ABOUT YOU BUT

I COULD USE THAT MONEY

AS MUCH AS YOU ALWAYS COMPLAIN
ABOUT BEING BROKE

WHAT ELSE ARE WE GONNA DO

LAWRENCE

THERE'S GOT TO BE A BETTER WAY OF
MAKING MONEY

IM NOT A THIEF MAN

MALCOLM

NO ONES SAYING YOU'RE A THIEF

THIS IS OUR Opportunity TO MAKE A
LITTLE MONEY AND WERE GONNA
TAKE IT

LAWRENCE

I DON'T KNOW IF I CAN DO THIS MAN

SOMETHING MAY GO WRONG, THEN
WHAT

MALCOLM

WHAT COULD GO WRONG MAN

ILL TALK TO THE STORE CLERK

KEEP HER BUSY

YOU PLAY LIKE YOUR LOOKING AT A RING OR SOMETHING

AND SNATCH A FEW ROLEX WATCHES WHAT COULD BE EASIER

BY THE TIME THEY NOTICE ANY THINGS MISSING

WILL BE TWO DAYS GONE

PIECE OF CAKE MAN RELAX

LAWRENCE
ROLEX WATCHES ARE EXPENSIVE

THEY COST OVER FIVE THOUSAND DOLLARS A PIECE

YOU WANT ME TO GRAB A HANDFUL OF ROLEX WATCHES

IF I GET CAUGHT

IT'S A FELONY OFFENSE

IM STILL IN HIGH SCHOOL MAN

I DON'T WANT TO RISK MY LIFE & FUTURE TO DO SOMETHING THIS STUPID

MALCOLM
IS IT STUPID TO MAKE A LOT OF MONEY, QUICK!

LAWRENCE
THE PRICE IS TO HIGH MAN

IF I GET CAUGHT

IM IN DEEP TROUBLE FOR A LONG TIME YOU

YOU WON'T GET ANY TIME AT ALL IT'S ME TAKING ALL THE RISK

ILL WORK & EARN MY MONEY COUNT ME OUT MAN

MALCOLM

OK MAN YOU DISTRACT THE STORE CLERK

AND ILL SNATCH THE WATCHES IS THAT BETTER MAN

LAWRENCE

DON'T THINK SO

COUNT ME OUT

MALCOLM

SO YOU DON'T WANT TO DO THIS

EVEN IF I TAKE ALL THE RISK?

LAWRENCE

NO MAN

THAT SHOE WAREHOUSE IS HIRING

LET'S APPLY FOR A JOB

MALCOLM
THEY HIRE KIDS OUR AGE?

LAWRENCE
YES

WE BOTH HAVE WORK PERMITS
BESIDES

WE CAN GET DISCOUNTS ON GYM
SHOES

MALCOLM
SOUNDS GOOD

WHEN DO YOU THINK WELL GET PAID

LAWRENCE
WE GET PAID WHEN WE DO THE WORK
MAN

MALCOLM
HEY LAWRENCE

YOU KNOW SOMETHING MAN

I REALLY DIDN'T WANT TO STEAL FROM THAT

JEWELRY STORE ANY WAY I WAS SCARED

LAWRENCE
NEITHER DID IMAN

NEITHER DID I

CONSEQUENCES

ALWAYS OUT WEIGH HEAVY WITH RISKS

IF YOU TAKE OF WHATS NOT YOURS

THEN ALWAYS REMEMBER THAT THERE ARE THOUSANDS UPON THOUSANDS

OF PEOPLE IN JAILS & PRISONS WHO

TOOK THE RISK OF TAKING FROM OTHERS AND FAILED!

WRITTEN BY EVERETT C BORDERS JR. @

THE COMPROMISE

DAVID
DAD!

ROBERT HAS MY WATCH

ROBERT

DAD!

I TOOK DAVIDS WATCH BECAUSE HE HAS MY BLACK SOCKS

DAVID

YOU DIDNT HAVE TO TAKE MY WATCH

YOU COULD HAVE TAKEN SOMETHING ELSE

ROBERT

YOU DIDN'T HAVE TO TAKE MY BLACK SOCKS

YOU COULD HAVE TAKEN SOMETHING ELSE

DAVID

GIVE ME MY WATCH

AND YOU CAN HAVE YOU BLACK SOCKS

ROBERT
OK

HERE'S YOUR STUPID WATCH

NOW GIVE ME MY SOCKS

DAVID
I CAN'T

IM WEARING THE SOCKS

ROBERT
WHY YOU DIRTY,

GIVE ME MY SOCKS

DAVID
CAN I BORROWTHEM.

ROBERT
NO

GIVE ME THE SOCKS DAD!

DAVID HAS MY SOCKS & WON'T GIVE
THE BACK DAD!

DAVID
WHATS THE BIG DEAL

ILL GIVE THEM BACK AFTER I VE WORN
THEM

ROBERT
YOU'RE CRAZY

IF YOU THINK YOU ARE GOING TO
WEAR MY SOCKS & GIVE THEM BACK,

ALL STINKY & DIRTY DAD!

DAVID
TELL YOU WHAT

IF YOU LET ME WEAR YOUR BLACKS
SOCKS TODAY,

YOU CAN WEAR MY NIKES THAT YOU
LIKE SO MUCH TOMORROW,

DEAL

ROBERT
DEAL

DAVID
HEY ROBERT,

WHERES MY TOMMIE HILL SHIRT

ROBERT
I LET RACHEL WEAR IT

ROBERT
WHAT

YOU DID WHAT DAD!

DAVID

WHATS THE BIG DEAL DAVID

RACHEL IS MY GIRLFRIEND

SHE WON'T LET ANYTHING HAPPEN
TO the SHIRT, CHILL

ROBERT

YOU CHILL,

WHERE DO YOU GET OFF GIVING MY
CLOTHES TO YOUR GIRLFRIEND,

I DONT EVEN LET MY GIRLFRIEND
WEAR MY CLOTHES

DAVID

REMEMBER THE TIME YOU GAVE MY
RING TO SHERRIN,

I NEVER DID GET IT BACK

ROBERT

SO WHATIS THIS JAPAYBACK

DAVID

NO MAN

I WAS GOING TO GET THE SHIRT BACK

ROBERT

YOU SAID THAT ABOUT MY RING
REMEMBER

DAVID

WHATS YOUR PROBLEM ANYWAY

NO HARM,

NO BIG DEAL, CHEER UP

ROBERT

YOU CHEER UP,

I WANT MY SHIRT BACK, TOMORROW,
UNDERSTOOD

DAVID
UNDERSTOOD

ROBERT
HEY DAVID

IF YOU CAME TO ME & ASKED FIRST, I
WOULDNT GET UPSET

DAVID
YEA

SORRY

ROBERT
NO PROBLEM BRO,

TELL YOU WHAT,

ILL GET THE SHIRT FROM RACHEL,
TOMORROW

DAVID
NO YOU WON'T

ILL GET THE SHIRT FROM RACHEL

YOU'RE NOT TALKING TO MY GIRL

ROBERT
HEY DAD

ME & DAVID WORKED THINGS OUT
YOU DONT HAVE TO COME IN HERE!

DAVID
YEA DAD

YOU DONT HAVE TO GET INVOLVED
OK

SIBLING RIVALRY

THE UPS & DOWNS OF LEARNING TO GET ALONG WITH YOU'RE BROTHER OR SISTER

YOUR BROTHER OR SISTER SEE YOU THE WAY YOU REALLY ARE

WITH ALL YOUR HANG UPS

ALL YOUR FAULTS

ALL THE THINGS THAT YOU ATTEMPT TO HIDE FROM THE REST OF THE WORLD

THEY SEE & KNOW IT ALL ABOUT YOU

SO TRY TO UNDERSTAND GET ALONG

FOR UNDERSTANDING THEM

YOU BEGAN TO UNDERSTAND YOURSELF

WRITTEN BY EVERETT C BORDERS JR. @

TEEN CLICKS CHEERLEADERS—

CHEERLEADER—1
LOOK IT'S THAT NEW GIRL CHRISTY

CHEERLEADER—2
SHE THINKS SHES SOO CUTE

CHIEERLEADER—3
I SAW HER WITH YOU BOYFRIEND AT LUNCH

CHEERLEADER—1
LARRY!

YOU SAW HER WITH LARRY!

CHEERLEADER—3
YES

AND THEY WERE ALL LOVY DOVY

CIIEERLEADER—2
LOOKS LIKE YOU HAVE COMPETION

CHEERLEADER—1
NO I DONT

CHEERLEADER—1
WELL SEE ABOUT THAT

CHRISTY
WALKS BY CHEERLEADERS

CHEERLEADER—2
HA CHRISTY

LARRY YOUR NEW BOYFRIEND?

CHRISTY
NO

JUST FRIENDS

CHEERLEADER—1
STAY AWAY FROM MY BOYFRIEND

CHRISTY
WHO LARRY

HES ONLY A FRIEND

CHEERLEADER—3
MESSING AROUND WITH SOMEONE
ELSES PROPERTY CAN BE HAZARDOUS

CHRISTY
WHAT DOES THAT MEAN

Cheerleader—2
IT MEANS

IF WE SEE YOU WITH LARRY AGAIN
YOUL BE VERY SORRY

CHRISTY
WHATS THE MATTER

YOU CAN'T KEEP YOUR MAN HAPPY

CHRISTY
CAN I TALK TO YOU IN PRIVATE

CHEERLEADER—1
ABOUT WHAT

CHRISTY
LOOK IM SO SORRY

I WAS JUST TALKING

I DIDN'T KNOW LARRY WAS YOUR BOY
FRIEND HE DIDN'T TELL ME HE HAD A
GIRLFRIEND & I

DIDN'T ASK

SORRY

I DIDN'T KNOW

CHEERLEADER—1
OK

NO HARM DONE

IVE HAD TRUST PROBLEMS WITH
LARRY BEFORE

CHRISTY
EVERYTHINGS COOL THEN
CHEERLEADERS HEY

EVERYTHINGS COOL GIRL

CHEERLEADER—1
WOULD YOU LIKE TO GET ON THE

CHEERLEADERS SQUAD I COULD VOTE
YOU ON

CHRISTY
ID LOVE TO GET ON THE TEAM

HEY

THANKS A LOT

CHEERLEADER—I
COME DOWN TOMORROW AT PRATICE
WELL SEE WHAT YOU GOT

CHRISTY
TOMORROW THEN

END

UNDERSTANDING TEAMWORK

ONLY WHEN A DIRECT CONFRENTATION TAKES PLACE MAY WE COME TO TERMS WITH THE MEANING OF LEARNING TO GETTING ALONG & UNDERSTANDING OTHERS,

SCHOOLS ARE AN OCEAN OF CONFUISON & MISUNDERSTANDINGS

IT'S A LEARNING PERIOD FOR FUTURE EVENTS,

TRY TO ALWAYS LOOK AT BOTH SIDES

WRITTEN BY EVERETT C BORDERS JR~

SUSPICION

GUY
HI BABY

DID YOU MAKE IT TO THE CLEANERS?

GIRL
NO

I WORKED LATE

BY THE TIME I GOT TO THE CLEANERS IT WAS CLOSED

GUY
REALLY

GIRL
WHAT DOES THAT MEAN

GUY
0H NOTHING

GIRL
HONEY

YOU ANGRY ABOUT THE CLEANERS

GUY
NO

GIRL
HONEY

WANT ME TO GO AND GET SOME
VIDEOS FROM THE STORE

GUY
OK

GIRL
HONEY

IM BACK

THOSE LINES AT THE STORE TOOK
FOREVER HONEY YOU MADE DINER
IM SO HUNGRY

GUY
YOU CHANGE YOUR COLOGNE

GIRL
NO WHY

GUY
YOU LEFT FOR THE STORE SMELLING
LIKE OBSESSION COLOGNE

AND NOW YOU SMELL LIKE POLO

GIRL OH

I SPRAYED SOME MENS COLOGNE ON
MY ARM TO CHECK IT OUT IN THE
STORE

GUY
HOW WAS IT

GIRL
I IKED IT

I WAS GOING TO GET YOU SOME

GUY
WHAT MOVIES DID YOU GET

GIRL
MATRIX & CRUEL INTENTIONS

GUY
GOOD

GIRL
DINNER WAS GREAT HONEY

GUY
ILL DO DISHES

GIRL
THAT'S SO SWEET HONEY

I REALLY LOVE YOU GUY

WHO IS VICTOR SIMMs

GIRL
WHY

HES a GUY THAT WORKS AT THE OFFICE
WHY YOU ASK?

GUY
HIS RENTAL SLIP FOR MOVIES ARE IN
OUR VIDEO BAG

GIRL
OH THAT

HE WAS IN THE VIDEO STORE IT WAS
NOTHING,

WE SPOKE WHY

GUY
OH NOTHING

GIRL
YOU JEALOUS HONEY

GUY
OVER WHAT

IM NOT INSECURE

GIRL
YOU COULD BE SECURE & JEALOUS AT
THE SAME TIME

GUY
NOT THIS GUY

BY THE WAY

I STOPPED BY YOUR OFFICE TO TAKE
YOU TO LUNCH

THEY SAY YOU TOOK OFF TODAY

GIRL
I DID FIELD WORK TODAY HONEY
WENT OUT MAKING SALES CALLS

GUY
SO

HOW WAS WORK TODAY

GIRL
IT WAS OK

WHAT TIME DID YOU STOP BY HONEY

GUY
10:30AM

GIRL
HONEY

IT WAS SO SWEET OF YOU TO DRIVE ACROSS TOWN TO TAKE ME TO LUNCH

WHERE WERE WE GOING TO LUNCH

GUY
THE PARKVIEW MOTEL

I HEARD THEY HAVE GREAT ROOM
SERVICE

GIRL
WHY THAT PLACE

GUY
THEY HAVE A GREAT BUFFET

I STOPPED BY AFTER LEAVING YOUR
OFFICE TODAY

GIRL
YOU DID

GUY
YES

I DID

BY THE WAY

DID YOU LOAN MY CAR TO ANYONE
TODAY

GIRL
NO WHY

GUY
IT WAS PARKED AT THE PARKVIEW
MOTEL

GIRL
WELL

I HAD A SALES CALL IN THAT AREA
WHAT ARE YOU TRYING TO SAY HONEY

GUY
OH NOTHING

THE HOTEL MANAGER CALLED ABOUT
3:30PM YOU LEFT YOUR PURSE IN ROOM
301 AT THE PEAKVIEW MOTEL

END

RELATIONSHIPS
THE CONTINUOUS COMPROMISE
BASED ON MERE TRUST & COMPASSION

TO COMMIT & GIVE OF ONES SELF

ONE MUST SEARCH THEIR HEART &
SOUL AND ASK THE QUESTION,

AM I READY FOR THIS,

IF YOU ARE READY TO EXPERIENCE
LAUGHTER THEN YOU MUST BE READY
TO EXPERIENCE PAIN,

ARE YOU READY

HOW MUCH ARE YOU READY

BE HONEST WITH YOUR SELF BE TRUE
TO YOURSELF FIRST

THEN YOU CAN BE TRUE TO ANOTHER.

END

WRITTEN BY EVERETT C BORDERS
JR. @

768

PUNKS

1ST—PUNK
THAT MR.GATES

GAVE ME AN F IN MATH

2ND PUNK
SO WHAT

I GOT AN F TOO

3RD punk

STARTS TO WRITE GRIFFITI ON THE LOCKER WITH A MARKER

4TH PUNK

I KNOW WHERE MR. GATES LIVES

2ND PUNK

SO

4TH PUNK

SO

WE GO OVER & TRASH HIS CAR & HOUSE

3RD PUNK

IM DOWN WITH THAT

1ST punk

HEY

YOU GUYS CRAZY

YOU WANT TO GO AND TRASH MR Gates HOUSE BECAUSE YOU FAILED MATH

THAT'S BEYOND STUPID

RISK GETTING CAUGHT

RISK GETTIING KICKED OUT OF SCHOOL FOR WHAT

THAT'S STUPID

DO IT BY YOURSELVES

4TH *PUNK*

HEY DOG

YOU DOWN WITH YOUR OWN OR NOT

IM NOT STUPID YOU WANT TO DO SOMETHING LIKE THAT COUNT ME OUT

WE ALL FAILED MATH BECAUSE WE DIDN'T

STUDY

LATER THAT NIGHT

4th PUNK

THAT DIDN'T SOUND LIKE FUN ANYWAY

2nd PUNK

YEA

3rd PUNK

LET'S DO SOMETHING ELSE

NEXT DAY

2nd PUNK

LET'S STEAL A CAR

AND GO RIDING

3rd PUNK

LET'S GO

4th -PUJNK

WHAT KIND OF CAR DO WE GET?

2nd PUNK

DON'T MATTER

WHAT EVER WE CAN GET OUR HANDS ON RIGHT

1st-PUNK

GO AHEAD FOOLS

THE POLICE STOP YOU THEN WHAT

YOU THINK YOU CAN OUT RUN THE COPS, GO TO JAIL,

GET KICKED OUT OF SCHOOL, FOR WHAT,

WE WANT A CAR WE CAN ALWAYS BORROW FREDDIES CAR

HES WORKING DOWN THE STREET

THEY STOP AT A 7-11

3rd...PUNK

READY

1st PUNK

STOP

WHAT DO YOU MEAN

4th PUNK

YOU KNOW WHAT WE MEAN DOG

4*th* PUNK

LET'S DO IT

1*st* PUNK

WERE NOT DOING NOTHING FOOL THAT MAN IN THAT STORE HAS A GUN

YOU GUYS ARE STUPID IF YOU THIINK CAN STEAL FROM THAT STORE & GETAWAY WITH IT

THERES CAMERAS THE MAN HAS A GUN

THERES PEOPLE IN THAT STORE WHAT

THAT IS THE MOST CRAZY & STUPID THING I EVER HEARD

YOU GUYS ARE CLOWNS

IM GOING TO PLAY BASKETBALL COMING OR NOT

3rd PUNK

COUNT ME IN

4th PUNK

IF YOU GUYS ARENT DOING ANYTHING ELSE WE MIGHT AS WELL PLAY SOME BALL

2nd PUNK

WHY EVERYTIME I COME UP WITH THINGS TO DO

YOU ALWAYS SHUT ME DOWN

1ST, PUNK

CAUSE YOU COME UP WITH STUPID IDEAS MAN

IM NOT GOING TO JAIL FOR YOU OR NOBODY HEY IF YOU GUYS WANT TO DO SOME POSITIVE COUNT ME IN

BUT USE YOUR BRAIN

IM NOT ABOUT GETTING INTO TROUBLE IM SMARTER THAN THAT **NEGATIVE PEER PRESSURE** IS DESTROYING THIS COUNTRY

PROBLEMS WITH YOUTH & VILOENCE CAN BE BEST SOLVED IN THE HOME

WITH THE PROPER PARENTAL GUIDANCE

YOUTH VIOLENCE CAN ONLY FLORISH IN AN ENVIROMENT THAT BREEDS VIOLENCE WE MUST CHANGE INTO A MORE PRODUCTIVE & SAFE ENVIROMENT THAT BREEDS MORE YOUTH OPPORTUNITY & USEFUL POSITIVE PROGRAMS

TALK TO YOUR KIDS

WALK WITH YOUR KIDS

SHOW & INSTILL GOOD VALUES ON TRUST & HUMILITY AND RESPECT.

REMEMBER

THE PROBLEMS OF TODAY

WILL NOT REMEDY THE SOLUTIONS OF TOMORROW

END SCENE

BY-EVERETT C BORDERS

PARENTAL ADVICE

DAD
KATHY

WHATS WRONG

KATHY
NOTHING DAD

IT'S JUST

DAD
WHAT

KATHY
WELL

I DIDNT MAKE THE TEAM

DAD
DID YOU TRY YOUR BEST

KATHY
NO

I DIDNT

I ATE BEFORE TRY OUTS & I DIDNT
FOCUS

DAD
WELL THEN

THE NEXT TIME YOU TRY WHAT MUST
YOU DO

KATHY
FOCUS AND TRY MY BEST

DAD
THAT'S MY GIRL

KATHY
DAD

I ALWAYS REMEMBER WHAT YOU TELL
ME

WHY DONT I ALWAYS LISTEN WHEN IT
COUNTS

DAD

CAUSE YOUR INDEPENDENT, YOU THINK YOUR OWN WAY, YOU'LL LEARN, WHEN IT REALLY COUNTS

YOU'LL AKE THE RIGHT DECISION

IM SURE OF IT

KATHY

FRIDAY IS THE NEXT TRYOUTS IM GOING TO MAKE THAT TEAM

DAD

THAT'S Y GIRL

YOU CAN DO IT

KATHY

HI DAD

DAD

WHATS WRONG

KATHY
I DIDNT MAKE THE TEAM DAD

DAD
DONT CRY PUMPKIN

IT'S ALL RIGHT

KATHY
I TRIED MY BEST DAD, I REALLY TRIED

DAD
DID YOU REALLY FOCUS

KATHY
YES I REALLY DID

IM JUST NOT GOOD ENOUGH

DAD
THAT'S NOT TRUE,

HOW DO YOU THINK YOU CAN BE GOOD ENOUGH

KATHY
BY GOING TO THE GYM FOUR DAYS A WEEK INSTEAD OF TWO

AND BY FOCUSING HARDER

DAD
THAT'S WHAT I WANT TO HEAR

AS LONG AS YOU HAVE TRIED YOU'RE BEST

YOU HAVE NOT FAILED,

YOU HAVE BEEN ENLIGHTEN TO STRIVED HARDER

KATHY
THAT'S RIGHT

IM GOING TO COME BACK & BE BETTER THAN BEFORE,

THAT'S WHATS IM GOING TO DO

DAD
THAT'S MY GIRL

BE PROUD THAT YOU AT LEAST TRIED YOUR BEST,

AND BECAUSE YOUVE SHOWN YOUR BEST YOU CAN ONLY GET BETTER REMEMBER THAT

KATHY
YES DAD

ILL REMEMBER YOU KNOW DAD

IM GOING TO PRACTICES RUNNING FASTER & JUMPING HIGHER

DAD
WOULD YOU MIND IF I GIVE YOU A TIP

KATHY
YES DAD

DAD
WELL

WHEN I WANTED TO JUMP HIGHER

I WOULD WEAR WEIGHTS ON MY ANKLES

AND WHEN I WANTED TO RUN FASTER I WOULD WEAR A CHUTE WHILE I RAN IN THE POOL

KATHY
THANKS DAD I THINK

ILL TRY THE WEIGHTS

DAD
KATHY

IN THIS WORLD YOU WILL HAVE MANY FAILURES,

IT'S HOW YOU HANDLE THEM THAT COUNTS

LEARN TO BOUNCE BACK PUMPKIN

THAT'S THE WAY OF THE WORLD

KATHY
BOUNCE BACK

YOU MEAN WHEN I FAILED THE TRYOUTS AND I TRIED AGAIN,

IF I KEEP ON TRYING AND TRYING TILL I MAKE IT,

THEN THAT'S WHAT YOU MEAN ABOUT

BOUNCING BACK, RIGHT DAD

DAD
RIGHT PUMPKIN

YOU'LL BE FINE, JUST FINE

KATHY
THANKS DAD

ILL TRY HARDER

CAUSE I WANT TO BE BETTER

DAD
I KNOW,

BE THE BEST YOU CAN BE, BECAUSE YOU WANT TO NOT BECAUSE I WANT YOU TO

KATHY
BUT DAD DONT YOU WANT ME TO

DAD
OF COURSE I WANT YOU TO PUMPKIN

I JUST WANT YOU TO REALIZE, BECAUSE YOU WANT TO

DOES THAT MAKES SENSE

KATHY
PLENTY DAD,

I LOVE YOU

DAD
I LOVE YOU TO PUMPKIN

THE RELATIONSHIP BETWEEN, FATHER & DAUGHTER IS VERY SPECIAL, LOVE ADVICE

COMPASSION

WISDOM & UNDERSTANDING PARENTAL AWARENESS TRUST

ARE ALL THE INGREDIENTS OF A STRONG BOND BETWEEN FATHER & DAUGHTER

WE MUST REMEMBER THAT ACTIONS SAID NOT ACTIONS HEARD

SHOULD BE ACTIONS WE LIVE BY & CARRY OUT

WRITTEN BY EVERETT C BORDERS JR. @

NEVER RUN FROM YOURSELF

RUDY
HEY RALPH

WHY DO YOU LOOK SO SCARED

RALPH
THOSE GUY ARE WAITING FOR ME AFTER SCHOOL

RUDY
FOR WHAT

RALPH
WHY DO YOU THINK TO BEAT ON ME

RUDY
WHAT HAPPENED MAN

RALPH
I TALKED TO ONE OF THOSE GUYS
GIRLFRIEND & THE GUY DIDNT LIKE
IT

SO HE & HIS FRIENDS ARE GOING TO
JUMP ON ME AFTER SCHOOL

RUDY
YOU WANT ME TO HELP MAN

ILL WATCH YOUR BACK

WANT ME TO GET SOME OF MY FRIENDS
TO HELP

RALPH
I DONT KNOW MAN

THOSE GUYS ARE MEAN

RUMOR HAS IT THAT THEY HAVE
WEAPONS

RUDY
WELL

WHY ARE YOU SO SCARED MAN I
KNOW YOU I GOT YOUR BACK MAN

RALPH
THOSE GUYS WILL WAIT FOR ME WHILE
I GO TO SCHOOL IN THE MOURNING

They'll WAIT FOR ME AFTER SCHOOL

THEY SAID THEY WILL FOLLOW ME
HOME & TRASH MY HOUSE,

WHAT AM I GOING TO DO MAN

RUDY
WHATS THE MAIN GUYS NAME THE
BOYFRIEND

RALPH
HIS NAME IS DAN

RUDY
WHY DONT WE TALK TO THIS DAN &
STRAIGHTEN THIS OUT

RALPH
I TRIED THAT

IT DIDNT WORK

LAST NIGHT WHILE I WAS COMING FROM THE GYM

DAN & HIS FRIENDS JUMPED ME & ALMOST BROKE MY RIBS

I CAN'T RUN FROM THESE GUYS FOREVER

RUDY
WHY RUN LOOK MAN

YOU KNOW HOW TO FIGHT PRETTY GOOD WHY DONT YOU & DAN HAVE IT OUT ONE ON ONE

YOU CAN BEAT THAT CHUMP MAN

RALPH
WHAT ABOUT HIS FRIENDS

RUDY

I GOT SOME FRIENDS AT THE KARATE CLUB

They'll LOVE TO GET DOWN WITH THIS ALL DAY ALL NIGHT

THIS IS WHAT THEY LIVE FOR

THEY CAN'T WAIT TO SHOW THEIR STUFF

ESPECIALLY TO SOME WANT TO BE TOUGH GUYS

RALPH

I DONT KNOW MAN

DON'T KNOW ABOUT THIS

RUDY

LOOK MAN

ALL THELL DO IS KEEP THE OTHER GUYS OFF YOU

AND ALL YOU HAVE TO DO IS
CONFRONT THAT DAN

WITH OUT HIS BOYS TO JUMP ON YOU
HE'S

NOTHING RIGHT

RALPH
RIGHT

DAN IS GOING DOWN

I TRIED TO TALK TO THIS GUY HE
DIDNT WANT TO LISTEN WITHOUT HIS
BUDDIES HE'S NOTHING

RIGHT!

RUDY
RIGHT

LETS DOITMAN

RALPH
HEY DAN

WHATS HAPPENING

DAN
WHO ARE THESE GUYS

RALPH
THEY'RE HERE TO KEEP YOUR BOYS
IN CHECK

NOW

YOU WANT A PIECE OF ME HERE I AM

DAN
HEY MAN

I JUST WANTED YOU TO LEAVE MY
LADY ALONE

YOU KNOW

RALPH
YEA MAN

I KNOW

ILL ASK YOU AGAIN MAN

DO YOU WANT A PIECE OF ME

CAUSE THIS TIME ITS JUST ME &
YOU HA,

LOOKS LIKE YOUR BOYS ARE LEAVING
WHATS THAT MATTER FELLAS

TO MUCH HEAT FOR YOU SO

DAN
WHAT ARE WE GOING TO DO

DAN
NOTHING MAN

I DONT WANT TO DO NOTHING
THE CASE IS CLOSED AS FAR AS IM
CONCERNED

COOL

RALPH
COOL RALPH COOL

RUDY
HEY RALPH

WHY DIDNT YOU GET DAN

WHY DIDNT YOU BEAT HIS HEAD IN
MAN

RALPH
DIDNT HAVE TO MAN

HIS BOYS SAW THAT I WAS NOT SCARED
THEY SAW HIM LOSE FACE AND THEY
LEFT

IT'S OVER

RUDY
YOU COULD HAVE

REALLY EMBARRASSED HIM MAN

RALPH
I DID MAN THANKS GUYS AND THANKS RUDY

I DON'T THINK ILL EVER BE SCARED AGAIN

RUDY
I CAN SEE THAT MAN

GO AHEAD RALPH GO AHEAD MAN

FACING YOUR FEARS

IS ONE OF THE MOST DIFFICULT? THINGS THAT ANY PERSON CAN DO

IF YOU ARE BRAVE ENOUGH TO FACE YOUR FEARS AND CONQUER them

YOU JUST MIGHT REACH THE ENLIGHTENMENT THAT YOU HAVE ALWAYS SOUGHT

LEARN TO FACE YOUR SELF FACE YOUR FEARS

IT IS NEVER AS BAD AS YOU THINK DONT BE AFRAID!

LEARN TO CHANGE YOUR MIND ABOUT THE WORLD AROUND YOU

FACE YOU FEARS!

WRITTEN BY EVERETT C BORDERS JR, @

MIMIC

SCOTT
WHATS WITH YOU PEOPLE

PAM
WHAT DO YOU MEAN YOU PEOPLE

SCOTT
YOU PEOPLE TRYING TO BE LIKE US

PAM
LIKE HOW

SCOTT
TRYING TO WEAR YOUR CLOTHES
LIKE US TRYING TO TALK LIKE US,
TRYING TO DO OUR MUSIC,

DON'T YOU PEOPLE HAVE ANYTHING
ORIGINAL ANYTHING

PAM

THAT'S NOT FAIR JUST CAUSE WE LIKE YOUR MUSIC & DRESS DOESNT MEAN THAT WE ARE TRYING TO STEAL ANYTHING

WHY ARE YOU SO MAD SCOTT

SCOTT

IM TIRED OF EVERY TIME I TURN ON AROUND, IM LOOKING AT YOU PEOPLE TRYING TO ACT LIKE US,

YOU DON'T SEE US TRYING TO ACT LIKE YOU PEOPLE,

NO MATTER HOW MUCH YOU PEOPLE WEAR YOUR CAPS TURNED BACKWARDS

YOU PEOPLE WILL NEVER BE AS COOL AS US

PAM

I KNOW

PAM

WHAT ABOUT WHEN YOU PEOPLE
WOULD STRAIGHTEN YOUR HAIR,

I SAW IT IN THE MOVIES AND
DOCUMENTARIES

SCOTT

THEY DIDN'T STRAIGHTEN THEIR
HAIR TO LOOK LIKE YOU PEOPLE,

THEY DID IT TO CHANGE THEIR HAIR
STYLE

PAM

WELL

WHATS THE BIG DEAL SCOTT

WHATS WRONG WITH US IDENT1FYING
WITH WHATS COOL

SCOTT
WE KNOW WERE COOL

WE HAVE ALWAYS BEEN COOL

SCOTT
WE DON'T NEED YOU PEOPLE TO
DEFINE US

PAM
SCOTT IM DOT TRYING TO DEFINE YOU

IM YOUR FRIEND

SCOTT
WHY BECAUSE IM A MUSICIAN,

BECAUSE IM COOL, ALL OF MY FRIENDS
ARE COOL,

WHY ARE YOU MY FRIEND

PAM
CAUSE YOUR SMART

AND I ADMIRE YOU,

YOU GIVE ME SOME GOOD ADVICE
SOMETIME,

THAT'S WHY YOU'RE MY FRIEND

YOUR WRONG ABOUT ME SCOTT

SCOTT
HEY IM SORRY PAM

IM, JUST MAD AT, WHAT, I SEE
ESPECIALLY IN THE MUSIC WORLD

PAM
HOW SO

SCOTT
IM NOT GOING TO MENTION ANY
NAMES

LOOK AT PEOPLE WHO HAVE GOTTEN
RICH BY MIMICKING OUR MUSIC,

OUR SOUND,

OUR DANCE STEPS,

YOU PEOPLE ARE LEACHES

PAM
THAT'S KINDA HARSH SCOTT

WHATS REALLY Bothering YOU,

THEIRS GOT TO BE MORE THAN THIS
MUSIC STUFF

SCOTT
IT'S EVERYTHING

I JUST SAW THE SPACE SHUTTLE ON TV THE OTHER DAY,

With THE FIRST WOMEN COMMANDER

THE LAST TIME I SAW A BROTHER ON THE SPACE SHUTTLE WAS WHEN IT BLEW UP MANY YEARS AGO

PAM
WELL

SO YOU THINK THERE SHOULD BE MORE BLACKS ON THE SPACES SHUTTLE?

SCOTT
NOT JUST THE SPACE SHUTTLE

IT'S THE WHOLE THING, WHY ARE WE ALWAYS CROSSING OVER CROSSING OVER IS NOTHING BUT A DOUBLE CROSS!

PAM

WHAT ARE YOU TALKING ABOUT
SCOTT

SCOTT

YOU REALLY DON'T SEE IT

YOU REALLY UNDERSTAND DO YOU

PAM

WHY CAN'T YOU JUST EXCEPT THAT

MUSIC WHERE EVER IT COMES FROM

IS A BIG PART OF OUR ENTIRE
AMERICAN CULTURE

IT DOESN'T BELONG TO YOUR PEOPLE
NOR MINE,

IT BELONGS TO ALL OF US

DON'T BE MAD that WE ADMIRE YOUR
MUSIC

ENOUGH THAT WE MIMIC IT,

DONT BE MAD THAT WE LIKE YOU STYLE ENOUGH THAT WE WEAR IT,

THE FACT THAT WE MIMIC YOU PEOPLE

MEANS THINGS ARE CHANGING FOR THE BETTER, DON'T YOU SEE THAT

SCOTT
HEY

MAYBE

I DONT KNOW WELL SEE ***END***

THINGS

ARE CHANGING

FOR BETTER OR WORST YOU AND I CAN'T DECIDE WE CAN ONLY SPECULATE ONLY HISTORY OR THE PEOPLE WHO INTERPRET IT CAN

WE LIVE IN AN OCEAN OF TIME

WHERE THE PAST IS LOST IN THE FUTURE WRITTEN BY EVERETT C BORDERS JR. @

MAKING THE GRADES

DEBBIE
ANGELA,

WE NEED TO STUDY IF WE ARE GOING TO PASS THAT HISTORY TEST TOMORROW

ANGELA
WHAT ABOUT THE DOUBLE DATE WITH LANCE & CHARLES TONIGHT

THE GUYS ARE GOING TO PICK US UP FOR THE MOVIES AT 6:00

DEBBIE

WHAT ABOUT THE TEST TOMORROW

ANGELA

WHAT ABOUT IT

WE CAN CRAM FOR THE TEST TOMORROW

DEBBIE

I NEED TO STUDY FOR THAT TEST

ILL TELL LANCE THAT I HAD TO STUDY

I THINK HE'LL UNDERSTAND

ANGELA

SO

YOU'RE NOT GOING

YOU JUST WANT TO LEAVE ME HANGING WITH CHARLES

YOU KNOW HOW HE IS WHEN WE GO TO THE MOVIES

IT'S LIKE HE HAS EIGHT HANDS

DEBBIE
WHAT DO YOU MEAN

LEAVE YOU HANGING

IF YOU DON'T WANT TO GO TO THE MOVIES WITH CHARLES

THEN DON'T GO

ANGELA
I LIKE CHARLES

I M NOT READY TO BE ALONE WITH HIM YET

THAT'S ALL

THAT'S WHY I WANT YOU TO GO WITH ME

DEBBIE

LOOK

ANGELA, I WANT TO GO TO THE MOVIES I JUST NEED TO STUDY FOR THE TEST

IM TRYING TO BRING UP MY S.A.T TEST SCORES

WE CAN GO THE MOVIES ON THE WEEKEND NOT A SCHOOL NIGHT

AND WE REALLY NEED TO STUDY FOR THIS TEST

DON'T KNOW ABOUT YOU BUT ILL FAIL IF I DON'T STUDY FOR THIS ONE

ANGELA

WHAT ABOUT THE GUYS

I WAS LOOKING FORWARD TO THIS DATE WITH LANCE

DEBBIE
THEY CAN HELP US STUDY

LANCE & CHARLES AREN'T EXACTLY
ACEING THEIR GRADES EITHER

SINCE THEY NEED TO STUDY FOR THE
SAME TEST

WE CAN ALL STUDY TOGETHER

THEN THE WEEKEND WE CAN ALL GO
TO THE MOVIES TOGETHER

ANGELA
YOU'RE RIGHT

GOING TO THE MOVIES WITH LANCE
ALONE IS A CHALLENGE

STUDYING IS SAFE

CAN'T GET IN TROUBLE THAT WAY

SOMETIMES YOU COME UP WITH
REALLY GOOD IDEAS GIRL

DEBBIE

WELL LETS STUDY & GET THIS OVER WITH

ANGELA

LET'S WAIT TILL THE GUYS GET HERE

DEBBIE

OK BUT,

WOULDN'T YOU WANT TO GET OUR WORK OUT OF THE WAY FIRST

THEN HAVE MORE TIME HELPING THE GUYS

ANGELA

YOU MEAN SPEND MORE TIME WITH THE GUYS DON'T YOU

DEBBIE IF I DIDN'T KNOW YOU BETTER

I WOULD GUESS THAT YOU'RE HAVING A STUDY DATE

DEBBIE
FIGURED IT OUT DID YOU

ANGELA
THIS IS A GREAT IDEA

THE GUYS ARE COMING OVER TO HELP US STUDY

AND AT THE SAME TIME IT'S LIKE A DATE AT THE SAME TIME

AND I CAN BE SAFE WITH LANCE

DEBBIE
GET YOUR PRIORITIES STRAIGHT GIRL

THE MAIN OBJECTIVE IS TO STUDY RIGHT

ANGELA
RIGHT

YOU'RE RIGHT

LET'S TURN UP THE LIGHTS

GET OUT THE POPCORN & SODA

AND SIT AT THE LIVING ROOM TABLE AND GET STARTED

DEBBIE
SURE YOU RIGHT GIRL

ALL THINGS COME AFTER WE GET OUR STUDIES RIGHT

WERE IN OUR SOUTH MORE YEAR

THEY'LL BE PLENTY OF DATES & OPPORTUNITY TO GO TO THE MOVIES

BUT WHATS REALLY IMPORTANT IS HOW YOU GO THROUGH IT

I MEAN SCHOOL IN ALL

IT IS POSSIBLE ANGELA TO HAVE FUN
WITH IT ALL

ANGELA
WHAT DO YOU MEAN

DEBBIE
STUDYING

DATING SPORTS
YOU KNOW, LEARNING

IN THE YOUNG YEARS
WE THINK WE SOMETIMES HAVE ALL
THE ANSWERS

ABOUT LIFE, RIGHT WRONG
RELATIONSHIPS, SCHOOL,
AND WHATS REALLY IMPORTANT

EVEN THOUGH IT IS IMPORTANT TO
SET A GOAL
WHERE YOU'RE GOING

AND HOW YOU GOT THERE

IT'S EVEN MORE IMPORTANT TO
REMEMBER
WHERE YOU HAVE BEEN

FOR IN ORDER TO PLOT ANY COURSE
N ANY SIX DIMENSIONAL SPACE

YOU ALWAYS NEED THE POINT OF
REFERENCE

WHAT WE MEAN IS

YOU CAN'T GET WHERE YOU'RE GOING
TILL YOU FIGURE OUT WHERE YOU
BEEN, THIS IS THE Essence of LEARING.
WRITTEN BY EVERETT C BORDERS
JR. @

LEARN FOR YOURSELF BARB

HEY WILLIAM,

GIVE ME THE ANSWERS TO THE TEST

WILLIAM

NO BARB,

YOU NEED TO STUDY LIKE EVERY BODY ELSE.
IT'S ONLY TWO DAYS BEFORE THE TEST & YOU NEED TO STUDY,

THAT'S THE ONLY WAY YOU'LL LEARN IT.

BARB

HEY,

I DON'T NEED A LECTURE FRO YOU,

JUST GIVE ME THE ANSWERS!

WILLIAM

NO BARB, NO.

BARB

ILL FIXES YOU!

WILLIAM

FIX ME HOW?

WHAT ARE YOU GOING TO DO BARB?

BARB

I WON'T SAY, YOU'LL FINE OUT.

WILLIAM

I CAN'T BELIEVE YOU, YOU'RE GOING
TO TRY TO DO SOMETHING TO ME,

CAUSES I WON'T GIVE YOU ANSWERS TO A TEST?

MAN ARE YOU A LOSER.

BARB

ILL TELL EVERY ONE, YOU'RE A FRUIT, ILL TELL EVERY ONE, YOU'RE A THIEF, AND WHAT DO YOU MEAN, IM A LOSER?

YOU BETTER TAKE IT BACK!

WILLIAM

NO,

I WON'T.

WILLIAM

YOU'RE GOING TO THREATEN ME OVER A TEST, BECAUSE YOU'RE TO LAZY TO STUDY, THEN YOU'RE A LOSER.

BARB

OK WELL THEN DON'T, GIVE E THE ANSWERS,

ILL TELL YOUR GIRLFRIEND, WE ARE TOGETHER!

WILLIAM

YOU WOULD DO ALL THAT FOR THE TEST ANSWERS?

BARB

YES,

I WOULD!

WILLIAM

WHAT DO YOU HAVE AGAINST STUDYING?

BARB

I DON'T KNOW,

I DON'T KNOW ANYTHING ABOUT
SCIENCE,

I NEVER UNDERSTOOD IT.

WILLIAM

WHY DOES THIS TEST MEAN SO MUCH
TO YOU?

BARB

CAUSE MY DAD TOLD ME,

IF I FAILED ANOTHER TEST HE WOULD,

TAKE MY CAR & CUT OFF MY
ALLOWANCES.

WILLIAM

WELL,

DO YOU WANT ME TO HELP YOU?

BARB

YES,

THAT'S WHAT IM ASKING FOR

WILLIAM

LOOK, BARB,

IM NOT GOING TO GIVE YOU THE ANSWERS, BUT I WILL HELP YOU WITH SCIENCE, ILL HELP YOU STUDY.

BARB

YOU WILL DO THAT FOR ME, AFTER WHAT I SAID ABOUT YOU

WILLIAM

YES,

ILL HELP YOU CAUSE,

I REALIZE YOU DON'T LIKE TO ASK
FOR HELP, OR YOU DON'T KNOW HOW.

BARB,

SCIENCE IS EASY, LOOK AT IT THIS
WAY, DO YOU KNOW WHAT THE TEST
IS ON?

BARB

YES,

PLANTS & ANIMALS & HOW THEY
COEXIST

WILLIAM

NOW LISTEN,

ALL ANIMALS BREATHE IN AIR OXYGEN, AND EXHALE OR BREATHE OUT CARBON DIOXIDE.

ALL PLANTS,

TAKE IN CARBON DIOXIDE, AND EXHALE AIR OR OXYGEN.

ONE CAN'T LIVE WITHOUT THE OTHER,

SEE WHAT I MEAN.

BARB

IS THAT ALL

WILLIAM

YES,

THAT'S ALL

BARB

THEN,

WHEN THE TEACHER SHOWS US THOSE
VIDEOS OF ALL THE RAIN FOREST,

BEING DESTROYED,

THAT'S DESTROYING PLANTS THAT
MAKE QUALITY AIR.

WILLIAM

YES

NOW YOU GET IT.

BARB

WHY ARE PEOPLE THEY DOING THAT?

WILLIAM

CAUSE THEY WANT TO CLEAR FOREST, PLANT CROPS & SELL TIMBER, WHO KNOWS

BARB

DON'T THEY KNOW, THEY ARE KILLING US,

I MEAN, THEY ARE HURTING THE WORLD.

WILLIAM

YES BARB, THEY KNOW,

SOME JUST DON'T CARE.

BARB

I WANT TO KNOW MORE WILLIAM

WILLIAM

WELL, PAY ATTENTION IN SCIENCE &
STOP CUTTING CLASS!

BARB

I WILL,

HEY WILLIAM,

IM SORRY I THREATEN YOU.

WILLIAM

I KNOW,

I JUST WANTED YOU TO SEE, AND DO
THE RIGHT THINGS, YOU NEED TO
KNOW ABOUT SCIENCE.

BARB

SURE YOU'RE RIGHT, LET'S STUDY

WILLIAM

OK BARB

KNOWLEDGE IS POWER,

BECAUSE BEING YOUNG

SOMETIMES, OUR THINKING MAY SEEM DISTORTED,

ABOUT WHAT IS REALLY IMPORTANT.

THE PATH THAT LIES BEFORE US,

IT'S SURE,

IT'S PROVEN,

AND IT IS JEST,

AS OUR FATHERS & MOTHERS,

AUNTS & UNCLES,

BROTHERS & SISTERS,

HAVE WALKED.

THE PATH OF KNOWLEDGE,

IS CONVEYED FOR ALL TO SEE & HEAR.

THERE ARE NO SHORT CUTS,

NO EASY WAYS,

ALL MUST INTAKE & CONTRIBUTE,

FOR THE PATH OF KNOWLEDGE,

ALWAYS LEADS TO YOUR ULTIMATE, INFORMATIVE, SALVATION & UNDERSTANDING.

WRITTEN BY EVERETT C BORDERS Ph.D.

INDIFFERENCE

SABRINA

HEY LOOK AT THOSE PEOPLE WEARING ALL THAT BLACK BLACK HAIR, C0MBAT BOOTS

BLACK FINGERNAIL POLISH & LIPSTICK TATTOOS OF SPIDER WEBBS

CREEPY!

ROSA

YEA

THEY ALL HANG TOGETHER IN THE LUNCH ROOM & AFTER SCHOOL, GROSS

SABRINA

HEY KATIA

WAIT UP

KATIA
HI

WHAT ARE YOU GUYS UP TO

SABRINA
WERE TALKING ABOUT THOSE GUYS
WHO ARE DRESSED UP IN ALL BLACK

KATIA
WHAT ABOUT THEM

THEY DON'T BOTHER ANYBODY

ROSA
SO WHAT

THEY LOOK GROSS

THEY SMELL & THEIR EMBARRASSING

SABRINA
DO YOU KNOW ANY OF THOSE GUYS KATIA?

KATIA
YES I DO

AND ALL OF THOSE GUYS DONT SMELL AND THEY DON'T CAUSE TROUBLE TWO WEEKS AGO

I WAS FLUNKING ENGLISH LINDA

WHO HANGS WITH THOSE GUYS OFFERED TO HELP ME OUT

AND I PASSED MY CLASS

KATIA
JUST LAST MONTH

YOU'RE LITTLE BROTHER ROSA WAS ABOUT TO GET BEAT UP BY SOME PUNKS, IT WAS ONE OF THOSE GUYS

THAT YOU DESCRIBED AS GROSS WHO
STOPPED THE PUNKS FROM BEATING
UP YOUR LITTLE BROTHER

SO DONT BE SO QUICK TO CONDEMN
PEOPLE WHO DRESS DIFFERENT THAN
WE DO

SABRINA
WHY ARE YOU DEFENDING THEM

YOU ACT LIKE YOU LIKE THOSE PEOPLE
I THINK THERE GROSS AND IF YOU
LIKE THE THEN YOU'RE GROSS TOO

ROSA
I HEARD ABOUT THE PUNKS TRYING
TO PICK ON MY LITTLE BROTHER

I DIDNT KNOW THOSE GUY HELPED
HIM I THINK IM GOING TO THANK
THEM I ALSO THINK

SABRINA

YOU ARE OUT OF LINE

THAT'S NOT RIGHT WHAT YOU SAID
ABOUT KATIA

SABRINA
IM SORRY I SAID THAT KATIA

I JUST DONT KNOW THEM THAT'S
ALL I'VE NEVER TALKED TO THEM
BECAUSE I ALWAYS THOUGHT THEY
WERE TOO WEIRD

LOOK IF YOU GUYS WANT TO BE
FRIENDS WITH THEM ITS COOL WITH
ME

KATIA
DOES THAT MEAN YOU WANT TO
INTRODUCE?

SABRINA

OK

I DON'T MIND

INTRODUCE US

ROSA

YEA

ID LIKE TO MEET THE GUYS WHO HELPED MY BROTHER

AS WELL AS LINDA

SABRINA

WHO'S THAT

ROSA

THE GIRL WHO HELPED KATIA WITH HER ENGLISH

IM FAILNG ENGLISH TO I COULD USE THE HELP

KATIA
IM PROUD OF YOU

SABRINA
FOR WHAT

KATIA
TAKING THE FIRST STEP

YOU CHANGED YOU ATTITUDE AFTER YOU HEARD THE FACTS ABOUT THOSE KIDS

SABRINA
YEA

SOMETIMES I GET BULL HEADED & OBSTINATE I REALLY DONT MEAN TO

ROSA
WE ALL HAVE SOMETHING

WHAT ABOUT THE CHEERLEADERS
THEY HATE US REMEMBER

SABRINA
YEA THEY HATE US CAUSE YOU STOLE
ONE OF THERE BOYFRIENDS

KATIA
YEA ROSA
YOU NEED TO STOP DOING THAT

ROSA
I KNOW

KATIA
ILL INVITE LINDA OVER THIS WEEKEND
& YOU GUYS CAN MEET HER OK

ROSA
OK

SABRINA
OK

END

WHAT CAN WE LEARN ABOUT OUTWARD APPEARANCE IF ANY THING,

WE LEARN NOTHING

IT'S ONLY THE EXPERIENCE THAT TEACHES US

WRITTEN BY EVERETT C BORDERS JR. @

4/15/2010

How not to be a <u>publican,</u> Tea.

Commentary Skit-1

Two guys in a pickup truck driving on the road wearing baseball caps a shotgun rack dipping skoal. The subject (Pete) is driving the truck wearing blue jean overalls

Vern,

Ha Pete,

Ever think about joining the Republican Party?

Pete,

You mean the tea party?

Vern,

No,

The Republican Party!

Pete,

What's the difference? They're both the same

Vern,

He spits out the window in the direction toward a car in the other driving lane.

Well one party is just as good as another isn't it?

Pete,

That's one way to look at it,

But I never thought of being against the government

That's what the tea party is.

Vern,

What about the Republican Party, What do they stand for?

Pete,

They're just angry they lost the election, Crooks, thieves who want keys to the safe,

They spent all their time complaining with no constructive answers & no solutions,

Trash talking the country

So they are the same

Vern,

What side are you on Pete

Pete,

Side,

IM not on anybody's side,

Hell, my wife & kids need health care, so does your family. It's like they never want us to have nothing!

I need a job and the ones that did all this have grabbed all the money & laughing at us like was fools or something.

Vern,

Laughing

Pete,

Laughing, at us,

We put them first, they put us last.

Think about justice and you'll find it, just- us

Vern,

I never saw it that way Pete,
Tea party want s to take back America back

Pete,

*Spits out the truck window & wipes his mouth
with his hand*
You mean clan tea party
Back to what Vern,
I never had anything to do with the any clan
tea party, I believe in live and let live,

Everybody has a right to live, just like you
Vern

Vern,

Well, what about the government take over &
everything being turned in socialism Pete

Pete,

What about it Vern,

Look, when your house is on fire, who do you call, When your kids need school, where do they go?

When you drive this truck, who controls traffic,

We all live under the protection and grace of the US government.

The president was elected by the people and he really is for all the people, that's why this country was formed and that's what Im gonna do.

The government took over when the constitution was written for all the people.

IM not gonna be lead by a bunch of greedy, power & money grabbing, back stabbing, race monger loudmouths who continue fooling us and laugh & lie in our face.

They just want to use us to get what they want & laugh at us afterwards.

Do you really think they care anything about your problems, your family, why do you think they fight so hard trying to keep you where you are in life?

Vern,

I was just think about it Pete,

Didn't say for sure.

Pete,

You want to be part of some clan tea party, go ahead, you can count me out.

Vern,

Well,

What about the other side Pete?

Pete,

Ha, the other side has tried to do more for you than any others in the history of this country.

Think about that Vern,

Don't be lead like a sheep

Vern,

Well

Pete,

What do you want to do Vern? Start another civil war?

You know before the civil war, blacks outnumbered the whites five to one.

Abe Lincoln (republican) freed them from slavery cause of fear of a revolt. Did you know that blacks turned the civil war? They built this country & railroads so what are you really trying to say?

Hell, between the mexics & blacks, we are the minority in this country can't start something we can't finish. Something like will never end & nobody wins. After all what we did to them, you don't see them trying to take over the government.

Vern,

No I don't want civil war,

Just want to take the country back

Pete,

Right,
Back to them stealing all the money laughing at us Back to another do nothing, shameful government, Back to another worldwide depression,

It ain't no difference in the way of the clan tea party and these greedy crooks that want to use & fool us once again, Why in the hell do you want to follow a maniac cause that's not your own?

Think for yourself Vern,
This President has tried more to help you & your family more than any other, is you that blind!

Has the president ever once said he wants just help his own people, no?

Is he trying to help all the people at the same time, yes? When he does something against the people, you can hoot & holler all you want.

You need to pay more attention,

Hell the man has only been in office a year & a half, What the hell do you want, tomorrow today!

Vern,

Spits out the truck window
Well,

Pete,

You want to follow a bunch of nut whack jobs that are religiously disguised behind the hood & think they are fighting a holy war against the evil, wake up.

This ain't about religion; this is about power, control, chaos & money that will never, ever end up in our pockets.

But don't take my word; take a look at every one of these hate/race mongers bank accounts.

The more they get you stirred up & listen & get mad, the more they get very rich laughing.

Who's fooling who Vern?

You will never profit from their thievery; we get only the filth from their gutters.

When you show up at these so-called K rallies, tea parties & hate meetings, you drive this pickup truck right?

Vern,

Well

Pete,
They always show up in jets and limousines
right,
Do you ever think that you're going to get any
piece of that Vern?

You should know better than to ask me what
I think about crap like this!

Vern,

Well,

Pete,

Anyway, were out of beer Vern

Vern,

Well,

I guess we need to pull over & get some then

End.

The above skit commentary is indicative of grossly distorted conversations spoken now all over the country & world.

United States of America has always been strong only because of our rich diversity.

If we are too truly survive as a strong & respective and prosperous nation, we must first speak in one voice of all people & for all people.

If we allow the vile distortions of the past to cloud possibilities of a bright future then America as we have always known it has truly lost its very heart & soul of any future humanity.

We start with empathy, common sense & learning heeds that the needs of the many always outweigh the needs of the few and never ever the one.

Historically, blind hatred & greed has always been a purported learned behavior.

This is the twenty first century as there are those who profit very highly in the business division of others acquisitions; there are those who convey convictions morality & the unlearning the past.

We must unlearn, only by unlearning can we all truly learn.

Our worldwide social society is tearing itself apart from help from those who would profit misery, suffering and division.

History has conveyed & recorded several catastrophic events throughout time. Before human comprehension it is recorded in the rocks and in the earth.

Are we just another species who are scurrying towards our own demise or can we all ever rise above the cloaked veil of intentional division and self-destruction.

We all live in an ocean of time, where our past maybe lost in our future.

Our own extinction may or may not be solely up to us. It is very difficult to say what the future is for this world or for this country.

What is very certain from history is that there is no future for any one, any group, any country, any world in division.

For those who tend to profit from the misery of the masses are counting on the ignorance in virtues & clarity of values in replacement with fear & contributing perpetual purported indecisions.

With the temerity to corrupt in collusion even at the very pinnacle of American Governmental officials, gives "in God we trust" all new meanings.

Written by E. Borders Ph.D.

HONOR THY PARENTS

CALEB
MOM
I WANT TO GO TO THE CONCERT TONIGHT

MOM

NO

THAT CONCERT IS DANGEROUS

THE RADIO SAYS GANGS WILL BE THERE, POLICE, PROTEST & FIGHTS YOUNG MAN YOU ARENT GOING ANYWHERE

CALEB

OH MOM

I WANT TO GO TO THE CONCERT

MOM

NO

LOOK SON

I HAVE NO OBJECTIONS TO YOU HAVING FUN AT CONCERTS

IT'S JUST THAT THIS CONCERT IS DANGEROUS,

I DONT WANT YOU TO GET HURT OR
ARRESTED,

BESIDES IT'S A SCHOOL NIGHT

CALEB
I'LL BET

IF DAD WAS HERE HE'D SAY I COULD
GO TO THE CONCERT

MOM
WELL HE'S NOT HERE

AND I SAID YOU COULDN'T GO! YOU
LISTEN TO ME YOUNG MAN, YOU WILL
DO AS I SAY, YOU ARE NOT GOING TO
THAT CONCERT TONIGHT

CALEB
WELL

CAN I CALL MASON & TELL HIM THAT
I CANT GO

MOM
OK

ANOTHER TIME SON

YOU CAN GO TO THE NEXT CONCERT

CALEB
HEY MASON

MY MOM SAYS I CAN'T GO!

MASON
WHAT! HEY MAN

YOU HAVE THE CAR

ALL THE GUYS ARE COUNTING ON
YOU TONIGHT

CALEB
I CANT HELP IT MAN

I CAN'T GO!

IM GROUNDED TONIGHT

MASON
LOOK MAN

YOU HAVE PEOPLE COUNTING ON YOU
HEY, IM COUNTING YOU COME ON
CALEB LET'S GO MAN

CALEB
SORRY MAN

IF I GO

MY MOM WILL TAKE MY CAR

MASON
GOT AN IDEA,

WHAT TIME DOES YOUR MOM GO TO
BED

CALEB
ABOUT

8:00PM

WHY

MASON
LET'S WAIT TILL SHE GOES TO SLEEP
& SNEAK TO THE CONCERT

SHE WILL NEVER KNOW

CALEB
WHAT IF MY MOM WAKES UP & FINDS
ME GONE,

SHE WILL TAKE MY CAR MAN

MASON
COME ON MAN

WELL HAVE FUN,

THIS CONCERT WILL NEVER COME TO THE CITY AGAIN THIS YEAR

BESIDES,

YOUR MOM WON'T TAKE THE CAR FOREVER

SHE WILL ONLY GROUND YOU FOR A WEEK

LET'S GO! MAN

CALEB
HEY MAN,

THE LAST THING I WANT TO DO IS MAKE MY MOTHER ANGRY, I TOLD HER THAT

I WOULD WOULDNT GO TO THE CONCERT

AND THAT'S THAT,

YOU & THE GUYS WANT TO GO THEN GO BUT IM NOT GOING

MASON
WELL LET US USE YOUR CAR THEN

WE'LL BE CAREFUL

CALEB
NO ONE

DRIVES MY CAR BUT ME!

MASON
WELL

HOW ARE ME AND THE GUYS GONNA GET TO THE CONCERT

CALEB

I DONT KNOW MAN TAKE A CAB OR BUS

BUT MY CAR IS STAYING HERE TONIGHT

MASON

HEY MAN

THIS IS FOUL

ID NEVER DO YOU THIS WAY

CALEB

WHAT ARE YOU TALKJNG ABOUT MAN I TOLD YOU MY MOM TOLD ME NO!

I CAN'T GO,

YOU GOT THAT,

AND IM NOT ABOUT TO GET IN TROUBLE OVER YOU, OR THE GUYS,

OR SOME CONCERT SO LAYOFF MAN

SEE YOU AT SCHOOL TOMORROW

MASON
HEY CALEB

DIDNT MEAN NOTHING

JUST WANTED TO GO TO THE CONCERT MAN SORRY MAN

SORRY

CALEB
HEY MAN

IT'S JUST THAT MY MOM AND ME ARE COOL

AND IM NOT GOING TO LET HERE DOWN

SO I CAN'T GO TO THIS CONCERT,

BUT I CAN GO TO ALL THE OTHERS

MASON
SEE TOMORROW AT SCHOOL MAN

END STRUCTURE

RULES RESPONSIBILITY TRUST

HONOR

THESE ARE SOME OF WORDS THAT ENCOMPASSES

FAMILY

PARENTS

SO IF YOU LISTEN TO THE REASON THAT PARENTS WHISPER,
THE WORDS NO!

YOU CAN BEGIN TO UNDERSTAND THAT WHAT THEY ARE REALLY SAYING IS WE LOVE YOU,

WE WANT TO KEEP YOU SAFE, WE CARE ABOUT YOU,

WE WANT YOU TO SUCCEED IN LIFE! WRITTEN BY EVERETT C BORDERS JR. @

GENDER WARS

ALEX
IVE HAD IT WITH GIRLS

FRED
GOT TURNED DOWN AGAIN HUGH

ALEX
SO WHAT

CAROL IS IMPOSSIBLE

EVERY TIME I THINK IM ABOUT TO GET WITH HER

SHE PULLS A DOCTOR JECKEL ON ME

FRED
THAT'S THE WAY GIRLS ARE

TRY DOING OR SAYING THE OPPOSITE

ILL BET SHE WILL LIKE YOU BETTER
THEN

ALEX
MAYBE

FRED
YOU KNOW SOMETHING

WHAT IF ALL THE GUYS GO ON STRIKE
ALL OVER THE WORLD FOR ONE
MONTH

ALEX
WHAT DO YOU MEAN

FRED

IF ALL THE GUYS DIDNT TALK TO GIRLS

DIDNT TAKE GIRLS OUT

DIDNT CALL GIRLS FOR ONE MONTH
WHAT DO YOU THINK WOULD HAPPEN

ALEX

NOTHING

THOSE GUYS WOULDNT HAVE GIRLFRIENDS

YOU'RE CRAZY

FRED

WHAT DO YOU MEAN

IM CRAZY

CAN YOU THINK OF A BETTER IDEA

ALEX
FRED

YOU ARE CRAZY IF YOU THINK

YOU COULD GET GUYS TO GO ON STRIKE FROM THEIR GIRLFRIENDS FOR A MONTH

YOU TALKING ABOUT ALL OVER THE WORLD

YOU COULDNT EVEN GET ANY GUYS IN OUR FIFTH PERIOD MATH CLASS TO DO THAT

FRED
I KNOW IT'S JUST A THOUGHT,

GIRLS ARE DRIVNG ME CRAZY, LAST NIGHT I WAS AT BURGER KING

I SAW DEBRA WITH SOME OF HER FRIENDS

SHE CAME OVER WHERE I WAS SITTING AND WANTED TO BORROW MONEY FOR A COKE

I SPENT ALL MY MONEY BUYING HER & HER FRIENDS FOOD

THIS MORNING SHE WOULDN'T EVEN SAY HELLO TO ME

ALEX
AND I THOUGHT I HAD PROBLEMS WITH GIRLS

FRED
YOU DO,

YOUR DATING CRAZY CAROL

ALEX
HEY

AT LEAST I HAVE A GIRL

YOU'RE STILL FISHING IN THE OCEAN

FRED
THAT'S ALL RIGHT

YOU NEED TO THROW CAROL BACK &
FISH FOR A FRESH ONE

ALEX
MAYBE

FRED
HEY ALEX

THAT GIRL RITA & HER FRIENDS ARE
LOOKING OVER HERE SMILING

ALEX
ARE THEY LOOKING AT ME OR YOU

FRED

DON'T KNOW & DON'T CARE

LET'S TALK TO THE

ALEX

NO LET THEM COME TO US

FRED

WHATS THE MATTER WITH YOU

TRY1NG TO PLAY HARD TO GET?

ALEX

NO

IF THEY WERE REALLY INTERESTED
THEY WOULD COME OVER & TALK

FRED

HEY MAN

RITA IS FINE

IM GOING OVER TO TALK

ALEX
GO AHEAD

FRED
HEY MAN

DO YOU KNOW WHAT SHE WANTED

FOR ME TO DRIVE HER & HER FRIENDS
HOME AFTER SCHOOL

ALEX
WELL WHAT DID YOU SAY

FRED
I TOLD THEM YES

ALEX
HEY MAN

THEY ARE USING YOU

THEY ONLY WANT YOU FOR YOUR CAR

FRED
SO THEY ALL USE US

THEY DO THE SAME TO YOU!

ALEX
NO MAN

YOU'RE NOT DATING RITA

SHE'S GOT A BOYFRIEND

YOU'RE GOING TO DRIVE SOME OTHER
GUYS GIRL HOME?

DON'T DO IT

FRED
SHE'S GOT A BOYFRIEND

I DIDN'T KNOW THAT

ARE YOU SURE

ALEX
YES

GIRLS LIKE THAT ALWAYS HAVE BOYFRIENDS

FRED
YEA

YOU'RE RIGHT

WHAT DO I LOOK LIKE DRIVING SOMEONE ELSES GIRLFRIEND HOME

ALEX
A FOOL,

A CHUMP I GUESS

FRED

IM NO FOOL

AND IM NOT DRIVING THOSE GIRLS HOME

ALEX

WELL GOOD FOR YOU MAN

WHEN A GIRL LIKES YOU

YOU'LL REALLY KNOW IF SHE LIKES YOU NOT FOR WHAT YOU CAN DO FOR HER SHE WILL LIKE YOU FOR YOU

IT'S LIKE CAROL

SHE LIKES ME FOR ME

SHE'S JUST CRAZY

FRED

HEY MAN,

I KNOW

GENDER WARS
SINCE MALE & FEMALE HAVE BEEN IN
EXISTENCE

THEY HAVE BATTLED WITH FEELINGS
& EMOTIONS FOR

LOVE WON & LOST

THAT HAVE PLACED EACH OTHER ON
THE EDGE INFINITE

PRESENT & PAST OBJECTIVELY
SPEAKING

HOPING THE NEW MILLENNIUM HOLDS
PROMISE FOR FUTURE GENERATIONS
AND GENERATIONS THAT MAY COME

THE GENDERS CAN ONLY SURVIVE BY
BECOMING ONE

AND THE FUTURE MAY ONLY BE
CERTAIN IF THE WAR SUBSIDES

WRITTEN BY EVERETT C BORDERS JR. @

DON'T PANIC IT'LL COME TO YOU

MR-RAY
MARTI N

WHATS WRONG

MARTIN
I DONT KNOW WHAT I WANT TO DO AFTER GRADUATION

MR-RAY
YOU KNOW SOME KIDS TRY & GO TO COLLEGE

THAT'S A GOOD START,

THAT'S SOMETHING TO THINK ABOUT

DONT YOU THINK?

MARTIN
YEA

BUT WHAT DO I DO AFTER THAT

MR-RAY
AFTER   COLLEGE   THEIRS   GRAD
SCHOOL

MARTIN
WELL WHAT DO I DO AFTER THAT

MR-RAY
YOU GETA JOB

MARTIN
THEN WHAT

MR-RAY
WHY DONT YOU TAKE ONE STEP AT A
TIME MARTIN,

TRY GElTING THROUGH YOUR JUNIOR
YEAR FIRST, ILL BET AFTER THIS YEAR
YOU'LL HAVE A BETTER HANDLE ON
WHAT YOU
WANT TO DO WITH YOUR LIFE MARTIN
MY DAD SAID THE MILITARY IS GOOD

MR-RAY
YES

THE MILITARY IS A GOOD CHOICE FOR
A YOUNG MAN LIKE YOU,

WAS YOUR FATHER IN THE MILITARY?

MARTIN
YES

HE WAS IN THE NAVY

MARTIN
AFTER HIGH SCHOOL

MY FATHER WENT INTO THE NAVY
AND LEARNED A TRADE HE SAYS IT'S
A GOOD DEAL

MR-MARTIN
YES

YOU COULD DO THAT

MARTIN
MY SISTER

GOT A SCHOLARSHIP IN SPORTS &
ATTENDED COLLEGE

SHE MAJORED IN ENGLISH SHE NEVER
LIKED ENGLISH WHY WOULD SHE
MAJOR IN A SUBJECT THAT SHE DIDNT
LIKE

MR-RAY
AS I RECALL

YOUR SISTER WAS OFFERED A BIG SPORTS CONTRACT,

SHE PROBABLY WON'T USE THAT ENGLISH DEGREE UNTIL SHE STOPS PLAYING SPORTS

IF SHE GETS HURT OR CANT PLAY ANYMORE SHE WILL NEED TO FALL BACK ON SOME THING,

A COLLEGE DEGREE WILL GO FAR

MARTIN
YEA

MR-RAY

COACH SAYS THAT IF I KEEP PLAYING BALL LIKE I HAVE,

THEN I COULD FOLLOW MY SISTERS FOOTSTEPS, BUT I DONT WANT BE LIKE MY SISTER I WANT TO BE LIKE MYSELF

MR-RAY
WHAT ARE YOU SAYING MARTIN

YOU DONT WANT TO BE SUCCESSFUL IN SPORTS LIKE YOUR SISTER,

LOOK, YOUR SISTER WAS GREAT IN SPORTS SO ARE YOU, BUT THE TWO OF YOU ARE COMPLETELY DIFFERENT,

IF YOU DONT WANT TO GET INTO

PROFESSIONAL SPORTS THEN DON'T,

GET YOUR EDUCATION,

THAT'S WHAT REALLY IMPORTANT

SOMEDAY YOUR SPORTS TALENTS WILL FADE, YOU NEED TO FALL BACK ON YOUR BRAIN YOU NEED TO GET AN EDUCATION

GET A DEGREE, OR DO BOTH,

GET YOUR EDUCATION AND GET INTO SPORTS,

IT WILL GET YOU FAR

YOU KNOW MARTIN

YOU CAN DO IT ALL

SPORTS, EDUCATION, MILITARY WHAT
EVER YOU WANT TO DO IN LIFE

JUST PUT YOUR MIND TO IT, YOU CAN
DO IT

MARTIN
YOU MEAN I CAN DO ALL THAT AT THE
SAME TIME

MR-RAY
SURE YOU CAN MARTIN

IF YOU GET A SCHOLARSHIP YOU'LL
BE IN COLLEGE,

YOU CAN JOIN THE R.O.T.C OR THE
MILITARY RESERVE,

AT THE SAME YOU'LL BE GETTING
YOUR COLLEGE DEGREE & PLAYING
SPORTS ALL AT THE SAME TIME AND
THAT, MARTIN

IS THE AMERICAN DREAM

MARTIN
BUT SUPPOSE I DONT GET A SPORTS
SCHOLARSHIP

MR-RAY
WHAT DO I DO THEN

MR-RAY
MOSTKIDSDON'THAVESCHOLARSHIPS

AND GO TO COLLEGE

A LOT CAN'T GET INTO THE MILITARY
BECAUSE OF ALL SORTS OF REASONS

MANY CANT GET INTO COLLEGE BECAUSE THEY CAN'T GET ADMITTED

MANY KIDS CANT PLAY SPORTS

YOU MARTIN HAVE THE Ability TO DO ALL THREE,

AND YOU CAN'T MAKE UP YOUR MIND

YOUR CONCERN IS NATURAL, BUT NOT THAT IMPORTANT AT THIS TIME WHEN YOU GET READY TO MAKE A DECISION ABOUT YOUR FUTURE

YOU'LL BE OK

MARTIN
WOW

MR-RAY

I NEVER THOUGHT OF THINGS THAT WAY I GUESS I HAVE A LOT TO LEARN

MR-RAY
YES YOU DO, SO, WHAT DO YOU NEED
TO DO

MARTIN
KEEP UP THE GRADES,

KEEP UP THE SPORTS

MR-RAY
BINGO

MARTIN,

I THINK YOU GOT IT,

LOOK,

IF YOU CAN MAKE IT IN SPORTS,
MILITARY OR EDUCAT1ON,

AS FAR AS IM CONCERN

YOU MADE SOMETHING OF YOURSELF

MARTIN

IM GLAD I TALKED TO YOU ABOUT THIS MR- RAY

THINGS ARE NOT SO CONFUSING NOW

MR-RAY

YES

WE SEE THINGS DIFFERENTLY WHEN THEIRS ANOTHER POINT OF VIEW

PICTURE YOURSELF AS A ROCKET

WHERE WOULD YOU GO IF YOU WERE LAUNCHED WITH OUT A GUIDANCE SYSTEM

MARTIN

IF YOU LAUNCH A ROCKET

IT'S NO TELLING WHERE IT MIGHT GO

MR-RAY

NOW

MARTIN IF IT HAD A GUIDANCE
SYSTEM

WHERE CAN IT GO?

MARTIN
WITH A GUIDANCE SYSTEM

IT CAN GO WHERE EVER IT'S GUIDED

MR-RAY
YES MARTIN

YOU ARE THE ROCKET

WE THE TEACHERS ARE THE GUIDANCE
SYSTEM

MARTIN
THANKS MR-RAY

MR-RAY
ANYTIME MARTIN

MARTIN
MR-RAY

ARE YOU GOING TO THE GAME
TOMORROW

MR-RAY
ILL BE THERE

SCORE A TOUCH DOWN FOR ME HUGH

MARTIN
ILL TRY MR-RAY ILL TRY

IT'S COMMON FOR AN ADOLESCENT
TO GET CONFUSED ABOUT THEIR
FUTURE
BUT WITH A LITTLE DIRECTION AND
COMMON
SENSE THEY FIGURE IT OUT

WRITTEN BY EVERETT C BORDERS
JR. @

DON'T MAKE FUN

SUSAN
HEY JACKIE

LOOK AT DARLENE

WHY DOES SHE EAT SO MUCH

LOOK AT ALL THE FOOD SHE HAS ON
HER TRAY

JACKIE
DON'T MAKE FUN OF PEOPLE

WHAT IF YOU WERE OVERWEIGHT

YOU WOULDN'T WANT PEOPLE TO
MAKE FUN OF YOU

SUSAN
I WOULDNT GET FAT EITHER

LOOK IF YOU DONT WANT TO BE FAT

THEN JUST DON'T EAT

JACKIE
IT'S NOT THAT EASY

SOMETIMES PEOPLE HAVE GLAND PROBLEMS OR THYROID PROBLEMS

IT MAKES THEM GAIN WEIGHT

IT'S NOT ABOUT EATING SOMETIMES

SUSAN
YOU SOUND LIKE YOU ARE DEFENDING HER

JACKIE
IF IT SOUNDS LIKE IT

YOU'RE RIGHT

SOMETIMES PEOPLE HAVE EATING DISORDERS DO YOU KNOW WHAT

I FOUND OUT THAT IT HURTS SOME
PEOPLE NOT TO EAT,

PEOPLE HAVE STOMACH ACHES IF
THEY DON'T EAT

SOME PEOPLE EAT OUT OF DEPRESSION
PEOPLE EAT WHEN THEY WORRY SOME
PEOPLE EAT TO FEEL HAPPY SO YOU
SEE

PEOPLE OVER EAT FOR ALL DIFFERENT
REASONS

SO BEING OVER WEIGHT IS NOT THEIR
CHOICE

SUSAN
WELL

I GUESS YOU TOLD ME

I DIDNT KNOW YOU FELT SO STRONGLY
ABOUT OVERWEIGHT PEOPLE

JACKIE
NO I DONT

IT'S JUST THE RIGHT THING TO DO,
MAKING FUN ISNT COOL

JACKIE
YOU SEE SUSAN

YOU'RE SLIM & TRIM FOR NOW

WHAT IF YOU HAD AN ACCIDENT OR
HAD A CHEMICAL IMBALANCE

AND SUDDENLY GAINED A LOT OF
WEIGHT HOW WOULD YOU FEEL THEN

SUSAN
ID KILL MYSELF COULD YOU IMAGINE
ME BEING FAT

JACKIE
YES I COULD IMAGINE SUSAN

NEVER SAY NEVER

NEVER SAY WHAT WON'T HAPPEN TO YOU

BECAUSE IT WILL

SUSAN
YOU MEAN YOU'RE OF THE OPINION THAT

WHAT GOES AROUND COMES AROUND

JACKIE
YES!

SUSAN

BEING PRETTY IS NOT JUST ON THE OUTSIDE

IT'S REALLY ON THE INSIDE

YOU SEE YOU'RE VERY PRETTY

YOU WANT PEOPLE TO LIKE YOU FOR YOU

BUT WHAT THEY SEE IS YOU BEING PRETTY

YOU'RE RUDE

YOU'RE SPITEFUL YOU'RE VINDICTIVE

I KNOW YOU WANT PEOPLE TO LIKE YOU FOR YOU

BUT THE ONLY REASON

ANYONE WOULD BOTHER IS

YOU'RE PRETTY

YOU KNOW IN A WAY

YOU ARE YOUR ONLY PROBLEM

SUSAN
JACKIE

I THOUGHT YOU WERE MY FRIEND

WHY DO YOU TALK TO ME THAT WAY

YOU'RE PRETTY TOO JACKIE

WHATS YOU PROBLEM THEN

JACKIE
YOU SUSAN

JACKIE
YOU ARE MY PROBLEM

GOOD FRIENDS ARE HARD TO COME BY

ANYONE THAT WOULD MAKE FUN OF PEOPLE IS NOT MY FRIEND

SUSAN
I WAS JUST KIDDING JACKIE

DONT GO

JACKIE
NO

YOU WERENT KIDDING

YOU WERE VERY SERIOUS

YOU MADE FUN OF DARLENE

WHAT DID SHE EVER DO TO YOU

SUSAN
NOTHING

I NEVER EVEN SPOKE TO HER

JACKIE
THAT'S WHAT IM TALKING ABOUT

IM GOING OVER TO HAVE LUNCH WITH
MY FRIEND DARLENE

SUSAN
JACKIE WAIT

I WANT TO COME TO

IM SORRY

I WAS WRONG

JACKIE
WELL

COME ON GIRL

ILL FORGIVE YOU THIS TIME

I DONT EXPECT YOU TO CHANGE OVER
NIGHT

YOU CAN BE PRETTY ON THE INSIDE
WHEN YOU WANT TO

JUST

DONT LET IT HAPPEN AGAIN

HOW DO WE OVERCOME OUR OWN
PREJUDICE

IF FRIENDSHIP & ACCEPTANCE CAN INSTILL PREJUDICE THEN

MAYBE GOOD FRIENDSHIP & ACCEPTANCE CAN END IT

EVERETT C BORDERS JR. @

DO YOU WANT TO

CHERYL
BOBBY I DON'T WANT TO

IM NOT READY

BOBBY
WHEN WILL YOU BE READY

DO YOU KNOW WHAT IM GOING THROUGH! I LOVE YOU, WHY CAN'T WE BE TOGETHER

CHERYL

IM NOT READY FOR THAT NOW

BOBBY

WHAT ABOUT ME IM READY NOW!

YOU SAY YOU LOVE ME

IF YOU REALLY LOVED ME

YOU'LL BE WITH ME NOW!

CHERYL

THERE'S MORE TO LOVE THAT SEX

YOU'RE TRYING TO MAKE ME FEEL GUILTY

IF I TELL YOU IM NOT READY WHY CAN'T YOU TRUST ME

BOBBY

TRUST

BABY I TRUST YOU

I JUST THINK THAT IF YOU REALLY LOVE SOMEONE,

YOU WOULD WANT TO BE WITH THAT PERSON,

SLEEP WITH THAT PERSON,

THAT'S WHAT LOVE IS TO ME

CHERYL
BOBBY,

DO YOU REALLY LOVE ME,

OR JUST TRYING TO GET ME IN BED?

BOBBY
CHERYL!

HOW COULD YOU SAY SOMETHING LIKE THAT TO ME,

DON'T I SHOW YOU HOW MUCH I CARE
ABOUT YOU,

DON'T I SPEND TIME WITH YOU,

DON'T I TAKE YOU PLACES & BUY YOU
THINGS,

YOUR MOTHER & FATHER LIKES ME
CHERYL

WHAT DO I HAVE TO DO TO PROVE TO
YOU THAT I LOVE YOU

CHERYL
BE MORE UNDERSTANDING

I WANT TO BE WITH YOU AS MUCH AS
YOU WANT TO BE WITH ME

BOBBY
I DOUBT THAT

CHERYL
STOP,

BOBBY STOP, BOBBY STOP IT, I TOLD YOU,

IM NOT READY YET!

BOBBY
BUT CHERYL,

YOU JUST TOLD ME,

YOU WANT ME AS MUCH AS I WANTED YOU

YOU'RE GIVING ME MIXED SIGNALS

CHERYL
I DON'T MEAN TO

BOBBY
YOU KNOW MARRY

SHE LIKES ME A LOT

SHE SAYS SHE WANTS ME TO TAKE HER TO THE DRIVE IN FRIDAY

CHERYL
THEN WHY DON'T YOU TAKE HER SINCE YOUR SO MUCH IN HEAT

BOBBY
MAYBE I WILL

CHERYL
SO THAT'S IT

YOU'RE JUST GOING TO DRIVE AWAY LIKE THAT

BOBBY
WELL

WHEN YOU REALLY WANT TO BE WITH
ME YOU KNOW MY NUMBER

CHERYL
THAT'S NOT FAIR

BOBBY

YOU KNOW I LOVE YOU,

WHY ARE YOU TALKING THIS WAY
IF IM NOT READY TO HAVE SEX WHY
ARE YOU PRESSURING ME

BOBBY
IF THAT'S WHAT IM DOING I DON'T
MEAN TO

IT'S JUST THAT WHEN IM WITH YOU

YOU DRIVE ME CRAZY

CHERYL
THAT'S TEENAGE HORMONES

BOBBY
YOU'RE RIGHT

IM SORRY

ILL BEHAVE MYSELF

AS WE ENTER THE THRESHOLD OF THE NEW MILLENNIUM

WE MUST REALIZE AND REMEMBER

THAT PREMATURE PERMISSQUITY ONCE WAS, AND SHALL CONTINUE,

IF WE ARE TO LEARN ANYTHING THROUGH EDUCATION FROM THE NINETIES

WE MUST LEARN & UNDERSTAND THAT MANY LIVES ARE AFFECTED THROUGH

TEENS HAVING SEX & UN PROTECTED SEX AIDS,

GETTING PREGNANT, DROPPING OUT OF SCHOOL,

FAMILY FINANCIAL STATUS BURDENS, SHATTERED & BROKEN CHILDHOODS

THIS IDEA MIGHT COME TO MIND

WHAT IS IMPORTANT TO YOU, FOR NOW!

IS IT GETTING WHAT YOU ARE STRIVING FOR IN LIFE OR FOR THE MOMENT VIEW THIS,

YOUR GOALS ARE ALWAYS UP RIVER YOU START OUT IN A BOAT WITH TWO ORRS,

LIFE JACKET,

JUST ENOUGH TO SUCCEED

WHEN YOU MAKE THE WRONG CHOICES YOU LOSE,

YOU'RE ORRS,

LIFE VEST,

THE ABILITY TO SUCCEED UP THE RIVER TO YOUR GOALS,

YOU GET LOST! REMEMBER

ALWAYS THINK OF AFTERWARDS FIRST!

END

WRITTEN BY EVERETT C BORDERS JR. @

COACH & JOCK

BOB
HEY COACH

WHY DID YOU PLAY Scott IN THE LAST GAME AND NOT ME

COACH

YOUR ENGLISH TEACHER PAID ME A VISIT BOB, YOU DONT STUDY,

YOU DONT HAND IN YOUR ASSIGNMENTS, YOUR GRADES ARE A SHAME

AND IF YOU FAIL THIS CLASS

THAT SCHOLARSHIP YOU WANTED IS OUT THE WINDOW

BOB

I DONT UNDERSTAND COACH I SCORE 25 POINTS A GAME

I PLAY BETTER DEFENSE THAN SCOTT IM NEVER LATE FOR PRACTICE

AND I NEVER GET HURT,

WHY ARE YOU DOING THIS TO ME COACH

COACH

BOB

YOU'RE NOT LISTENING

YOU NEED TO IMPROVE YOUR GRADES

SOME DAY YOU WON'T BE ABLE TO PLAY BALL WHAT WILL YOU DO THEN?

BOB

NOT ABLE TO PLAY! COACH

IM GONE ALWAYS PLAY BALL

THERE WAS TWO TALENT SCOUTS CHECKING ME OUT LAST WEEK

COACH

THAT WAS THEN

THIS IS NOW LOOK BOB

WE ALL KNOW THAT YOU HAVE A NATURAL ABILITY TO PLAY BALL,

YOU'RE SMARTER THAN WHAT
YOU HAVE SHOWN YOUR ENGLISH
TEACHER,

LISTEN

HIT THE BOOKS

OR AS FAR AS YOUR SCHOLARSHIP
GOES

YOU'LL BE HITTING THE ROAD

YOU SEE IT TAKES MUCH MORE THAN
TALENT TO SUCCEED IN THIS WORLD

BOB
WHAT DO YOU MEAN

COACH
ILL GIVE YOU AN EXAMPLE

I SAW YOU PLAYING POOL LAST NIGHT
AT MICKYS WITH YOUR FRIEND BOB,

YEA, SO

COACH
I STOPPED AND WATCHED YOU SHOOT

BOB
I KNOW IM GOOD IN POOL

I ALMOST RAN THE TABLE ON THAT
GUY

COACH
ALMOST DON'T COUNT

RIGHT!

EITHER YOU WIN OR YOU LOSE

BOB
I DON'T FOLLOW

COACH

YOU DID ALMOST RUN THE TABLE ON THAT GUY LAST NIGHT,

YOU WERE READY TO SINK THE EIGHT BALL BUT THE TEN BALL WAS BLOCKING YOUR SHOT

BOB
RIGHT

BUT COACH

I CAN'T MAKE THOSE SHOTS IT'S TOO HARD

COACH
WHY IS THAT BOB

BOB
CAUSE

THE ONLY WAY TO MAKE THAT SHOT
YOU NEED TO HAVE A LOT OF ENGLISH
ON THE BALL

COACH
WHAT DID YOU SAY?

BOB
YOU KNOW COACH

YOU NEED TO PUT ENGLISH ON THE
BALL

TO MAKE THOSE GREAT SHOTS AND
WIN EVERY GAME

COACH
EXPLAIN

HOW ENGLISH WORKS?

BOB

IT'S LIKE WHEN IM PLAYING BALL

AND IT'S THE LAST SECONDS OF THE BIG GAME

AND THEY PASS ME THE BALL

AND I DRIVE TO THE BASKET & FINGER ROLL A LAY UP AND DRAW THE FOUL

WELL

ENGLISH MEANS

I CAN SEE THE PLAY BEFORE I DO IT

I CAN SOME HOW WILL THE BALL IN THE BASKET

COACH

WHAT DO YOU CALL IT AGAIN?

BOB

E, N, G, L, I, S, H

SO WHAT YOUR SAYING IS ENGLISH APPLIES TO EVERYTHING

BASKETBALL, POOL, LI FE

HEY COACH

THANKS

TIME TO HIT THE BOOKS HARD

COACH
YOU'RE A SMART KID BOB

YOU HAVE WHAT IT TAKES TO MAKE IN THIS WORLD

REMEMBER ALWAYS APPLY THE ENGLISH AND YOU'LL NEVER GO WRONG

BOB
I NEVER THOUGHT OF LEARNING IN THAT WAY PRETTY CLEVER

COACH

WE JUST WANT YOU TO BE THE BEST YOU CAN BE

THAT IS WHY IM THE COACH!

END

WRITTEN BY

EVERETT C BORDERS JR. @

CAN I

DEE
MOM

CAN I BORROW THE CAR
ME & IRISH ARE GOING TO THE MALL

MOM
NO

DEE
BUT MOM WHY NOT,

ILL TAKE CARE OF THE CAR YOU KNOW I ALWAYS DO

MOM
YES YOU DO

BUT YOUR PROBLEM IS

YOU DONT KNOW WHEN TO COME
HOME

DEE

I KNOW HOW TO COME HOME MOM

WHEN HAVE I HAD PROBLEMS COMING
HOME TOO LATE

MOM

REMEMBER THE TIME WHEN YOU &
KIM WENT TO THE MOVIES

YOU DIDNT GET HOME TILL TWO AM

AND REMEMBER WHEN YOU & JUUA
WENT TO THE CONCERT

MY CAR HAD ALL THOSE SCRATCHES
ON THE DOOR,

THEN THERE WAS THE TIME WHEN
YOU & MICHAEL HAD THAT DATE AND
MY CAR WAS STOLEN

DEE
MOM

THAT WASNT MY FAULT THAT TIME
AT THE MOVIES, I LEFT THE KEYS IN
THE MOVIES & HAD TO FIND THEM,

THAT TIME AT THE CONCERT WASNT
MY FAULT

I PARKED IN THE PAY LOT & PEOPLE
PARKED TOO CLOSE TO THE CAR

WHEN THE CAR WAS STOLEN, ME &
MICHAEL WERE IN THE MOVIES

PLEASE MOM,

CAN I BORROW THE CAR PLEASE MOM

MOM
DEE

WHY WON'T YOU LET KELLY BORROW
ANYTHING OF YOURS

DEE

BECAUSE KELLY DESTROYS EVERYTHING SHE PUTS HER HANDS ON, THE LAST TIME I LET BORROW MY TAN BLOUSE SHE PUT A STAINS ON IT THAT I CAN'T GET OUT, IT'S RUINED,

I KNOW SHE'S Y SISTER BUT SHE'S IRRESPONSIBLE WITH MY STUFF!

MOM

IS THAT ALL

DON'T YOU LOVE YOUR SISTER DEE

DEE

YOU KNOW I LOVE KELLY MOM

THAT'S NOT FAIR

IT'S JUST THAT SHE DOESN'T TAKE CARE OF Y STUFF LIKE I DO

MOM

ARE YOU SAYING THAT KELLY CAN NEVER BORROW ANYTHING FROM YOU AGAIN

THAT'S KINDA HARSH ISNT IT

I KNOW THAT YOU WEAR SOME OF KELLYS CLOTHES,

YOU BORROW HER PERFUME & JEWELRY

WHAT IF SHE SAID THAT YOU COULDNT BORROW ANYTHING FROM HER,

YOU WOULD BE KINDA UPSET WOULDN'T YOU

DEE

YES I WOULD

LOOK AT ALL THE THINGS I DO FOR KELLY MOM

MOM

NO MORE THAN SHE DOES FOR YOU

DEE

OK MOM

IM BEGINNING TO SEE YOUR POINT

YOU'RE COMPARING BORROWING AS A REFERENCE AND YOU'RE USING ME & KELLY T0

GET ME TO SEE THE POINT ABOUT BEING RESPONSIBLE WITH OTHER PEOPLES PROPERTY

NAMELY YOU'RE PROPERTY

VERY GOOD MOM

MOM

OH

DO YOU BEGIN TO SEE THE COMPARISON

DEE
MOM

BORROWING A CAR FROM YOU AND
KELLY BORROWING SOMETHING
FROM ME

IS TWO DIFFERENT THINGS

MOM
REALLY, HOW SO DEE

DEE
MOM I DONT LET KELLY BORROW
ANYTHING CAUSE SHE DOESNT TAKE
CARE OF MY STUFF

MOM
AND YOU DON'T SEE THE COMPARISON

DEE
NO MOM

IM NOT KELLY

MOM
NO YOU ARE YOU

KELLY MAY HAVE BEEN A LITTLE
RECKLESS WITH YOUR THINGS

BUT SO HAVE YOU WITH MY THINGS

SO DONT PUT YOUR SELF ABOVE YOUR
SISTER, YOU MAKE MISTAKES JUST AS
KELLY DOES

DEE
SORRY MOM,

I DIDN'T MEAN TO PUT MYSELF OVER
KELLY,

IM SORRY

MOM

HERE'S THE KEYS TO THE CAR IT'S TWO P

I WANT MY CAR BACK AT NINE PM YOU GOT THAT YOUNG LADY

DEE

NO PROBLEM MOM

MOM

AFTER ALL THE THINGS THAT HAVE HAPPENED TO MY CAR IN YOUR POSSESSION

IM TRUSTING YOU AGAIN

DEE

THANKS MOM

I WON'T LET YOU DOWN

SOMETIMES THE BOND BETWEEN MOTHERS TO DAUGHTER

IS STRAINED DUE TO ADOLESCENT INDEPENDENCE,

TALKING AT SOMEONE IS VERY DIFFERENT THAT TAKING TO THEM,

ALWAYS REMEMBER

ESTABLISH A COMMON GROUND AND WORK FROM THERE

WRITTEN BY EVERETT C BORDERS JR. @

BROTHER TO BROTHER

BIG BROTHER
HEY LITTLE BROTHER WHERE YOU GOING?

LITTLE BROTHER
IM GOING WITH RAMON & YORK

BIG BROTHER
WHAT ARE YOU GUYS UP TO

LITTLE BROTHER
DON'T TELL MOM & DAD

RAMONS GOT SOME B.B GUNS

WERE GONNA SHOOT CARS ON THE FREEWAY

BIG BROTHER
WHO IDEA WAS THAT

LITTLE BROTHER
YORK

BIG BROTHER
IF YORK TOLD YOU TO JUMP OFF A BRIDGE WOULD YOU?

LITTLE BROTHER
NO

IM NO FOOL

WHY YOU COMING LIKE THAT

BIG BROTHER
LISTEN

ONE TIME I WOULD THROW ROCKS AT SCHOOL WINDOWS

THE SAME SCHOOLS THAT I Attended SCHOOL, WE FROZE IN THE WINTERTIME!

LITTLE BROTHER
COOL

BIG BROTHER
NO

IT WASNT COOL

IT WAS IN THE WINTER TIME

AND THE CLASS ROOMS WERE COLD
KIDS GOT SICK

A GIRL THAT I LIKED A LOT ALMOST
DIED NO BRO IT WASN'T COOL AT ALL

LITTLE BROTHER
WHAT HAPPENED

BIG BROTHER
WELL

TWO OF MY FRIENDS GOT CAUGHT
ONE TIME BREAKING WINDOWS IN
THE SCHOOL

LITTLE BROTHER
DID YOU GET CAUGHT?

BIG BROTHER
LATER I DID

MY FRIENDS TOLD ON ME

LITTLE BROTHER
WHAT HAPPENED

BIG BROTHER
I WAS EXPELLED FROM SCHOOL

DAD GAVE ME A BUTT WHIPPING YOU
WOULDNT BELIEVE,

I HAD TO DO COMMUNITY Service

AND THAT GIRL I TOLD YOU ABOUT
REFUSE TO SPEAK TO ME

LITTLE BROTHER
I WON'T EVER GET CAUGHT LIKE THAT

BIG BROTHER
THE ONLY WAY IS TO NOT DO IT

WHAT IF MOM IS RIDING IN A CAR YOU
HIT WITH A BB GUN

WHO IS THAT GIRL YOU LIKE SO MUCH?
DEBBIE,

WHAT IF SHE WAS RIDING IN the CAR?

HIT WITH A BB IN THE EYE BY YOU OR
YOU'RE FRIENDS,

WOULD YOU LIKE THAT

LITTLE BROTHER
I DIDN'T THINK OF IT THAT WAY

BIG BROTHER
REMEMBER

EVERYTHING YOU DO AFFECTS OTHERS GOOD OR BAD

LITTLE BROTHER
WHAT DOES THAT MEAN

WE WERE JUST GOING TO HAVE FUN

BIG BROTHER
FUN

ARE YOU HAVING FUN OR FOLLOWING SOME GUYS WHO AREN'T VERY SMART

LITTLE BROTHER
WHY YOU WANNA TALK ABOUT MY FRIENDS LIKE THAT

BIG BROTHER
HA BRO

YOU'RE SMARTER THAN THAT

YOU WANNA HANG WITH ME

YOU WANNA SEE WHAT BETTER THINGS YOU CAN DO THAN THAT GARBAGE

LITTLE BROTHER
YOU REALLY MEAN IT

I RATHER HANG WITH YOU

BIG BROTHER
YES

BUT NOT DRESSED LIKE THAT

LITTLE BROTHER
WHATS THE MATTER WITH HOW I AM DRESSED

BIG BROTHER
IF YOU WANT TO IMPRESS DEBBIE YOU NEED TO DRESS COOL, CLEAN LIKE THIS

LITTLE BROTHER
HEY BRO

TEACH ME TO BE COOL With THE GIRLS

BIG BROTHER
NO PROBLEM

LITTLE BROTHER

LISTEN TO ME AND YOU'LL BE ALL RIGHT

LITTLE BROTHER
HANGING WITH RAMON & YORK IS STUPID

WHAT WAS I THINKING

BIG BROTHER
DONT KNOW BRO

JUST DONT thinks STUPID, DEAL

LITTLE BROTHER
DEAL END

***WRITTEN BY EVERETT C BORDERS
JR. @***

AT THE MOVIES

DAVID
HEY STEVE
WE STILL GOING TO THE MOVIES

STEVE
ONLY IF YOU DON'T BOTHER PEOPLE

WHILE THEY TRY & WATCH THE MOVIE

DA*VID*

WHAT ARE YOU TALKING ABOUT

I LIKE TO HAVE FUN AT THE MOVIES
WHATS WRONG WITH THAT?

STEVE

THAT'S WHAT IM TALKING ABOUT

YOU HAVE TOO MUCH FUN

PEOPLE GO TO THE MOVIES TO WATCH
THE SHOW

NOT ACT LIKE A CLOWN!

DAVID

HEY MAN

IF YOU DONT WANT TO GO

THEN DON'T GO

STEVE
ILL Go DAVID

JUST DON'T EMBARRASS ME

OR GET IN TROUBLE, OK

DAVID
NO PROBLEM MAN

STEVE
LET'S CHECK OUT STAR WARS

DAVID
SOUNDS LIKE A PLAN

DAVID
WHERE DO YOU WANT TO SIT

I LIKE TO SIT IN THE BACK IN THE MIDDLE ROWS

STEVE
OK

DAVID
HEY MAN

THAT'S THE FOOL WHO WAS TALKING
TO MY LADY YESTERDAY

STEVE
WHERE

DAVID
THEIR

IN THE THIRD ROW RIGHT!

STEVE
SO WHAT

IF ALL HE WAS DOING IS TALKING
WHATS YOUR PROBLEM

DAVID
HEY MAN HE'S NOT SUPPOSE TO TALK
TO MY WOMEN

STEVE
HEY MAN

WHY DID YOU THROW THAT CANDY
AT HIM

DAVID
I FELT LIKE IT

STEVE
LISTEN

YOU GOT A PROBLEM WITH SOMEBODY
YOU NEED TO TALK TO THAT PERSON
AND FIND OUT WHATS GOING ON

NOT THROW THINGS YOU GOT
THAT MAN!

DAVID
I KNOW MAN

THIS CRAP IS MAKING ME CRAZY

STEVE
HEY MAN THAT GUY IS LOOKING AROUND

TRYING TO FIND OUT WHO HIT HIM IN THE HEAD WITH THAT CANDY

DAVID
YOU'RE RIGHT

ILL FIND OUT WHAT THAT FOOL WAS DOING WITH MY LADY AND IF I THINK HE IS TRYING TO GET WITH HER, IM GOING TO

STEVE
YOUR NOT GONNA DO ANYTHING

YOUR MOUTH IS WRITING CHECKS
THAT YOU'RE BODY CANT CASH!

YOU SEE THE SIZE OF THAT GUY

DAVID
IM GOING

STEVE
OK FOOL

DAVID
HEY STEVE THAT GUY

HE'S MY LADYS COUSIN

STEVE
I HAD NOTICED

HE DIDNT BEAT YOUR BRAINS OUT

NOW DON'T YOU FEEL REAL STUPID

DAVID
WELL

NOW I KNOW THE TRUTH

STEVE
DID YOU TELL HIM THAT

IT WAS YOU THAT HIT HIM WITH THAT CANDY

DAVID
YOU CRAZY,

IM NOT STUPID

HEY MAN LOOK OVER THEIR

THAT'S CINDY

SHE TURNED ME DOWN

WHEN I ASKED HER TO GO OUT WITH ME!

STEVE

WHY ARE YOU STARTING THIS CRAP AGAIN WHY DID YOU THROW THAT CAN'T YOU JUST WATCH THE MOVIE!

DAVID

HER BOYFRIEND JUST SAW US

BACK ME UP STEVE

HE'S COMING OVER HERE

STEVE

WHAT DO YOU MEAN BACK YOU UP

I DIDNT DO ANYTHING!

DAVID

HEY MAN

YOU'RE NOT GOING TO BACK ME UP BRO

STEVE
NO

I TOLD YOU

NOT TO ACT LIKE A CLOWN

BUT YOU DIDN'T LISTEN DID YOU!

DAVID
THINK ILL GO OVER AND APOLOGIZE
TO HIM

STEVE
GOOD IDEA

DAVID
HEY MAN

CINDYS BOYFRIEND IS ALL RIGHT

HE'S NOT EVEN MAD OR NOTHING

STEVE
SO

YOU DID APOLOGIZE?

DAVID
NO MAN

I TOLD HIM THAT YOU HIT HIM BUT HE
FORGIVES YOU

STEVE
HEY MAN

IM NEVER GOING TO THE MOVIES
WITH YOU

DAVID
WHY NOT STEVE

HEY,

IM SORRY

IT WON'T HAPPEN AGAIN

STEVE
FORGET IT MAN WATCH THE MOVIE

HOW DO WE MEASURE FRIENDSHIP IS IT TOLERENCE & PERSONAL PAITENCE OF OTHER PEOPLE WE ADMIRE,

ARE FOND OF OR IS IT THE OVERWELMING TRAIT OF ALL OF US TO WANT TO BELONG,

TO BE LIKED & RESPECTED

END

WRITTEN BY EVERETT C BORDERS JR. @

ABSTAINANCE

KATHY
HEY LINDA

DID YOU HAVE A DATE WITH MICHAEL
LAST NIGHT

LINDA
YES

ME & MICHAEL WENT OUT

KATHY
WELL

WHERE DID YOU GO WHAT DID YOU
DO TELL ME

LINDA
HE PICKED ME UP AT SIX

WE DROVE & TALKED A WHILE THEN
WE HAD SOME CHINESE FOOD AND
WE DROVE TO THE DRIVE INN MOVIE

KATHY
WELL WHAT DID YOU SEE

LINDA
JAW BREAKER

KATHY
I HEARD IT'S A GOOD MOVIE

WAS IT?

LINDA
WE DIDN'T LOOK AT THE MOVIE

TO MUCH

KATHY

WHAT DID YOU DO GIRL

DID YOU & MICHAEL... DID YOU

LINDA

YES

KATHY

WHAT WAS IT LIKE?

DID IT HURT?

YOU MEAN YOU DID IT IN MICHAELS LITTLE CAR?

LINDA

TO ANSWER YOU'RE QUESTIONS

MICHAEL HAD HIS FATHERS FORD EXPEDITION AND IT WAS UNCOMFORTABLE AND YES IT HURT A LTTLE

KATHY

DID MICHAEL USE CONDOMS

LINDA

HE USED MINE

KATHY

WHAT

WHAT ARE YOU DOING WITH CONDOMS

LINDA

MICHAEL DIDNT HAVE ANY

HE DIDN'T WANT TO USE ANYTHING

BUT I WOULDN'T, UNTIL HE USED A CONDO

I GOT TWO CONDOMS FROM MY BROTHERS WALLET BEFORE I WENT OUT WITH MICHAEL

KATHY
GUESS IT'S BETTER TO BE SAFE THAN SORRY

LINDA
YEA

IM SORRY I DID

I COULD HAVE WAITED

MICHAEL IS OK BUT

I SHOULD HAVE WAITED TILL I WAS OLDER

KATHY
WHY

YOU DIDNT RISK ANYTHING MICHAEL WORE A CONDOM

LINDA
YOU DON'T UNDERSTAND

MICHAEL KEPT PRESSURING ME I SHOULD HAVE WAITED

I REALLY WASNT READY

KATHY
I THOUGHT YOU LOVED MICHAEL

LINDA
I DO

BUT I STILL COULD HAVE WAITED

TILL I WAS REALLY READY

KATHY
SO

YOU REGRET IT HUGH

LINDA
YES I DO

AND I WON'T DO IT AGAIN TI1LL IM OLDER

KATHY
HOW OLD

LINDA
AT LEAST EIGHTEEN

A GIRL SHOULDN'T HAVE SEX TILL SHE'S AT LEAST EIGHTEEN YEARS OLD

KATHY
YOU'RE ONLY FIFTEEN LINDA

ANYWAY

I ALWAYS THOUGHT IF IT'S WITH SOMEONE YOU REALLY LOVE

IT'S OK

LINDA

IS THAT HOW YOU THINK

NO!

WHAT IF I DIDNT BRING CONDOMS

WHAT IF THE CONDOM BROKE

WHAT IF MICHAEL GOT ME PREGNANT

WHAT IF HE GAVE ME AIDS OR SOMETHING

WHAT IF WE GOT CAUGHT BY THE POUCE

WHAT IF PEOPLE FROM SCHOOL WOULD HAVE SAW US OR MY PARENTS FOUND OUT

KATHY

I NEVER WOULD HAVE THOUGHT OF ALL THAT

THINK ILL TELL RANDY TO HOLD HIS
HORSES

LINDA
YEA

TELL RANDY TO HOLD EVERYTHING
TILL AFTER HIGH SCHOOL OR COLLEGE

KATHY
WHAT IF RANDY STARTS TO PRESSURE
ME LIKE

MICHAEL PRESSURED YOU

LINDA
THEN TELL RANDY THAT YOU WONT
DO IT

IF HE STILL LIKES YOU & RESPECTS
AFTER THAT

THEN YOU'LL KNOW THAT HE REALLY LIKES YOU

IF RANDY DOESNT LIKE YOU THEN

IT'S REALLY NO BIG DEAL

KATHY
IF IT WASN'T A BIG DEAL,

WHY DID YOU DO IT

LINDA
CURIOUS I GUESS

KATHY
WELL GIRL

YOU REALLY GAVE ME SOMETHING TO THINK ABOUT

DONT THINK ILL BE DOING ANYTHING SOON

LINDA

YEA GIRL

IF GUYS LIKE YOU

THEY'LL LIKE YOU FOR YOU.

NOT WHAT THEY CAN GET FROM YOU
Wait TILL YOU ARE REALLY READY
WAITE. TILL YOU ARE OLDER

KATHY

EIGHTEEN OR TWENTY OR SOMETHING
HUGH

LINDA

YEA

SOMETHING LIKE THAT

KATHY

WHAT IF MICHAEL WANTS TO DO IT
AGAIN

WHAT WILL YOU TELL HIM

LINDA
ILL TELL HIM TO TALK TO THE HAND

KATHY
YOU'RE FUNNY GIRL

LINDA
YEA

FUNNY

TEENS HAVING SEX

IT IS VERY NECESSARY TO HAVE ALL THE FACTSIF YOU HAVE OR THINK ABOUT HAVING UNPROTECTED SEX YOU RISK GETTING AIDS & SEXUALLY TRANSMITTED DISEASES & UNWANTED PREGNANCY

AND MASSIVE FINANCIAL BURDENS PLACED ON YOU & YOU'RE FAMILY, YOU RISK ALL THIS WHEN YOU HAVE UN PROTECTED SEX.

THE BEST WAY TO AVOID RISK FOR TEENS IS NOT TO DO IT!

UNTIL YOU'RE OLDER TO HANDLE THE RESPONSIBIUTY

WRITTEN BY EVERETT C BORDERS JR. @

APPEARANCE

966

969

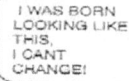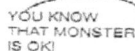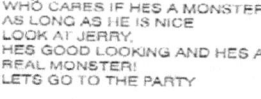

APPEARANCE

We as human beings are affected and stimulated by outward appearances.

Infatuation is, brief, to accept and reject, seems only second nature, and some affects can last a lifetime.

Facing life as, it faces you; one would say that physical looks are a matter of individual, interpretation. Although norms differ from one group to another, most of the wise, would agree that, true beauty, lies within.

It's like, looking at a piece of beautiful pastry, Unless you experience the final sensation of taste, You might not know if you like it.

After having a bad experience, with beautiful pastry, may affect your perception of beautiful pastry in the future.

Perception, the most powerful paradox of the human experience, has people focusing on only, outer layers. Concentrating, using your inner primal, mind and trusting your senses, you may reveal your true ability to see beyond the constructs of deliberate masks.

Think of a pretty woman in a sexy dress; now imagine her without, makeup, no sexy skirt, with a terrible hangover. Does that sound appealing?

Facts, support, most beautiful woman are selfish, self centered, arrogant and greedy.

Perception, can you see beyond it?

Do you have the knowledge and the ability to?

WRITTEN BY

Everett C Borders Jr. Ph.D.

Friends

977

Conclusion

Kinship,

Hardship,

Friendship,

In our day to day struggles of survival in dealing with the opposite sex.

We must heed the messages our elders have always spoken of.

We must abide, by the proper interactive, etiquette that has passed down from all times.

And the message is,

Never mix work or business with pleasure, And never,

Ever,

Ever,

Attempt to chase the wind.

WRITTEN BY

Everett C Borders Jr. Ph.D.

The needs of the many, always outweighs the needs of the few, or the one, fore never have so few, owed so much to so many.

END of all written material.

Written by;

Everett C Borders Jr. PhD.

2019

CPSIA information can be obtained
at www.ICGtesting.com
Printed in the USA
BVHW070801240619
551796BV00001B/2/P